MARC CAMERON

ACTIVE MEASURES

A JERICHO QUINN THRILLER

PINNACLE BOOKS
Kensington Publishing Corp.
www.kensingtonbooks.com

PINNACLE BOOKS are published by

Kensington Publishing Corp.
119 West 40th Street
New York, NY 10018

All Kensington titles, imprints, and distributed lines are available at special quantity discounts for bulk purchases for sales promotions, premiums, fund-raising, educational, or institutional use. Special book excerpts or customized printings can also be created to fit specific needs. For details, write or phone the office of the Kensington sales manager: Kensington Publishing Corp., 119 West 40th Street, New York, NY 10018, attn: Sales Department; phone 1-800-221-2647.

First Pinnacle premium mass market printing: December 2019

10 9 8 7 6 5 4 3 2

ISBN-13: 978-0-7860-4269-2
ISBN-10: 0-7860-4269-9

Printed in the United States of America

Electronic edition:

ISBN-13: 978-0-7860-4270-8 (e-book)
ISBN-10: 0-7860-4270-2 (e-book)

For Amy

*In yon strait path a thousand may well be
   stopped by three:
Now, who will stand on either hand and keep the
   bridge with me?*

   —THOMAS BABINGTON MACAULAY,
      "Horatius at the Bridge"

Prologue

November 29, 1962
Santiago de Cuba

Colonel Miguel de la Guardia knew well the white bone of war. He'd watched his friends be blown into pieces, seen women defiled and children burned—but never in his life had he witnessed anything so heart-breaking as this convoy driving out of the forest. Across Cuba under cover of darkness, other commanders stood and wept in similar clearings at the unfolding of the same sad event.

History would judge the Russians for this insult. Of that, Colonel de la Guardia was certain.

The Soviet Union had once believed in the revolution. For fifty-nine glorious days, Cuba had been a nuclear power. Fidel was able to shake his fist at the American president, secure in the knowledge that if push came to shove, he could repel an invasion by the imperialist—and render the stolen base at Guantanamo Bay a glowing pit of radiation.

But no more. Khrushchev, the once-loyal Soviet older brother, had decided this was not to be. Cuba was too young and impetuous to be trusted with nuclear weapons.

De la Guardia squared his shoulders, steeling himself against despair.

Eight MAZ trucks squealed and groaned in the darkness, pulling heavy trailers out of the clearing and disappearing into the forest. The hulking trucks ran without headlights, security against American attack. Four KS-19 100mm air-defense guns would be the last to roll away. One could never be too careful—*Yanqui* spies were thick as weeds on the island. Cuba had won the revolution, but the war with the U.S. smoldered on. And the Russians had still decided to abandon them.

Colonel de la Guardia stood ramrod straight in the purple shadow of an abandoned poultry house. He was flanked by his driver and one of his aides. Both were mere boys, barely a decade older than his own son. In their late teens, they had more than once proven themselves fiercely devoted to the revolution and, more important, to de la Guardia. The colonel had zero doubt that, had it been light enough to see, tears of abject sadness would have been apparent on the young men's exhausted faces.

Dozens of men coughed and cursed in the blackness of night, tired and, like their commander, despondent to the point of weeping. Kits rattled, wooden crates thudded against one another. Even the trucks seemed to register the wrongness of what they were doing. Springs squeaked and gears groaned in protest as they disappeared down deeply rutted roads.

The last six FKR tactical nuclear missiles were leaving the island.

The idiot *Yanquis* had chewed their collars over medium- and intermediate-range missiles in Cuba, but they'd had no idea about the short-range weapons the Soviets had deployed right under their noses.

Then Khrushchev had decided he wanted all his missiles back, along with the four Soviet regiments meant to operate them.

It was all de la Guardia could do to hold his head upright. A tall man with the chiseled look of an American film star, he was a son of the revolution, proud of his close friendship with the *comandante*, though he didn't care much for that blowhard Ernesto "Che" Guevara. Colonel de la Guardia did not fear death, but this Soviet insult was far worse. To be weak was one thing, but to know real power and then have it stolen by those who professed to be your friends—that was emasculating.

At a sudden crunch in the gravel, his training took over and brought him out of his moping. His hand dropped to the Makarov pistol at his side.

"Ah, there you are, Comrade Colonel," Major Vasili Capuchin said. There was no moon, but intermittent brake lights and the periodic flash of torches were enough to illuminate Capuchin's smile. His world had not turned upside down.

"Do not look so glum, my friend," the major said. "All is not lost. This is not the end of everything."

"I do not blame *you*, Comrade Vasili," de la Guardia said. "But I fear that you are wrong."

De la Guardia's counterpart in the Soviet forces in Cuba, Capuchin was the *de facto* man in charge of the regiment tasked with the FKRs pointed at the American base at Guantanamo Bay. The Russian was only a major, but it was an unspoken truth that a Soviet major outranked a Cuban colonel by exponential proportions.

De la Guardia sighed, attempting to remind himself

that his friend was in fact guiltless. Major Capuchin was only following orders from the Presidium of the Supreme Soviet, but as the one tasked to oversee the logistical details of the missile removal, did he not bear some responsibility for leaving Cuba vulnerable to another *Yanqui* invasion?

The Russian put a hand on de la Guardia's shoulder and gave it a brotherly squeeze. A nearby truck hit its brakes, and for a brief moment, a line of perfect teeth gleamed under a thick salt-and-pepper mustache. Had it been any other Soviet, de la Guardia would have been tempted to cut his hand off with a machete.

"Come with me, my friend," Capuchin said. He nodded toward the hulk of the farthest poultry barn, some hundred meters away. They were all abandoned, but the ammonia smell of chicken manure still hung like razor blades on the humid air. "There is something I want to show you."

De la Guardia groaned. He'd been awake for over thirty-six hours. There was little point in doing anything other than finding a bed. Still, he followed dutifully, motioning for his aide and his driver to accompany him with a flick of his hand.

Capuchin nodded to the two younger men before looking back at de la Guardia to raise a wary eye.

"Do you trust these men?"

"Without question," de la Guardia said. "They would die for me."

Both boys puffed their chests at the show of trust from the colonel.

"Ah," Capuchin said. "Dying is often the easy part."

The boys glared at the Russian. De la Guardia gave a wan smile in spite of himself. Capuchin had been a boy during the siege of Stalingrad. Two pimple-faced teenagers could hardly intimidate him.

"Comrade Fidel trusts them," de la Guardia said. This returned the smug grins to the boys' faces and put the matter to rest once and for all.

"As you wish." Capuchin turned on his heels.

Twenty minutes later, Colonel Juan de la Guardia emerged from the poultry barn, smiling for the first time in a week. He inhaled deeply, oblivious to the stench of ammonia. The night air was immeasurably sweeter than it had been only moments before. He wanted to sing, but he thought better of it. There were still too many soldiers loading gear and supplies. A Soviet jeep rattled up and screeched to a stop. The driver, a young lieutenant named Ivchenko, gave Capuchin a crisp salute.

The major turned to de la Guardia and extended his hand. "My car is here."

De la Guardia smiled. "You must stay and celebrate with me."

"As far as my people know," Capuchin said, "there is nothing for us to celebrate. Day after tomorrow, my ship departs Mariel Harbor for Severomorsk with the last of our special weapons. There is much to do before we leave."

De la Guardia gripped the other man's hand in both fists. Tears welled in his eyes. It was an uncharacteristic display of emotion in front of his staff, but he did not care. "You are a true comrade of the revolution," he said. "I do not know what to say."

Capuchin gave him a soft smile. "Whatever it is, it

would be better if you said it to Castro. He should know
that there are those of us who believe in your cause,
strongly enough to leave one of our little girls behind."

The major often referred to his missiles as females.
The FKRs in particular were "little girls."

"And what if Fidel decides to utilize your gift sooner
rather than later?" de la Guardia asked.

Capuchin shrugged. "Then someone will be shot,"
he said. "And that someone will very likely be me. As I
told you: Given the right circumstances, dying is not so
difficult."

"Very well." De La Guardia almost bounced with
pent-up excitement. "I need to see to my men here and
make a quick telephone call to my wife. Then I will
follow you back to Havana on the next flight so I can
inform Comandante Fidel in person. The Americans are
everywhere. This is not the sort of information one
sends via unsecure lines."

The prospect of a bullet to his neck still lingered in
Vasili Capuchin's mind as he fastened his lap belt in the
Antonov An-2 forty-five minutes later. The "Annushka"
biplane took off from Antonio Maceo Airport south of
Santiago and made a lumbering turn back to the northeast, over the dark expanse of tree-choked hills below
and unlit homes. Tensions with the United States were
high, but it was the lack of electricity in these rural areas
that kept them blacked out, not attention to security.

The major leaned his forehead against the window,
half thinking he might see the shadow of his friend's
jeep speeding along the silver-gray road on its way to
the airport.

What he saw instead caused his breath to catch hard in his throat. Orange flames a thousand feet below sent a spiraling plume of sparks and smoke into the night air.

Capuchin kept his eyes glued to the scene but barked over his shoulder to Lieutenant Ivchenko. "Check with the pilots," he said. "Find out what they are hearing on the radio."

The Annushka carried only twelve passengers, so Ivchenko crossed only a short distance before reaching the cockpit and leaning inside, shoulder-deep. Two minutes later, he made his way back down the narrow aisle bearing news.

"A Cuban convoy has been attacked coming out of the forest."

Capuchin gave a weary groan. "Our missiles?"

"The weapons are already past." As he spoke, Ivchenko bowed his head, then glanced upward like a guilty child. "The assassins were killed."

"Good," Capuchin said. "What else?"

"I am very sorry to inform you, Comrade Major, but it appears that Colonel Miguel de la Guardia's jeep was hit by a rocket-propelled grenade. There were no survivors."

Capuchin rubbed his eyes with a thumb and forefinger. War in one part of the world or another was all he'd ever known. A man might get used to bloodshed, but good friends were hard to come by.

Ivchenko patted the headrest in front of Capuchin, half turning to go. "I will tell the pilot to return to Santiago."

The major thought for a moment, then shook his head. "No, Lieutenant," he said. "Our mission is before us, not behind."

The young man protested. "If Colonel de la Guardia was killed . . . what of the weapon?"

The Antonov banked west, toward Havana and away from the fireball. With nothing but black out the window again, Capuchin turned in his seat to fully face the lieutenant. "My dear Petyr," he said, through a tight smile. "The records of inspection and the ship's bill of lading show all of the missiles accounted for. I will personally sign off on them when our ship reaches Severomorsk. There is no time to tell Castro directly. Honestly, apart from you, I trust no one but Colonel de la Guardia with information about a nuclear device that should not be in Cuba in the first place."

Ivchenko chewed on his bottom lip, then cocked his head to one side. "She is well hidden. Perhaps she is lost for good."

"It may not be until you and I are bones in the ground, but mark my words. Someone will find her," Capuchin said. "The little girl I left behind will not stay hidden forever."

Present day
Florida Straits

Freedom lay off the bow, close enough to smell.

Alejandro Placensia had never ridden a wild horse, but he had flown a MiG-23. This sleek Bahamian cigarette boat slamming against the waves of a confused sea was surely a close approximation of both. The vessel shot through the ink-black night as if fired from a cannon, sending up a chattering spray that drenched everyone on board.

Alejandro's wife, Savina, sat on the floor of the boat. One slender hand gripped their small daughter, while the other held a wooden effigy of Elegua, the Santeria deity that her godmother had given her. Two-year-old Umbelina squirmed and whined, trying to escape her mother's python grip, but Savina looked forward, chin up, the outline of her oval face barely visible in the darkness. Alejandro was sure she was smiling.

The Cuban ran a hand over his spray-drenched hair and crouched deeper in the back of the cigarette boat. He felt incredibly small on the great, black sea. Alejandro estimated that they must be crossing the Gulf Stream by now. Umbelina giggled at the pounding ride, misreading her father's terror for excitement.

Their captain, a slender Haitian man named Deveaux, sat behind the wheel, a black silhouette against a blacker night. Only the glow of his cigarette, whipped into an orange coal by the wind, illuminated his face.

Ocean currents pushed the waves in a great arc to the northeast, while prevailing winds blew due north across the water, muddling the seas and adding to the chop. Alejandro had once been a pilot, flying a MiG-23 for the 2661st Attack Squadron at San Antonio de los Baños. One of his commanders, observing that Alejandro had the mind of a scientist, had recommended him for the prestigious Aerospace Engineering University of Moscow. It meant no more money—everyone in Cuba except for politicians and generals made essentially the same salary. But his mother could brag about his education, and he got a place to live with floors that were not completely uneven, so that was something.

Placensia did the calculations for speed and drift in his head, praying Deveaux had made the necessary course corrections. He would have said something, but the sullen Haitian did not invite idle talk. The captain had hardly spoken ten words since he'd picked them up just after midnight on the Bahamian rock known as Cayo de Sal—Salt Cay.

The tiny chain of uninhabited islands was a well-known stopover for *balseros*—desperate souls fleeing Cuba on flimsy homemade rafts cobbled together with inner tubes or blocks of Styrofoam. Alejandro had first considered hiring one of the human smugglers from Mexico who helped Cubans escape the island. But the going rate for one of these *lancheros* had been somewhere around 10,000 American dollars *before* the smuggling of Cuban baseball superstars to the U.S. had inflated the fare to more than two hundred thousand per person. Even with his side job driving rich Canadian and European tourists around Havana, Alejandro knew he could never afford that price for his entire family. And no one would front him the money because he didn't have a lucrative sports contract waiting on the other end. It was just as well, though. He'd heard that many *lancheros* had ties to Mexican drug cartels. Subjecting his little family to the dangers of the sea seemed far better than chancing a double-cross or ransom scheme of the violent Zetas drug cartel.

But he had to leave. There was no question about that. In the end, he split the difference and piloted his own small, rubber raft as far as Salt Cay, meeting Deveaux to take them the remainder of the way. The United States Coast Guard made regular patrols of Salt Cay, but the approaching hurricane seemed to be keeping them in ports back home, preparing for the rescue work ahead.

The Cuban coastguard had their own fast boats, but the same storm was predicted to shave the northern coast, so most of these patrol crafts had fled to the south, on the Bay of Pigs side of the island. In fact, Alejandro and his family had encountered no other vessels since slipping away from the island. Most people who were caught fleeing Cuba—traitors to the revolution, the government called them—were thrown in prison for reeducation.

Alejandro would be shot.

In truth, he'd thought about leaving for more than a decade. He'd just been too much of a coward to follow through until now. Cubans were a beautiful people, *his* people, but Cuba was an island of smoke and mirrors— garish, flaking paint over rotten wood and rusted metal.

Revolution had once appealed to him, as he supposed it did to all young men of conscience. He and his friends were proud Fidelistas. They hated the *Yanquis* and their wicked capitalist ideology with a righteous purity that astounded even their communist parents. He had been a child during the *Período Especial*—the Special Period of rationing and shortages that followed the Soviet abandonment in 1989. Creeping over the wall of the Havana Zoo with his father to "liberate" the peacocks from their cages had seemed a great adventure. He'd been too young to understand the desperation his parents had felt when having to eat zoo animals and the unnamed meat that he found out much later was feral cat. It had been easy to blame the problems of the Special Period on the *Yanquis*.

Communism seemed a wise enough notion when that was all he knew. But the older he got, the more he saw. The more he saw, the wider his eyes began to open. A beautiful woman did not have to beg to be courted. A government should not force you to believe.

Then he'd been allowed to leave the island for an engineering conference in Chile.

If capitalism was so bad, why were those who lived under its wicked umbrella so happy? The greedy residents of Valparaíso had bread and meat in their grocery stores. The new vehicles that teemed along the *avenidas* had plenty of fuel. Bit by bit, Alejandro's notion of what was right and what was wrong began to shift. He hated the rich *turistas* he drove around in his cab not because they were bourgeois, but because they did not want his island to change. "We had to come here before progress ruins you," they said. Alejandro knew the hardships of the ancient cars and broken streets that they called "quaint."

He'd finally decided to leave in the coming December, after hurricane season was well behind them, but Zayda de la Guardia, Major General of the Intelligence Directorate, had summoned him to Santiago, and Alejandro's fate was sealed on the day he'd arrived. Even if he did exactly what they ordered, he would eventually be killed. Death was the way men like General de la Guardia kept secrets.

It was the way of things in this quaint island paradise.

Alejandro was able to slip away from de la Guardia's staff and catch a flight from Santiago back to Havana, where he picked up his family without being arrested. The small inflatable boat was hidden in the mangroves near the resort beaches of Cayo Blanco, where his contact had said it would be. They'd left under cover of darkness and, using Alejandro's mobile phone as a GPS, navigated the fifty kilometers across Nicholas Channel to the Cay Sal Banks. To Alejandro's astonishment, Captain Deveaux had been waiting at the agreed-upon spot.

When he finally saw the winking lights of Marathon Key on the horizon, the Cuban's throat convulsed. The "wet foot, dry foot" policy of the United States had changed in recent years, making asylum nearly impossible. *Balseros* who were lucky enough to make it onto dry land before arrest had once been able to remain in America as refugees. Now, they were routinely sent back to Cuba.

But Alejandro had seen things. Surely the *Yanquis* would welcome his family with open arms when they heard what he had to say.

Deveaux slowed the cigarette boat a mile offshore. The following wake shoved the stern as it caught up with them, causing the boat to wallow in the sea and throwing everyone forward. Savina looked up in alarm.

Alejandro gave a forced smile to the captain, hoping to conceal his fear.

"Everything is okay?" he asked in accented English. Deveaux had made it abundantly clear that he did not speak Spanish.

"*Tout bon*," the captain said, a freshly lit cigarette clenched between his teeth. He nodded toward the side of the boat. "Off you get."

Alejandro drew his wife and child closer now. The air was hot and muggy, but he had to concentrate to keep his teeth from chattering.

"Off?"

A sudden gust of wind extinguished Deveaux's cigarette. The flame of his lighter showed the look of cruel indifference on his face as he puffed the cigarette back to life. He cupped his hand over the new coal to shield it, shrugging.

"I have no wish to see the walls of an American

prison." He gave an impatient flick of his wrist. "So, as I say to you before, off you get."

Alejandro was taller, stronger, and had much more to lose. Deveaux seemed to read his mind and drew a black pistol from his pocket.

"But . . . it is too far," Alejandro stammered. "We will drown."

Deveaux gave a deep belly laugh, looking like the pirate that he was. "*J'en doute*," he sneered. "I doubt that. You Cubans are . . . how do you say? *Les cafards* . . . the cockroaches. I think you outlive us all." His dark eyes narrowed, flicking the pistol again. "Get off, before I decide to keep your woman." His voice softened inexplicably, as if he'd not just threatened to kidnap Savina. "Mind the current. It will push you up, along the coast. Swim at an angle, and you shall be fine."

Alejandro stood, pulling his wife to her feet. "But . . . our child . . ."

Deveaux shrugged again. "I am happy to take her with me, but if I am honest, she stands a better chance in the sea with you." He threw the boat into gear, nodding again toward the choppy water. "I am leaving. The longer you put this off, the farther from land you will be."

Alejandro stepped to the rail, pulling Savina with him. He gazed sadly at the flickering city lights, so near, yet so very far away. Taking little Umbelina in his arms, he blew in her face so she'd hold her breath—then jumped, willing himself not to think of the sharks that hunted these waters at night.

Santiago de Cuba

General Zayda de la Guardia's driver stepped on the squealing brakes, bringing the rusted Lada sedan to a stop in front of the abandoned poultry house. Fifty feet wide and two hundred feet long, the old hulk of a barn was the easternmost of four identical houses. They were all built sometime in the early thirties to provide chicken for the many casinos and fancy restaurants that had crowded the island.

It was just before five-thirty in the morning, almost two hours until sunrise, but the general had his people on a strict timetable. Work continued throughout the night.

The air was hot and sticky. It always was on the island, though sometimes it was much hotter and far stickier. The smell of ammonia from the nearby sewage lagoon bit de La Guardia's nose, causing his eyes to tear up as soon as he opened the door. It could not be helped. Something had to be done with three decades of chicken manure. Generators and pumps wheezed and slurped, keeping the slop at bay in the toxic soup of the burbling lagoon.

Time had reduced the other three barns to little more than skeletons, but de la Guardia had made this one much more substantial. Thick timbers buttressed the plywood retaining wall that kept the sewage lagoon from reaching the barn, and his men had fitted the interior with blackout screening, cobbled together from scraps of whatever they could find. Bits of weathered, Soviet-era lumber and repurposed roofing material were tacked up on the walls.

The Lada finally came to a stop. The driver set the parking brake and rushed around to open the door. De la Guardia could never remember the man's name. It was Russian—Madic, or Madiv, or some other boringly Slavic name, a remnant of Soviet soldiers who had fathered many children on the island. These men had married their Cuban paramours long enough to give them a Russian surname, then promptly abandoned them when they were recalled to the motherland. This young driver knew of the secret bunker, but he was too terrified to pose any threat in the short term. The long term would take care of itself. In any case, the man would wait in the car.

De la Guardia had considered running a chicken operation in the other barns. But such an endeavor would mean turning soldiers into chicken farmers, and he feared that chicken farmers would not make good coconspirators.

The front door was unlocked. One of de la Guardia's soldiers, dressed in civilian clothing, hastily put out a cigarette and braced to attention. The periphery of the general's flashlight beam illuminated glossy female legs on the pages of a pornographic magazine. It seemed the guard had attempted to bury it in a mound of decades-old chicken dung when he'd heard the squealing brakes. De la Guardia raised an eyebrow at the magazine and growled a few words about the dereliction of duty, but he left it at that. Like the driver, this man did not have enough value to warrant a formal rebuke.

Under normal circumstances, soldiers could rest easy under the notion that anyone with enough authority to have them shot was likely sleeping off a night of overindulgence, probably snoring beside his mistress. But Zayda de la Guardia was a man on a mission— a mission that saw him dressed in a cheap cotton shirt and riding around in a rusty Lada that was older than he was.

The only thin thing about the piggish general was the

mustache above a mouth that seemed a few centimeters too long for even his wide face. The dark Spanish eyes, inherited from his great grandfather, were small, like specks on a dinner plate. His thick black hair was combed up in a slight pompadour, like the photograph of his father that his mother kept above her dining room table. Where Colonel Miguel de la Guardia's dashing looks had seen him rise in the revolutionary army, Zayda had been promoted for the opposite reason. He was smart and driven, to be sure, but his odd look made certain that he could never outshine the Castros—an offense that had been the downfall of many handsome men in Cuban politics. Where Zayda's father had looked like a man to lead other men, the younger de la Guardia's visage said he would simply kill them if they did not get out of his way. It didn't hurt that Zayda's father had been a hero of the revolution, murdered in his prime.

De la Guardia looked the sentry up and down, just to make him nervous. "Ring down to Dr. Placensia," he snapped. "I want to see him at once."

The guts of the building were hidden beneath a trapdoor of rough lumber in an earthen bunker under the old barn. Right now, only a ladder led down from the trapdoor, but de la Guardia had arranged for the crane that would bring out his prize in coming days.

The sentry stammered, staring into the empty building. "I would be most happy to do so, General, but Dr. Placensia is not here."

De la Guardia's stomach began to knot. "Where is he?"

"This I do not know, General. He has not been here for the better part of two days."

The general spun on his heels, stalking outside to his

Lada. He snatched a mobile phone from his pocket and punched in a number as he walked.

A youthful Cuban coastguardsman answered immediately, audibly bracing when the general informed him who he was.

De la Guardia launched into his demand. "Radar signatures of vessels heading toward Miami. What do you see?"

"We observed one approximately four hours ago, Comrade General," the coastguardsman said. "It was small, moving quickly. Likely an inflatable or other small craft. We believe this vessel met up with a larger, faster vessel near Cay de Sal, which continued toward Florida. At present, it is stopped two kilometers offshore from Marathon Key."

De la Guardia sputtered, furious. "No one thought to intercept this vessel in Cuban waters?"

"Our patrols have all moved to the lee side of the island, out of the predicted path of the hurricane."

"I see," de la Guardia said, grinding his teeth. "Tell me, what is this vessel doing at this very moment?"

"It is motionless, Comrade General," the coastguardsman said. The man's voice trailed off. "My apologies. It appears to be moving again."

"Toward the shore?"

"No, sir," the coastguardsman said. "On a bearing toward the Bahamas."

"I want this boat stopped," de la Guardia fumed. "I do not care if you have to invade Nassau." He ended the call before the coastguardsman could protest.

De la Guardia checked his watch, then punched a second number into his mobile.

The man on the other end of the line picked up on the third ring.

"Where are you?" de la Guardia snapped.

"Precisely where you sent me," the voice whispered, absent the fawning deference others showed.

"You have finished then?"

"I have not."

"That is too bad," de la Guardia said. "I have another mission. Marathon Key. How long until you can get there?"

"A half an hour if we leave at once," the man on the other end of the line said.

"Make it twenty minutes," de la Guardia said.

"What am I looking for?"

"A very wet man clamoring up from the beach," de la Guardia said. "His wife and child may accompany him. At this moment, I believe he is swimming from a boat that has deposited them approximately two kilometers offshore."

"Swimming?" the calm man repeated, as if taking notes. "How old is the child?"

The phone crackled with static, as it often did over Cuban telecom systems.

"What does that matter?" the general snapped. "One or two, perhaps."

A contemplative sigh. "Two kilometers is a long swim with a baby."

"Yes, yes, so it is," de la Guardia said, struggling to keep the pitch of his voice from rising. "This traitor must be stopped. I will send a secure message with the particulars. Let me talk to Fuentes."

"We split up," the man said, his voice registering a hint of disgust.

It was saying something if Colonel Joaquin Mirabal, a cold man who hunted and killed other human beings for a living, considered Fuentes a soulless animal—the very qualities for which de la Guardia employed both of them.

"Very well," the general said. "I will call Fuentes directly. Get on with your job, Joaquin. This traitor must be stopped."

"The sharks will probably get him," Mirabal offered.

"See that they do," de la Guardia said. "One way or another."

Key Largo, Florida

Ted Schoonover saw the little girl first, standing in the surf, backlit by the rising sun. Her shadow was absurdly long across the swath of golden sand that stretched below the line of condos. Black hair plastered to her chubby little face, she stood at the tideline, water draining from a sagging cloth diaper. Schoonover and his wife did not have children, so he was no expert, but this one looked about two years old, maybe younger. A man staggered out of the water behind her, dragging a sputtering, half-conscious woman by the arms. Moving woodenly, he dropped the woman on the dry sand and then collapsed to his knees beside the child. He'd obviously deposited the girl on the shore and gone back for the woman.

Cubans, Schoonover thought. *Almost dead Cubans*.

He dropped his tape measure, hurdled over the row of newly planted palmetto shrubs, and sprinted to help the exhausted family.

In his mid-thirties, Schoonover was much too young to be as rich as he was. He'd lived in Florida for the past six years, earning his first million in real estate shortly after he'd separated from the Air Force. A former F-22 pilot, he could have flown in civilian life, but driving what was essentially a winged commuter bus back and forth across the sky at 40,000 feet was the last thing he wanted to do after the high-speed, low-drag stuff he'd grown used to in the military. Luckily, it turned out that risking his ass in real estate kept his blood pumping nearly as fast as prepping for a 7-G turn.

Schoonover made it to the exhausted family in half a dozen long strides. He pantomimed drinking something, and then pointed toward the condos. His Spanish was usually passable, but in the heat of the moment he couldn't manage to dredge up a single word beyond *agua*.

The wet man surprised him by speaking accented English. His voice was breathless and raspy. "Water," he said, nodding emphatically. "Yes, please, for my little girl and my wife. My name is Alejandro Placensia." He looked up and down the beach. "There were spotlights a short time ago, shining across the water. Did you see them?"

Schoonover shook his head. "I didn't see anything, but I just got here to check on my property."

Placensia gulped in another breath. He gave an uneasy nod, continuing to look over his shoulder. "I was pilot for Cuban Air Force . . . and an aeronautical engineer . . ." Tears streamed from his sad brown eyes. The man swallowed hard, summoning up the energy to continue. "I . . . have information . . . vital to United States. I wish to request asylum for my family."

Schoonover ran a hand through his hair, still wet from a morning shower. "I'm not sure how that would work," he said. "But I'm a former pilot myself." He shook the Cuban's hand. "Welcome to the United States, brother. I can call the police for you, if you want."

The man shook his head, hugging his wife closer. "Please, no. Cuban intelligence has many contacts inside Miami police. I would prefer to speak with someone higher."

Schoonover clapped his hands and pointed an index finger at the Cuban. "You know what?" he said. "I got a buddy from the Air Force Academy. He'll know what we should do."

Chapter 1

Virginia

Jericho Quinn knew the sound of fear when he heard it. His back against the door of the Cracker Barrel restaurant north of Dulles International Airport, he took a scant moment to survey the parking lot, homing in on the direction of the scream. It was early, a few minutes after six in the morning. The breakfast rush was just starting, the lot less than half full.

Beside Quinn, Marine Master Sergeant Jacques Thibodaux froze as well, his tremendous bulk eclipsing the rising sun over Washington, D.C., to the east. The big marine tugged down his tan baseball cap—a recent addition to his wardrobe—and rubbed a freshly shaven jaw that was sharp enough to cut glass. He turned his head slightly to search the lot with his good eye. The other, covered with a black patch, had been injured at Quinn's side in a firefight in Bolivia.

One Marine and one special agent for Air Force OSI, the two men were accustomed to moving toward the sound of danger, but not blindly or without any strategy.

"What do you reckon, Chair Force?" The big Marine said, rarely missing an opportunity to chide Quinn for his chosen branch of service. Jacques Thibodaux was originally from Louisiana, and his Cajun accent and playful attitude came through loud and clear. "I count three goons standing by that red Mustang."

"Yep," Quinn said. He moved his head along with his eyes as he scanned so he wouldn't miss any details. He'd shaved after his 0500 workout, but his cheeks were already beginning to show a dark stubble. This, combined with his scruffy hair, gave him an unkempt, predatory look that was intensified by its contrast with the recruiting-poster-sharp Marine. "There are two more coming up from behind," he added, moving again.

Fifty meters away, a young couple stood facing the three men in forest green T-shirts on a small grass island in the middle of the restaurant parking lot. Quinn couldn't be sure, but it looked as though the couple had just gotten out of the Mustang. The tallest of the three men had squared off, shoulders flared like a cobra and fists doubled at his sides, spoiling for a fight. The sandy-haired kid from the Mustang raised both hands. His spitfire girlfriend wasn't helping matters, peeking around from behind him and giving an earful to the three aggressors. Two others, also in green T-shirts, made their way toward the little group from between the parked cars.

"Get a load of their matching clothes," Thibodaux muttered. "Looks like a bunch of Batman villains. You reckon that one with the blond dreadlocks could be a girl?"

"Yep," Quinn said again. He zipped up his armored, black leather motorcycle jacket as he stepped around a row of rocking chairs so he could hop off the end of the restaurant's long covered porch. Conventional wisdom dictated he leave the jacket unzipped to provide easier access to the Kimber 10mm pistol in the holster over his right kidney, but Quinn didn't want to introduce a gun into what was likely just a fistfight. The leather jacket was heavy enough to provide an extra level of protection and supple enough to lift out of the way with his nondominant hand should the pistol become necessary. The weather was warm, but he'd worn the jacket and Kevlar-lined Tobacco Jeans anyway.

"Dammit," Thibodaux spat as they neared the altercation. "I don't wanna hit a girl if there's any way around it. Do me a favor, Chair Force. You hit her if she needs hittin'."

Quinn shot his friend a look, but didn't say anything. Jacques had a tendency to philosophize up to and even during a fight. Luckily, he never seemed to require an answer, just a listening ear. Quinn had trained and fought alongside the big Marine countless times over the last half decade—enough times to know he would get down to business when the time came, no matter who he had to hit.

The hard truths of real-world conflict had taught both men to employ the same basic strategy—surprise, speed, and overwhelming force. The Cajun relied on his size and tremendous strength, where Quinn's boxing and jujitsu background gave him more finesse.

Quinn noted a University of Maryland Terrapin sticker beside a decal of a Union Jack on the Mustang's bumper. None of the group looked much older than twenty, and he thought maybe this was some beef over school rivalry. Once he was close enough to hear the invective spewing from the green-shirt crowd, though, it was clear this was something different than a fight over football.

"Here now!" Thibodaux barked, adopting the disciplinary tone he used on his seven sons. "Looks like we got ourselves a misunderstanding." He sidestepped to the right, while Quinn moved left, flanking the group.

The green-shirts didn't have enough sense to care.

The tallest of the five, their apparent leader, continued to focus intently on the Mustang driver. He addressed Thibodaux without looking up.

"Haul ass, Grandpa," he said. "We got this."

Quinn took a step closer, less than ten feet away now, a hair nearer to the leader than Jacques. "You got what? Five against two? Looks like assault to me."

The leader's apparent aide-de-camp took an aggressive step toward Quinn, met his eye, and then froze, trying to build up his nerve. He was smart enough to stop, but couldn't keep from yapping like a dog.

"You're not cops," the kid sneered, "or you would have told us already. And anyway, like you said, there are five of us . . . so you should go."

The Mustang driver kept his hands raised. He spoke with a decidedly educated British accent. "I've never spoken with these people in my life. Apparently, they think I'm some kind of fascist."

The green-shirt leader opened his mouth to respond, but the girl behind the Mustang driver began to scream at him again, defending the honor of her boyfriend in language strong enough to make even Thibodaux grimace.

The leader glanced sideways at Thibodaux, his face screwed into a dismissive sneer. "I thought I told you to get your ass outta here, old man."

Thibodaux shrugged, letting the comment about his age slide. Neither he nor Quinn had reached forty yet. He maneuvered so the nearest thug was between him and the hood of the Mustang.

"How about you explain to me what's goin' on here, boss?" Thibodaux said.

The chubby girl in dreadlocks pointed a finger at Thibodaux. "You're either with us, or you're pro-fascist."

"Just anti-dumbass," Thibodaux said.

"You talk like you're from the South," the girl said. "Pretty sure you're a fascist, too."

"Nope," Thibodaux said, heaving a long sigh.

"Well, shithead here sure is," she said.

The Brit raised his hands even higher. "Why do you all keep saying that?"

The leader began to breathe through his nose, a sure sign that he'd worked himself up to attack. The entire group looked and acted like amateurs, but Quinn had learned a long time ago that amateur elbows to the nose hurt just as bad as elbows belonging to trained professionals.

Quinn's hands came up to his chest, palms out—a purely tactical move, not one of contrition. There was no signal between Quinn and Thibodaux, but he knew that Thibodaux would spring into action, too. They'd decided early on what they would, and would not, tolerate from these people—or anyone else, for that matter.

Quinn drove forward, straight through the leader's startled aide-de-camp, taking just enough time to throw a lightning-fast one-two-three combination of left jab, right cross, and left uppercut. The last punch was overkill, but Quinn was already committed. He yanked the Brit out of the way with his right hand, throwing him to the ground in the process. The green-shirt leader threw a single, glancing blow to the Brit's chest, but quickly reverted into the posturing phase. Quinn slapped him on the ear, driving him sideways into another right cross as the third green-shirt in line stepped up. This one fancied himself an actual fighter. He squared off in a fists-up, Sherlock Holmes–style bare-knuckle boxing stance.

Quinn was vaguely aware of Thibodaux, bouncing someone's head off the hood of the Mustang while he wore the screaming, dreadlocked girl like a banshee-backpack. Jacques yowled, probably bitten. He was always getting bitten—he had a tendency to pull his punches when he fought females, even when they were trying to kill him. He let loose a string of Cajun curses and reached over his shoulders in an attempt to peel the screeching woman off his back. Finally succeeding, he raised her high above his head. It looked like something out of a *WWE SmackDown* match.

Quinn wanted to watch what happened next, but his opponent turned out to be slightly more skilled than his stance suggested. Quinn loved boxing, and he rarely stood toe to toe in a real-world fight. But an explosive attack might kill this hapless kid, so Quinn circled instead of crashing in. He put the kid's back to Jacques, just in time to watch the big Cajun toss the woman, a little too gently, to the ground. It did the trick, though, and she gave up—for the moment.

The door to a nearby Mazda creaked open, and a sixth green-shirt climbed out. This one was at least six four, and almost as thick as Thibodaux.

Jacques chuckled. "Oh good," he said. "I've leveled up in this game."

Quinn's green-shirt feinted with a left jab, a little too

deeply, presenting the point of his chin on a silver platter. Quinn rewarded the mistake with a cross elbow to the nose, dispensing with Marquess of Queensberry rules now that Thibodaux might need some help.

He needn't have worried. Jacques drove a knee into the big guy's groin, and then, when the guy doubled over, used the fender of the Mustang to great effect once again.

Quinn took a step back, scanning for other attackers. That which didn't kill you often had friends waiting in the wings to kill you when you thought the fight was finished.

All the idiots appeared to have shown themselves.

With all six green-shirts out cold or pretending to be, Thibodaux stooped to pick up the ball cap that the girl had knocked off his head.

Quinn smiled. "You should think about losing the hat. It's just not you."

"That's the whole point of it, Chair Force," Jacques said. "I wear the cover to make me look less like a Marine."

Quinn's smile broadened. "Let me know how that works out for you. And don't keep calling it a 'cover' if you want to sound like a civilian." He reached down to help the Brit to his feet. "You okay?"

"I'm fine," the kid said, his jaw hanging open. "That was nothing short of amazing." He looked up. "I must tell you, there is not a racist bone in my body. Why did these people think I was a fascist?"

"Let's ask 'em." Thibodaux goaded the initial insti-gator with the toe of his motorcycle boot. "What's your beef with Mr. Mustang here?"

"He's got a Confederate flag," the green-shirt leader said.

The Brit looked confused. "No, I don't."

On a hunch, Quinn stepped around to look at the Mustang's bumper, whistling Jacques over at what he saw.

Thibodaux rolled his good eye at the green-shirt. "Not that a Stars and Bars bumper sticker is worth gettin' your ass kicked over, but that's a British Union Jack, genius."

Chapter 2

Soon after, after they'd made sure the British student and his girlfriend were back in the Mustang and safely on their way, Quinn and Thibodaux stood beside their BMW GS Adventure motorcycles at the other end of the parking lot. They'd need to leave quickly if they didn't want to become embroiled in a quagmire of statements and interviews with law enforcement.

Quinn slipped a beaked Arai dual sport helmet over his head. The helmet was gunmetal gray to match his bike, with *Death Dealer* war axes airbrushed on each side to match his personality.

Thibodaux threw a leg over his own bike, which was a more vibrant red and black. "I don't mean to put too fine a point on it, *mon ami*," he said, helmet poised above his head. "But I didn't exactly hit that gal back there. She hit the pavement."

"Tomato, to-mah-to," Quinn said, pushing the Beemer's ignition switch with his right thumb. Two minutes later, he rolled on the throttle and made a left turn onto Old Ox Road toward Reston. As usual, Thibodaux's philosophical meanderings began to pour through the Cardo Bluetooth speaker inside Quinn's helmet almost as soon as they were on the road.

". . . you ask me, marry Ronnie, have a passel of kids, and channel your inner grandpa—"

"You mean my inner dad," Quinn said, taking the bait.

"Nah," Thibodaux said. "Skip the dad part and just be a grandpa. I've decided not to sweat the normal stuff dads are supposed to worry about. Camille hates it."

Quinn chuckled, chewing on that. "I never figured you for an inner grandpa," he said. "An inner child, maybe."

"Well, I'll tell you, Chair Force," the big Cajun drawled, passing Quinn's motorcycle on the left. "Turns out, my inner grandpa is pretty cool, but my inner child is a mean little bastard."

Quinn couldn't help but smile. "Mine too," he said.

His cell chirped in the headset, rescuing him from further discussion. He tapped the controls on the outside of his helmet, then rode forward to make a telephone gesture to Jacques, letting him know he was handling a call. A familiar voice spilled through the speakers.

Quinn smiled, recognizing an old Air Force Academy squadron mate from the Tough Twenty Trolls. Teddy Schoonover had gone the pilot route, while Quinn pursued a career as a Combat Rescue Officer and led a team of PJs, the Air Force's elite pararescue personnel. By the time Quinn had made the switch from Special Ops to the Office of Special Investigations, Schoonover was teaching a new cadre of pilots to fly F-22s at Tyndall AFB in Florida. The two men saw each other at periodic reunions, and they still kept in touch via the close association of men and women who'd endured the same Beast Summer during their freshman year in the thin air of Jacks Valley above Colorado Springs.

"Well hey, Ted," Quinn said. He kept his voice low and even, despite how happy he was to hear from a former classmate. The Academy had a way of cementing friendships, and Schoonover was one of the best. They exchanged quick pleasantries, skipping the usual banter about the food at Arnold Hall and any number of things neither of them missed about USAFA. Schoonover was rattled and jittery—no small thing for a man accustomed to strapping himself into a hunk of metal flying faster than the speed of sound. Quinn listened without interrupting.

"I'll do what I can," he said when Schoonover finished. "I'll check with a friend at Customs and Border Protection."

"I'd appreciate that, Jericho," Schoonover said. "This guy acts like somebody had the proverbial red dot on his forehead. Know what I'm saying? He's scared shitless, and I don't mind telling you, that's got me spooked. According to him, Cuban Intelligence has Metro-Dade wired from the inside, if you know what I mean. I've got a lot of friends in local law enforcement, and I've heard the same thing from them."

"That's a strong possibility," Quinn said, thinking of what he knew of Cuba's Intelligence Directorate. He glanced at his left mirror, shoulder checked to made doubly sure his lane was clear, and accelerated around a poky Ford Fiesta as he continued to speak. "This Placensia guy, he seems legitimate?"

"I think so, yeah," Schoonover said. There was noise in the background and muffled conversation as Schoonover spoke with someone else, presumably the Cuban refugee. He came back on the line a moment later. "He keeps saying he has information vital to the United

States. Listen, Jericho, Customs and Border Protection is all well and good. But don't you know anyone in . . ." He lowered his voice. "I don't know, the intelligence community?"

Quinn smiled in spite of his friend's anxiety. "I might know someone," he said. "Let me make a couple of calls, and I'll get back to you."

"Right away," Schoonover said. "I'm serious, Jericho. There's something about this guy. I mean, he was scared enough to swim in from a mile offshore carrying a little kid . . ."

"I'll get back to you in a flash." Quinn hit the Cardo control on the left side of his helmet to disconnect. He voice dialed the next call.

Five minutes later, Veronica "Ronnie" Garcia repeated Quinn's words back to him from her cubicle on the Russia desk at CIA Headquarters, just fifteen miles away. "Cubans, you say?"

Ronnie, the product of a Russian father and a Cuban mother—and Jericho Quinn's girlfriend—had a special affinity for refugees who were attempting to escape the thumb of the Castro regime, since she'd done it herself as a teenager. Now, her voice was rough with nostalgia. "Of course we'll help this guy. I've got a friend who's a case officer in Miami. He'll let ICE know the Agency will run point on this one, for the time being at least. He can arrange a neutral pickup and get the family to a safe house." Her tone grew softer, less businesslike. "Jericho, tell your Academy buddy to be careful. Miami stinks with Cuban DI operatives. Most of the time, my outfit underestimates how sharp they are. If this refugee knows something important to the regime, and they know he's run off, they'll be on his tail *muy pronto*. You got me, mango?"

"I'll pass that along," Quinn said, then relayed the address to the condo where Ted Schoonover was waiting.

"Good deal," Ronnie said, the richness of her accent coming across through the phone. "All this talk of the old country has me jonesing for some *crema de plátano*. How about you take me to Cubano's in Silver Spring tonight?"

Quinn smiled at the memory of their first quasi-date. He was very nearly banned from the place for a hellacious fight where he'd demolished the restaurant's men's room while defending himself from an attack. In the end, Ronnie had smoothed things over with some rowdy—and highly suggestive—Cuban jokes with the management. There seemed no end to what she could accomplish with a smile and few bats of her dark lashes.

"Who could say no to plantain soup?" Quinn said. "Okay, I promised Ted I'd call him right back. I'll let him know you're setting something up through your people and he can rest easy."

"Copy that," Garcia said. "Who loves ya, mango?"

Quinn shot a glance at Thibodaux, who rode just ahead and to the left in the same lane, glad he couldn't hear, then whispered into the helmet mic, "Voodoo."

"Damn right, me do," Garcia said.

"Me, too," Quinn said.

Quinn redialed Ted Schoonover as soon as he ended the call with Garcia. It rang once, then went immediately to voice mail. He tried again with the same result.

He'd expected Schoonover to pick up on the first

ring. The fact that he'd let two calls go unanswered gnawed at Quinn's gut. And if he'd learned anything over the course of his violent career, it was that his gut never lied.

Chapter 3

Six minutes earlier

Most operatives of *Dirección de Inteligencia* focused their efforts on recruiting agents from among the youth of Miami. Younger Cuban Americans tended to lean much further left than their parents. DI's chief recruitment weapons were a healthy capacity for salesmanship and, in the case of the female operatives, an oozingly stereotypical Latina sexuality. All of these provocateurs had been trained in defensive and offensive combat at the spy school known as Camp Matanzas, but few bothered with firearms, preferring social engineering to gunplay.

Joaquin Mirabal was not a recruiter. He was a hunter. The white scar that crossed diagonally from forehead to chin like a jagged white lightning bolt on his angular face was a testament to that.

Heavily influenced by his KGB trainers, Colonel Mirabal armed each of the other three members of his team with suppressed Pistolets Besshumnyy. The silenced handgun was based on the tried and true Makarov 9x18mm. It had come into service in the late 1960s, a decade before Mirabal was born, but was still issued to Russian Spetsnaz and FSB operatives who needed to kill quietly. While not completely silent, the small handguns were effective, and a little gunfire rarely raised much suspicion in southern Florida so long as the shots were kept to a minimum.

An avid hunter of big game since his early postings in Africa, Colonel Mirabal was by far the best shot in his four-person squad. As such, he gave himself a little more latitude with his choice of sidearm. Instead of the PB, he carried a tiny Beretta Bobcat in .22 caliber, outfitted with a small suppressor not much larger than his thumb. The "can," as the Americans called it, was just under eight centimeters long. Subsonic ammunition and a locked slide rendered the weapon as quiet as any he had ever used. Of course, he had to get close to employ it, but that was rarely a problem for a true hunter. He left the slide unlocked to allow for follow-up shots, but the gun was still no louder than a vigorous slap.

Each member of his team carried a blade for close work, or if they were making a statement. Mirabal's own knife was a simple hunting affair he'd been given by a tracker and friend in Angola. It was a homely thing, with a weathered acacia handle and a carbon steel blade that rusted easily if he didn't keep it oiled. But it held an edge, and he got it bloody often enough that remembering to oil it was not an issue.

The muscular Mateo Duran and voluptuous Serafina Lopez both carried heavy Soviet FSB daggers called *Karatels*, or Punishers. Guns and knives were easy to conceal inside heavy nylon fanny packs, conveniently popular with the older set in Florida who didn't want to fish items out of their pockets.

Estrada, the youngest of the four at twenty-two, carried a geologists' rock pick instead of a blade. It was roughly the same dimensions as a hammer, too big for the fanny pack. Estrada hung it from his nylon belt, where it blended easily with the blue and gray of his board shorts. The heavy pick was brutally lethal and had the added benefit of sending a clear message to any defectors who watched the news: They might assume a dead body containing the roundnose bullets from a Makarov pistol were from a Cuban assassin, but the spike of a rock pick through the teeth was a definite reminder to everyone to keep their own mouths shut. It was a practice that even Mirabal, who had seen much blood and bone over the course of his forty-six years, found disgusting. But Estrada did not seem to mind, so the duty fell to him.

As soon as he'd received the call from General de la Guardia, Mirabal brought up a weather report on his mobile phone while Duran drove. He needed something more specific than the basic weather report, so he used a website called Windy.com that displayed forecasts for wind speed, direction, wave height, and ocean currents. More important, it gave Mirabal the measurements for right now, not just the forecast, allowing him to make the necessary minute-by-minute computations. Once de la Guardia had relayed the last known radar location of the traitor's boat, it had been a straightforward process to deduce where the man would likely come ashore. Even the mightiest swimmers were subject to the wind and tide.

The traitor had jumped off the boat somewhere off Marathon Key, but the currents would sweep him northward toward Miami. If he was any kind of swimmer at all—and only a good swimmer would brave these dark, shark-infested waters with his wife and child—Alejandro Placensia would make landfall on Key Largo.

Mirabal worked time and distance calculations for drift as if he were charting a sailing course rather than trying to determine where the victim of his next bullet would founder on the sandy shores of the United States.

Duran parked their rented black Silverado pickup on a small side road, just beyond a tennis court in the neighborhood up the beach from where Mirabal guessed Placensia would make landfall. The sun was coming up, and people were beginning to stir. Few took the paper anymore, streaming what little news they read over the Internet, but some of the older ones—mostly women with brightly dyed hair and big Hollywood sunglasses— would be out soon to take their morning walks.

Mirabal made sure his team dressed to blend in. All the men wore pastel board shorts and polo shirts. Serafina's tennis dress would show off toned legs and distract any would-be witnesses from the specifics of her face. The Silverado was classy enough to fit in with the rest of the bourgeois *Yanqui* cars and trucks.

"I see him, Joaquin," Serafina whispered from the shadows. Her voice buzzed against her left fist as she held the portable infrared scope to her eye. She meant no disrespect by addressing her superior officer by his given name—too many people in the United States spoke Spanish, and it would arouse suspicion if anyone overheard her calling him "Comrade Colonel." She passed him the scope, then gestured with the blade in her right hand. "There, perhaps a hundred meters away beyond that row of palmettos, in the shadows beneath the shaded lanai."

Mirabal scanned the shoreline through the scope, locating the glowing forms of a tall man, a smaller woman, and a much smaller child. Even at eighty degrees, the ocean had sent most of their blood inward to keep their cores warm, leaving their skin to show the ghostly blue of a natural gas flame. A fourth form, this one bright red, stood some twenty feet distant from the others, arm up as if talking on his phone.

"Excellent work," Mirabal said. "Their recent swim has made them difficult to detect."

The Cuban woman smiled. Like the rest of the team, she'd worked all night on the earlier, unresolved assignment. She'd dampened her short black hair, making it look as though she'd just stepped from a morning shower. It was not a flattering look, Mirabal thought. It gave her the flint-hard visage of a woman who'd been wronged by too many men, adding a decade to her twenty-five years.

She spoke without looking away from their prey. "The far wall of the lanai should provide cover from neighbors to the west," she said. "The row of palms will shield our approach."

Mirabal gave a slow nod. "Placensia is bound to be watchful," the colonel said. "He knows someone is after him."

Estrada scoffed. "Do you think he expects us so soon?"

Mirabal nodded. Once they engaged the target, he would expect immediate obedience and nothing less, but he encouraged open discussion at the beginning of an operation. "What you say is true," he said. "But you must always put yourself in the skin of your quarry. This man Placensia is an engineer, which means he is accustomed to thinking in a linear manner. He is also a traitor. Traitors are burdened with an oppressive guilt, even when they feel their cause is just. You must always remember: men who run naturally assume they are being chased."

Estrada gazed down the beach and chewed on the thought. He was an able student who absorbed things quickly. Were it not so, he wouldn't have been included in the colonel's squad. Anyone could master the gross motor skill of hitting someone in the mouth with a hammer, but getting close enough to do so, and then escaping without getting caught . . . that took skill. And practice.

Colonel Mirabal shot a quick glance at Serafina. "Muss your hair, please," he said.

She did so without hesitation. It was one thing to address him as Joaquin for security reasons, but no one on the squad had a slightest trouble remembering that Mirabal was a colonel in the Intelligence Directorate, capable of having any one of them shot with a whisper, or even shooting them himself if he wished, from a very long way off.

"Exquisite," he said, smiling as Serafina's hair took on a more natural look in the pink morning light. He could smell the coconut of her shampoo. Though she was by no means rich, her position with the Directorate gave her access to the good stuff—like real soap from an unopened bottle. Mirabal's stomach knotted in momentary tension at the thought of his mother and her half-used bottles of hotel shampoo from the pitiful care packages sent by American do-gooders who could not be bothered to supply anything but their trash. It was humiliating. What did they know of life in Cuba?

Serafina cleared her throat, drawing Mirabal out of his thoughts. She blinked large, doe-like eyes, the picture of an innocent student waiting for further instruction.

The colonel chided himself for the momentary lapse

from his usual mission focus. "You and I will approach along the beach," he said. "We will merely be another couple out for a morning walk." He nodded toward the small gun pack over her belly. "May I?"

"Of course, Colonel." Her cheeks flushed. "I mean, Joaquin." She held up her arms, allowing him easy access.

Mirabal removed the diminutive Beretta .22 from his own fanny pack and screwed the suppressor onto the threaded barrel. The suppressor gave the superb little pistol even better balance than it already had, all while retaining the easily concealable profile. He tipped up the barrel to make certain there was a round in the chamber, then traded the gun for Serafina's suppressed Makarov so her pistol was in his pack and the Beretta Bobcat was in hers. He then slid the belt around so the pack rested at the small of her back.

Mirabal explained his plan quickly, then sent the other two men around to approach from the street while he and Serafina began to walk down the beach toward the doomed Alejandro Placensia.

Mirabal and Serafina took a full three minutes to cover the hundred meters of beach to their target, allowing Duran and Estrada time to move in. They paused to look at seashells, stopped now and then to gaze out at the sunrise, and meandered back and forth like they had no place else in the world to be. Serafina played the part of misty-eyed lover very well, which was not surprising. It was hardly a secret that she worshipped her commander like he was some sort of saint. Her hip brushed against his thigh as they walked, and she squeezed his hand a little too tightly. Mirabal pulled away, looking down with a soft smile. They reached the row of palmettos in front of the condominium.

"Now," he whispered.

At his signal, Serafina jerked up a foot. She gave a little yelp, pitiful, as if she'd stepped on something sharp. Mirabal stooped to check her foot, then stood, looking back and forth up the beach. His gaze stopped on the people under the lanai, as if by happenstance.

He waved, giving them a nervous smile.

"Hello!" he called, staying put as if he didn't want to abandon Serafina. His English was perfect, and though he was obviously Latino, he sounded like he might easily have grown up in Florida, or Texas, or anywhere else in the United States. "My girlfriend stepped on a piece of glass. Can she wait with y'all while I run back and get the truck?"

A *Yanqui* man with blond hair stood and waved back with his mobile phone. "I . . . We're . . . we're kind of in the middle of something."

"Come on, man. She's bleeding pretty bad." Mirabal said, pleased with the twang of his accent. "You got a first aid kit?" He helped Serafina hobble toward the house without waiting for an invitation, letting his right hand drop out of sight to the small of her back.

Mirabal wondered for a fleeting moment if they had the right target. But the woman stared with her lips set in a tight line, sensing that something was not right. Her hair was still wet from the ocean, plastered to her cheeks and neck. The wild look in her eyes left no doubt that the man beside her was the fugitive, Alejandro Placensia. A small child wandered around from behind a chair, confirming the thoughts. Placensia pushed the little girl behind him as if he knew exactly what was coming.

A smile tugged at Mirabal's lips as they got closer—thirty, twenty, then seven feet away. His hand dipped into the fanny pack and wrapped around the grip of the Beretta. He unsnapped his own fanny pack with his left hand, passing it, and the pistol inside, to Serafina.

"You keep the cell phone, my love," he said. "I'll be—"

Serafina took a step to her right as Mirabal moved left and lifted his gun, giving him room to fire.

Placensia bounded forward, attempting to intercept any bullet meant for his wife.

Very brave, Mirabal thought, turning slightly to adjust his point of aim. The suppressed Beretta spat once, the tiny, 32-grain projectile tearing into Alejandro Placensia's left eye. Swaying momentarily, the engineer toppled over onto his wife.

At that same moment, Duran and Estrada rounded the corner. They shot the woman and the blond American before they had time to turn. Serafina pointed her pistol at the child, but Mirabal pushed the muzzle downward.

"No," he whispered. "It is not her fault she was born to a traitor."

The American and the woman died instantly, but Placensia writhed on the floor. The surgically small wound in the center of his eye was invisible but for the tiny tear of blood on his cheek. He opened his mouth, gasping fishlike, reaching for his little girl.

Duran turned to face outbound, pistol behind his thigh, ready to silence any witnesses who happened to walk past on the beach.

Serafina searched Placensia's sodden pockets, then did the same with his wife and crying child. Finding nothing, she checked the American to make certain nothing incriminating was left at the scene. She left a set of car keys and a folding knife with the body, but passed his wallet to Mirabal. He sighed, then nodded to Estrada, giving him leave to get on with the messy business with his rock pick.

Under the cool shade of the lanai, the colonel took a moment to punch a number into his mobile while Estrada did his gruesome work. He waited for the tone, then gave a passcode and was immediately put through to General de la Guardia.

"*Terminado*," he said. He moved his thumb to end the call, but de la Guardia was having none of that.

"Did he speak to anyone?"

"Yes," Mirabal said. He was eager to hang up and move on, but one did not school the head of the Intelligence Directorate in security protocols.

"Who?"

"That person in no longer a problem," Mirabal said. "Everything has been contained."

"And a message was left for other traitors?"

Mirabal stifled another sigh. "This too is done."

"Carry on then," de la Guardia said. The line went dead. The Americans had ways of monitoring cellular traffic, especially those that went outside the confines of U.S. borders.

"Finished." Estrada turned, wiping spatters of blood of his forehead with the back of his hand.

Mirabal was not squeamish, but he considered it a blessing that Estrada's thick physique shielded from sight the "message" left by driving the rock pick through the engineer's mouth.

The American's mobile phone began to play a military march the colonel recognized but could not quite name. Serafina took a handkerchief from her fanny pack and used it to lift the phone from the ground beside the dead man's hand, careful not to answer. It stopped ringing, going to voicemail.

Mirabal flipped open the wallet.

"Theodore James Schoonover," he muttered, reading from the Florida driver's license.

The mobile phone in Serafina's hand began to play the ringtone again. This time, Mirabal recognized it as the song of the U.S. Air Force. *Off we go, into the wild blue yonder* . . .

He tipped his head toward her hand. "Does it name the caller?"

Serafina held up the device.

The word *Jericho* displayed for a moment, before the ringtone stopped and the screen went dark.

"Jericho." Serafina said. "A place, perhaps? Or maybe Schoonover's office."

"Perhaps." Mirabal glanced at his watch. They'd been on scene for three minutes. "It probably does not matter. We should go at once."

The team left the kill site without another word, back-tracking along their original routes—he and Serafina on the beach, and the others on the street. This time, they jogged to cover the distance back to the truck more quickly.

"Jericho," Mirabal said aloud as he ran along the soft sand. It was an interesting name, but this mission was over. It was of no further consequence to him.

Chapter 4

Jericho Quinn leaned his BMW into an arcing turn, taking a hard right onto Reston Parkway. He tapped the button for the Cardo system mounted on the side of his helmet and used his voice to call Ted Schoonover for a third time.

Still nothing.

Wanting to concentrate more fully on the phone call, he pointed to a Navy Federal Credit Union ahead and motioned to Thibodaux that they should pull over. The men rolled to a stop alongside each other. They dropped the side stands at the same moment, but stayed on their bikes. Quinn hung his helmet on the right handlebar and took his phone out of his pocket to try Schoonover's house next. He was good with numbers, better than average, but it was only by luck that he remembered Schoonover's home number. Ted had always been big on fitness—and mnemonics. The last time he and Quinn had spoken, he'd been proud of how the last four digits of his home phone (2348) spelled out BFIT on the keypad.

The house phone yielded nothing but more voicemail, this time in Mrs. Schoonover's relaxed Georgia accent.

"Hey, Shayna," Quinn said, deciding at the last minute

to leave a message. "Just talked to Ted a few minutes ago. I have the information he wanted. Have him give me a shout."

Quinn ended the call and looked over at Thibodaux.

"What you thinkin', *mon ami*?" The man said in his gumbo-thick drawl. "I know that look of consternation when I see it. It takes an awful lot to get you this worried."

"Probably nothing," Quinn said. "I—"

The phone chirped again. He put it on speaker.

Shayna Schoonover's frantic voice poured out.

"Jericho," she said. "I . . . I'm afraid something awful has happened. I hope I'm wrong, but . . . your message said you were just talking to Teddy. Are you in town?"

"No," Quinn said, his stomach knotting. "I'm in D.C. Ted called me with a question. What do you mean, something has happened?"

"I'm on my way to the condos right now," Shayna said. The pitch of her voice grew more strained with each word. "But the lady who lives next door said she heard noises like shooting, and then she saw some people running away. Now I can't get ahold of Ted."

"Shayna," Quinn said. "You should call the police."

"I did," she said. Her voice was tremulous, like it might shatter. "That's who I was talking to when you called. I thought you might be Teddy, so I hung right up." She paused. "Jericho, he better be okay. Do you hear me?"

"Just do me a favor and wait for the police."

She hung up, panicked nerves getting the better of her. Five minutes later, Quinn's phone chirped again.

It was a courtesy call from a Sergeant Robbins of the Monroe County Sheriff's Office.

They had sent a grief counselor to talk with Shayna Schoonover.

"That's some awful shit, *mon ami*," Thibodaux said after Quinn heard what little information the sergeant would give him and hung up. "When do we leave for Florida?"

Quinn gave a small smile, consoled by the fact that his friend would get involved without a second thought. "There are at least a half dozen laws that preclude us from getting involved in a murder investigation on U.S. soil."

Thibodaux tilted his head to one side, peering hard with his good eye. "So you're not going?"

"Of course I'm going," Quinn scoffed. "Ted Schoonover was my friend. I'm just not prepared to get you involved in something so obviously against the rules."

"Hell, Chair Force," Thibodaux said. "I got lots of friends who stand beside me when I follow the rules. I expect you'd have my back when I don't."

Quinn nodded. "Of course."

"Then shut your piehole and tell me the damned plan."

Quinn decided to call Ronnie again—if only for the calming effect of her voice. Again, he put the phone on speaker so Thibodaux could be a part of any decisions that came out of the conversation.

"I'm so sorry, Jericho," she said after he brought her up to speed. "I'll have my contact in Miami check in with Monroe County. See what he can find out before we get down there."

Quinn shot a glance at Thibodaux, who gave him a knowing nod. "You're coming with us?"

"Did you think I wouldn't?"

Quinn sighed. "We're on the bikes. If you don't mind booking us three seats on the first flight out of Reagan, I'll call Palmer and tell him what we're up to. You sure you want to go to Miami during hurricane season?"

She laughed out loud. "It's been stormy weather ever since I met you. I'm starting to get used to it. You tell the boss I'm going, too, even if I have to take leave."

"Copy that," Quinn said, ending the call.

Quinn's boss, Winfield "Win" Palmer, also happened to be the President's national security advisor. Four years earlier, he'd recruited Quinn and Thibodaux from their respective agencies to work directly for him as what he called "OGAs," or Other Governmental Agents. He'd later added Ronnie to the group. Quinn, who recently pinned on Major in a private ceremony at Andrews Air Force Base, was already accustomed to working counterintelligence cases with the Air Force Office of Special Investigations. Master Sergeant Jacques Thibodaux spoke Italian and French, though he pretended only to speak a rough Cajun patois that made him sound more redneck than he actually was. His assignment as an OGA working directly for the President's right-hand man made his eye injury less of a problem than it would have been if he were still assigned to Quantico. It screwed with his depth perception a little, but his wife liked the damned thing, and to Quinn's chagrin, the big Marine often joked that if there ever was a child number eight, it would very likely be conceived while he was wearing the patch.

Ronnie Garcia was relatively new to the clandestine side of the CIA. She'd fled to the United States after the Soviets abandoned Cuba and her parents had passed away. She'd caught Palmer's attention as a member of the CIA's uniformed security division during a shooting spree inside Langley by three moles from Central Asia. Garcia had killed all three men, but only after they'd caused dozens of deaths—including those of many of her friends. Palmer had brought her aboard his small team, using her on a case-by-case basis and promoting her to clandestine work, but leaving her in place so she could continue to learn the ropes.

Palmer answered Quinn's call on the first ring.

The parking lot in front of the Navy credit union was deserted, and Quinn turned up the volume so Thibodaux could hear what was going on from the adjacent bike more easily.

Palmer gave a long sigh after he'd listened to Quinn's quick, "bottom line up front" briefing.

"The timing for this couldn't be more wrong," he said.

Quinn gave a series of quiet grunts to show that he was listening while Palmer explained. He'd heard rumors of talks between a special envoy and the Cuban government. Somebody in government was always talking about talks with one enemy state or another. It was the way area experts kept themselves relevant.

Thibodaux shook his head. "Quinn's Air Force Academy bud said this Cuban defector . . ."

"Alejandro Placensia." Quinn filled in the blank.

"Yeah," Thibodaux said. "That guy. He supposedly

had some secret that is all-important to the U.S. Does that name ring a bell?"

"Not to me," Palmer said. "But I'll do some checking with the folks at Liberty Crossing." The Director of National Intelligence—a position Palmer himself had previously held—had his offices at Liberty Crossing. The ODNI acted as a clearinghouse and brain center for the sixteen other U.S. intelligence agencies. "Our Cuban refugee policy has tightened up some. There's always a chance that this guy was just blowing smoke to get asylum."

"True enough," Thibodaux said. "But the timing suggests otherwise."

"And someone killed Ted Schoonover along with Placensia." Quinn said. "There's a chance they thought Placensia had passed on whatever information he had. I'd like to follow up on it."

"Go," Palmer said.

"Garcia wanted me to let you know that she's coming too," Quinn added.

"I have no doubt," Palmer said. "But listen up. This could very well lead you to Cuba. The fact that she was born on the island adds a layer of complexity to the trip, not to mention the added danger. They don't recognize the right of anyone to give up Cuban citizenship, so they'll want her to have a Cuban passport. She's young enough that there's always a chance she could be pressed into the Cuban military if they decide they want to screw with her."

Thibodaux grimaced. "That would suck hind titty," he said.

Quinn gave a contemplative nod. "Right now, our

plan is only to go to Florida, check in with the sheriff's office in Key Largo, and take a ride out to where my friend and the Cubans were killed."

"Understood," Palmer said. "But if the Intelligence Directorate was involved, the killers are already back in Cuba, and I know how determined you get. We have underestimated Cuba's intelligence apparatus for too long. Don't make that mistake here."

"Garcia could travel under an alias, if we do end up going," Quin said. "Or we could give her an alternate background. She lived in Florida from middle school onward. It would be fairly easy for her to pretend she was born in Hialeah."

"That could work," Palmer said. "So long as her relatives play along. All the Cubans I've ever met are on the boisterous side. One of them says, 'I haven't seen you since you were a little girl,' and the wrong people hear it . . .'"

"Understood," Quinn said. "I'll leave it up to her."

"You do that," Palmer said, almost—but not quite—giving an uncharacteristic chuckle. "The more I get to know Veronica Garcia, the more I realize pretty much everything is up to her in the long run. Just make it work. With these bilateral talks going on, I want the entire team on this if you do go over. I won't get too deep into your operational planning, but with Jacques and Emiko, you'll have enough overwatch."

Thibodaux held up his gloved hand, frowning like a fourth grader who just saw his math teacher in the grocery store. "Now hang on, boss. There's no need to call in Miyagi."

Palmer scoffed. "Emiko said you guys are getting along much better."

"My ass, we are," Thibodaux groused. "Sir. If by getting along, you mean she only kicks me in the nuts a couple of times a week now, then we're practically dating."

"Work it out," Palmer said, ending the call.

Chapter 5

Santiago de Cuba

Multiple coats of whitewash and gallons of industrial cleaner did little to mask the pungent odor from years of poultry excrement. At times, especially after a hard rain, ammonia and other noxious gases threatened to overwhelm even those aboveground. Inside the bunker, workers were often brought to tears. Liquid from the sewage lagoon just on the other side of the wall seeped and oozed through virtually every seam. A makeshift gutter had been laid in the raised metal grate that served as a floor, allowing the sewage to drain down to where the sump pumps could reach it without flooding the workspace.

Overhead fans were meant to make the work environment more comfortable, but fans cooled by evaporating sweat, and everyone's sweat was contained inside their rubberized radiation suits. Rather than going to the trouble to install costly air-conditioning, de la Guardia opted to cajole and threaten his team into finishing their tasks more quickly.

Seven men in full orange suits huddled around the device as if in an operating theater, blocking it from full view. Two paid special attention to the new guidance system Placensia had been installing before he defected. Others busied themselves on the body of the rocket itself.

The warhead they avoided completely.

De la Guardia had not known of the existence of the missile until his mother, just before her death, mentioned offhandedly that his father had telephoned her the night he was murdered. His call had been cryptic, she said, something about a child Major Capuchin had left behind in Cuba—a "little girl." His mother died furious that the Russian, a man whom she'd counted as a dear friend, would abandon his own flesh and blood without so much as a backward glance.

But Mama was old and prone to overreaction. De la Guardia hadn't thought much of it again until he found one of his father's old journals. In it, Miguel de la Guardia mentioned his friend Major Capuchin, an officer in the Soviet 584th FKR regiment. According to the diary, Major Capuchin often referred to the short-range nuclear missiles as his "little girls." De la Guardia knew from his studies that Khrushchev had, for a short time, left tactical nuclear missiles in Cuba to counter what Castro believed was an imminent U.S. invasion. The 584th was in charge of these weapons, some of them reportedly bunkered in the woods near Santiago de Cuba, the very place where de la Guardia's father had been murdered in 1962.

Once the general knew of its existence, the secret bunker had been amazingly easy to locate. He found it astonishing that a local farmer hadn't already stumbled upon the thing while stealing tin from the old barns.

With the blood of the revolution long dried and

faded, Zayda de la Guardia often wondered if his life had any true purpose at all. But that day, after he'd made his way down the decaying timber ladder and into to the cave-like bunker for the first time, the heady ramifications of his discovery hit the general with full force. Standing ankle deep in a soup of rainwater and chicken dung, he played the beam of his light across the sweeping wings and rounded lines of Major Capuchin's "little girl" and saw his future with absolute clarity.

Why would Capuchin leave a nuclear device in Cuba if he had not intended that it eventually be fired at the United States? Surely it was de la Guardia's responsibility, his *fate*, to continue his father's work. The plan almost wrote itself. It would be so easy, so direct. The difficulty, he'd thought at first, would not be in deploying the weapon, but in doing so without directly implicating Cuba. Arab terrorists would be blamed first. De la Guardia laughed at the thought. ISIS was a doomsday cult, and they would be more than happy to take the credit. The U.S. would suspect Cuba, at least enough to suspend the normalization talks—but they would have no proof.

It was a solid plan, known to only a few like-minded associates. Operational security became his top priority.

His first step was to assign a small platoon of guards to rotate through duty aboveground, standing post in the surrounding trees to keep away accidental interlopers. A larger number would have drawn unwanted scrutiny. Only fourteen people—one of those his own son— were privy to what was hidden underground. He needed one more, but Fuentes was busy in Florida taking care of that one. The small number made for grueling hours in the cramped and often toxic confines of the underground bunker. Apart from the noxious ammonia fumes, they also had to contend with radiation leaking from the decades-old device.

The missile had remained hidden through many storms over the years. Rainwater had fallen into the enclosure for decades, percolating through manure and rotten poultry feed to form a caustic soup that dripped down on the bunker below, leaving the device's aluminum fuselage badly corroded. The bulk of the damage was on the tail fins and one wing, though, and the rounded body of the missile, though streaked and thin in spots, was deemed airworthy for a short flight after a few minor patches.

Most important of all, the warhead itself looked to be in working condition. Radiation had consumed much of the internal wiring and contact points, but those could be repaired. Placensia had assured him that the guts of the device were still very much alive and well. The expert they'd brought in from Tashkent replaced the warhead wiring and made certain it could be armed to detonate when the time came.

Alejandro Placensia's sudden betrayal had left them short an engineer. Colonel Pedro Luna had spent the past fifteen years of his life in politics, but he'd been trained as a flight engineer, and now the general had pressed Luna into service for his expertise, however stale.

Luna had bushy eyebrows and the curt manner of a politician who was pretending to remember how to be an engineer. He surveyed the refurbishing and fabrication on the FKR and looked up at the general. He pointed to the extensive work on the aircraft's wing as he spoke, his voice hollow and distant behind the respirator of the protective suit.

"Do you see this five-centimeter section here?"

De la Guardia leaned closer and nodded, studying the small bead of melted metal where the wing attached to the fuselage. It was a tiny fraction of the aluminum welding that had been accomplished on the missile. "Does this need to be redone?"

Luna shook his head. "No," he said. "That small piece of work is the only portion that looks to be acceptable."

The corporal in charge of welding wilted visibly.

De la Guardia clenched his teeth. "We are not attempting to reach the moon, Colonel. Will it fly a hundred and fifty kilometers?"

Luna continued to cluck and peck around the airframe for a moment, running the glove of his suit along the rivets and welds. At length, he shrugged. "I believe so, but the original engine propels the missile at just over five hundred miles per hour. The augmentations should boost it to very near Mach One. It is my duty to remind you, General, this launch vehicle is extremely old. It will be subjected to tremendous stress in order to reach that speed."

"I understand," de la Guardia said. "Do Placensia's augmentations look appropriate?"

"As far as I can tell," Luna said. He did not ask where Placensia was. He did not need to. It was obvious from the nature of this operation that infractions in security would be eliminated.

The group around the missile stepped back for the first time in a day, allowing de la Guardia a full look at the device. Old and ragged or not, the FKR was a thing of singular beauty.

As a boy, de la Guardia had envisioned missiles looking like rockets for outer-space travel. Even as a young man at the University of Havana, he had thought of all nuclear missiles as something like the Jupiter ballistic missiles he'd read so much about as a child. With its sweeping wings, the Soviet *Frontovaya Krylataya Raketa*—called a *Meteor* by the soviets and a *Salish* by the West—looked more like a smaller version of an MiG 15 fighter. The large, semicircular air intake resembled a smile under the blunt nose. Propelled by an SPRD-15 rocket strapped to the back, this Frontline Combat Rocket carried a fourteen-kiloton nuclear payload and had a range of just over a hundred miles. The atomic bomb the Americans had dropped on Hiroshima had roughly the same explosive yield, so this one was plenty big enough to obliterate downtown Miami—which was just what General de la Guardia intended to do.

The chime of a mobile phone caused everyone in the group to look at each other in horror. De la Guardia had made it extremely clear—anyone who brought a camera into the bunker would be thrown against *el paredón*— the execution wall—and summarily shot. They breathed sighs of relief into their individual respirators when they realized the phone belonged to the general himself.

De la Guardia was expecting the call. He moved toward the ladder without a word of explanation, letting the mobile continue to ring until he'd climbed to the upper floor and he'd removed his hood.

"*Sí.*"

"She arrived at work early," Roberto Fuentes said. His venomous voice crackled over the airwaves. "But we have located her vehicle." The phones were encrypted, hopping frequencies every few seconds, but like a good intelligence operative, de la Guardia always wondered if he was under surveillance. Placensia's defection had rattled him into being much too open in his conversation with Mirabal. With any luck, any American intelligence operatives had been sleeping on the job.

"Very well," the general said. "Extend our invitation as soon as possible. Let me know when you are on your way back."

De la Guardia ended the call. Fuentes wouldn't make a move until later. The sort of invitation he was about to extend was best made after dark, without any witnesses.

Chapter 6

Shayna Schoonover sat on her living room couch, hugging a pillow to her chest. Long, sandy hair was pulled back in a mussed ponytail. Her eyes were swollen and red. Quinn sat across from her in an overstuffed loveseat that matched the couch. Two female Monroe County Sheriff's Office detectives took up positions in leather chairs at the arched opening to a large kitchen. The Schoonovers had only recently moved into the Sunset Point home. Freshly laid carpet and brand-new furniture only added to the emptiness now that Ted was gone and Shayna had to live here alone.

One of the detectives held a small notebook and pen while her partner sat with empty hands, maintaining eye contact with Shayna. Quinn was there to support her, but the sheriff's detectives were there to see if she had a motive of her own. It was a sad reality in homicide cases that any domestic partner had to be considered a suspect, at least in the beginning.

Ronnie Garcia was outside, talking on the phone to her Miami CIA counterpart. Thibodaux waited outside as well. He knew his size could be intimidating, so he chatted up a few of the other sheriff's deputies under a magnolia tree out by the pool.

Shayna gazed at nothing in particular, her chest giving way to periodic shudders of emotion.

"Why, Jer?" she suddenly asked, her Georgia drawl exacerbated by grief and fatigue. "Teddy's got no enemies whatsoever. He's the most decent man I ever met—and certainly the most honest guy in the real estate business."

The older of the two sheriff's investigators, a forty-something detective with short straw-colored hair, gave a sympathetic nod. She wore khaki slacks and a white polo shirt. A gold badge was clipped to her belt next to her Glock pistol. She had introduced herself to Quinn as Jane Lister when he'd arrived.

"I'm so sorry, Mrs. Schoonover," the detective said. She leaned forward with her cell phone to show a photograph of the dead Hispanic woman from the scene. "I apologize for putting you through this, but do you have any idea who this is?"

Shayna shook her head. "The police were taking away a little girl when I got there. One of the officers said her parents were killed. What . . . what . . . happened to the child?"

"She's with protective services." Detective Lister shot a glance at her partner. "Safe. I need you to focus on the female right now."

Quinn's OSI credentials had smoothed things enough with Monroe County that the detectives had already shown him the crime scene photos. The rock pick buried in the Cuban's mouth was far too brutal to show Shayna.

Detective Lister had even floated the idea that Ted Schoonover might be involved in human trafficking. It was her job to look at all possible angles, so Quinn cut her some slack. After all, he was holding back information of his own that could have helped steer her toward a more correct investigative theory. Lister knew he'd been the last to talk to Schoonover, but Quinn had left out the part about the Cuban's knowledge of something "vital to the United States."

Lister folded her hands across the lap of her khakis. "So you can't think of anyone that might want to hurt your husband?"

Shayna sniffed. "I really can't. He was so sweet." She looked up at Jericho. "Do you think this might have something to do with drugs?"

He shrugged.

"It might," Lister said. "We have yet to ID the Hispanic man and woman but if, as Mr. Quinn says, they turn out to be Cuban, there's a strong possibility that they were running from a *lanchero*—someone who had brought them across. Your husband may have been a tragic victim of circumstance."

The front door opened, sending a swath of bright light across the tiled living room floor. Ronnie leaned in and jerked her head at Quinn. "Could I talk to you a sec?"

Quinn excused himself, drawing a raised eyebrow from Detective Lister, who was probably assuming (rightly) she was about to miss something important. It was no wonder feds and locals often got crossways.

"What's up?" Quinn said once he'd followed Garcia back to the relative privacy of the driveway and their rented four-door Jeep.

Ronnie Garcia bounced a spectacularly round hip against the fender. In her late twenties, she was tall with rich, caffè-latte skin and thick black hair that fell around athletic shoulders. She had a sultry air that would have made perfect bait for a honey trap, if she'd been that kind of spy. Her Russian father had described her as *zaftig* when she was a child. Her ex-husband had said she had a ghetto booty—but only once to her face.

She put a hand on Quinn's arm, smiling softly in spite of the horrible situation. "You owe Geoff Sharp dinner at Morton's when he comes back to D.C."

"Who's Geoff Sharp, and why do I owe him dinner?"

"CIA station chief in Valparaíso."

Quinn leaned against the Jeep beside her. "Chile?"

"The very one," Garcia said. "I had our contact with AFIS grab a copy of the fingerprints Monroe County submitted. The woman isn't on file, but the fingerprints for the guy with the rock pick in his face came back as belonging to an Alejandro Placensia."

AFIS was the FBI's Automated Fingerprint Identification System. The Sheriff's Department had rolled each victim's fingerprints at the scene.

Quinn threw his head back and gave a long sigh, taking in the new information. "So Placensia was known to the Agency?"

"Yes indeedy." Garcia moved dark eyebrows up and down, almost giddy at being able to help Quinn during his time of need. "He attended a Latin American conference on jet propulsion and guidance systems in Valparaíso two years ago, along with five other Cubans. Sharp had his guys grab some latent prints off the wineglasses at one of the cocktail parties. Alejandro Placensia was registered as a professor of aeronautical engineering from *Universidad Tecnológicia de La Habana José Antonio Echeverría*—'Havana Polytechnic' for short. I checked the address. It's in Marianao, a few miles west of Havana."

"Anything out of the Cuba desk?"

Garcia shook her head. "Not anything they're willing to spill. Information is likely pretty sparse, considering how actively the Intelligence Directorate hunts down moles. I'll call Palmer and see if he can get any tidbits they might be holding back from me."

Quinn looked up and down the block at the million-dollar homes. New BMWs, Mercedes-Benzes, and Porsches sat in the driveways of every other house. Those without a fancy car on display certainly had one (or three) in the garage. Out back, along the canal that connected to the sea, every home had a slip with a boat that likely cost as much as Quinn's first house. It was idyllic, calm—absent even the whiff of murder.

Thibodaux came around the side of the house from the backyard, his good eye peering at Quinn. "I know that look, *mon ami*. You got yourself a plan."

"Havana Polytechnic?" Quinn mused, half to himself.

"That's right," Garcia said. "Marianao is close to what they call the hospital district. We used to pass near it when my father drove us to Marina Hemingway. He would tell us stories of Ernesto, the famous author."

Quinn sighed. "We're not getting anything here. Let's go see what we can find out."

Garcia bit her bottom lip. "Really, mango? Go to Cuba?"

"Why not?"

She shrugged. "Oh, I don't know. Being shot as spies with our backs against a wall. Interrogations with battery cables clipped to our tender parts. Twenty years of hard labor in a sugarcane field. You name the punishment. You'll find it in Cuba."

Quinn stood away from the Jeep and rubbed his

hands together. "It's settled. We'll leave as soon as we work out the details and brief Palmer."

Garcia draped a brown arm around Quinn's shoulders. "Did I happen to mention the part about us getting shot as spies?"

"Oh ye yi!" Thibodaux heaved a heavy groan. "Are you kidding, *cher*? That's what pushed him over the edge." He held up his cellphone and wagged it back and forth at Quinn. "How about you tell my bride I'm going to Cuba posing as Emiko's husband? Truth be told, I think it would suit her better if they shot me as a spy."

Chapter 7

Quinn said goodbye to Shayna Schoonover and promised to check back with her in a day or two. Detective Lister protested when he left without giving a statement but was savvy enough to realize that there was something going on well above her pay grade. It wasn't every day that counterintelligence types camped out in her bailiwick, but Monroe County's proximity to Cuba meant such circumstances weren't exactly unheard of, either.

Garcia drove, while Thibodaux, who was too large to fit comfortably in the back, took shotgun. Quinn sat in the middle of the backseat, leaning forward with the phone flat in his hand with the national security advisor on speaker.

An old West Point man, Win Palmer liked to have a good battle plan, even though he knew full well that such plans crumbled at first contact with the enemy. Any American traveling to Cuba who was remotely suspected of working for the government would be followed and, at the very least, subjected to a long interrogation. At worst, they would be imprisoned, tried, and (as Garcia had so eloquently put it) placed "backs against a wall."

Canadian and European tourists regularly visited the

island, but Americans had to have a reason other than personal pleasure, usually cultural education. Still, several thousand U.S. citizens traveled to Cuba every year. Thibodaux and Miyagi would go as a couple—a mixed martial artist from Louisiana with his pretty Asian wife. The eye patch didn't exactly help the big man blend in, but they hoped it might make Cuban intelligence believe he couldn't possibly be a government operative. Quinn would travel with a U.S. passport under the cover name James Shield. Generally speaking, it was better for operational and personal security to choose a legend that included the same given name as your real one, but having a first name like *Jericho* made that problematic, so Quinn usually picked given names that were easy to remember under stress.

"Honestly," Palmer said. "The more I think about this, the more I hate the idea of any of you going over."

"I'm assuming we have assets in place," Quinn said.

"Of course." Palmer remained vague, even though the phones were encrypted.

"Risky," Garcia said. "We don't exactly have a great track record of keeping agents in Cuba from turning double."

"True," Palmer said, going on to reiterate his earlier fears. "I'm most worried about your legend. You're still a Cuban national in their eyes, and your aunt might—"

"I haven't been back since I was fifteen," Ronnie said. "My Auntie Peppa is the one who helped me get out. She's . . ." Ronnie paused, as if trying to come up with the right set of words.

Palmer, never comfortable with gaps in the conversation, prodded. Operationally, he was trained to expect the worst. "If she's going to be a risk, we'll have to rethink."

Ronnie cut him off, looking sideways at Quinn for moral support. "That's not it at all. She's rock solid in the trust department. She's just sort of . . . eccentric. That said, she'll help point us in the right direction. I'm sure she'll be cool with pretending I was born here in the U.S."

"Very well," Palmer said, sounding unconvinced. "Miyagi is on her way down. She has a new birth certificate for you. Take that along with the passport, just to be on the safe side. Though I'm not entirely certain there is a safe side. I don't suppose you would consider just returning to Langley and letting Quinn and Thibodaux check this one out."

Ronnie's face screwed into a fuming scowl, but she kept her voice even. "All due respect, sir, but they'll need a guide. Neither of them speak Spanish. Snooping around for info on Alejandro Placensia without the language will only draw more attention."

Quinn took advantage of a lag in conversation. "Placensia was bringing us something important enough to get him killed. I'd say a trip is worth the calculated risk. We'll tread lightly, I promise."

"I'm not sure treading lightly is in your skill set," Palmer said. "I'm serious, Jericho. This president doesn't quite understand you like Chris Clark did. He'll have my ass if we do something to screw up the talks."

"Roger that," Quinn said. The boss had said "we," which meant he was on board, doubts and all.

"Okay, then," Palmer said, ready to drill down on the details. "Weather guessers have this hurricane passing north of the island day after tomorrow. Evidently, some American adventure travelers aren't that adventurous. The opportunity to look a tropical storm in the teeth has more than a few canceling their flights. That leaves some open seats in the tour group that leaves this afternoon, and a few more tomorrow. Quinn, Emiko booked you and Garcia with a people-to-people tour arriving in Havana at sixteen-thirty this evening. Unfortunately, that doesn't give you enough time to get back here to pack."

"I'm already packed," Garcia said. "Sorta thought this might happen." She glanced over her shoulder at Quinn and mouthed so Palmer couldn't hear, "I packed for you too, mango."

"Thibodaux," the national security advisor continued. "You and Miyagi will leave tomorrow at 0900, traveling as Mr. and Mrs. Jacques Dubois. You'll stay at the same hotel with Quinn and Garcia, providing them with overwatch. All of you listen to me. This trip is for information gathering only. Nothing active. Understood?"

"Understood," Quinn said for everyone.

Palmer's voice grew distant, ready to move on to something else. "You'll have to go in slick. Leave your guns and other weapons with Garcia's Agency buddies in Miami. Emiko has your emergency exfiltration contingencies if this all turns to shit. We'll broadcast corresponding numbers on VHF."

"Copy," Quinn said, nodding to himself. Marine radios should be easy enough to find, even in Cuba. Times and locations of various pickup points would be read out over an open channel using a series of six to eight numbers that Jericho and the others would memorize. When they heard a number, they would have twelve hours to get to the corresponding location.

"We'll do you proud, boss," Thibodaux said. "But I

got a teensy little beef about me and Miyagi traveling as a married couple—"

"You'll do fine, Mr. Dubois," Palmer said. He disconnected without another word.

"Well, ain't that some peachy shit?" Thibodaux groused, banging his head against the side window of the Jeep. "Which one of you want to call and tell Camille I have to play house with Emiko Miyagi on a Caribbean island? I'm pretty sure if there's an active volcano anywhere around Spotsylvania, Virginia, she'd just as soon throw me in it."

Quinn raised both hands. "I'll leave that one to you, bud."

Garcia shot a glance of mock terror at the big Cajun "Not a chance, my friend," Garcia said, taking the exit to a steakhouse near the airport. "Here's an idea. Camille has got to be used to a few secrets by now. How about you just don't tell her?"

"Yeah, right," Thibodaux hung his head. "Like that would work. I ain't gotta worry about sonic attacks and that other shit going on over there. The noise my Cornmeal's gonna make will be enough to give me 'drain bamage.'"

For Ronnie Garcia, freedom held an enormous amount of guilt. As the American Airlines 737 made a slow bank to the south of Havana toward José Martí International Airport, she pushed her forehead against the side of the aircraft and stared out the window. Few people were inbound to Havana because of the hurricane, and most of the middle seats were empty.

Quinn had been able to sleep seemingly the moment

he closed his eyes, and he rested peacefully in the aisle seat of the same row. He'd said goodbye to his little girl, Mattie, on the phone before they left. That meant he'd also said goodbye to her mother—his ex-wife. Ronnie didn't exactly need spidey senses to know that Jericho still loved his ex. He made no secret of the fact. He had, though, promised that it was a nonissue. And Kimberly Quinn was a good person, which made it impossible to hate her. Ronnie banged her head softly against the side of the airplane to get these thoughts out of her mind. She had more important things to ponder.

It was almost impossible for Ronnie to fathom that she'd not been back to the red dirt of her little island for almost fifteen years. A scant ninety miles from Miami, it had taken longer to board the airplane than it had to fly across the Florida Straits and reach Havana. She'd only seen it from the air one other time—not counting her frequent nostalgic trips via Google Earth back to her auntie's house.

At first glance, Havana looked like any other city of medium size, a suburb of Miami or maybe Fort Lauderdale. A closer inspection on the airplane's descent revealed damaged streets and crumbling buildings just off the main thoroughfares. Plus, you didn't see donkey carts in Fort Lauderdale. Crumbling gray concrete seemed to be the prevailing motif, just as it had been when Ronnie left. She leaned back in her seat, closing her eyes and remembering the way it had been—and how it likely was still.

Her mother's younger sister, Josefina Garcia— everyone called her Peppa—was only a decade older than Veronica. Bright and full of energy, Auntie Peppa glowed in person and in spirit. The two of them shared the same physique, which had always seemed to gall Ronnie's shorter and rounder mother. Ronnie's earliest memories of her pretty, young aunt were of thick black hair tied up in a red scarf, a radiant grin, and a fat cigar clenched between white teeth. Ronnie's Russian father hated the cigars, thinking them unfeminine. It didn't matter. Ronnie turned the most awful shade of green the first time she lit up her first Cohiba, so she'd left the things to her auntie. Somehow, Peppa had been able to pull it off and remain the most beautiful woman Garcia had ever seen.

For some unfathomable reason, Peppa Garcia had never married. Oh, she liked men and understood them better than most. As she grew older, Ronnie suspected that this might have been Peppa's problem. Perhaps men did not really want to be understood, least of all by a woman with Peppa's beauty.

Whatever the reason, the bright and beautiful Peppa Garcia remained single. She'd provided a willing confidant for her teenage niece. The two of them conspired almost every day—about boys, womanhood, the future, the revolution, and the hardship and wonder of living on their beautiful island. And after Ronnie's mother and father died, they began to talk of escape.

Ronnie's mother had another sister who'd already crossed the Florida Straits on a leaky boat made from the hood of an old Chevrolet sedan. Pursuant to the U.S.'s "wet foot, dry foot" policy, Auntie Madonna was allowed to remain once she made it to shore. Had the Coast Guard apprehended her at sea, they would have sent her right back to Cuba as an illegal alien. Madonna lived in Hialeah, where she worked in a T-shirt factory and eventually married her foreman, a kind man named

Rodrigo Villanueva. It was nothing short of amazing that Madonna, who also smoked fat cigars but did not look nearly as pretty doing it, found a husband so quickly when Peppa had not.

Ronnie thought it must be easier to get married in America, and she said so. Peppa assured her that it was something else entirely.

Auntie Madonna soon offered to take care of the or-phaned Ronnie, begging Peppa to bring the child over on the next available boat. But Auntie Peppa did not care for the water, and she was certainly not going to chance her luck on a flimsy raft. Her favorite niece would not leave Cuba as a *balsero*. They would go, but they would go on an airplane to Mexico as tourists, from which they could then cross into Texas on foot. Ronnie thought it a great adventure, unaware at the time how expensive and dangerous the undertaking was.

The Americans called refugees who came up from south of the border "dusty foot" Cubans. Like the "dry foot" variety, these, too, were allowed to stay, so long as they made it into the country. It was an odd rule, but Ronnie was happy for it—until she made it across and Peppa was apprehended at a checkpoint in Matamoros, Mexico. They'd agreed beforehand that Ronnie would run and Peppa would follow later if they were to get separated, but Peppa never came.

As per their plan, a frightened Ronnie took a bus from McAllen to Miami, looking like the runaway that she was. Auntie Madonna and Uncle Rodrigo met her at the Greyhound bus station and took her back to their small but comfortable home in Hialeah. Auntie Peppa was deported back to Cuba, and there she remained, only ninety miles away from Ronnie. For years, Peppa was watched closely by Cuban authorities, unable to ever leave the country again. She did not even call at first, and Madonna explained that she'd probably been sent to an education camp. It was a term much easier for a teenage girl to swallow than the hard truth that her best friend and confidant had gone to prison for helping her escape the regime. Ronnie and Madonna wrote letters regularly, and after two years, Peppa finally called. They spoke frequently now, at least once a month, but their conversations were never the same as when Ronnie was young. Over the years, Ronnie had come to realize in part what had happened to her auntie. It was difficult to know what to say to someone who had done hard time because of you. Ronnie always suspected the calls were monitored, and she guarded what she said, especially after she applied to work with the CIA.

The plane touched down on José Martí's single runway, bouncing once. A round of cheers from the passengers pulled Garcia back to the present and roused Quinn from his short nap.

"Hey," he said, throwing his shoulders against the seat in a groaning stretch. He turned his head to the side against the headrest and met her eye. "You okay?"

"Honestly," she lied, forcing a smile, "I could not be *bueno*-er."

Their weeklong cultural tour package included accommodations at the luxurious Hotel Sevilla, two dinners at a *paladar*, meals at a private home, and concierge service should they have any questions or need assistance with their people-to-people experience.

That was a joke, Ronnie thought. The twentysomething kid who was their concierge would pee his pants if he knew the kind of assistance they were likely to need.

They were responsible for their own cab to the hotel. Taxis were, their tour operator had told them, part of the mystique and charm of Havana. Quinn grabbed two SIM cards for their phones from a kiosk in the airport and changed some money into CUC, the convertible Cuban currency used by tourists.

The air in Havana was thick enough to chew. It amazed Garcia how a small island, just miles offshore from Miami, could seem even more humid than Florida. She supposed the hurricane bearing down from out in the Atlantic had something to do with it.

Quinn, a dyed-in-the-wool motorhead, was mesmerized by the vintage cars. Havana rush hour was light compared to traffic on the Capital Beltway. Still, it inched along at a leisurely, island pace, slowed by the broken roads, human-powered pedal cabs, and occasional bony horse dragging a ramshackle cart. Every driver seemed acutely aware of the cost of fuel and tires. The twenty-minute trip cost twenty CUC, around twenty U.S. dollars, but Quinn tipped the driver ten CUC— almost half of what the man made each month as a dentist.

Even by American standards, the architecture of the Hotel Sevilla was opulent, a throwback to the glitzier times before the revolution when movie stars and mobsters poured endless money into the Cuban economy. Ronnie's Soviet father had been a respected teacher, so she had enough money for a few niceties growing up, but she'd never been inside one of the downtown Havana hotels. They were for rich politicians and military leaders who needed to relax.

Thinking back, as they walked across the rich Moorish tiles and between potted palms, made Garcia sick to her stomach. Her father was a smart man. How could he have believed such political garbage?

Check-in went smoothly, with the only problem being a lecherous bellman who eyed Ronnie in such a way that he very nearly earned what Quinn called the "axe handle to the nuts" treatment. She squeezed Quinn's hand and ushered him up the room before they got booted out of the country.

Quinn used his cell phone to take a few flash photos of Garcia from various angles while she unpacked and hung up their clothes. It was an easy way to look for hidden surveillance without being too obvious. Lenses from pinhole cameras tended to sparkle in flash photographs. He found three likely spots, one on every wall but the one with the bathroom door. Quinn held up the phone so Garcia could see each photo and pointed to the spots where he suspected the cameras were as he scrolled through. Garcia found one more behind the mirror that faced the bathtub. It didn't quite fog the way it should have when she turned on the hot water. The creeps who installed surveillance cameras always seemed to put one in the bathroom—a hell of a lot of valuable intel to be gained there . . . Perverts. It made things awkward, but Ronnie was glad to find them. If they'd found none, it would have meant they weren't looking hard enough. Being watched and aware of it was far preferable to being unaware and compromised.

Now the trick would be to live as if they had no idea

they were being watched, and listened to, while doing nothing they didn't want on film.

Ordinarily there would be no way of knowing if the cameras were passive—just recording on a hard drive— or if a set of eyes leered on the other end. Ronnie was self-aware enough to realize that the shady-looking bellman who'd given her the lustful once-over was surely telling someone at this very moment that he had to check out the hot *chica* in 503.

The last thing out of her suitcase was a black nightgown worthy of a Bond girl. The cameras made her want to sleep in a pair of sweatpants and a T-shirt, but couples vacationing in the Caribbean islands needed to do what couples do when visiting the Caribbean—or face the scrutiny of the intelligence community.

Jericho was rarely one for public displays of affection—not because he was a prude, but because he liked to keep his eyes open and his gun hand free. Behind closed doors was a different story, and he didn't even have to act to play the part of lustful boyfriend.

She held the nightie up for his approval, but he tossed the nightgown aside, as he often did at home. He leaned in close, as much to have a moment of private conversation as to nibble on Garcia's ear.

"I don't want to spoil the mood," Garcia whispered, "but I need to warn you about my auntie."

Quinn pulled back for a moment, taking her shoulders in both hands. He looked into her eyes for a long moment, and then returned to kissing her on the neck.

"Warn me?" he said, lips buzzing again her skin. "Warn me of what?"

Garcia's eyes rolled back in her head. She groaned. "I'll give you five minutes to stop doing that."

"Warn me of what?" Quinn said again.

"Oh . . . I . . . oh, yeah, that," Garcia panted. Her shudder was no act for the camera. "Oh, shit . . . Seriously, mango, it can wait."

"Warn me of what?"

Garcia groaned. "Okay, but it's gonna kill the mood. My mother's sister . . . my Auntie Peppa . . . ummm . . . the uninformed might call her a witch."

Quinn froze, lips to her neck.

"No kidding?"

"She's not," Ronnie said, her eyes still closed. "A witch, I mean. Not really, anyway. She's more of a high priestess."

"That makes me feel a lot better."

"Honest," Ronnie said. "She's really cool, but when you meet her . . . there's liable to be a lot of chicken blood."

Chapter 8

Under the night sky, Violeta Cruz pushed off the wall of her swimming pool with chubby, tanned toes whose nails were painted a conservative, mother-of-pearl pink. She'd been hoping for some stars, but she knew the massive low-pressure system swirling out in the Atlantic had whipped up a pile of clouds like a gigantic cotton-candy machine at a state fair. Floating lazily on her back in the cool water, a welcome respite from the muggy day, she saw nothing but black through the screen that completely enclosed *her* pool and *her* lanai. Paddling with her hands, she felt her thick hair—much of it dyed an iridescent turquoise—floating around her face. *That's right, suckas*, she thought. She had her own swimming pool and her own three-bedroom, two-bath ranch house in the comfortable Hammock Lakes West neighborhood south of Cape Canaveral. The locals in the industry—her industry—called it the Space Coast.

She'd left the pool lights off, preferring to swim under the cover of darkness. Mr. Goldberg, the sweet old dude from the house next door, liked to stand in his too-tight boxer shorts and pretend he was watering his scabby lawn whenever he saw her get in the pool. For some reason, the previous owners had never built a privacy fence.

Violeta looked like her mother. That is to say, she had a pleasant face, was just a hair over five feet tall, and was nearly as round as one of the rusted fuel drums that her father had used to cobble together the raft that had brought the family across the strait from Cuba. Violeta was twenty-seven years old and the first member of her family to graduate from college—let alone earn a master's degree in Aeronautical Engineering.

She'd shown promise in math at an early age, memorizing insanely long numbers after looking at them for just a few minutes. She surpassed her instructors in advanced algebra at Santa Clara Primary School Number 3 when she was ten years old—and it would have been earlier, had she been exposed to the right sort of problems. She was doing calculus and analytical geometry at thirteen. The Cuban government stepped in at that point, explaining to her parents that for the good of the state, their only child was to be ripped from their arms and carted off to live in a dormitory at the University of Havana. Rosario Cruz had been wise enough to agree with a fittingly sad but understanding nod. He promised over the tears of his wife that he would deliver young Violeta to Havana in one week's time.

The Ministry of Science, Technology, and Environment vehicle had barely driven away from in front of their home when the Cruzes began throwing clothing into two cardboard suitcases. Violeta wept huge tears at the idea of leaving her friends during the thirty-kilometer drive to the coastal fishing town of Isabela de Sagua. Her father and his friends worked for the next four hours on a makeshift raft, and they cast off from shore under an inky new moon. The seas were calm that night. It was quiet enough to hear the lapping of water on the metal barrels, and Violeta's mother had to clap a hand over the mouth of her sobbing daughter to silence her.

Their family had always kept to the rules. They attended communist rallies alongside their neighbors. At six years old, Violeta had been part of a school choir that sang at the interment of Che Guevara's remains in a special mausoleum in Santa Clara. Fidel himself had made a speech to the masses. And now her parents were breaking the law—defying the *comandante*. They were traitors to the revolution. Until her dying day, Violeta would never forget her complete astonishment when her father had spat in the water as he paddled their raft, cursing Castro and "that son of a bitch, Che."

It took her only three days in Hialeah to make new friends, and to realize that the United States was not the boogeyman her teachers in Santa Clara had made it out to be. Jobs were plentiful, and the electricity in their new house worked twenty-four hours a day. Most important, she was able to attend a special school for kids who excelled in math without having to leave her parents.

She received her high school diploma a year later—a formality, her counselors explained. She went on to get her undergraduate, masters, and doctorate degrees at Embry-Riddle, focusing her dissertation on artificial intelligence in Global Positioning Systems. Her parents moved from Hialeah to Daytona Beach, where she lived with them until she was eighteen. For a time, she dropped the "a" in her name. Her parents hadn't been too happy about it, but *Violet* was still bad enough. *Violeta* made her sound like a ballet dancer. Not there was anything wrong with dancers. Executing a perfect plié was all well and good, but her professors had big, linear brains that tended to think of her as a girl first and an engineer second—if at all. If she could have changed her name to Vern, she would have.

Then a cute guy in her section at work had called her Violeta, so she let the "a" reattach itself. Easily considered the smartest person on her team, if not the entire company, Violeta had nothing to prove.

And now she had her own house.

Her stomach growled, reminding her that she had half a pepperoni and mushroom pizza waiting for her in the fridge. She'd only been home for half an hour, and she wanted to get a swim in before it was too late.

Her group supervisor at XplorDyne had the team working on incredibly interesting projects that had to do with all sorts of fascinating issues like launch stresses, miniaturization, and a thousand and one other problems. In truth, she never wanted to leave work until she remembered that she had her own house with real appliances and an honest-to-goodness swimming pool.

A muffled thump, like the sound of a car door in her driveway, caused her to lift her head out of the water. She heard it again and swam to the edge of the pool, crossing her forearms on the warm concrete of the deck. She kicked her legs behind her, listening, expecting to hear her doorbell at any moment. Nothing but the chirp of crickets in the palmettos—and the whistling sound of Mr. Goldberg's garden hose. He must have seen her through the window. Violeta rested on the lip of the pool and watched a lime green anole lizard scramble in fits and starts along the brick ledge of her kitchen window, hunting one of the monster skeeter eaters that were drawn to the light.

She checked the time on her Fitbit. Almost 8:00 P.M.—

too late to eat pizza without having terrible dreams. And she needed a good night's sleep. Some grand pooh-bah from NASA was coming in tomorrow for a progress check on a new guidance system. She pressed up from the pool with both hands. People were always surprised when they saw her do that. Chubby girls shouldn't be strong enough to lift themselves out of the pool. But Violeta took after her mother in the strength department too. Water drained off her one-piece suit. She would have liked to have gone skinny-dipping, but the old man's constant lawn care next door put the kibosh on that.

She grabbed her towel off the pool deck and wrapped it around her waist. *Odd*, she thought. The light in Mr. Goldberg's kitchen window illuminated a garden hose spraying unmanned in the grass.

"Hey," Violet called through her screen and into the darkness. "You left your water running, Mr. G."

She shrugged. Not her problem. Maybe he got a phone call or something. She'd check back before she went to bed.

Violeta left the wet towel in a puddle inside the back door—you could do stuff like that when it was your house. The A/C sent a chill up her back, and she peeled the wet suit off her shoulders, pulling it down to her belly as she walked to the front window to peek out through a narrow gap in the drapes. A light blue Tahoe was parked across the street. It hadn't been there when she got home. She tugged at the seat of her swimming suit, still peering through the crack in the curtain.

"Wonder whose car that is," she murmured.

"It is mine," a deep voice said from behind her, quiet and even.

Violet's breath caught in her throat. She tried to scream, but managed only a gurgle.

"Who . . . ? What are you doing?" She was hyperventilating. "This is my house!" Speaking freed her diaphragm enough that the scream finally came, shrill and ragged. It took her a moment to register that there were three men in the room. One sat on the couch. He looked like he might be around forty, but he was fit. He had a lot of grease in his slick, black hair, and a small mustache was trimmed down to a thin, down-turned line, like an extra frown above his cruel mouth. The other two—the muscle, from the looks of them—stood on either side of him. All three wore jeans and dark T-shirts.

Violeta screamed again, but the guy with the slick hair held up his hand.

"You waste your breath, my dear," he said, still calm. He rested his hands on his knees, relaxed, as if he'd just dropped by for a visit.

"You need to leave." Violet's chest heaved, then shuddered. "Mr. Goldberg has a gun!"

"Really?" Slick said. "Was he the one watering his lawn?"

Violeta nodded, mouth half open.

"Well, then." Slick lifted the tail of his T-shirt, displaying the butt of a black pistol. "I, too, have a gun. And unfortunately, I have already shown mine to your friend Mr. Goldberg."

Violeta tugged at the shoulder straps of her swimsuit, trying to pull them up to cover herself. They were wet and hopelessly twisted at her waist. "Please, don't . . ."

The man with slick hair patted the cushion beside

him on the couch. "We are not here to rape you. Come sit. I will explain."

She shook her head, feet rooted in place, covering her exposed breasts with crossed arms. "I—I just moved in," she said. "I don't have anything worth stealing."

Slick patted the cushion again. "The man I work for, he thinks otherwise."

The two other men moved in, not touching her, but close enough to drive her toward the couch. One of them pushed her down beside Slick.

Violeta struggled to make sense of all this. If the men weren't there to hurt her . . . And what had they done with poor Mr. Goldberg? "Your boss," she stammered. "What does he want with me?"

Slick gave a little shrug, then turned to face her. She saw for the first time that he held a syringe in his right hand.

"He wants you to come home."

Chapter 9

It was dark by the time the cab carrying Quinn and Garcia turned off of the paved main street and squeaked to a stop in Peppa's neighborhood near the Rio Almendares. The oppressive weight of the humidity made it feel even darker. Their driver spent the trip from the hotel making several back-and-forth turns at Garcia's instructions, like a mouse looking for a piece of lost cheese. Streetlights, iffy even on the major road, were completely nonexistent in many of these neighborhoods, even ones like Auntie Peppa's that were considered middle class by Cuban standards.

A dog growled somewhere in the shadows. A muggy wind kicked up a skiff of trash and dust that forced Quinn to squint while he paid the cabbie. The taxi pulled away, tires popping on the dirt and gravel, cracked taillights throwing odd shadows onto the buildings as it slowed to make a turn back toward the city, where the doctor hoped to pick up more foreigners.

Ronnie, who ordinarily did little but throw on her clothes and run a brush through her hair before calling it all good, had spent more than forty-five minutes primping in front of the hotel mirror. She fairly bounced with giddiness at the notion of seeing her favorite aunt again after so many years. A crisp white cotton blouse hung off her shoulders, and her bright yellow skirt came down to mid-calf. She rounded off the ensemble with a pair of Chaco hiking sandals in case she had to run and a yellow flower for her hair. Quinn stuck with a loose, short-sleeved island shirt with an understated palm tree design woven into the linen, khaki slacks, and a comfortable pair of Rockports.

Ronnie crowded next to Quinn's elbow, as if afraid he might leave her alone. He wanted to ask if she was alright, but it made her grouchy if he acted like she needed him to swoop in and save her. Instead, he stood with her at the bottom of the crumbling steps of a two-story concrete block house and held her hand while she pulled herself together. The place was a mansion, or had been at one time when it belonged to someone of prominence. Quinn imagined dinner parties on the open roof, dominoes and daiquiris on the full-length front porch, fine gardens in the back, and an opulent façade. Now it slumped, eaten by decay like so many homes in old Havana, graying and in desperate need of new paint. High shutters and a great wooden door, at least ten feet tall, suggested the place had raised ceilings. Orange lamplights glowed in the ground-floor windows.

Quinn took a half step back as a door flew wide and a female figure in a white skirt charged out. A long machete trailed down from her right hand, a dark silhouette against the interior lights.

Quinn braced himself at the sight of the blade, but Ronnie squealed and yanked her hand away. She broke into a string of machine-gun Spanish, elated, as if her aunt always met her at the door with a sword.

The woman buried the machete into a stump on the porch—which seemed to be set there for that purpose—

and wiped her hands on an apron. She embraced Garcia in the pool of light from the front door, speaking loudly enough to set dogs barking up and down the deserted street.

Quinn chuckled. So much for slipping into Cuba unnoticed.

A few moments later, two young men, one Hispanic, the other black, appeared at the doorway. Both looked to be somewhere in their early twenties. Both were also dressed in white.

Peppa held Ronnie out at arm's length, peering around her to get a long, squinting look at Quinn. "So this is the one you tell me about?" She spoke in English, something Quinn hadn't expected.

Ronnie nodded vigorously. "It is." She leaned in, confiding some secret, before stepping back for the benefit of the two young men. "Auntie, I want you to meet, Jim. Jim Shield."

Backlit by the open door, Peppa continued to peruse Quinn without speaking while she swatted at least a half dozen mosquitos on her neck and arms. Like Ronnie, she was tall, but it was hard to tell much else in the dark. At length, she turned to the helpers behind her. "Please fetch some *cafécito* for my niece and her cruel boyfriend. They have come all the way from America to meet her auntie."

The young men turned on their heels and vanished into the house. Arm around Ronnie, Peppa did the same. Quinn followed, though uninvited. He wanted to see what this chicken blood thing was all about.

The blades of a palm-leaf fan turned lazily on the high ceiling of the foyer, as if they didn't want to get overheated from too much effort. A row of nine candles burned on a rough wooden shelf along the wall to the right, the kind where someone might leave car keys in the U.S. There was a squat effigy of clay, about the size of a large potato, at the far end of the candles. Cowrie shells had been pressed into the clay to form two eyes with a single shell as a mouth. The candles and a bare bulb in an old, ornate sconce on the wall provided enough light for Quinn to get his first good look at Peppa Garcia.

She'd grabbed the machete from the stump as they came inside, and it hung now from long fingers at the end of a bronze arm, standing out in sharp contrast to the white skirts. She passed the blade to the darker of her two helpers. From their white clothing and nodding deference, Quinn assumed them to be some sort of acolytes.

Not much past forty, Peppa Garcia looked at Quinn with the eyes of an ancient soul. The short sleeves of her simple white peasant blouse were fringed with delicate lace. The neckline plunged, exposing the swell of her large bosom—a trait that was apparently common to Garcia women of all generations. Quinn couldn't help but notice the ring of perspiration that moistened the neckline of Peppa's blouse. A maroon scarf pulled her hair up in a neat turban, complete with a pink plastic flower. With the same pronounced hips and smooth, full figure, she looked like a slightly matured version of Ronnie.

Peppa swatted another mosquito on her chest and then met Quinn's eye.

"You were expecting someone older."

It wasn't a question.

There was no right way to respond, so Quinn stepped forward to shake her hand. She pulled him in for an enveloping embrace common to aunts the world over. She smelled of cigar smoke and chocolate pudding—surprisingly complementary and comfortable smells.

"Come," Peppa said, stepping back to gesture at two green coconuts on a small table along the wall opposite the candles. The tops of each fruit had been hacked away with the machete to create a small hole, through which a paper straw had been inserted. "Please, have something to refresh yourselves after the long journey. You should not drink the water around here, but the coconuts are fine." She gave Quinn another up-and-down look as she spoke. "Ramón and Iggy will bring the *cafécito* to us in the parlor. I hope you like your coffee strong and sweet, Mr. . . . Shield. That is the way we do it here in Cuba. Is that not right, Veronica?"

Ronnie grinned as if she were about to burst.

The room at the back of the house that Peppa Garcia called her parlor had twin palm-leaf ceiling fans. Large, floor-to-ceiling windows in the opposing walls were open to the night cross breeze. Mosquito coils—probably bought through the black market—burned in front of each window, keeping the bugs at bay. The room was well lit by a lamp in each corner, much brighter than the foyer. Another clay effigy, this one with bits of feather, colored cloth, and shells, occupied a low table next to a horsetail flyswatter and a glass candleholder depicting an image Quinn recognized as Saint Therese. A woven basket full of deep purple eggplants sat before it as an offering. Dried coconuts, strings of beads, and a pile of a dozen or so cowrie shells took what looked like a place of honor along the back wall. An assortment of thick velvet floor pillows and several plush chairs, all a deep burgundy, told Quinn this was likely where Peppa met with her customers to divine their futures.

"So," Peppa said, taking a seat in the chair nearest the basket of eggplant. "This is the dangerous one?"

"This is him, Auntie," Garcia said. "Jericho—"

The creak of a door hinge caused Peppa to raise her hand, cutting her niece off mid-sentence.

Ramón, the acolyte of Afro-Cuban heritage, came in ahead of the one called Iggy. Ramón carried a wooden serving tray with the small porcelain cups of *cafécito*, the sweet Cuban espresso and milk. Iggy followed with a similar tray of fried plantain chips and potato croquettes.

Ramón smiled brightly as he served the espresso, but Iggy, shorter and with thick hair swept up in a 1950s-style pompadour, kept his eyes cast toward the floor. Peppa watched in silence until both Ronnie and Quinn had taken some of the offered snacks on folded cloth napkins.

"Oh, Ignacio," she said, as if it were an afterthought. "Would you please cut some fresh melon for me and our guests?"

"*No hay*—" The young man stopped, nodding as he remembered he was supposed to speak English. "We have . . . no melon, señora."

Peppa gave a nonchalant shrug. "Felipe had some nice ones when I walked past his shop this morning. Please go and buy us a melon. When you return, Ramón will fetch the speckled rooster. We will make a sacrifice to Oyá and see what she has to tell us." She looked up at Quinn and gave him a little nod. "Do not worry, Jim Shield. It will not be a waste. The rooster's blood will feed Oyá, the goddess who assists me with my questions, and then its flesh will be tomorrow's dinner."

"Of course," Iggy said, apparently used to accommodating his teacher's whims.

Peppa waited for him to leave before she bit off the end of a large cigar. She rolled the bitten piece of tobacco around in her hand, examining it carefully, and then, striking a wooden match, puffed the cigar to life. Quinn noticed for the first time as he watched her manipulate the cigar that her nails were painted maroon to match her headscarf.

Peppa took a moment to study the growing ash of her cigar, then looked up to eye Ronnie carefully.

"It is good to see you, child," she said, somber, direct. "But I must ask. Why have you come? It is certainly not for me to tell you that this man you have chosen has a dark past. I suppose you already knew that. In any case, you could have asked me about him on the phone."

Ronnie sighed. "One of our friends was killed in Miami early this morning, along with a young family of Cuban refugees. We plan to take a look around the CUJAE." Garcia used the colloquial term for the university where Alejandro Placensia was supposed to have been a professor. "We have reason to believe that our friend's death may have been connected to someone with the department of aeronautical engineering."

"Aeronautical engineering?" Peppa repeated. She took a pencil and notepad from a nearby table and, holding the cigar in her teeth, wrote a series of directions. "I know of no such program at CUJAE. But I will tell you this. If murder and rocket science are involved, you will want to look at this address. The military has a school here that I have heard is connected to CUJAE in some way. Perhaps you could pass this information on to someone, and they would check it for you."

Quinn smiled. "We're here in an unofficial capacity."

"Unofficial?" Peppa said, rolling the idea around in her head as she considered the burning end of her cigar. She leaned forward, lowering her voice in a tone of mock conspiracy. "Do not all intelligence people come here unofficially?" Puffing the cigar again, she broke into a broad smile. "Anyway, I should have warned you earlier, Ignacio is certainly a . . . *chivato* . . ." She looked at Ronnie. "How do you say it?"

Ronnie's mouth fell open. Her eyes widened, alarmed. "An informer?"

"Ah," Peppa said, nodding through a massive cloud of smoke. "Yes. That is the word. He reports to the Committee for the Defense of the Revolution—the CDR. His mother and I are good friends."

Ronnie cocked her head. "So we don't have to worry, then?"

Peppa puckered her full lips and held the cigar out to one side, blowing a perfect smoke ring. "Oh, you must be careful of that one, to be sure. The CDR have his *cojones* in a vise of some kind. Who knows what they have on him. Maybe they threaten his parents . . ." She winked at Ronnie. "Or his favorite auntie."

Peppa saw Quinn shoot Ramón a quick glance. She gave a dismissive flick of her free hand. "Do not worry about him," she said. "This one's *cojones* fly free as birds."

The dark youth smiled and nibbled on a fried croquette.

"Speaking of aunties," Ronnie said, changing the

subject. "Do you know if my father's sister is still on the island?"

Peppa simply looked at her and continued to smoke.

"Ludmila Dombrovski," Ronnie prodded. "You remember her."

"Oh, yes," Peppa shrugged. "Of course I do. But we have not kept in touch over the years. She must have returned to Russia after your father passed on."

Ramón suddenly spoke up, earnest, wanting to be helpful. "I know of a woman with that name, Odesa Dombrovski. I think her auntie is called Ludmila."

Peppa shook her head. "You must be mistaken."

"No," Ramón said. "I am certain, now that I think on it. Ludmila Dombrovski."

Peppa blew another smoke ring. "A common enough name. This one must be a different Ludmila."

"Perhaps," Ramón conceded. "The one I am thinking of lives in Santa Fe."

Ronnie sat up straighter. "My Auntie Ludmila lived in Santa Fe. That's west of the city. Right? She was a teacher, like my father."

"To the west." Ramón nodded. "Near Marina Hemingway. This one is a teacher as well."

"It has to be her," Garcia said. "A niece with the surname Dombrovski seems unlikely, though, since she and my father were the only siblings."

"Perhaps." The young man shrugged. He looked Ronnie up and down, clearly taking stock of her figure. "But if I am to be honest, Odesa Dombrovski does have your . . . nose."

Peppa cleared her throat in an obvious attempt to put an end to the conversation.

Ronnie turned to stare at her.

"What is going on?" she asked. "You are hiding something."

Her auntie picked a piece of tobacco off her lips and closed her eyes. "It does no good to lie. My sister is the one who wished to keep a lid on this trash."

Ronnie shot to her feet. "Keep a lid on what trash?"

"Okay, then." Peppa blew a cloud of smoke toward the ceiling. "Since you leave me no choice, I will just say it."

"Say what?"

Peppa groaned. "When you were five years of age, your father had a very short affair with a young teacher at his school. He regretted it immediately and confessed to your mother, but . . . the damage, as they say, was done. The young woman was already pregnant. The divorce was your mother's decision."

"Divorce . . ." Ronnie put a hand on top of her head, dumbfounded. Quinn got up to comfort her, but she pulled away. "But my parents were married to each other."

"No," Peppa said. "They lived as man and wife, but they were divorced. Your father was, in fact, married to Soleil Perez until the day he died. Your mother had money of her own, but Soleil stood to lose her teaching job over the affair and subsequent child. At your mother's insistence, your father divorced her and married the girl. He never lived with her, though he did support the child—and give her his surname."

"A sister . . ."

"Odesa Dombrovski has a small charter boat in Marina Hemingway, where she caters to rich tourists. You must get any further details from her. I imagine that she knows much that I do not." Peppa glared at Ramón and sniffed. "One apprentice is all ears, the other is all mouth."

Peppa Garcia stood at the threshold of her tall front door while her stunned niece and the dangerous boyfriend departed in a yellow cocotaxi. Ignacio had just made it home in time to hear the last of the conversation about Veronica's half sister.

"Iggy," Peppa said, without turning around. "Fetch me the speckled rooster." She raised the stub of the dead cigar so the apprentices could see it. "Do you recall how to discern the ash?"

Ramón gave a somber nod. "The burn was uneven, señora—on one side only."

"That is correct." She watched the taxi pull away. "Meaning?"

"Bad luck," Ramón said, as if reciting the answers to a test, his voice husky and low. "Misfortune. Pain."

Peppa gave a deliberately slow nod.

"Death."

Chapter 10

Ignacio "Iggy" Baca waited until Madam Peppa had cut the throat of the speckled rooster and made her blood offering to Oyá before he excused himself to go for a walk.

The ceremony had not been a pleasant one for Ignacio. Peppa did not trust him. But what could he do?

On one hand, Señor Alacrón at the Mercado del Mundo had caught him stealing tennis shoes. They were Chinese tennis shoes and not even very good ones, but stealing was stealing, and Ignacio did not want to go to prison. Señor Alacrón, who was the leader of the local Committee for the Defense of the Revolution, said Ignacio could make everything right by reporting subversive activity by his employer or his neighbors.

On the other hand, Ignacio was apprenticed to the fiercest human being he had ever met. He was certain she'd petitioned Oyá to curse him. She'd uttered his name when she killed the speckled rooster, catching herself in time to send him for an extra bowl to cover her slip.

It was not lost on Ignacio that his teacher aligned herself with one of the strongest orishas in the Santeria pantheon. Oyá, the warrior goddess who sat on Peppa's head, was owner of the marketplace, keeper of the cemetery gates—bringer of change, both bad and good. She rode the wind into battle, a lightning bolt in one hand and a machete in the other.

Peppa Garcia, friend of this powerful goddess, was not the sort of person you wanted to cross—and yet Ignacio was forced to do it every day.

Ignacio walked five blocks in the black night before stopping to sit on a broken wooden bench. The shop behind him was closed, which was too bad, because he could have used one of their *batidos*, the Cuban version of a fruit smoothie. It was almost midnight, and there was not another soul on the narrow street. Ignacio took the mobile phone from his pocket and held it in his hand, staring at the cracked screen. "Oh, señora," he whispered. Peppa Garcia treated him fairly. She made sure he was well fed and carefully taught him the ways of the orisha—and he repaid her with this.

Perhaps he could give a report on the foreigners but leave Señora Peppa out of it altogether. Yes, that's what he would do. He owed nothing to these *Yanquis*. The woman was somehow related to Peppa, but that could not be helped. Betraying them would be better than betraying his patron. Surely Oyá would understand that.

He punched the memorized number in with his thumb, taking care not to leave it in the history of his phone in case Ramón decided to snoop. Being unworthy of trust himself, Ignacio trusted no one, least of all his friends.

"It is me," he said when Alacrón picked up.

"What have you got for me?" Alacrón yawned. "I hope it is something good."

"I believe it is, señor," Ignacio said. "There are two foreign visitors in my neighborhood. I only got portions of their conversation, but they seem like people who would interest you." All of what he said was true, though he did conveniently leave out where he heard the conversation. Alacrón grunted to show that he was listening. It was not uncommon for the man to sit through an entire report without speaking an actual word. "One of them," Ignacio continued, "is a good-looking woman. She appears to have relatives in Cuba. I do not think the man speaks Spanish, but the woman is fluent. This man is very dark."

"Afro-Cuban?"

"No," Ignacio said. "I mean his spirit. He is extremely dangerous."

This seemed to interest Alacrón. Ignacio could hear the scratch of a pen on paper. "Their names?"

"I do not know their names or where they are staying." Ignacio paused, knowing that once he said the rest, there would be no going back. "But I do know where they will be tomorrow morning. Marina Hemingway."

Chapter 11

Jericho Quinn's mother owned an emerald ring that had a lot in common with Marina Hemingway. Both were stunning—so long as you kept them at arm's length. Closer inspection of his mother's ring revealed chipped facets and a large crack running down the center of the stone.

It was still possible to get a postcard-worthy photo of Marina Hemingway, but only if you stood on just the right spot and aimed your lens at just the right boat, cropping out the surrounding rot. Nine miles west of Havana on Santa Fe Harbor, the marina should have been a jewel—and, no doubt, it once had been. Now, one hotel was completely shuttered. The other had a nice enough exterior, but was shabby and smelled faintly of mildew on the inside. Whitewash peeled and flaked from the apartment buildings and shops that ran along the fingers of land beside the marina's four channels. Red tiles on the roofs were broken and often missing completely.

The cab ride from the Hotel Sevilla took twenty minutes. He'd considered having the cabbie go a couple of other places first, doubling back a few times, but he changed his mind. Running surveillance detection routes in a cab was problematic at best. At worst, it made you look guilty. Sometimes it was better to go about the business of being a tourist with open eyes, fully aware that you were being followed.

"Okay," Quinn said to Ronnie once the cab drove away. "You visit your sister, and I'll catch a bus to the hospital district."

Ronnie stared out at the marina as if rooted to the concrete. "You think it's fate that our fathers have the same first name?" she said, stalling for time.

Quinn chuckled. "I don't know. Peter is a common enough name in Ireland and Russia."

"You don't speak Spanish," she said without looking up. "I should come with you. I can take care of this personal stuff later."

Quinn put one hand on her shoulder and tapped his temple with the other index finger. "Your auntie's map is right here," he said. "I take the bus down Calle 222 and get off at the immunology center. From there, I'll spend a few minutes just ambling around to see if I've been followed. Then it's a short walk over to the military aeronautical science building. I'm just going to look. No funny business."

She turned to follow him. "Still—"

"Talk to your sis, Ronnie. You should meet her." He smiled. "I'd be a third wheel—and I'm a two-wheel kind of guy."

Ronnie sighed. "Okay. But be careful."

"You bet," Quinn said. "You know me—'careful' is my middle name."

She grimaced. "Your middle name is 'deep shit.' You're just too cultured to admit it."

"I'll be careful," Quinn said. "Won't be gone long. I'll find you on the docks in an hour or so. Her slip's on the north side of Channel Number 2, right?"

"Right," Ronnie said, sounding uncertain.

Angel Diaz ducked behind the covered bus stop across Avenida 5 and pressed the speed dial on his mobile phone. A forty-one-year-old former baseball shortstop, he had wispy, thinning hair and a hefty paunch. He looked nothing like a spy, and he wished for an actual two-way radio and a covert earpiece like the ones spies in the movies used to contact their handlers. His surveillance gear looked exactly like what it was: a flimsy earpiece connected to a cheap mobile phone from Cubacel with a blue plastic wires. Señor Alacrón didn't want to be called a handler and strictly forbid Diaz from referring to himself as a spy. He was merely a good citizen, doing his duty by reporting subversive activity to the Committee for the Defense of the Revolution.

A good citizen, indeed.

Diaz had briefly thought of going to the United States. He didn't see it as defecting. He only wanted to play baseball. His mistake was to confide the dream to his girlfriend, who also happened to be Alacrón's younger sister. He should have known something was wrong when she asked him to tell her his thoughts a second time. She captured the entire conversation on tape—and Alacrón had captured him. Now, twenty years later, the man who was not his handler still called every few weeks for information.

Today, Angel's civic duty was to work with Sammy Meduro, a fellow CDR stooge, to intercept two Americans. As a former boxer, Meduro was supposed to be the muscle. That meant Diaz was to be the brains, which meant there had been no one else available for the task. Their targets were described only as "a beautiful Latina *chica*" and "a dangerous-looking man with a dark beard." It wasn't much to go on, and both Diaz and Meduro had said as much—but only to each other, certainly not to Alacrón.

And then the cab arrived, and the descriptions made sense at once.

"They are here," Diaz said, the moment Alacrón answered his call.

"Excellent," Alacrón snapped. "Follow them, and report back what you discover."

It certainly sounded like something a handler would say to a spy. Diaz thought spying far preferable to being a rat.

Diaz wanted to melt into the asphalt when the dangerous man kissed the beautiful Latina and then turned to walk directly toward the bus stop.

"The man is coming toward us," Diaz stammered, motioning for an annoyed Meduro to walk with him up Avenue 5. "But the woman remained behind at the marina. They are going separate directions."

"Follow the man," Alacrón said. "I will have the police bring him in for questioning after you find out where he is going. We can see what the woman is up to later."

Diaz cupped a hand over his mouth to shield his conversation, though the dangerous man had yet to make it across the street. One could not be too careful. "What if he tries to elude us?"

"He should not even see you," Alacrón said.

Diaz pressed the issue, risking the wrath of his boss. "But suppose he does?"

"Well," Alacrón sighed, "you must stop him. If he tries to get away from you, that means he is up to no good."

"Clear," Diaz said, thinking maybe that sounded a little bit like a spy.

"Idiot!" Meduro said after Diaz relayed Alacrón's message. They'd stopped to loiter under an elm tree twenty meters from the bus stop. "You have to call and ask for instructions on the smallest of matters. We could have stayed with the woman. Following behind that ass would be much better than staying with the man." The boxer gazed across the street, raising a lecherous eye. The mess of cartilage that was the man's cauliflower ear made Diaz a little sick to his stomach.

"The bus is here," Diaz said, ignoring his partner. "Keep your eyes down so he does not see you. He will remember your ugly face if he looks at you too long."

Meduro doubled a fist and bobbed his head, pretending he was going to punch, the way he always did when he wanted to intimidate someone.

"You are the idiot," Diaz said under his breath, quietly enough so Meduro could not hear.

The two good citizens of the Committee for the Defense of the Revolution boarded after the dark man, remaining at the front of the bus so they could keep an eye on both doors. They were not actually trained as spies, but they knew it would be less suspicious if only one of them left the bus at the same time as their target. The other one could get off at the next stop, coming back quickly to join the surveillance. With any luck, the dangerous man would never even know they were there.

Quinn spotted the two men tailing him the moment they got on the bus. The human brain was remarkable in its ability to distinguish between the tiniest relative differences of white to iris in the human eye. Someone staring, even for only a moment and from dozens of yards away, was painfully obvious.

The paunchy guy with the wispy comb-over engaged in conspicuous ignoring, averting his eyes to look everywhere on the bus except for where Quinn stood. Conversely, the big guy with the torn-up ear couldn't keep from glancing in his direction. This one caught Quinn's eye a half dozen times in the first two minutes, then looked quickly away as if he'd been caught committing some crime. *Definitely not Cuban Intelligence*, Quinn thought. When it came to following someone unnoticed, there was little intelligence about either of these guys.

Following Auntie Peppa's instructions, Quinn stepped off the bus in the medical park on Calle 222, a few blocks from the Center of Molecular Immunology. Only Paunchy followed him off, but he was so obvious that Quinn couldn't help but feel a little like he was being punked. He kept an eye peeled for someone conducting a more professional, secondary surveillance.

Quinn was fluent in five languages but spoke very little Spanish. He had a good ear, though, and he had quickly absorbed a great deal from listening to Garcia. She'd taught him the Spanish version of his often-repeated motto, "See one, think two," early on: *Ver uno, pensar dos*. And seeing two always made him wonder if there were more.

This time, anyone else out there was too well trained for Quinn to identify them. He made it to the campus of the International Center for Neurologic Restoration, four blocks away, before he came to the conclusion that he was dealing with either the Cuban version of the Keystone Cops or a pair of counterespionage operatives who possessed such incredible cunning as to completely take his mind off the invisible professionals that were really following him.

It was probably the former, but Quinn kept his eyes peeled nonetheless. At least half the scars on his body had been caused by people who didn't know a thing about strategy or technique.

Chapter 12

"**H**oly buckets," Thibodaux said under his breath. "You got us booked at the Cuban Alamo." The '57 Buick Century taxi dropped him and Emiko Miyagi in front of the opulent stone entrance to the Hotel Sevilla on Trocadero.

A uniformed bellman gave them a broad smile from under his curling gray mustache as he took their bags. They followed him through the cavernous lobby and up the blue tiled steps between twin statues of lions. The abundance of statuary and high ceilings reminded Thibodaux of Vegas, without the painted sky.

There was no line at check-in, and Señor Mustache stepped aside with a polite flourish while he waited with the luggage.

The heavyset man behind the mosaic tiles of the reception counter couldn't keep from leering at the tiny blossom of a tattoo that peeked from the top of Emiko Miyagi's black bra. She was more than capable of taking care of herself, and Thibodaux had no reason to feel protective, but he did, and that annoyed him. Much to Thibodaux's chagrin, he and Miyagi made a handsome couple. She was at least eight years his senior, somewhere in her mid-forties—maybe even older. He made it a point not to hazard a guess into such deadly minefields. And anyway, near flawless skin and an ultra-fit body allowed her to pass for decades younger.

Traveling as Mr. and Mrs. Jacques Dubois from Montreal, they would be under slightly less scrutiny than Quinn and Garcia—so long as they remembered to reel in the intensity of their personalities. Thibodaux's imposing height and mountainous build drew second looks in any crowd. The black eye patch tended to focus the power of his already severe gaze, causing even casual observers to take a startled step backward if he happened to look at them too long. Camille called it his eye-burn and warned him about it every time they met with one of the boys' teachers. He knew he was the sort of man other people noticed. His favorite Mambo brand surfer shirt, with a pattern of spark plugs firing into bright red hibiscus flowers against an electric blue background, showed he did not care. And if he didn't care, he didn't matter because such a man obviously had nothing to hide.

Emiko Miyagi was just over five feet tall and a hundred and five pounds, but if anything, her visage was even more withering. The mysterious tattoo playing peekaboo with the desk clerk added to her cryptic persona. Thibodaux wondered if the air of danger was because her favorite weapon was a blade. Did hacking an enemy to death with a sword turn you into a badass, or did being a badass render the hacking easier to do? He supposed it was a chicken-or-egg thing.

Killing someone with a sword, even a long one, meant getting close. It was a personal act, not something you could accomplish from a hill a thousand meters away. Miyagi had done it many times since Thibodaux had known her. Emiko Miyagi hardly weighed as much as his leg, but he wasn't ashamed to admit that the little Japanese woman scared the shit out of him.

She tugged on his hand, nearly sending him into a panic until he snapped out of his internal philosophy session and remembered where they were.

"Honey," she said, in the slightly nasal purr of a stereotypical Japanese wife. "The bellman can take the bags to the room. I want to walk along the ocean."

Thibodaux shrugged, trying to act as if he was used to such behavior from this killer. They'd rehearsed, but subservient wife was so out of character for Miyagi that Jacques was sure he'd never get used to it.

"Whatever you want, sweetheart."

He gave the bellman a five-CUC tip to take their bags—Miyagi's a rolling case with a disconcerting pink Hello Kitty design. Acting as if they didn't realize that the bellman might go through their bags only added to their legend as trusting Canadian tourists.

Five minutes later, Miyagi sidled up next to Thibodaux as they walked along Trocadero toward the Malecón seawall.

"I think I did very well," she said. "People will believe you and I are husband and wife. Don't you think?"

"So long as we remember to argue now and again," Thibodaux frowned. "And don't call me honey. It creeps me out."

"What do you wish me to call you? Jackie?"

He wagged his head. "Jacques will do nicely, thank you very much." He stared out at the ocean. "I wish we could call and check on the kids."

Miyagi knew he was talking about Quinn and Garcia.

They stopped at a shop that sold gaudily painted

coconuts and shellacked conch shells. Emiko lowered her sunglasses, pretending to look at the postcards on a revolving rack while she took the opportunity to check and see if anyone was following them. She shook her head as if she didn't like any of the cards, letting Jacques know she didn't see anyone. Both of them were smart enough to know that meant little. Cuban intelligence was capable of deploying an army of officers and agents who would blend into the fabric of society. For all they knew, the fat guy behind the shop's chipped Formica counter was on the Intelligence Directorate payroll.

Miyagi lowered her glasses. "I'm sure the kids are fine without us."

She took his hand again and they continued to walk.

Thibodaux looked down at her. The nearest person was a lone fisherman casting a makeshift pole fifty feet ahead, but he kept his voice low anyway.

"This has gotta be hard for you, pretending to be my wife when you don't even like me."

Miyagi smirked. "You merely remind me of someone."

Jacques walked on in silence for a time, then waited for a group of Chinese tourists to amble past before he said, "Well, I told Camille that you don't like me. That way she's got nothin' to worry about, with us sharing a room and all."

Miyagi laughed again. "Your wife certainly has nothing to worry about. If I can share a bath with Quinn-san and nothing inappropriate occurs, I can certainly share a bedroom with you."

Thibodaux stopped in his tracks. "Hang on. You had a bath with Chair Force?" He closed his good eye and shook his head, walking again. This was too much to fathom. "Never mind. I don't even want to know."

"It became necessary that I show him my tattoo," Miyagi said. "To explain about my past. My daughter. As I said, nothing happened but for two humans sitting and talking together."

"Yeah," Thibodaux said. "Naked, in a steamy tub."

"We Japanese have a different view of nudity than Americans."

"Maybe so," Thibodaux said. "But I reckon we'll just keep this little factoid from Camille. What she don't know will let me keep my nuts intact."

"I had not planned to ever bring it up," Miyagi said. "And, I should point out, I am the one who should be nervous, given the situation."

"How's that?"

"Well," Miyagi said. "Your poor wife appears to get pregnant every time you walk past her. I am much too old to have six or seven children."

The big Cajun peered down with his good eye as they walked. "You know human babies aren't usually born in litters, right?"

Miyagi's face fell into a frown of mock astonishment. "I will have to remember that."

"Outstanding. Now let's you and me just work on looking like we're a happy couple."

Emiko gave a playful grin. "Should I act a little more jealous of other women?"

"Just other beautiful Japanese badasses," Thibodaux said.

Miyagi squeezed his hand a little tighter. "Thank you, Jacques-san. Men do not say such things to me very often."

"It's part of my cover."

"I know," Emiko said. "But it is, nonetheless, nice to hear."

There was no posted sign out front, but the presence of a military checkpoint on the paved road between the four white stucco buildings led Quinn to believe he was outside Cuba Polytech's aeronautical engineering satellite campus—or at least something more important than just another hospital. The streets were fairly crowded here, with residents of the nearby apartment buildings and patrons of the sundry shops and tiny cafés. Some carried flavored fruit drinks or juice, dispensed into small plastic water or cola bottles they had saved for that purpose. Many held handmade bags of bread, and what little they could find in the way of tinned food. Probably to get ready for the approaching hurricane, Quinn thought. Others waved their rolled morning issue of *Granma*. The state newspaper was named for the yacht that had carried Fidel and his revolutionaries back from Mexico in 1956. The boat had been named for the previous owner's grandmother, but that translation seemed to have given way to revolutionary history.

Quinn couldn't help but notice the stark difference between this place and the glitzy tourist areas along the Malecón. Here, bicycles outnumbered cars of any vintage. Quinn counted a dozen donkey carts between the neurology center and the school campus. There were no touts offering bicycle tours or directions to the finest *paladar*, no one hawking merchandise, no fancy cabs, no one begging for money. The residents here had nothing extra to sell. Their clothing was colorful and even stylish—though a more discerning eye would have noticed even the newest items were at least a decade behind the latest fashions in the U.S. The men wore slacks and faded, short-sleeved shirts of thin cotton. Many of the women wore colorful shorts against the heat and tight T-shirts with gaudy logos. Most of the clothing showed significant wear and the odd stain here and there, like something that had been washed by hand. Quinn had little idea what people said as they walked by, chattering, laughing, and gesturing wildly to make their point. These were the middle class of Havana, if there was such a thing. The actual poor lived in more rural areas, without access to many of the niceties like shops or clean drinking water. The people walking by Quinn on this cracked, uneven sidewalk had little, and what they did have was generally made up of the worn-out, the run-down, and the necessary rather than anything frivolous.

Quinn used his peripheral vision to pay attention to the satellite campus. There was a frenetic pace to the people coming and going, as if no one was immune to arrest. This nervousness was common around secure facilities in countries run by a powerful military. The security police posted at the gate on Edwards Air Force Base had guns, but that didn't keep some colonel's wife from stopping to chat them up about how hot the day was. The soldiers in front of this mundane campus didn't look like they were in the mood to talk about anything.

Quinn slowed his pace a half step but kept walking. Now that he had an idea of where to focus, he could get the address to Palmer and ask him to check satellite surveillance for odd activity. He didn't expect to see anything as damning as missiles being snuck in under the cover of darkness, but satellites also showed other things—like the arrival of a large complement of uniformed officers when there had been none for weeks or months. Even a change in the daily routine might add a vital piece to the puzzle, once they figured out what sort of puzzle they were looking at. A local agent might be able to dig up something concrete.

Quinn glanced at the checkpoint as he passed, careful not to make the same mistake as the goons on the bus by avoiding it altogether. The sentries were considerably older and more seasoned than soldiers he'd seen on the street up to this point. They met his gaze with glares. He sped up, raising his eyebrows and ducking his head to demonstrate the appropriate amount of obeisance. A quick backward glance, ostensibly away from the soldiers, told him Paunchy had picked up his pace as well and was now less than half a block away. The idiot held the cord to his earbuds up to his mouth, apparently talking to someone on his cell phone.

Unfortunately, Quinn caught his eye. Instead of smiling as if it were a coincidence, Paunchy's jaw dropped in panic, caught red-handed.

Quinn made a quick right, habitually swinging a little wide so as not to go in blind. He had no idea where Cauliflower Ear was at the moment. There was a corner store at the end of the block with an alley running behind it. Paunchy dogged his steps a few meters back. Quinn darted right again, hopping over a stack of wooden banana crates. He smiled to himself when the plodding gallop of the man's footsteps slowed, then stopped, hesitating before tentatively following him into the shadows.

Chapter 13

Going into an unexplored alley wasn't Quinn's first choice of strategies. There were too many variables. It could be a dead end. The paunchy guy might have some friends. Or there might be more Cubans with no connection to Paunchy who would see no problem at all giving an American a beatdown.

Light at the end of the alley made Quinn think it continued out into the next block. Instead of an exit, though, he found a pile of twisted steel and concrete rubble where a building had collapsed. A slab of the second story lay across the end of the alley, forming a barrier that looked more like a deadfall trap than a viable route of escape. Given time, Quinn could have picked his way over the debris, but trying to get through it quickly was a recipe for a broken ankle or a case of lockjaw from a rusty wound.

An old woman with her hair piled up in a loose scarf stepped out the back of her bakery with a bag of trash. She took one look at Quinn and the oncoming Paunchy, then ducked back inside. It was a relatively safe bet that she wouldn't call the police. A fight between two strangers in the alley would work itself out quickly. Police involvement would cause everyone hours of problems.

Quinn spun when Paunchy was less than twenty feet away. A quick glance around the alley shadows revealed several possible weapons—a mop handle, a coil of heavy rope. There was a length of rusted chain with a three-inch meat hook attached to the end. Paunchy didn't appear to be armed, but pistols had a way of turning up quickly.

Quinn grabbed the broken mop handle, keeping the chain and meat hook behind him in reserve, just in case things got more serious. He held the three-foot shaft in his right hand down along his leg and raised his left hand, palm open.

"Hey, *amigo*," he said. "You speak English?"

Paunchy lumbered forward tentatively. His face twitched. A low growl rumbled deep in his belly.

Quinn had fought men like this before. He was obeying orders, caught between the rock of disobedience and the hard place of a battle he didn't want to join. He was more afraid of whoever gave him his orders than he was of Quinn, but only by a hair.

Quinn stepped deftly to the side, letting the man continue past a half step before swinging the mop handle so it took him across the trailing calf muscle. The effect on Paunchy's morale was immediate. He yowled in pain, hopping forward to arrest his fall as he transferred all the weight to his good leg. Quinn reversed course with the mop handle, crashing into the side of Paunchy's forward leg with a vicious backswing. It was like getting a dead leg on steroids. The mop handle lit up the common peroneal nerve that ran roughly under the outer seam of a man's slacks, overloading the nervous system and causing both legs to buckle. Quinn reversed trajectory with the stick once again, impacting the man's floating ribs with a sickening crack. Less than three seconds after he'd rushed Quinn, Paunchy lay on his back clutching his side and sucking for air like a fish out of water.

The back door to the bakery opened again, and the same old woman stuck her head out. She frowned when she saw the fight had not moved elsewhere and ducked back inside. Quinn smiled, heard a crunch of gravel behind him, and turned in time to catch a powerful right hook square on the jaw.

Quinn fell back with the blow, narrowly avoiding a left hook from the guy with the cauliflower ear.

That must have been who Paunchy was talking to on his cell.

Fully committed to the attack, the big guy ran at Quinn and pressed him against the rubble, intent on tripping him up as he backpedaled. Quinn himself was a boxer and enjoyed forays back into the sweet science when the circumstances dictated—usually when he wanted to make a point, though, not to counter an attack. Boxing was violent, even deadly, but it was still a sport.

Cauliflower Ear, on the other hand, was married to his training. He relied on skill and finesse to set Quinn up for a devastating combination and a quick knockout.

Quinn capitalized on this devotion. He threw a couple of jabs to keep the man on his toes. It wasn't that Cauliflower Ear wasn't able to fight dirty. He was more than willing to punch below the belt or use one hand to drag Quinn into a Cuban version of an Irish hug. His weakness lay in the way he failed to employ his feet. It seemed unthinkable to Cauliflower Ear that he could use something besides his hands, or maybe his forehead, as a weapon. His feet were shod in heavy leather boots and would have been devastating, but they were destined for nothing other than keeping him upright.

Quinn threw another jab-cross combination, then began immediately to chop the other man down. He started by planting his instep to the side of his opponent's knee. Meant to bend only one way, the joint was particularly sensitive to lateral stress.

Cauliflower Ear yelped, sidestepping quickly and dragging his injured leg. Quinn followed his own momentum, clawing at the other man's exposed kidney through his shirt as if he meant to rip away the flesh. Far from devastating, this "horse bite" did little but direct the Cuban's energy, making him light on his feet.

Exploding upward, Quinn slammed the heel of his open hand into the other man's chin, intent on following it up and over to slam the man's head backward and down, much like spiking a volleyball. Cauliflower Ear had more energy—and savvy—than Quinn anticipated, and he turned his head at the last moment, letting Quinn's hand graze by. Quinn earned a slap to his ear for his trouble. The Cuban hit him again, hard in the temple, sending a shower of sparks into his brain. For a moment, he had the all-too-familiar sensation of the lights dimming, but he shook it off. Luckily, the Cuban was too slow to deliver a follow-up shot before Quinn could regain enough of his senses to scramble out of the way.

Quinn blew out a hard exhale, bringing his vision back into focus. He couldn't afford another mistake like that against a man this powerful. Pressing in, Quinn rejoined the fight quickly to let an angry, unfocused right scream by, inches from his jaw. He snapped a hammer fist into Cauliflower's groin. The larger man slumped, his jaw hanging open like he might vomit. Quinn seized the moment and pummeled him in the floating ribs, paralyzing his diaphragm and robbing him of his ability to breathe. Grabbing the larger man behind the head with both hands, Quinn yanked hard, multiplying the applied force as he bashed his forehead into the Cuban's already crooked nose.

Cauliflower Ear staggered backward and hit the wall, slithering to the ground in a heap, out cold. The paunchy guy with the comb-over croaked for air a few feet away—conscious, but out of the fight.

Quinn held up his wallet and then wagged a finger back and forth. He shook his head at the men as if chiding a couple of disobedient children. "*No robar! No carterista!*" he said, mimicking the phrases Garcia used on him when he took the last piece of gum from her purse.

Three minutes later, Angel Diaz wheezed into his phone, "He thinks we were trying to rob him."

Sammy Meduro leaned against the concrete wall on the opposite side of the alley, his head was back, trying to stanch the river of blood that flowed from his shattered nose.

"Rob him?" Señor Alacrón whispered, as if he did not want anyone in his office to know of the debacle. "Tell him you are undercover policemen."

Diaz grunted for air. "We cannot tell him anything, sir. He is not here."

The line fell silent for so long Diaz thought Alacrón had hung up.

"Hello?"

"Where is he?" Alacrón demanded.

"I do not know," Diaz said.

"Do you not suspect he might return to Marina Hemingway, to meet with the woman?"

Diaz rubbed his aching ribs. Two of them were certainly broken, and his leg felt as if it were on fire. "Of course," he said. "That is where he would go."

"Very well," Alacrón said, as if it were oh so simple. "You say he believes you were going to rob him?"

Diaz nodded, bringing a stab of pain to his neck. He must have injured it when he fell. "He called us pickpockets."

"Then see to it that he is robbed," Alacrón snapped. "I want to know what this man who can best Sammy Meduro in a fight is doing in Cuba."

Chapter 14

Ronnie Garcia was sitting on a bench under a ratty palm tree eating a sandwich when Quinn got off the bus. The sun-bleached wooden bench had no back, so she leaned forward, elbows on her arms, toes pointed inward, and head down as if in defeat.

"How'd it go?" Quinn asked, taking an swig from the glass bottle of Jarritos Mexican cola she'd handed him.

Ronnie sighed. "I decided to wait," she said. "I've gone this long without even knowing I had a sister. There's no need to rush into things." She cocked her head to study his face as he sat down beside her.

"Are you okay?"

"Why wouldn't I be?" Quinn asked.

"Because you have blood on your cheek, smart-ass."

Quinn reached up and wiped his face with his forearm. "Don't worry. It's not mine."

"Is that supposed to make me worry more or less?" Ronnie asked. "Considering where we are."

"Stop trying to change the subject." Quinn reached toward the sandwich, suddenly starving. "What's this?"

"*Hamburguesa de Cerdo,*" Garcia said. "I used to love them when I was a kid. It's a pork burger with strawberry marmalade and cream cheese."

"Sounds mysteriously delicious." Quinn raised the

sandwich to take a bite, but shoved it back to Garcia immediately after he took one look. "It's raw!"

"Not raw," she corrected. "Pink."

"Yeah, well, pink equals raw."

Garcia shrugged. "I guess I'm hoping my Cuban gut is still immune."

Quinn grimaced. "I'm not sure anyone builds up an immunity to tapeworms. Anyway, poisoning me isn't going to let you off the hook."

"Cut me a little slack, mango." Ronnie took a sullen bite of the medium rare pork burger. "I need the nourishment. Some jerk stole the seats off all the women's toilets here at the marina. I had to hover in the air. That takes a lot of energy out of a girl."

"Again with changing the subject," Quinn said. "We're not leaving here until you meet your sister."

"Aren't you worried about the guy whose blood was on your cheek?"

"I'm concerned," Quinn said. "But there's a chance it was just an unrelated street crime."

"Really?"

"No," Quinn admitted. "Not likely. But they were definitely not sharp enough to be from the Intelligence Directorate."

"They?"

"There were two," Quinn said. "Anyway, if they knew we were coming here, they probably know where we're staying. You should meet your sister while you have the chance. We may only be in Cuba a few more hours."

According to Auntie Peppa's talkative apprentice, Odesa Dombrovski moored her boat on the north side of Pier 2. Quinn couldn't remember the exact slip number. It didn't matter. There could be no doubt that the blond woman working on the back deck was Garcia's sister.

Garcia leaned sideways as they walked, speaking under her breath. "I always thought I inherited the ghetto booty from my mother," she said. "But apparently, my father had something to do with it."

"Hadn't noticed," Quinn lied.

"Maybe my dad had a type," she said, sounding glum.

Odesa had a lot more in common with Garcia than the propensity toward athletic hips. She was tall, with the same broad shoulders and full figure. Her complexion was much lighter than Ronnie's, though still tan in contrast to the dusky blond hair she kept pulled back in an elastic headband. She wore khaki shorts and a tawny, sleeveless T-shirt darkened with perspiration along the plunging neckline and underarms. Leaning over a long-handled mop and a plastic bucket of soapy water, she worked to scrub black marks off the deck of an old but well-kept wooden fishing boat. Quinn had spent enough time around boats to know the black marks had been left by some careless passenger's shoe soles.

The vessel was moored parallel to the concrete pier, but they'd approached from the stern. The boat's name, *DANOTRIA*, was painted in ornate red letters on the white transom. Quinn looked at Garcia for a translation, but she only shrugged.

"I got nothin'," she whispered.

"I cannot take you out today," the woman said in English without looking up from her chore. "The sea is too rough. Too dangerous."

Quinn stepped closer to the stern and dipped his head toward the marks on the deck.

"Some people."

"And they did not even give me a tip," the young woman said in time to the rhythm of her scrubbing. She was not rude, but a long way off from friendly.

Quinn waited for Garcia to say something, but she just stood there, arms folded as if she were freezing to death.

"Your English is very good," Quinn said. He was honestly surprised.

"My father was a . . . how do you say it? A stickler for languages."

Ronnie spoke. "My father as well," she said. "You might have heard of him. His name was Peter Novakovich Dombrovski."

Odesa's head snapped up. Dark eyes flitted back and forth from Garcia to Quinn. She sneered, then resumed her scrubbing.

"So this is my wicked stepsister, come from the ball to observe me while I scrub cinders."

Garcia stared blankly. "What?"

"*What?*" Odesa looked up from her scrubbing and gave a mock frown. "They do not have fairy tales in *Yuma?*" She used the colloquial Cuban word for all places foreign, especially the United States."

"Of course they have fairy tales," Garcia said. "I just . . . I'm not your step—I mean, I am, but I'm not wicked . . . Look, I didn't even know you existed until last night."

"It does not matter," Odesa said. "We have nothing to discuss, you and I." She pointed the dripping scrub brush at Quinn. "You, on the other hand. I could talk to you for hours on end."

"Forget it," Garcia spat, letting fly what Quinn took for a string of Spanish curses. "You're right. We have nothing to talk about."

Quinn ignored Odesa's come-on. It was obvious she was just flirting to anger her sister. "Of course you have things to talk about," he said. "If I met someone who knew my father, I'd want to spend at least five minutes comparing notes, even if I did hate her guts."

"I hate every part of her," Odesa said. "Not only her guts."

Ronnie stood on the pier pouting, arms still folded, while Odesa continued to scrub as if she meant to dig a hole in the deck.

Quinn heaved a heavy sigh. "What does the name of your boat mean?" he asked in an effort to break the rapidly forming ice.

"*Danotria*?" Odesa said. "It means 'freedom' in Russian."

"No, it doesn't," Ronnie snapped. "*Freedom* in Russian is *svoboda*, or maybe *volya*."

Odesa looked up, a conspiratorial smile creeping across her lips. "If you must know, it means 'freedom' in my secret language. I tell Russians *danotria* is a Finnish word. To the Finns, I explain it is Croatian. I tell the harbormaster it is antiquated Russian as if it is . . . how do you say it . . . common knowledge. No one wants to look as if they do not already know. It is my own personal little revolution. I call my vessel by the name *I* choose, even if that name means nothing at all. I think that is freedom. Do you not agree?"

"I like it," Quinn said. He dug an elbow into Garcia's ribs.

"Okay. It's ingenious," she said, almost as if she meant it.

Odesa dropped the brush into the sudsy bucket and stood, arching her back against the stiffness brought on by her work. Like Garcia, she appeared to have no idea how beautiful she truly was. She tossed her head toward the cabin door. "Come inside if you wish." The chip on her shoulder was still prominent in her words. "I will put on some coffee."

Garcia turned to go. "She wants us to leave."

Quinn looked from one sister to the other. "She said she's putting on coffee . . ."

"That means we're supposed to go," Ronnie said. "It's a polite Cuban way to say 'time for you to leave.'"

Odesa chuckled. "Or it means that I will make you some coffee. I'm sure it will not be so good as your American coffee, but we Cubans are merely trying our best to be adequate."

Odesa Dombrovski turned out to be an eloquent, if bitter, young woman. Her English was very good, though some of the colloquialisms were a little dated—from reading old books, Quinn guessed. There was a bit of an Eliza Doolittle from *My Fair Lady* naivety to her pattern of speech. Canadian visitors she took out fishing were probably too polite to critique or correct her, likely finding her quaint.

"So anyhow," she said, drinking the dregs of *cafécito* from her tiny cup. "I got our father's name, but you had the man." She slammed the cup on the wooden dinette

as if she'd just won a drinking game. "Oh, he came
to visit us every fortnight or so, but he would never
stay. Not even once. I always wondered why my mother
never tried to woo him back. I suppose her heart was
broken. Anyhow, a name is nothing more than a few
letters on paper. You are the lucky one. I was ten when
I heard you'd gotten out. Do you know how I spent my
mornings when you escaped to America?"

Ronnie shook her head.

"Oh, those were marvelous times indeed," Odesa
said. "For at least an hour each morning, my job was
to crumple up small squares of the newspaper—
smoothing them out, then crumpling them again, over
and over until they were soft. Toilet paper was nowhere
to be found, so we had to use the latest editions of
Granma and *Invasor*." She chuckled. "We Cubans like
to say ours were the most well-read asses in the world."

"I'm so sorry for you," Ronnie said softly.

"I do not need your pity," Odesa snapped. She looked
at Quinn. "Do you know what Cubans want?"

"Danotria?" he said.

A smile flickered in Odesa's eyes, but she closed
them immediately, as if she didn't want to be discovered. "We want the rest of the world to stop treating us
like shit. We want our government to stop treating us like
shit. Is that too much to ask? A boy I know . . . my boyfriend if you ask him, but he is just my friend . . .
anyhow, an American college student hid some *titi* in
my friend's backpack at a police checkpoint."

"What's *titi*?" Quinn asked.

"Beats me," Garcia said.

"Ritalin." Odesa blazed ahead with her story. "The
American student was put on a plane back to the U.S.,

and my friend is in jail. Do you see what I mean? It is shit. Sometimes in Cuba, your . . . *abogado* . . . the lawyer, he comes to the jail to tell you there was a trial and you were judged guilty."

Quinn gave a slow shake of his head.

"Of course you will be judged guilty," Odesa continued, "if you are not able to defend yourself. I do not think this is how you do it in America." She was still talking only to Quinn, ignoring Ronnie. "I have read all the Perry Mason books, and even some John Grisham."

"You're right," Quinn said. "That's not the way we do things in the U.S. Look, this is a lot for both of you to digest. Odesa, why don't you let us buy you dinner at our hotel?"

Ronnie's head snapped up. Odesa noticed her discomfort and accepted immediately.

"I would like that, Mr . . ."

"Shield," Quinn said. He looked out the cabin window at two men who loitered a hundred feet up the pier, looking from boat to boat. "Jim Shield."

Odesa followed his gaze. "CDR," she mumbled, her voice dripping with disdain. "I can spot the lousy *chivatos* from here." She stood. "Thank you very much for the visit. Now they will come and grill me for simply talking to Americans. They say relations between our two countries are getting better, but someone should tell that to the CDR idiots. Nice to meet you, Veronica, but I don't need the trouble that people like you bring with them."

"People like me?"

"Yes," Odesa said. "People who have CDR informers following them around. You will be happy to know that I must pass on dinner." She opened the companionway door and gestured out on deck with a flourish, hurrying them along. "Now please, do not go. Wait for the coffee." She looked at Garcia with a sneer. "And that means exactly what you think it means. *¡Chao pescao!*"

Paunchy and Cauliflower Ear turned to walk the other direction as soon as Odesa opened her door. They were hiding behind the bus stop across the street when Quinn and Garcia reached the marina entrance.

"That blood that was on your face," Ronnie said. "Would it have anything to do with why these guys have marked us?"

"Maybe," Quinn said. "Pretty sure it has something to do with why they're keeping their distance."

Ronnie chewed on her top lip, the way she did when she was fretful. "What if they question her? She could tell them I was born in Cuba."

"I think she's got more sense than that."

"She might do it just to hurt me."

"You have the same father," Quinn said. "Who, by all accounts, was a good man. I'm willing to bet you both inherited his qualities."

"There's no way to know if we can trust her."

Quinn nodded at the sign above marina, noting the name of the famous author. "Papa Hemingway himself had something to say about that. 'The best way to see if somebody is trustworthy is to trust them.'"

"Big words," Garica scoffed. "You don't trust anybody."

"Not true," Quinn said. "I trust the Dombrovski sisters."

Chapter 15

Odesa stood inside the door of her freedom boat, taking maybe a little too much joy in watching the squeaking CDR rats scamper up the pier away from her sister and the handsome boyfriend. As enjoyable as it was, one thing was certain: If the *chivatos* were involved, then something was about to happen—and it wasn't going to be good.

Odesa leaned her forehead against a window that sparkled in Bristol fashion, like a good skipper's boat should. "Why have you come, princess?" she whispered, her breath blowing a puff of fog on the glass. "Beautiful, privileged Veronica . . . Is your visit a good omen or a bad one?"

Hate was not exactly the word to describe her feelings, Odesa thought. Jealousy? Maybe. Especially with that *mangon* boyfriend.

Odesa's mother had slapped her face the first time she'd spoken the name of her half sister—as if she'd uttered a blasphemous curse. Twenty years later, she still felt the heat of the blow against her cheek.

Her father brought sweets when he came to visit. He would hold her on his knee and tell her jokes and call her *milaya*. But she wanted none of that. She only wanted him to stay. Instead, he left nothing but the woody leather smell of his Russian cologne, to return to the daughter he actually loved. The lucky daughter. The daughter who was not an embarrassment.

Perhaps *hate* was the correct word after all.

Peppa Garcia looked down from her second-floor balcony at the three women standing at her front door. If *Radio Bemba*—the grapevine, literally "lip radio"— had a switchboard operator, it was Peppa Garcia's old friend, Maria Mendoza, who now stood in the center of the little group.

Maria had a gorgeous body, round hips and full breasts that rivaled even Peppa—and that was saying a great deal. Even when she was a child, men would whistle at her when she was walking away. But it was a different story when she turned to face them. She'd suffered from terrible acne as a child and, worse yet, genetics that left her facial features oddly oblong, with one eye slightly larger than the other as if she were beginning to melt in the island heat. Most of their classmates in secondary school had called her *cebolla*, because any boy would have to pull her dress over her head and tie it in a knot like an onion to stomach being with her, they said. Peppa had treated her kindly, even shared a few boiled eggs with the lonely girl at lunch. To Peppa, it was nothing, a kind word, a boiled egg. But to Maria it had been everything, and brought with it her unbreakable devotion.

Maria grew no prettier as she matured, but what she lacked in traditional beauty, she made up for in intelligence and wit. Even the mean girls recognized it—as did Javier Mendoza, the neighborhood mechanic and handyman who eventually married her. Virtually every vehicle in Havana teetered on the razor's edge of complete disintegration. Javier was a genius who could manufacture rubber gaskets out of old Soviet tires or restore the snap to a spring with some heat and a bucket of used motor oil. Peppa once saw this maestro of "shade tree" manufacturing make a small internal part for an oscillating fan from an old plastic hair comb that was missing most of its teeth. People came in droves to his small shop with everything from broken toasters to Russian Ladas. While they waited, Maria sold them small homemade cakes and caught up on the local news.

Ronnie had asked Peppa to keep her ear to the ground about Alejandro Placensia. Her niece had warned her to be careful, to go slowly, but that was not in Peppa Garcia's nature. She did not live in a world of *rejas*—iron bars over her windows and doors—either literally or figuratively. Oyá looked after her. She would be smart about it, but that did not mean she had to be slow.

She'd asked a few trusted friends if they knew of the Placensia family, though not over the phone. That would have been beyond careless. If the U.S. was looking for this man, then Cuban intelligence authorities would be monitoring telephone calls and email traffic. Peppa had heard they had some sort of sniffer sold to them by North Korea that could zero in on a mobile signal to within three meters.

Peppa had her own network—the smaller, and more secure, *Radio Bemba*. These were people who believed in the orisha, the way of the saints, and trusted Peppa to guide them. Maria Mendoza was among the most informed, and she knew a woman who was familiar with Alejandro Placensia's mother.

It did not take long to find out that Señora Placensia was distraught over something. Maria suggested to her friend, a woman named Celeste Cardenas, that she bring Señora Placensia to Peppa for a consultation with the orishas.

Ramón ushered the three women in while Iggy prepared tea. Peppa had considered sending him away during the ceremony, but he knew nothing of the name Placensia. He would see this as nothing more than the priestess performing a ritual, as she did almost every day. If she sent him on a make-work errand, he would smell a secret—the way *chivato* did—and gnaw at it until he discovered what it was.

Maria was dressed in a long, lemon yellow skirt and sleeveless white blouse. Her hair, like Peppa's, was pulled up in a colorful scarf. Her friend Celeste, also brightly dressed, was as round as a football and only a little taller. Señora Placensia wore a powder blue, double-knit pantsuit—dated, even by Cuban standards. Somewhere in her early sixties, she looked thin and frail as a weathered cornstalk. Sweat beaded on a pinched upper lip. Her eyes were red and rheumy—a worried mother at her wit's end.

Maria leaned in to kiss Peppa on both cheeks. "*Holá Mamita*, may I present Mrs. Cardenas and Mrs. Placensia? I have informed them that you may provide some guidance through your relationship with the saints."

Peppa gestured down the hallway with an unlit cigar, held between the fingers of a perfectly manicured left hand. Her long nails were painted a rich aubergine purple and glistened under the light of the ceiling fan. Eggplant was a favorite food and color of her patron orisha. Like

Oyá, the Santeria priestess wore a nine-colored sash and carried a sharp machete in her right hand.

A large part of any ceremony was show—at least in the beginning. It was important to instill in the person who wanted the reading that this was serious business. They were, after all, communicating with the gods. If Peppa's stern smile failed to drive the point home, the sight of the machete always did. Ramón and Ignacio retired to the far end of the room ahead of the group and began to thump on the taut skins of their hourglass-shaped drums. Two cigars were already burning in front of the altar, Monte Carlos that smelled of rich earth and fine chocolate.

The rhythmic drumbeats and pungent cigar smoke settling in layers through the candlelight beckoned the women forward. Maria Mendoza had seen it before during a reading for her husband's business, but even she stood and stared at the clucking rooster across the dimly lit room, mouth agape.

"Welcome," Peppa said. She gestured with her machete toward three straight-back chairs, arranged to face a fourth that was placed beside the altar. "Please, be seated. Señora Placensia, what troubles you?" The weight of already knowing that the woman's son was dead pressed against Peppa's belly like a hot stone. She was no charlatan, no carnival fortune-teller. If the cowrie shells spoke of evil and death, then so be it. She would not use information gleaned from Veronica to make Señora Placensia believe she could foresee the future or know the unknown. That was the purview of the orisha and the saints.

"My little granddaughter," the frail woman said, a cotton cloth pressed to her quivering lips. "My treasure,

Umbelina. I am afraid my son and his wife have taken her away."

Peppa bit the end of her cigar and struck a match, breathing it to life. "Away?"

"To *Yuma*," the poor woman wailed. Her chest heaved with pent-up sobs. "She is . . . only two years of age. Such a . . . a dangerous journey . . . for a small child. I must . . . absolutely must know if my Umbelina is safe."

"We will inquire," Peppa said, puffing on the cigar. "Your son and his family, do they live with you?"

The woman nodded, sniffing into her hankie. It was a rag really, but in Cuba one made do with what one had. "My Alejandro once flew MiG fighter jets, but the government sent him to be an engineer. One would think that would bring him home more often, but he only travels more. Overseas, then to other parts of the country. I have seen him only once since he left for Santiago de Cuba some weeks ago. And then his clothing reeked of chicken manure." She leaned forward, eyes wide. "Perhaps such a noxious smell is a bad omen?"

"I do not know," Peppa said. "Omens do sometimes manifest themselves as odors."

"Oh, *dios mio*," the older woman sobbed. Though Castro had decreed Cuba an atheist country, it was not uncommon for people to reverently invoke the name of God when grieving or frightened. "I do not think they would leave this old woman unless the journey was much too strenuous." She looked up, giving an explanatory nod. "I have a bad bladder, you see. I could never sit in a raft for so many hours." She began to cry again. "But if such a journey is strenuous for me, imagine how bad it would be for my poor little Umbelina . . ."

Peppa blew smoke rings toward the women. Maria looked on in rapt attention, still yet to close her mouth. Feet dangling on stubby legs, Celeste held on to her chair with both hands on either side of her thighs, looking as if she might roll away.

"How long has Alejandro been in Santiago?" Peppa asked.

"Some weeks now," the grieving woman said. "He is working on something he cannot talk about."

"Perhaps he has moved his family there so they are nearer to him."

"Oh, if that were only the case," señora Placensia said. "Some very serious men from the army came looking for him yesterday. They said he and his wife have gone missing. Defected." She hung her head. "No . . . he has gone away."

Peppa used the machete to kill the young chicken, directing the arterial spray of blood into a bowl, which she then placed on the altar to feed Oyá, imploring the goddess to communicate through the cowries. Peppa read the shells twice.

"I do not know what has become of Alejandro," she lied. "I am told nothing about him." Señora Placensia swelled up as if to protest, but Peppa raised a hand, flicking her fingers, clawlike, to hush the woman. It worked like a spell. Placensia wrung the piece of cloth in her hands, preparing herself to hear the worst. Maria swallowed hard, finally shutting her mouth. Celeste continued to grip the sides of her chair, clearly terrified.

"Umbelina is in good health," Peppa said. "And she misses her grandmother." Surely the last was not a lie. Señora Placensia seemed as if she would be a pleasant enough woman were it not for her grief—and what little girl would not miss her grandmother?

It was not good to rush the orisha. Oyá might have had much more to say, but Peppa clenched the half-smoked cigar between her teeth and shooed the women out the front door. She had to talk to Veronica—and the conversation could not be held over the phone.

Chapter 16

General Zayda de la Guardia strode down the pier with murderous purpose. Yellow soot from the nearby cement plant stained the weathered wood. Gray clouds hung low and brooding over a choppy black sea. Palm fronds chattered in a humid wind. There were few vessels moored in this portion of the Marlin Marina in Santiago de Cuba, the vacancies due to a fortunately timed government construction project brought about by de la Guardia's good friend in the Cuban coastguard. De la Guardia should have been going over the many things he needed to do, but it was impossible to think of anything but the traitor's sudden defection. Thick smoke, as black as the general's rage, belched from the Antonio Maceo power plant across the bay, throwing a greasy haze over the city of half a million. De la Guardia's father had told him stories of his time with Comrade Fidel in the Sierra Maestra mountains. Zayda's father had been an *escopetero*—a skirmishing scout who launched campaigns against Batista loyalists and reported back to the rebels' mountain headquarters.

Adventurous times, those. Zayda would never be his father, but he could live up to the *el credo de escopetero* to win at all costs, to fight until victory. Not as romantic as guerilla war in the Sierra Maestra mountains, his fight was in the details of rivets and welds and new electronic guidance systems. Today, he was at the pier to check the launching mechanism that would fire the FKR-1 from on board a Dominican fishing vessel. A set of steel I-beams on an electric lift that could be raised and lowered at an angle, the launcher looked relatively straightforward.

It was anything but. The traitor Placensia had been an integral component in marrying the rocket's newer, stronger propulsion with the launching system on the boat, essentially making certain that the weapon did not blow up in their faces at the time of launch. Now they would have to do without him.

The Dominican boat that was the objective of his visit lay at the far end of the docks, moored between two much larger military patrol vessels that blocked it from casual view. De la Guardia used his time during the walk to get a report from Colonel Mirabal via his secure mobile phone. In truth, the general found Mirabal off-putting. Such profound lack of pretense was, after all, a sort of pretense in and of itself. No one could be that calm, that self-aware, that precise under fire. De la Guardia had killed more than a few men, but his heart fluttered in his chest like a wounded chicken's wing each and every time. Surely Mirabal had similar feelings. He must.

Mirabal answered on the second ring, the same way he always did: calmly, with a single word. It was maddening.

"Yes?"

"I read your report," de la Guardia said.

Mirabal was silent.

"I wish to check on the child," the general continued,

panting now as he walked. The journey from the vehicle was a relatively long one on legs more accustomed to sitting behind a desk.

"The child, General?" Mirabal asked. "I am not sure I understand."

"The child," de la Guardia said again. He hated having to explain himself. "You assured me the traitor and his wife have been . . . seen to."

"As indeed they have," Mirabal assured him.

"The same with the child, then?"

"Of course not," Mirabal said, his voice even, absent even the slightest spike in emotion.

"Of course not," de la Guardia repeated. He would not allow this hired assassin to claim the higher ground. He quickly changed the subject. "Was the traitor searched for documents?"

"He was, General," Mirabal said. The man had no idea of de la Guardia's conspiracy and probably assumed Placensia had stolen something that might embarrass Cuba.

"You searched the man and his wife personally."

"I did not," Mirabal said.

"Ah," de la Guardia said. "Do you trust your men with such an important task?"

"I do," Mirabal said simply. "If it were otherwise, they would not be my men."

The matte gray hull of the thirty-meter Guarda Frontera patrol vessel loomed closer now. Mercifully, the project boat was just a few steps beyond. De la Guardia swallowed, wishing for some water. "What do you make of this word you saw on the American's mobile phone?"

"Jericho?"

"Jericho," the general said. "A code word, perhaps?"

"Perhaps," Mirabal said. "But this American smelled like an amateur. Not a person who would use code words."

De la Guardia scoffed. Mirabal often spoke of a person's smell, as if it could be used as a litmus test for their character. "A name, then?"

"That is more likely," Mirabal said. "A name in the man's address book. My contact at AT&T Miami tells me the number associated with this Jericho is registered to a car dealership in the state of Virginia, but there appears to be no such dealership."

"A fictitious government cover," de la Guardia mused. The Intelligence Directorate often used such false identities in other countries. "You are absolutely positive Placensia gave nothing to the American?"

"It is possible," Mirabal said, his tone a verbal shrug. "But his clothes were dripping seawater when we arrived. It appeared that he was still seeing to the safety of his family."

De la Guardia wanted to make a joke. Placensia was a traitor, lacking honor. He deserved no respect, even in death. Mirabal did not go in for such jokes, so he kept the thoughts to himself.

"Be watchful," he said instead. "American spies are everywhere." He was growing exhausted, both of walking and of this conversation. "Take a break. Hunt some birds or utia. You are not happy unless you are chasing something."

"Indeed," Mirabal said.

De la Guardia reached the end of the pier. "I will have another trip for you soon, so do not go far." Mirabal would understand that "a trip" meant an assignment. Someone to kill.

"A trip off-island?" Mirabal asked, sounding a little like he was stifling a yawn, the heartless bastard.

De la Guardia dipped his head toward a North Korean working on the launcher as he came up alongside the fishing boat. "No," he said into the phone. "Quite near."

The missile would have to come out of the ground and be transported here. That could be done by workers who had no idea what they were dealing with. The majority of people involved need know only that they were handling a heavy wooden crate. A conventional weapon. But there was no way to keep his plans hidden from the men who helped with the launcher. In order for the machinery to work, they had to know exactly what they were doing. There would be several loose ends to clean up before this was over.

De la Guardia would have to be cautious. Burning loose ends often caused the entire rope to catch fire.

Chapter 17

Quinn stared wide-eyed at Paunchy and Cauliflower Ear as if their presence on the bus alarmed him. He jumped off just before they pulled away from the curb, as someone would when he'd seen the men who'd just tried to pick his pocket. The two CDR guys were trapped, hemmed in behind the rest of the passengers. With no reason to pretend they were unaware of the tail, Quinn and Garcia ducked around the corner, hailing a cab out of sight of the bus.

Quinn had the cab drop them a full ten blocks from Peppa's house, on the off chance Paunchy or Cauliflower Ear had seen the license plate. Their taxi appeared to be individually owned, without a dispatcher, but it would be easy enough to question the driver about where he'd dropped the pretty Latina and her scruffy American boyfriend.

Surveillance detection runs worked relatively well to find out if you'd grown a tail, but they were never intended to shake one. There were a lot of beautiful women on the planet, Junoesque women with plenty of curves. Garcia had something else. A brilliance. A chemistry. A magnetism that made most men and many women want to be around her. It also made it fairly easy to follow her in a crowd.

Quinn could dampen his intensity with wide eyes and a crooked smile, but Garcia couldn't conceal her sex appeal if she was dressed in a burlap sack. Some things were impossible to hide. So she didn't try, instead using it to their advantage.

They met Peppa five blocks from her house, stopping to chat at a small grocery that sold sandwiches made from freshly shaved, translucent slices of roast pork. It was well after lunch, and Quinn was happy to find that the meat was fully cooked. The two women chatted in Spanish while Quinn bought two of the sandwiches for himself. They were small, and he'd used up a great deal of energy in the alley fight—not to mention negotiating the emotional minefield of Ronnie and Odesa's first meeting.

The sandwiches were fine, as far as sandwiches with paper-thin meat went, tasting more of pickle and bread than pork. It was peasant food in a country where many went hungry, so Quinn didn't complain, even to himself. He walked around the shop while Ronnie and Peppa talked, gawking like an interested tourist. The effects of the U.S. embargo on the island were obvious. A half dozen cans of lonely-looking mackerel had an entire shelf to themselves. There were flavored ramen noodles from China and some Russian sweets here and there, along with a few bags of pork rinds. Competition was virtually nonexistent, and most items were represented by a single brand.

Quinn spent the equivalent of twenty cents on a glass of sugarcane juice to wash down his sandwiches. As long as he kept his mouth shut, shopkeepers didn't realize he was a foreigner and didn't charge him *turista* prices.

Peppa relayed her information quickly, interspersed with the quiet laughter of longtime friends who'd happened on one another at the bodega. Even so, Quinn was able to look at everything in the store twice before the meeting was over. He gave the last of his sandwich and half of the cane juice to Garcia.

Peppa disappeared up the street toward her house, while Quinn and Garcia went north, back toward the Malecón to find a taxi.

"Santiago de Cuba," Garcia said. "You know where that is?"

Quinn nodded. "South."

"Yep," Garcia said. "Jacques says Cuba looks like a big vacuum cleaner. Santiago is right on the sucky part."

"Not far from Guantanamo Bay."

"Yep," Garcia said again. "I don't like this sound of this."

Quinn rubbed a hand across dark whiskers. "Me neither. An aeronautical engineer with information vital to the United States, working on some secret project fifty miles from an American naval base . . . We'll need to get this to Palmer. It may be a piece of a bigger puzzle that he already knows about."

Garcia shot him a look as they walked, nodding. "I'll write it up on the way." She put two fingers in her mouth and whistled at a passing Plymouth Valiant taxi. The driver, a twentysomething kid in a snazzy white Panama hat, was already slowing down to look at her anyway. Garcia's figure might not help her blend in, but it didn't hurt when it came time to get a cab.

Quinn opened the door and let her slide in first. The driver said hello, offering in Ricky Ricardo English to show them the "*muy* wonderful sights of Havana." To his chagrin, Garcia ignored him, completely engrossed in thumb-typing a message on her cell phone.

Quinn gave the young driver a sad shrug, as if he wouldn't mind a little tour, but the señora was having none of it.

"Hotel Sevilla," he said.

"That is a very nice hotel," the driver said, stepping on the gas and eliciting a belch of black smoke from the Plymouth's little slant-six engine.

Quinn had the kid in the Panama hat drop them off two blocks down Trocadero from the hotel, hoping to get an eye on Paunchy or Cauliflower Ear before they saw him. Neither was visible, but that didn't mean anything. They might be watching from an unseen window, or could have passed the job to other CDR operatives. Quinn only hoped anyone new was as clumsy as the first pair. They'd probably originally followed him because he was an interesting American. The events in the alley might have raised the level of scrutiny.

Garcia had finished typing out her message in the cab. She walked beside Quinn, her left hand clasping his right—loosely, in case he needed it—while the fingers of her right trailed along the brick and stone and stucco of every building they passed. It was as if she wanted to touch everything, to feel the essence of Cuba. In truth, she wanted anyone who happened to be watching to be used to her dragging her hands. It made it much easier to place the tiny NFC—near-field communication—sticker on the mosaic tile floor in front of the lion statue on the right side of the lobby steps.

A quick Internet search had allowed them to choose

a likely spot for the drop before they left Miami. The roaring lion was in plain view, making it less suspect to foreign intelligence watchers than some shadowed hallway or remote bench on the seawall. They would all pass directly beside it, every time they came and went from the hotel, making it much easier to "load the drop." The best magic tricks happened right under everybody's noses.

Generally used to tag merchandise or control building access, the hair-thin coil of copper in the square inch of NFC paper could hold eight kilobytes of data. A small device attached to their smartphones that looked like a credit card reader allowed them to encode the stickers.

Each couple would send the data to Palmer via an encrypted email, but the handoff ensured that any information was not compartmentalized, and therefore lost, should something happen to either party.

Palmer already knew from the CIA Chief of Station in Chile that Placensia was an aeronautical engineer. Garcia kept her message clear and concise.

Delta working on unknown project somewhere near
Santiago de Cuba. Nothing follows. rD

The lowercase initial for Ronnie followed by the uppercase initial for Dombrovski would let Palmer know all four of them were safe. A supremely stoic man, Palmer rarely showed his concern, but Garcia knew he worried constantly.

Quinn saw Thibodaux and Miyagi seated off the lobby in the poolside café, facing the door. Quinn scratched the back of his head with the knuckles of a closed fist, alerting the big Marine that there was a message in place.

Garcia snuggled in next to him, burying her forehead against the hollow of his shoulder.

"I'm tired," she said. "Wanna lie down for a little while before dinner?"

Quinn raised a wary eyebrow and whispered, "Don't forget the cameras."

Garcia batted long lashes and gave a sultry shake of her hair. "Just lie back and think of England, Mr. Bond."

Chapter 18

The grilled marlin at Buffet la Giralda on the first floor of Hotel Sevilla was good, but a little heavy on black beans and white rice for Thibodaux's taste. He was Cajun to the core, and as such, he liked his beans red and his rice dirty.

Miyagi and Thibodaux saw Quinn's signal at the same time. Now they would wait to see if anyone peeled off from following Quinn and Garcia to watch the drop point.

Miyagi was an interesting enough woman, if she would ever talk. Thibodaux had thought they were making some real headway during the walk on the Malecón seawall, but she'd clammed up as soon as they got back to the hotel, as if she'd thought better about revealing any semblance of a human side. Dinner had been a real killer, with more noise from her fork clinking against the plate than there was coming out of her lips. Now, operational necessity said they had to kill more time, sitting across from each other in silence—an excruciating prospect for someone as talkative as Master Sergeant Thibodaux.

She gave him a sleepy-eyed wink and dabbed a cloth napkin to her lips. Their regular conversations centered on the strategic and tactical, both defensive and offensive. She was particularly hard on Jacques during their training sessions, picking apart his every mistake while heaping compliments on Quinn for his near superhuman intuition when it came to battle. Chair Force was smaller and, though the Marine would never admit it out loud, the better fighter—but he was also teacher's pet.

"Jacques-san," Miyagi said. It was the pip of a tiny bird, missing her usual sharp edge. Thibodaux had to force himself not to open his good eye in dismay at the stark difference in this strange woman.

"What is it, *cher*?"

"I can see in your face that you are perplexed."

Thibodaux's brow shot up, Spock-like, trying to keep from giving away any emotion that would make him look weak. She was almost showing a soft side. "I'm fine."

"Okay," she said. "I suppose couples often experience moments of tension between themselves."

"True dat," Jacques said. "Now that we're talking, I gotta ask—you said you don't like me much because I remind you of someone? Did this someone hurt you?"

Miyagi gave a matter-of-fact shake of her head. "On the contrary." The corners of her smallish mouth perked into a sly smile. "You and Quinn are so much like brothers. It surprises me that he has not told you of Kenichi Miyagi, my boyfriend from long ago."

"Well, old boyfriends ain't something he's likely to mention," Thibodaux said. "Fact is, I do most of the heavy lifting when it comes to conversation. I believe he prefers it that way." He rubbed his chin, genuinely interested. "So I remind you of Kenichi?"

"Just so," Miyagi said, eyes sparkling. "He was a

muscular young man, quite cocky. Afraid of nothing. Murdered by the man you saw me kill when we were last in Japan."

Thibodaux had seen her kill several men in Japan, but he kept that thought to himself.

Miyagi appeared to read his mind and clarified. "The father of my daughter."

"Let me get this straight." Thibodaux's face screwed into a pouting frown. "I remind you of a muscular and overconfident boyfriend?"

"Yes," Miyagi said. "In any number of ways, some good, some not so good. Perhaps you will now see why I have chosen to keep you at a distance."

"Are you pullin' my leg?" Thibodaux said. "Is this . . ." He leaned in across the table. "You know. Part of your cover?"

"No," Miyagi said. "This is simply the uncomfortable truth."

Thibodaux waved the waiter over for the check and charged it to the room. He helped Emiko with her chair, and they walked together into the lobby, toward the statue of the roaring lion and the dead drop. Arm in arm with the enigmatic woman, the big Marine breathed in a great lungful of air. This was one revelation he wouldn't tell anyone, not even Chair Force.

Miyagi took out her phone and pointed to the statue where Garcia had left the NFC tag.

"Jacques," she said. "I want to get a picture." She dragged him over to stand on the landing of blue and white tiles, shoulder level to the statue, then handed him the phone. "Your arms are longer," she said. "You take a selfie of both of us."

Hearing the normally stoic Emiko Miyagi, emotionless assassin, martial arts master of untold disciplines, say a word like "selfie" made Thibodaux feel like the world had suddenly started turning the other direction.

Thibodaux raised the phone up to take a photo, but Miyagi pushed his arm down. She gave a disgusted motherly cluck and hooked a finger in the V of his collar, pulling his head down to her level. Wetting her thumb with her tongue, she rubbed a bit of imaginary grilled marlin off the corner of his lips. Jacques had always hated spit baths as a child, but this one was supremely intimate and gave him the wrong kind of chills. Forcing himself to focus, he nonchalantly let the hand that held the phone rest on the polished wood flooring at the base of the statue, allowing it to read the message on the NFC sticker. Now it would be a matter of sending it via ultrafast, encrypted communication to Palmer.

He extended the camera again and took a quick selfie. Miyagi's smile was particularly impish. She was having way too much fun torturing him.

He put an arm around her smallish shoulders as they walked away, feeling the ripple of cable-like muscles. Drawing her close, he leaned down as if to whisper something sweet in her ear.

"I don't mind tellin' you," he said. "That was just plain weird."

Chapter 19

No matter what else happened, Angel Diaz didn't want to get hit in the mouth again. Walking through the lobby of the Hotel Sevilla, he limped past a giant man with short hair arguing with a small Asian woman. He turned when he reached the top of the steps, watching the couple for a short moment, mostly to check out the Asian woman's ass. The big guy shot him a jealous stare, the way a man should when he had a woman who was worth bothering with. Such a challenging look would not normally have bothered Angel, but the earlier fight with the American had shaken him. He didn't remember getting hit in the mouth, but he must have, because he had two loose teeth. The attack to his ribs he remembered—every time he took a breath.

Ignacio hadn't paid attention to the American's entire conversation, but he thought he'd heard "Trocadero." That left a finite number of hotels and homestays to check. This was a nice place—at least by Cuban standards. Compared to the shithole Angel lived in with his sister and her three brats, it was a palace. It seemed like the kind of place the American would bring his *chica* girlfriend.

In truth, Angel had been overjoyed when the Americans had given them the slip on the bus. It gave him time to change into a different shirt, this one a foamy green guayabera. It wasn't clean—his lazy sister hadn't done the wash in days—but at least it didn't have any bloodstains on it. Along with a scowl that could clot cream, Sammy Meduro wore the same nasty T-shirt he'd had on during the fight. He said all the bloodstains made him look tougher. Angel Diaz though they made it look like a bird just shit on his shoulder. Still, even gimping along on an injured knee, Meduro was an incredibly strong man, so Angel kept this opinion to himself.

There were two people behind the gleaming tile reception desk, a heavyset man who was less able to look down and see his toes than Angel Diaz and a blond *chica* who was cute, but also a little on the heavy side. The big guy's name tag said he was Franco, the night manager. The *chica* was young, maybe nineteen, and had one of those wide-eyed smiles that made her look eager to please. Naturally, Angel approached her.

She wore a white, short-sleeved shirt, the buttons of which were stretched tight across a chest that had probably gotten her this job, if the leering night manager had had anything to do with hiring. Her plastic name tag said her name was Esmerelda.

"Good evening," she said in Spanish. "How may I help you?" Her smiled flickered but did not quite fade when she saw the blood on Meduro's T-shirt. Maybe the dumb shit was right. Maybe it was good to have a little something extra that made people have second thoughts about not cooperating. People who worked for the CDR didn't carry badges. They rarely asked questions, relying on snooping and a keen ear trained toward the

Radio Bemba to keep them informed of any behavior that appeared to go against the revolutionary cause.

Meduro saw the look and turned up the volume on his silent menace, standing mutely beside Angel.

"We're looking for an American," Diaz said. "Need to get him a message."

"We have several Americans here," Esmerelda said. "If the man you are looking for is among them, I would be more than happy to deliver the message."

"That's good . . ." Angel let his eyes fall to her name tag, then linger there just long enough to make her uncomfortable. "Esmerelda. May I call you Elda?"

She nodded.

Angel leaned both forearms on the counter, taking some pressure off his aching ribs, hiding the pain with a sneer. "This guy we're looking for, Elda, he's a little taller than me. Skinny. Dark skin, black beard . . . like an Arab. Moves like a policeman or a soldier."

"As I have told you," Esmerelda said. "We have many Americans staying here as guests. You will need to be more specific."

The fat night manager sidled up next to his blond protégé, nudging her sideways with a hairy arm. "Do not be so difficult," he snapped, before looking up with a tight but accommodating "we want no trouble" smile. "Would the man you are looking for be in the company of an attractive Latina?"

Meduro nodded.

Angel said, "He would indeed."

The manager slid two pieces of computer paper across the counter, copies of the passport photo pages for James Shield and Veronica Gomez.

Angel gave a smug nod. "That is the one."

Meduro stepped past the planter at the end of the reception desk, moving behind one of the large white columns. He drew the mobile phone from his pocket like a gun.

"Happy to be of service," the fat night manager said.

The blonde glared sideways at her boss, gritting her teeth as if to keep from saying something she'd regret. There was obviously some history between the two. Angel wished he had the time to learn more. That was really the only good thing about working with CDR—getting to know all the nasty little secrets about people.

The *chica* took a deep breath, moving her name tag up and down enough to momentarily take Angel's mind off the mission.

"The message, señor," she said, bringing him back on task. She stood ready to write, pencil poised above a sheet of blank paper.

Angel gave a shrug that hurt his ribs. "More of a delivery."

He took a heavy, eight-by-ten envelope from his back pocket and set it on the counter. It was damp and folded in half lengthwise. Smoothing it out with the flat of his palm, he snapped his fingers for the pencil in Esmeralda's hand.

She handed it over as if it were about to bite her.

Across the front, Angel wrote: *James Shield/Urgent* before sliding the pencil and the sealed envelope across the counter.

"I will see that it is delivered," Esmerelda said.

"Excellent." Angel shot a glance at Meduro, who'd

stepped back up beside him. The boxer held up five fingers.

Esmerelda said, "Is there anything else I might assist you with, señor . . . ?"

"Oh, Elda, Elda, Elda," Angel said. "I know *your* name. You don't need to know mine. When I say so, I will need you to call James Shield and let him know he has a package."

Esmerelda pushed a lock of blond hair out of her eye and turned toward the office door behind the counter.

"No," Meduro grunted, stopping the girl in her tracks. The suddenness of it made even Angel jump. "You stay out here with us, *chica*," the boxer said.

Five minutes turned into ten, and even the fat night manager—who had made a career of standing around doing nothing—began to get bored. He had smelled the Committee for the Defense of the Revolution rats as soon as they squeaked in off Trocadero. Though not an informer himself, Franco Gutierrez had gladly pocketed more than a few CUC from both CDR and the Intelligence Directorate. Local police had no money to pay him, so they simply got what they wanted with threats of getting him fired from his easy job.

For a moment, Gutierrez considered telling the two men across the counter about the cameras in Señor Shield's room. The Dirección de Inteligencia had installed cameras all around Havana. Franco knew of others in at least two hotels where he'd worked before. No frowning DI operative had told him about the monitor room behind the false wall in this office, but his experience at the other hotels had taught him where to look. Esmerelda was much too committed to her boyfriend to make the night shift anything close to interesting, so Franco had spent his time behind the closed office door, wiggling molding and rapping on the hollow wall until he'd found the way in. It was extremely simple—a nail that, when pulled, extended to become a handle, allowing a counterweighted door to slide open. Five split-screen color monitors were recessed into a cabinet above a single chair. A flat DVD recorder sat on the desk at the base of the monitors beside a very official-looking red telephone. All the instructions were written in Cyrillic, but Franco was enough of a natural voyeur to suss out the operational procedures. It hadn't taken him long to figure out which five rooms had cameras. He assumed there was audio, too, but he had no idea how to turn that on. When anyone checked in who struck his fancy—like the tight little Filipina woman in 303, the scarily handsome Japanese woman in 802, or Jim Shield's busty Latina girlfriend, they went in one of those five rooms. Night shift became a little less boring—though he lived in mortal fear that someday, the official-looking red phone might ring and put an end to his little game.

Until then, he wasn't sharing his secret room with anyone, especially not these two idiots.

The guy with the bad ear's mobile phone suddenly rang. He answered it, then nodded. "*Listo*," he said to his partner. *Ready*.

The slimy one leaned across the counter again. "Okay, *chica*," he said. "Call Jim Shield and tell him to come down and get his package." He snapped his fingers at the fat night manager. "I need the key to your elevators."

Franco searched around behind the desk until he found a ring with a dozen keys. He didn't care if these guys ate Jim Shield for dinner. Whatever he could do to get them to leave. He found the one for the elevator and held it up, letting the rest of the ring dangle.

"The car on the left does not work," he said.

The big one snatched the ring away and shook it. "Good."

Ronnie Garcia's toenails were painted a deep red according to Jericho's opinion that polish should always be the color that would look good on a sports car. She lay back on the bed in a black silk chemise, one leg draped over the other, curling and then uncurling her toes as if clenching a fist, bleeding off energy the way a cat flicked only the tip of its tail when getting ready to pounce. A tiny dress, small enough to make Quinn's throat convulse and blacker than the chemise (if such a thing were possible), lay spread like a mysterious, Ronnie-shaped void against the white sheet.

Jericho stood in front of a half-length mirror on a mahogany desk. Like the rest of the room, the furniture had once been grand but was long past its use-by date, shabby and worn at the edges. The desk smelled strongly of fake-lemon wood polish. The mirror, missing a good deal of its glazing, showed several smoky patches of chipped paint on the wall behind it instead of an unbroken reflection. The overhead light didn't work at all, and one of two bulbs in the standing lamp was burned out, leaving the room in shadows. Quinn assumed there would be several infrared light sources at strategic points around the room in order to get good video when the lights were out, but he hadn't risked tipping his hand by overtly looking for them.

He took a half step sideways, taking advantage of the single bulb to adjust one of the gunmetal cuff links in the cloudy mirror while he kept Garcia's pretty toes in full view over his shoulder. His mother had given him the cuff links when he got his early acceptance letter to the United States Air Force Academy the winter of his senior year of high school. Simple brushed metal with no jewels, monograms, or design, they were his favorite pair—which wasn't saying much, because he only owned one other. Cuff links were customarily worn with ties, and Quinn hated ties with the heat of a thousand suns. He'd opted for tropical dinner dress, which, by his personal definition, meant polished Rockport loafers, khaki linen slacks, an open-collar shirt with cuff links, and a navy blazer of lightweight wool.

The rooftop Torre del Oro restaurant in the shadow of the dome of *el capitolo*—the former Cuban national capitol building—didn't require formal attire, but acting like a couple who was rich enough to fly to Cuba for a hurricane party meant dressing for dinner.

Still, Quinn felt naked without his usual everyday carry. No Kimber 10mm. No stubby Riot fixed blade, or even a more vicious Gentle Hand—the Japanese killing dagger. Nothing more than a small folding Böker that his kid brother, Bo, called a granddad knife. It was good for little but whittling willow flutes and opening letters, but it was a blade, and Quinn could not bear to be completely without. He rounded out his meager EDC with a tiny Streamlight flashlight and a disposable butane cigarette lighter he'd bought as soon as they'd gotten off the plane. Blade, light, fire. Tools, not weapons, but it was the best he could do.

The fact that management had put them in a room

with cameras didn't put Quinn any more on guard than usual. He was relatively certain that no one from Cuban intelligence was aware of his true identity. Had he just been another American traveler out on a holiday with his wife or girlfriend, the authorities might have reviewed the tape at a later time—or, at the most, pulled up the feed once or twice during their stay. Ronnie's presence, though, made the odds of an active surveillance rise exponentially. Quinn was a pipe hitter, not a scientist, but he considered it a mathematical certainty that several sweating men were now packed into some closet, crowded around a series of monitors. He pictured a low man on the totem pole left to sit and watch the empty room for hours, directed in no uncertain terms to call his seniors the moment the curvy Latina returned. Especially now that her toes were exposed on the end of long, muscular legs.

The phone beside the bed trilled like something out of an old movie about spies in Cold War Europe.

Both Quinn and Garcia turned to look at it for a moment, surprised by the noise. On this sort of job, an unexpected call rarely brought good news. The phone trilled a second time. Garcia, who was closer, groaned as if getting ready to roll over and reach for it. Her long hair lay across the pillow, and Quinn wanted to keep it that way as long as possible. He motioned her to stay put, striding in a pair of white terrycloth hotel slippers across the threadbare carpet.

"Hello?" he said.

"Señor JimShield." The female voice said it without pause, as if the name were all one word. "You have an envelope at the front desk." She sounded bothered, a little pissed that she was having to speak English.

"Okay," Quinn said. He waited a beat for her to offer to have it delivered. When she didn't, he said, "I'll be down to pick it up. Can you tell me who delivered it?"

"I sorry, sir," she said, a little too quickly. "I do not have that information . . . right in front of me."

Quinn hung up the phone and looked at Garcia. In truth, he'd never taken his eyes off her.

"What was that about?" she asked.

"An envelope for Jim Shield at the front desk."

Garcia sat up at the news. She mouthed the word, "Peppa?" taking care to face away from the cameras.

Quinn took her hands and pulled her to her feet as if to kiss her before going downstairs. "Maybe," he whispered. "Could be from Odesa." He felt Ronnie tense at the mere mention of her half sister's name. "I need to hurry. Sounds weird, but from the tone of her voice, I think the lady on the phone was trying to tell me that the person leaving the envelope was standing 'right in front of her.'"

He pecked Ronnie on the end of her nose and slipped into the Rockports.

"Be right back," he said.

"Who loves you, mango?"

"*Vous* do," he said, giving her a final wink before doing a habitual quick peek into the hallway, then padding quickly toward the stairs.

Chapter 20

The snap of Quinn's jogging footsteps echoed off the concrete walls of the stairwell. He slowed at each landing, peeking over the painted metal rail before continuing down. An elderly British couple met him coming out of the heavy fire door at the third floor. The man, who wore a dive T-shirt from the Bahamas, jumped back a half step when he saw Quinn. His wife, a thin woman with short, steel-gray hair, rolled her eyes.

"The lift appears to be broken," she said. She realized Quinn was going faster and gestured for him to go ahead.

He felt none of the familiar tingling in his gut. The Japanese called it *haragei*—art of the belly. The man had an elastic bandage around his knee. His leathery, tanned bicep wept dots of blood from a newly applied tattoo—a stylized shark. Not averse to tattoos, Quinn couldn't think of too many places in the Western Hemisphere he'd be less likely to let someone stick him repeatedly with a needle than Cuba.

He gave the couple a smiling nod and continued down the last three floors, rounding the corner in the lobby toward the registration desk. He'd thought he might see Thibodaux and Miyagi, but they were probably down on the seawall, shooting flash traffic on the covert communications phone that the Navy would relay back to Palmer. A few guests milled in the lobby, looking at the architecture or flopping down in chairs after long walks along the Malecón. There was no one at the desk other than the female clerk. Esmerelda, her name tag said. Quinn remembered her from the evening before. She was thumbing absentmindedly through a glossy magazine that featured Cuba as a wedding destination.

Quinn reached into the front pocket of his slacks to get his passport.

The woman shrank back a hair, as if trying to distance herself from Quinn and the manila envelope on the counter.

"Mr. JimShield," she said, before he had a chance to show his passport or even speak.

That in and of itself was not out of the ordinary. Many hotels prided themselves on memorizing guests' names. The Hotel Sevilla was not even remotely full. But this was something else. Esmerelda had been all smiles and bubbles earlier in the evening. Now, her expression was flat, humorless.

He held up his passport.

"That will not be necessary," she said. "We know who you are."

Quinn nodded, waiting, but she just stood there, looking at him.

"You said you had an envelope?" he finally prodded.

"Ah, yes." She handed him an eight-by-ten yellow envelope with his name scrawled across the front. It was fairly thick. Quinn guessed there were perhaps two dozen pages inside. Fingers white with tension, she grasped the envelope for a moment too long, before letting him pull it away. "I am *so* sorry." Still no emotion.

Quinn wondered if she was sorry for forgetting about the envelope or if it was something entirely different.

He fished a five-CUC note from his pocket and slid it across the counter. He started to go, but then turned back, nodding at Esmerelda's travel magazine. "My girlfriend," he said. "She would be interested in seeing that. May I buy it from you when you finish with it?"

Esmerelda pushed it to him. "Please," she said. "I am finished. Perhaps you can get some use from it."

Quinn gave her a polite nod and took the magazine, heading for the stairs. The elevators were in-op for the time being, but he wouldn't have used them even if they'd been working. Standing in a steel box with only one door when you had no idea who was waiting on the next floor was a good way to catch an inordinate amount of lead in the belly. Stairwells offered their own variety of danger, but Quinn vastly preferred them, especially when he was armed—which he now was, having rolled the thick travel magazine into a tight tube.

He made it as far as the fourth-floor landing before he met Cauliflower Ear walking slowly down the steps from the fifth. The big thug was smiling cruelly, as if he'd just bitten the head off a tasty puppy. Another half step brought Paunchy into Quinn's view, coming down from the landing above.

"Hey, guys," Quinn said. He slowed but didn't stop moving. He didn't want the boxer to stop. He kept the rolled magazine down behind his thigh. "*No carterista.* I told you before. You can't have my wallet." He ignored Paunchy for the moment to focus on the big guy, nodding toward the demolished ear. "I can help you with some moves, if you want."

The man's smile faded and he kept coming, dragging his injured knee.

"And footwork," Quinn said. "Your footwork sucks."

Paunchy's voice reverberated from above in the concrete stairwell, rattling something off in Spanish.

Cauliflower Ear cut him off. "I speak English!" He moved faster now, trotting downward from five steps above Quinn, counting on momentum and his larger stature for the attack.

Quinn relied on the same things.

He sprang upward the moment the boxer's lead foot was within reach, hitting the oncoming freight train at a forty-five-degree angle inside the knee with the point of his shoulder, stretching tendons and snapping cartilage in the process. The man yowled, instinctively shifting his weight backward. Quinn grabbed a handful of pant inseam and spun. With no good legs left to support himself, Cauliflower Ear toppled backwards. All Quinn had to do was help him, dragging the inseam and the leg along with it, leveraging the other man's head downward to crack against the lip of the nearest stairs. The muffled groan was enough to tell Quinn he wouldn't offer any more problem.

Paunchy spun on his heels, scrambling back up the steps toward the landing and the door that would be his escape. Quinn bounded after him, reaching out to snag the cuff of the fleeing man's slacks. He hauled upward, slamming Paunchy's face against the landing and dragging him down, his head bouncing like a bowling ball in a pillowcase as he slid down the steps.

Quinn rolled him over as soon as they reached the fourth-floor landing. "Why are you after me?"

Paunchy loosed a vehement string of Spanish curses through a slurry of saliva, blood, and broken teeth.

Quinn patted both men down, hoping to find something he could use as a weapon. Nothing. Neither of them had so much as a pair of toenail clippers. Quinn resolved as he worked to go downstairs from here instead of up, leading anyone else away from Garcia. He put the toe of his Rockport in Paunchy's exposed ribs, pushing a muffled woof from the man's chest. "Who are you?"

The man gave a half-hearted groan, like the sound of air leaving a punctured tire. He spoke a single word in English.

"Bait."

The clomp of heavy boots rolled down from the fifth floor. A slamming door echoed up from the second. Quinn set his jaw. Two, maybe three coming from above. He couldn't tell how many below.

He'd fought multiple opponents many times, sometimes armed, sometimes empty-handed. At best, it was a recipe for broken ribs. At worst . . . He preferred not to think about that. He glanced at the door that exited out to the fourth floor. They'd left him only one avenue of escape—and he was absolutely certain that was the way they wanted him to go. They'd probably thought he would run from the big boxer.

Three more Cubans, street thugs from the looks of them, poured down the stairs. More boots echoed from below.

Quinn's breath was relaxed, regular, despite the earlier fight. The tight confines of the stairwell gave him a slight advantage, allowing him to stack his opponents. He shot one more look at the door. It was impossible to know how a fight here would end up, but he was sure of one thing. If he went where they expected him to, he was certain to lose.

The three men above came at him all at once, raining fists and feet, seemingly unaware that they were hitting the wall and each other as much as they connected with Quinn. Two more joined the scrum from below, swarming Quinn like angry wasps. He caught a knee to the belly and returned the favor with a vicious elbow to a different person. Something heavy hit Quinn in the calf—a stick or a pipe, he couldn't tell, but it sent a shock pain up his legs, giving him a dose of his own medicine. Nausea blossomed through his stomach and he staggered forward, slumping to his knees. The door swung open and someone barked an order in Spanish. His right eye was already swelling shut. Another knee connected, this time at the point of his hip, bringing another wave of gut-churning nausea.

Powerful hands grabbed him by both arms and hauled him to his feet.

"Señor JimShield," a booming voice said. It was the one who'd come through the door, the one in charge. "*Usted arrestado*. You are under arrest."

"*Arrestado*?" Quinn groaned. He started to say something else, but a heavy fist drove hard into his kidney. Through the haze of his rapidly swelling eyes, he saw Cauliflower Ear, standing to one side, blood dribbling from his ear. The guy could dish out a punch, even when he was wobbled.

Quinn felt a pinch in his neck. Warmth spread down his spine. His field of vision narrowed, and he found it impossible to keep his feet. They'd injected him with something. Cauliflower Ear hung on to the railing and wound up for another blow. Quinn groaned again, trying in vain to cover up as his world went dark. He fell unconscious against the stairs, but they kept hitting him all the same.

Ronnie looked at her watch for the fifth time in as many minutes. It was a ladies' TAG Heuer Aquaracer that Quinn had given her. She walked to the window to look down at the street, then sat back on the edge of the bed, bouncing on her feet, tamping back the litany of awful thoughts. How long did it take to go pick up an envelope? Was he in the lobby, bullshitting with Thibodaux? If that was the case, and he hadn't had the decency to call, she was going to punch him in the face. No, that wasn't it. Operational security dictated they maintain separation from Jacques and Emiko—and Quinn would never violate OPSEC without an awfully good reason.

She checked her watch again. Ten minutes. He should have been back by now.

Garcia ignored the hidden cameras and stripped the black chemise over her head, pulling on a T-shirt and jeans. She slipped into her sandals as she walked out the door, giving her hip pocket a pat just as the door closed to make sure she had the room key. Both elevators appeared to be out of order—not surprising—so Garcia trotted down the hall to the stairwell. It was well lit, but like many places in Cuba, it carried the sickeningly sweet odor of sewage and mildew. *Ah*, she thought, *the smell of revolution*.

Ronnie was perfectly able to handle herself in a pinch, but she was also a realist, and waltzing into a deserted stairwell went against her better judgment. She peeked inside, relieved to find the place empty, and then made her way down quickly toward the lobby.

She pulled up short on the fourth floor.

Blood—a lot of blood—was spattered across the landing and steps. Quinn had a way of leaving a trail of bloody footprints wherever he went, sometimes his, more often someone else's. Garcia shot a quick glance over her shoulder to make certain she was still alone, then stooped to examine the spatter more closely. She found a tooth with a gold cap—definitely not Jericho's. Whatever happened, Quinn had gotten the best of someone. She found a spot near the tooth where a head had hit the concrete, leaving a small puddle of blood and saliva. Some of the blood spatter had small trails, where something—or someone—had been dragged across them.

Garica's heart caught in her throat when she found a second pool of blood, this one about three or four inches in diameter. It was in the middle of the landing, surrounded by black scuff marks—from multiple pairs of boots. Halfway down the stairs to the third floor was a manila envelope and a tattered magazine. The pages were torn, and a dark boot print had landed square in the center of the smiling bride on the front cover. Garcia ripped the envelope open, hoping to find a clue. Even a ransom note would be something.

There was nothing but pieces of newspaper, ripped in uneven squares to fill out the package and make it look like something official.

Garcia flew down the stairs, hitting the door to the lobby at a dead run, slowing only when she came out of the stairwell so as not to make a scene. She went directly to the registration desk. A young woman peeked around the corner of the office from where she was having a heated conversation with the leering slob who had checked them in. She started to come out, but the fat man beat her to the counter, wearing his fake smile. His cheeks twitched when he spoke—obviously jumpy about something.

Garcia willed her heart rate to slow. The CIA offered entire courses at Camp Peary that were dedicated to the art of maintaining a relaxed demeanor.

"I'm trying to find my boyfriend," she said. "Jim Shield. Someone called him to come down to pick up a package."

The letch's thick eyebrows shot skyward. "Ah, yes, an envelope. He has already retrieved it. Did he not return to your room?"

You know good and well he didn't, you fat piece of shit, Veronica thought. *You're probably the one with your eyes glued to the cameras*. She took another deep breath and counted to five. "Sadly, no," she said. "Did you see which way he went?"

"I am sorry," the man said. "But I did not. May I help you with something else?"

"As a matter of fact, you may," Ronnie said. "Who left the envelope?"

"I can't say."

"Can't, or won't?" Ronnie said in Spanish, fuming now. She opened the envelope and spread the worthless newspaper across the counter to make her point. In the States, she would have preserved it for fingerprints, but the last thing she wanted to do was have Cuban officials running Quinn's latents.

The young woman stuck her head out of the office, catching Garcia's eye.

Ronnie started to say something about the bridal magazine, but held her tongue at the last second. Quinn had mentioned that he thought the woman was trying to tell him something over the phone. There was a chance she might have some information if Ronnie could somehow get her separated from her slob of a boss.

The man pushed the newspapers back as if they were on fire. "What is all this to me? I have no power over what is or is not inside a message someone leaves the front desk."

Ronnie took a deep breath. "Do you have any cameras?"

"Madam," the man said through clenched teeth. "I do not know what you are trying to imply, but we are not that sort of hotel."

Ronnie rolled her eyes. "I'm talking about security cameras here in the lobby," she said. "What did you think I was talking about?"

The man's cheeks flushed red. "No security cameras." He grabbed Esmerelda by the sleeve to make sure she followed him. "Come. We have work to do."

Ronnie strode back to the stairwell, hoping that she might run into Quinn as she rounded the corner. Instead, she saw more blood, a telltale smear at shoulder level on a set of heavy wooden doors. Her heart sank when she opened the doors and found that they led into an alley and loading dock. Whoever had grabbed Quinn could have taken him out of the hotel unseen, without much trouble, provided they'd been able to get him under control.

Sprinting back up the stairs, Ronnie shielded herself

from all the cameras she knew about. She grabbed a small dive knife from her luggage and shoved it in her pocket. The blade was only three inches long, but it was sharp and it made her feel better. She threw a long-sleeved nylon beach cover over her T-shirt and put on a pair of socks and some leather Rockport high-tops. They were more sensible than her sandals in case she needed to run—or kick the fat desk clerk's ass.

She scrawled a quick note for Quinn in the unlikely event that he came back, telling him to call her phone. She signed it "ronnie," using a lowercase *r* to let him know she was not in immediate danger herself but that the situation was less than ideal. Going down to the lobby again, she began to agonize over what to do next.

OPSEC was one thing, but Quinn was in trouble. She had to do something—even if it was wrong.

Chapter 21

Garcia found Emiko and Jacques eating dinner in the alfresco café near the pool, pretending to listen to a quartet of Cuban musicians. There was a vacant table beside them, plenty close enough for them to exchange pleasantries. She kept her face passive as she filled them in on what little she knew, which wasn't much.

Thibodaux set his fork down on his plate and rubbed his face. "He's likely gone off followin' somebody and will walk through the door any minute."

Garcia told them about the blood spatter.

Thibodaux attempted to shrug that off. He kept up his French accent for appearances. "I took my own walk around the neighborhood, sister. No disrespect to this wonderful country, but there's more blood and piss on the walls around here than there is fresh paint."

The Cajun put on a brave face, but it was obvious even he didn't believe his own rosy picture. He of all people knew Jericho's propensity for getting himself into hot water.

Ronnie started to say something else but stopped when she saw the woman from the front desk coming around the corner.

Esmerelda turned her back to Thibodaux and Miyagi,

shot a furtive glance over her shoulder, and then knelt beside Garcia's table.

"I should not be telling you this, señora," she said, "but your boyfriend, Mr. JimShield, I know what happened."

Garcia gritted her teeth, fearing the worst.

"He has been arrested," Esmerelda said.

"Arrested." Garcia repeated. That wasn't as bad as being kidnapped. Probably. Maybe.

"Arrested for what?" she managed to say.

"Robbery," Esmerelda said. "And for striking a policeman."

Garcia fought tears of frustration and fear. She was not usually a crier, and it really pissed her off when it happened.

"Do you know where they took him?"

"I am sorry, señora," Esmerelda said. "But no. Perhaps they will tell you at the main station." She used the edge of Ronnie's table to push herself to a standing position. "I must go before my supervisor begins to look for me."

"That jerk?" Ronnie said. "Kick him in the nuts for me when you get a chance."

Esmerelda cocked her head to one side. "The nuts?"

"*Huevos*, *cojones*," Garcia explained.

"Ahhhh," Esmerelda said, eyes brightening. "One day, I will do that very thing."

Miyagi waited for the young woman to get out of earshot.

"If the authorities suspected us of doing anything wrong, we would all be in jail."

"Yeah." Garcia agreed, but it didn't make her feel any better. Quinn was still behind bars under false pretenses, in a country whose regime would throw him in a very dark hole if they had even the slightest inkling of who he really was—if they didn't simply have him shot.

Chapter 22

Violeta Cruz awoke to waves slamming against the bottom of a speedboat. She didn't know how long she'd been out but, judging from her sore neck, suspected it was a while. The boat slowed, the motor burbling and ride smoothing as they moved into protected waters. She pretended to be asleep as one of the men threw her over his shoulder and carried her up a ramp to toss her in the back of an old van. It was only then that she realized someone had dressed her in sweats and a T-shirt while she was unconscious, a thought that made her feel like throwing up.

She'd heard it said once that highly intelligent people lost their minds more quickly than others. She didn't know if it was true, but she did know she was smart—and that she was about to go crazy by the time the thugs dumped her in the corner of a basement in what she guessed was a government building. She kept her eyes glued shut, but Slick leaned down close, his breath uncomfortably moist on her ear.

"I know you are faking," he said. Then he left with the other thugs.

They left her there all day, hands cuffed behind her back, sitting on a mildewed mattress in the corner of a dark room. The only light came from a high window, much too small for her to get out of, and anyway, from the shadow on the floor, it looked to be barred. After a few hours of crying, tears and snot gave way to intense anger that made her jaws ache. She began to beat her head against the wall, screaming now—demanding a restroom break. Slick came in and shuffled her down a dim, tiled hall to a room with a single stained toilet. He laughed in her face when she'd asked him to remove the handcuffs, then shoved her to the door, telling her she had two minutes.

Slick took her to the toilet every two hours, she estimated. She made three trips before the general showed up.

Violeta didn't meet too many men who were shorter than her, but she had the beady-eyed general by a good inch, maybe more. He sat rigidly upright, as if he wanted to milk every last centimeter out of his height. He wore civilian clothes—an open-collar, charcoal dress shirt and a pair of blue slacks—but everyone referred to him as Comrade General. *Comrade General*? How bizarre was that? She vaguely remembered such talk from her childhood, but it seemed weird now, like something from a spy movie. He'd introduced himself as General de la Guardia, but she thought of him as the Penguin from *Batman*, no matter what his name was.

He talked her head off during the drive—asking her about her thoughts on Cuba and the United States, as if to gauge her loyalty. There was never any chance to respond before he launched into more questions or another long, philosophical monologue.

Slick was driving the old Russian Lada. One of his musclemen sat in the front passenger seat, while Violeta found herself sandwiched in the back next to the little general. The other muscle followed in a beater jeep.

The springs on the Lada protested as Slick turned off one bad road onto a worse one. The transmission chattered as he downshifted, lugging the engine. As an engineer, Violeta tended to think of the individual parts of a machine rather the machine itself. "That engine has a nice car," she would sometimes say to her father, demonstrating how she viewed the world.

Funny, Violeta thought, the places her brain went while she was kidnapped.

Slick had to restart the squealing Lada twice as he negotiated his way over and around deep ruts of red earth, slippery and of indeterminate depth due to the water collected from the intermittent rain. Forests of spindly pine and elm ran along either side of the road, threatening to overgrow it completely, and kept Slick confined to the rutted single track.

General Penguin fell silent long enough to take a few breaths, turning to look out the window. Gray clouds, dark green trees, and soupy red earth. Violeta had to glance down at her own blue sweatpants to assure herself that there were other colors.

When the general turned back to her, his face was dark, eyes pinched. His small mouth twisted as if he'd seen something outside that suddenly enraged him.

"Your father abandoned his country," he said. "Had he not done so, I would not have had to resort to . . ." He swept his hand toward her, illustrating her condition as a captive. "These draconian measures."

"The government was taking me away from my family," Violeta said.

The general dismissed this with a flick of his stubby

fingers. "I have read your file," he said. "They were not taking you away. You were being given better opportunities, opportunities that would benefit the revolution as well as you and your family."

Violeta didn't respond. She was handcuffed in the back seat of a Soviet-era car with a madman who'd ordered her kidnapped. There was nothing she could say to win this argument.

"You know," the general said, "Cuba does not recognize your *Yanqui* citizenship. You were born on this island, so you will always be a citizen of Cuba, subject to her rights and responsibilities. Your father and mother knew this, but still they took it upon themselves to commit treason and kidnap you from your own nation. Contemptible traitors—"

"Stop it!" Violeta fumed. No one spoke of her parents like that, least of all this slimy thing.

The general ignored her outburst, rolling his eyes. "You do not think it, but that does not make it any less so." He shrugged. "But we are almost there. We must move to the meat of the matter. Once you see what you are about to see, there will be no going back."

Violeta gasped. "Then don't show me!"

"I think you misunderstand," the general said. "My wife is always telling me that I should be more clear. There is no going back to the United States already. What I mean to say is, once you see what is around this corner, you will not leave this forest alive unless you agree to fulfill your responsibilities to the island of Cuba—which are your responsibilities by virtue of where you were born."

Violeta's head spun. She wanted to scream. "I can't—"

"Ah." The general cut her off. "But you can. And you will."

The Lada turned through a gap in the pines and squealed to a stop in front of a huge, dilapidated barn.

"It is too late," the general said. "We are here."

"What do you want from me?"

"Simple," the general said. "You are an expert in GPS guidance. Cuba—your country—needs you to build such a system. We are still in the experimental stages, so the rocket on which you will be working, an older Soviet model, would only be used for test purposes."

Violeta knew the Cuban military already received plenty of missile and rocket technology from Russia, North Korea, Iran, and half a dozen other governments that didn't have the same compunctions against trade held by the United States. If General Penguin needed to kidnap someone to work on his rocket, he was orchestrating something outside the normal chain of command— going rogue.

"I design guidance systems for satellites," Violeta said. "I'm not comfortable working on a weapon."

"Do you think this matters to me?" The general sneered. "I do not care what you are comfortable with."

"Well . . ." Violeta set her jaw, as stubborn as she was smart. "You went to a hell of a lot of trouble to bring me back to Cuba just to shoot me. Because I'm not doing it."

The general slumped. "Very well," he said. He looked directly at her with the most intensely evil eyes she'd ever seen. "But I must warn you. Your death will not come quickly." He leaned forward a little, tapping Slick on the shoulder. Violeta could see the driver's leering smile in the rearview mirror.

"Fuentes," the general said, snapping his fingers. "That item we spoke about earlier."

Fuentes bent forward to reach down by his feet and produced a crumpled paper sack. He passed it back to his boss.

The general reached inside the sack, like a magician getting ready to pull a rabbit out of his hat.

Violeta nearly threw up when he removed his hand.

Only a month before, her mother had gone with her to the stylist and gotten her own version of Violeta's signature bright turquoise streak in her steel gray hair. It was called Voodoo Blue. There was no doubt that the eight-inch braid the general tossed into Violeta's lap belonged to her mother.

Violeta began to hyperventilate. "How . . . ?"

"She is safe," the general said. "For now." His face grew dark again. "But the next time you tell me you will not do this or you will not do that, there will be flesh attached to the hair I bring you." He leaned across the seat, pressing a hand on her knee. "A great deal of flesh."

Chapter 23

The drugs had made it impossible for Quinn to fight back during the beatdown in the stairwell. By some miracle, he'd been able to avoid most of the boots directed at his head and keep his teeth intact. His brain was addled, but functioning. Excess adrenaline and whatever drug they'd pumped into him wore off by the time they dragged him out of the unmarked metal box van into this cell. The right side of his body had taken the brunt of the attack, and he was pretty sure his kidney looked like Garcia's raw pork hamburger. At least a couple of ribs were broken. In addition to making him stagger like a wino, the drugs had robbed Quinn of his sense of direction. There were countless jails in Cuba, none of them good, and he had absolutely no idea where he was.

His legs felt boneless, uncontrollable, but a slap from a rubber truncheon to his thigh pushed him up on to his toes as they half dragged, half escorted him inside. The sliding steel bars, once painted yellow, were now flaking and running with rust stains. Quinn tried to look around to get his bearings, but that earned him another sickening slap on the thigh and an order in Spanish that either meant "eyes front" or "I'm about to beat you to death." The effect on Quinn was pretty much the same.

A slender young man in a sweat-stained, olive green uniform sat behind a concrete counter. This booking area was painted to match the iron bars—and in the same sad state of disrepair. The walls leading in looked like they were made of blocks, but the area behind the intake guard was covered in dark wood paneling. Any molding was long gone, leaving the rusted nailheads naked at the seams. The sickeningly sweet smell of body odor and urine hung heavy in the dank air. Uncontrolled sobs drifted up the hall, almost as if they were being piped in for ambiance. Water—or more likely sewage—gurgled through unseen pipes below the brushed concrete floor. The lighting in the cramped booking area was bad, or else the beating had done something to his vision. It was probably a little bit of both.

The gaggle of arresting officers—Quinn counted five, once his vision cleared—pressed in, surrounding him while their apparent leader filled out a form the young guard had slid across the counter. The leader was an older man with a wide mustache and hints of gray in his curly black hair.

The young man stood, craning to get a better look at Quinn, then turned to the lead officer and said something in Spanish. The older man shrugged and kept filling out the paper, copying information from the "James Shield" passport. The jail guard shook his head, apparently unimpressed by the arresting officer's seniority. He reached behind the counter and produced a small digital camera, with which he began to take photos of Quinn's injuries.

"Lift shirt," the young man said, letting go of the camera with one hand to pantomime with the tail of his own shirt.

"I'm still handcuffed," Quinn said in English, rattling the chain behind his back.

The jailer glared at the arresting officer, who barked something to his thugs. One of them unlocked the cuffs, giving them a cruel yank out of spite. Quinn had done something to piss these guys off. Maybe one was related to Cauliflower Ear. The two CDR goons were nowhere to be seen.

Quinn complied with the jailer's instructions, lifting his shirt to show a football-sized bruise that grew darker by the minute.

The jailer put down the camera and gave an emphatic shake of his head, speaking firmly to the guy with the mustache. Quinn got the gist of the Spanish. The jail wouldn't accept him until he saw a doctor. Luckily for the arresting thugs, there happened to be one on-site. The jailer pointed down a dark hall to his right, beyond the naked wooden paneling. A rivulet of something wet trickled down the center of the concrete floor, disappearing into a drain.

Quinn's arms were wrenched behind him again and the handcuffs ratcheted back on, this time even tighter. The group moved down the hall like a single-celled organism with Quinn as the nucleus. One thug held each arm, two behind shoved him forward every few steps. The guy with the mustache led the way.

A redheaded Cuban woman greeted them in the sick bay with a series of grunts. She wore a stained lab coat that had probably once been white, but was now yellowed by smoke from the cigarettes that overflowed the ashtray on her desk. Not tall to begin with, she stooped at the shoulders as if from some injury to her neck. Her brusque manner made Quinn think she'd received her sensitivity training from the KGB.

The guy with the mustache spoke to her in rapid Spanish, tossing his head back toward booking as if looking for some sympathy.

"He would have had to see me anyway," the woman said in accented English. Her voice was hoarse, like she'd been hit in the throat. She looked directly at Quinn. "I am Dr. Gamboa. Please open your mouth."

Quinn complied. She looked it over and then nodded. "Are you ill?"

"No," Quinn said.

She eyed his bloody knuckles and the boot prints on his shirt. "Injuries?"

"Bruising, maybe some broken ribs."

Dr. Gamboa examined the injuries to his side, then drew enough blood to fill three vials. She muttered to herself as she worked, jotting notes down with a stubby yellow pencil, the type common in prisons where guards are fearful of improvised weapons.

"No claimed illnesses," she mumbled as she wrote. "Bruising and trauma on left side—"

Quinn coughed, grimacing at the effort. "Right side," he said.

One of the thugs behind him drove a fist into Quinn's left kidney, sending him to his knees. He gasped, dry heaving, then climbed back to his feet without being helped.

Dr. Gamboa raised an eyebrow and looked at him a moment before turning back to her paper. She shook her head, then raised her arm so the lab coat fell back and exposed the plastic bracelet on her bony wrist. She was a prisoner as well.

"Bruising over lower ribs and kidneys on left *and* right sides."

She wrote in silence for two full minutes before looking up at the guy with the mustache. "He is fine."

Another trip back down the stinking hall brought Quinn back to the booking counter, where the cuffs were removed and the thugs left the way they'd come in. The steel door slammed shut, and Quinn found himself alone with the young jailer, who rolled his fingerprints and a took few more photos. He took Quinn's Aquaracer dive watch and had him sign a receipt—though he kept both copies. Quinn was made to strip down to his shorts standing at the counter. The guard's mouth fell open when he saw all Quinn's scars, but he quickly regained his composure. He'd likely seen worse but hadn't been prepared for it on the American.

Quinn was issued a stack of bedsheets, a pillowcase, and a prison uniform—gray pants, white T-shirt, and gray vest. Half a full-size bar of soap sat on top of the folded pile.

Quinn knew other guards would arrive any minute to take him to wherever he was being housed and decided to take a chance with this jailer, who seemed at least slightly approachable.

"May I speak?"

"Go ahead," the man said.

"Should I call an attorney?" Quinn asked.

"That is up to you."

"May I make a call to let my friend know where I am?"

"In time, perhaps."

"Can you tell me why I was arrested?"

The jailer consulted the paper the guy with the mustache had filled out. "Hitting a police officer," he said, sounding bored. "I will now explain to you the rules of your confinement."

Two other jailers, both large men with bellies that stretched the buttons of their shirts and hung over their uniform belts, emerged from an office behind the counter to act as witnesses. One carried a tattered magazine with a photo of a naked woman on the cover. The other twirled a two-foot length of gray rubber hose. This one sneered at Quinn.

The booking officer continued. "From this point, you are number three-two-zero." He reached across to affix a plastic hospital-type bracelet to Quinn's wrist, crimping it in place with a pair of pliers. The bracelet bore Quinn's photograph, his ID number, the date of his arrest, and the numbers 15-2. The booking officer caught his eye to make sure he was listening, then continued. "You must never look directly at a guard. If you do, you will be punished. When you are ordered to move, walk slowly on the left side of the hall, head down, hands clasped behind your back. We know you carry your sheets at this time, but after this, if you look up or unclasp her hands, you will be punished. The revolutionary government of Cuba guarantees that you will be fed three times a day. You may not trade or share food with other prisoners. If you do, you will be punished. You are required to work at your assigned job. Fail to work, and you will be punished. Sexual activity with other inmates is prohibited. If you engage in this activity, you will be punished. Giving or receiving a tattoo or possessing tattooing equipment is prohibited. If you engage in this activity, you will be punished . . ."

The list went on for two solid minutes. Quinn stopped listening, keeping his head down, suspecting he was going to be punished one way or another no matter what he did or didn't do. He tried to focus long enough to formulate some semblance of a plan—not for escape, but for survival.

"Do you understand the rules of your confinement as I have explained them to you?"

Quinn coughed. "I understand."

"Excellent," the booking officer said.

With that, the two fat guards stepped around the counter and hustled Quinn back down the dark hall, past the doctor's office and a section of holding cells with black, flat, iron bars. Quinn couldn't see inside, but it was apparent that this was the origin of the sobbing he'd heard earlier.

"Keep moving," the guard with the hose growled, though Quinn hadn't slowed down.

The sounds and smells grew louder and stronger. Thick cigarette smoke curled out of the cells, forming a green cloud halfway between the concrete floor and the dark metal grate of the ceiling. Gnarled hands held rusted bars, timing it just right so they pulled back an instant before the guard smacked them with the hose. The prisoners seemed to know just how much taunting they could get by with, jeering in Spanish, probably more at Quinn than the guards. The shaven heads and hollow eyes made the prisoners look like victims in a concentration camp. Their normally brown complexions had faded to a chalky yellow from lack of sunlight.

Quinn's beard and shaggy hair made it painfully obvious that he was new meat, but the guards solved that by stopping at a small cell halfway down the hall. Most of the cells housed dozens of men, but this one held only three, plus a skinny Cuban woman in nothing but a pair of white panties who sat on the far bunk playing cards with one of the prisoners. Posters of girls in swimsuits papered the walls. The smell of coffee pushed back the jailhouse odors. These had to be the trustees.

A beady-eyed, guinea pig of a man with large jowls shaved Quinn's head and beard with a pair of electric shears. The clippers had probably never been cleaned or sharpened, and they yanked out nearly as much hair as they cut.

The guard gave his porn magazine to the barber, then shoved Quinn back into the hallway.

The one with the hose leaned in close enough that Quinn could smell cooked onions and bad teeth.

"Head down," the guard said in broken English.

"I understand," Quinn said. He wanted to say more, to defy authority. Hitting a guard would, no doubt, gain him prisoner cred, but at this stage of the game, it might also get him beaten to death.

The guard opened the metal door with a large key on his belt, then tapped Quinn's wristband with the hose, pointing at the 15-2. He nodded to the long row of three-level cots situated along each wall of the roughly fifty-by-one-hundred-foot bay. Almost all the cots were occupied by shirtless men—and all of those were staring directly at Quinn, who was dressed in nothing but his newly issued boxer shorts.

"*Quince-dos*," the guard said, tapping the number on the wristband again. He spoke loudly and slowly, as if that made it easier to understand in Spanish, and then pointed the hose at the cots and started counting. "One, two, three, *quatro*, *cinco* . . ." He then aimed the length of hose at the bottom cot of the nearest bunk, moving upward. "One, two, three. *Quince-dos*. One-fife-two."

"I understand," Quinn said, counting halfway down the row along the left wall of the cellblock until he got to fifteen. He clenched his teeth and nodded. Of course the biggest guy in the block would be sitting on the edge of the bed that was assigned to him. A huge scar ran diagonally from above the man's right eye, disappearing into a thick black beard that covered his chin. A riot of tattoos on his muscular chest gleamed with sweat under blinking fluorescent lights. The look on his face was clear—*I know this is your bunk. Come and take it.*

The guard stifled a smile. "Rule three-fife: you must sleep in correct bunk." He prodded Quinn forward with the hose. "Or you will be punished."

Chapter 24

Ronnie Garcia took a cab to her auntie's, leaving Jacques and Emiko to relay what little they knew of Quinn's situation to Palmer. Hopefully, the approaching storm hadn't chased the Navy intel ship back to Miami.

Peppa's dark-skinned apprentice, Ramón, answered the door. Ronnie didn't wait for him to open the door completely, but shouldered her way inside, walking past him. Iggy, the little worm, held up both hands to stop her, but he shrank away like fluff before a wildfire as she kept walking.

"Señora, por favor, please . . ."

Peppa appeared at the end of the hall, a lit cigar in her hand. Her hair was tied up in a wine-red kerchief. She wore a simple multicolored skirt and a white peasant blouse that hung off both shoulders. As Ronnie drew nearer, she noticed a fine spray of blood covering the front of the blouse and Peppa's chin.

Peppa shook her head at Iggy. "Relax," she said. "Veronica is always welcome here. Anytime. Do you understand?"

"I need to talk to you," Ronnie said. "Something's happen—"

Peppa raised her empty hand. "Iggy, Ramón, please go to the market and fetch me some coconut water."

Ramón turned to go but Iggy protested.

"We have a fresh box in the refrigerator," he said.

"Then go buy us another one," Peppa said. "Please go at once."

Iggy gave her a hard look, as if thinking of a challenge, then turned on his heels.

Ronnie started to speak again, but Peppa kept her hand raised until she heard the door close. Even then, she walked to the front to look out the window, assuring herself that both apprentices were well down the street.

"What is it, my dear?" she finally said. Her face darkened. "Has someone hurt you?"

Barely holding back tears, Ronnie filled her in on Quinn's arrest and the fact that she had no idea where he was.

"I think Odesa betrayed me," she said.

"That is doubtful."

"You didn't see her, Auntie. She hates me."

Peppa set the cigar in an ashtray beside her loveseat and took Garcia's hand in hers, patting it softly. "She does not hate you. I have looked into her eyes. She would never betray you. You are blood, both daughters of the same good man."

Ronnie scoffed, wiping a tear from her cheek. "The same good man who betrayed my mother?"

Peppa leaned back in her chair and stared at the ceiling. "Your father made a mistake," she said. "Terrible, to be sure. But he owned this mistake and paid the price of it until the day he died. What you are talking about is different. Odesa knows that telling the CDR anything would be throwing you to the wolves."

"I'm sure she knew exactly what she was doing," Ronnie said. "I swear to you, Auntie, if I find out she had anything to do with Quinn's arrest . . ." She stopped, chest heaving.

"I know," Peppa said. "You are your father's daughter, but you are also your mother's child. Believe me, I know all too well what kind of temper your mother had. But Odesa did not betray you. I am sure of it."

"How?" Ronnie asked.

"Because I know who did."

"Ignacio?" Ronnie guessed.

"I fear that is the case," Peppa said. "I thought we were careful, but I am afraid he heard too much."

A window shutter flew open, causing both women to jump and letting a howling wind into the room.

"The coming storm is a bad one," Peppa said, walking over to latch the shutter.

Ronnie closed her eyes, pounding the cushion beside her with a clenched fist. "I have to find him, Auntie. Where do we start?"

Peppa moved to the loveseat so she was sitting beside her niece. "I will ask my contacts. If the authorities have truly arrested your friend for robbery, he may be at one of the police stations, a pretrial facility, or even a prison. If they have arrested him for something else, then . . ." She shook her head, as if clearing it of the thought.

"What?" Ronnie pressed. "Tell me what you're thinking."

"If your friend is in custody for something political, they may have taken him to Villa Marista. I will check with my contacts, but if he is held there, it will be more difficult to get to him."

The thought of Quinn in the Villa, as it was called, made Garcia's heart sink. Formerly a Catholic seminary, in the early 1960s the KGB had helped Castro transform the place into the Cuban version of Lubyanka. It was a dungeon where secrets—and toenails—were extracted with sadistically scientific precision.

Peppa put her hand on Garcia's shoulder. Her lips quivered as she spoke. For the first time in her life, Ronnie saw her auntie's hands shake.

"Veronica, my dear," she said. "Even if your friend is in the Villa, you must not lose heart. This is what they want you to do—to rob you of hope. But I . . . I cannot go there."

"Auntie Madonna told me they arrested you after you helped me get to the United States," Garcia whispered. "Is that where they took you?"

Peppa nodded. "Seven months," she whispered. "Your friend is strong. I can see this in his eyes. I was not so strong." She sniffed, remembering. "They call the Villa a place of instruction, but it is really a place of constant violation and . . ." She shook her head, steeling herself. "I am being awful. We have no idea where your friend is. They do not send people arrested for robbery to the Villa."

Ronnie looked hard at her auntie, seeing a reflection of the anguish Ronnie herself had felt after horrific torture on a black-site prison boat less than two years before.

"I cannot explain in detail," Ronnie said. "But I have been in similar circumstances."

"I can see that," Peppa said. "I hope you were able to kill the men who did it."

Ronnie nodded, startled at her aunt's bluntness.

"Some say revenge is a bad thing," Peppa continued. "But you and I know all too well that most such philosophers were never violated with an electric prod."

Ronnie's jaw hung open, revealing her astonishment. "How did you know?"

Peppa gave a sad shrug. "It is what men like that do to women."

"Did you?" Ronnie asked. "Get revenge, I mean."

"After the fact," Peppa said. "I did not let them break me. Two of them were the worst. One has been . . . taken care of."

"If you see the other," Ronnie said. "Please point him out to me."

"I will be happy to," Peppa said. "But as much as I enjoy plotting revenge, we must figure out how to help your friend. To do that, we need to know where he is. I will make a few calls. Even jail guards need occasional help from the orishas. Someone will be able to help us find him. You go talk to your sister. Her boyfriend is in jail. If she has been to visit him, she will know better than I how to navigate the system."

"I—"

Peppa raised a hand to shush her. "Trust me," she said. "And trust her."

Ronnie gave a sullen nod. This entire ordeal was insane. Quinn locked up in a Cuban jail while she relied on her father's love child and a Santeria priestess to help her find him.

The front door opened, then slammed shut.

"Forgive me!" Ignacio yelled from down the hall. "The wind got it."

Peppa rose to her feet and picked up the smoldering cigar. "In the meantime," she said. "I will deal with my apprentice."

Ronnie clenched her teeth, barely tamping back her anger. "If he is the one who turned in Jericho . . ."

"You must understand something," Peppa said. "He is not a bad boy. They are surely blackmailing him with something. That is the way they do things. Even his mother says his soul was a bit watery from the time he was a small child."

"His fault or not," Ronnie said. "He has to tell us what he knows."

Peppa picked up the machete she used to dispatch her sacrificial rooster, then stuck the burning cigar between her perfect, white teeth. She puffed the coal to life. "He will tell me what we need to know." She spoke around the clenched cigar, holding up the blood-rusted blade and turning it back and forth. "Because I will explain to him that the rock is more terrifying than the hard place."

Chapter 25

Quinn took a slow breath, suppressing the uncertainty that writhed in his gut like a snake. This was the Serengeti plain, and he had a finite amount of time to establish himself as something other than a wounded antelope. His ribs were on fire. White-hot pain pulsed in the back of his head. His left eye was nearly swollen shut. No matter how much bravado he showed, he *was* wounded. And everyone in this place could see it.

He counted his breaths—in for three seconds, hold for three, out for three. The technique was called by different names: combat breathing, tactical breathing. At the moment, Quinn didn't care. The exercise helped to control his adrenaline—to manage his fear.

Fear was normal. A healthy dose of it was natural and kept you on your toes—alive. But runaway fear could grow into full-blown, debilitating terror. That was deadly. Physical training helped. Experience helped more. Quinn had a ton of each under his belt. But there was no training, no experience that could have prepared him for the realities of this gauntlet he was having to walk in this Cuban prison.

He ignored the catcalls, the taunts in Spanish that he couldn't literally understand, but knew full well meant he was "new meat." Instead, he looked through the gloom of cigarette smoke and scanned the faces of the men staring at him from their beds. He counted nineteen bunks on either side. With three beds per bunk, that made space for one hundred and fourteen prisoners. Four or five beds on either side stood empty, but the block was very near capacity.

Every prison block around the world had a shot caller, the guy who ran the most powerful gang and decided what went on in his domain. A tenuous mixture of politics, prison economics, and open warfare decided who was in charge—and how long he stayed in power. Shot callers kept the peace, so guards were often a little more forgiving of their behavior. The guy sitting in Quinn's assigned bunk was the only man in the block with a full beard, so he was likely the boss. That couldn't be helped. One thing was certain: Quinn had a few milliseconds to get his bearings and start moving.

Nearly naked and carrying the meager gear he'd been issued, Quinn began his walk down the jeering aisle. He moved slowly, head up, shoulders hunched slightly, ready to attack the first person who looked at him wrong. It was vital that each man here saw loud and clear in his demeanor that this was not his first time in lockup.

The booking officer had stacked his issue gear in order of size, with the folded sheets on the bottom, then the uniform pieces, then the pillowcase, and finally half a bar of what looked like Dial soap—probably part of a humanitarian donation from some church group in the U.S. or Canada. Quinn estimated the soap to weigh a little over two ounces. Not optimal, but better than nothing. He'd nudged it into the mouth of the pillowcase while the inmate barber shaved his head, and now he pushed it farther as he walked, getting ready for what he felt sure was ahead of him.

A man on the top bunk to his immediate right gave a low wolf whistle and waved him over. Quinn kept walking, but the man slid to the floor. "Hey *muchacha!*" the man said, crossing the open bay. "I talking to joo."

Quinn held his bundle of gear in place while he turned to face the oncoming man. This guy wouldn't require a weapon, makeshift or otherwise. He probably didn't even want to fight but was a tester, someone assigned to feel out the new arrival.

Quinn kept his weight balanced on both feet, watching the rest of the prisoners with his peripheral vision in case one of them decided to jump on his back and make it a free-for-all. He held the stack of gear under his left arm, ready to drop it if he needed to.

He didn't.

The mouthy prisoner stopped five feet away. He eyed Quinn's scars but kept talking. Quinn couldn't understand what he said, but the challenge was evident in the tone. No, this one wasn't a fighter, but Quinn decided he'd use him anyway to make a point.

A snap kick to the man's groin bent him over at the waist. Quinn didn't wait for him to cry out before rechambering his kick and delivering another snap, directly to the base of the guy's nose, standing him up again. He teetered there for a moment, too stunned to defend himself, while Quinn kicked him in the groin again, this time sending him staggering back to the nearest bunk, where he collapsed on top of another prisoner.

Quinn turned and kept walking toward his assigned bunk, greeted with more jeering—and a few cheers—

like the out-of-town fighter at a local boxing match. A few people rooted for him—but very few.

The man sitting in his bunk dangled his feet and looked on impassively.

Three bunks away, another man—this one on the left, one bed away from the shot caller—eyed Quinn. He too wore nothing but shorts, showing off a powerful torso and thick arms. He moved his head back and forth, then interlaced his fingers, extending his arms to pop his knuckles, limbering up for a fight.

Quinn kept walking, wrapping his fingers around the pillowcase.

The big boy was up on his toes now, fists at his sides, right leg back for power.

Quinn dropped everything and grabbed the open end of the pillowcase, swinging it upward like a war hammer. The bar of soap caught the big bruiser on the point of his chin. Quinn adjusted the angle of his swing just slightly as the soap arced upward, looping the pillow-case behind the big guy's neck when it came around a second time. Grabbing the soap end as it came over the other man's shoulders, Quinn yanked backward, pulling the man to him at the same time as he propelled his own forehead into the bridge of the big guy's nose.

Quinn stepped back, using the unwinding momentum to swing the weighted pillowcase around a final time, thumping the big guy hard in his left temple. Quinn's attack lasted less than two seconds—and made the fluid statement he wanted to make. He knew how to fight.

Quinn kept his eyes up, watching for threats in his peripheral vision as he stooped to pick up his sheets and uniform.

The bearded shot caller studied him for a long moment, then got to his feet, yielding bunk 15-2 with a flourish of his open hand.

The prisoner in 15-1 stayed in the shadows of his lower bunk, unwilling to get involved.

A lanky guy wearing his vest but no shirt walked over from bunk 22-1 across the bay and stuck out his hand.

"*Yuma*?" the man asked. Garcia had explained to Quinn that *Yuma* meant the United States.

Quinn shook the offered hand, but warily. He still had the makeshift mace if things got out of hand.

"I am Red," the other prisoner said. "Do you know the *Shawshank* movie?"

Quinn nodded.

A smile spread over 22-1's face. He put the flat of his hand to his chest. "I here a long time. So I am called Red, like in *Shawshank* movie. I help you like Red help Andy."

The man lying in 15-3, the bunk above Quinn's, laughed out loud from behind an issue of *SuperBike*. He lowered the magazine and peered down at 22-1.

"Don't listen to Vargas," 15-3 said. His English was near perfect, as if he'd learned it in a British boarding school. "They call him Red because he is more of a communist than any revolutionary on this damnable island. He is a stinking informant who will pass along your every word to the guards."

"He lies," Vargas said. "No one in here likes him."

"Look around you, Andy." The guy in the top bunk chuckled. "If no one here likes me, that should tell you about my character."

"I just want to get some rest," Quinn said to Vargas. "We'll talk later."

Red Vargas gave him a thumbs-up and offered a bizarrely garbled quote from some movie that he must have thought was *The Shawshank Redemption* but sounded like it was from a Spaghetti Western.

The man on the top bunk lowered his motorcycle magazine as Quinn situated his sheets and prisoner uniform. Standing next to his own bed put Quinn nearly eye to eye with the other man. He looked to be in his late fifties, pale, with a scruff of gray stubble and a little curl to the silver hair that was starting to grow out from his buzz cut. He was gaunt, like most of the other inmates. Bruises from a recent beating decorated his forearms and shins with purple blotches. He chewed on his bottom lip while he studied Quinn, then returned to his magazine without a word.

"Your English is very good," Quinn said.

"I was a professor before they locked me in here." He lowered the magazine again and Quinn saw the broken blood vessels around his right eye. He'd definitely been roughed up. "Academics never fare well in a revolution." He winked the bloodshot eye. "We know too much shit and refuse to shut up about it."

"The revolution was a long time ago," Quinn said.

"If you believe that, then you do not know Cuba. Here, we fight a revolution every day." He shrugged. "I got tired of it. Stopped fighting nine years ago. Some *chivato* shithead like your friend Red let one of his other *chivato* friends know, and I was picked up the next day."

"I'm not trying to make any enemies," Quinn said. "But Red is a long way from being my friend." He shook his head. "Nine years . . ."

"It seems like twenty," 15-3 said. "You have made a

good decision pertaining to Red. Truly, it is best that you don't trust anyone in here, even me. Fernandez—the man who was in your bunk—he is El Jefe. He would be all too happy to take you under his wing now that he sees you are a good fighter. So you can help him enforce his will among the other prisoners when they don't pay up for the prostitutes or drugs he runs with the fat, son-of-a-bitch guard who brought you in here." He let the magazine fall to his chest and extended a hand. "I am Jorge Santana."

"Jim," Quinn said. "Jim Shield."

"*Mucho gusto*," Santana said, shaking Quinn's hand. "May I ask what they have accused you of, to get you locked inside the notorious Valle Grande Prison?"

Quinn sighed. At least he knew now where he was being held—though it did him little good, since he had no way to communicate that fact.

"Hitting a police officer."

Santana raised a silver brow. "I sincerely hope these charges are true."

Quinn shrugged. "How about you?"

"Pre-criminal dangerousness," Santana scoffed. "The words sound insane when they leave my tongue. Though, if I am to admit the truth, my revolutionary captors knew whereof they spoke. I have done things these nine years that I would never have dreamed of doing before my arrest. And it only gets worse." He rubbed the bruises on his arms, looking up at the ceiling as he pondered some deep thought. "It is a point of fact that no one leaves Valle Grande an innocent man, though many arrive that way. One must do the unimaginable just to survive." The old man looked at Quinn with his blood-shot eye and gave a long, resigned sigh. "One day, they will have to shoot me—and when they do, I will surely deserve it."

Ignacio lay facedown on his narrow bed, using a sodden pillow to muffle his sobs. He'd confessed to Señora Peppa as soon as she confronted him. The words and tears and snot spilled out all at once, adding to his shame. For a moment, he thought she meant to cut his throat with the machete. He certainly deserved it. The blade would only have put him out of his misery. Instead, she'd killed a young pullet, spilling the chicken's blood in a bowl and asking Oyá to intercede in the matter. Ignacio needed healing, Peppa said. The blood and carcass could help with that. Unlike other sacrifices, the flesh of this bird held his sickness, his sins, so it would not be used as food.

But it did not hold all his sins, because Ignacio could not bear to tell Señora Peppa everything.

He could still picture the lifeless bird, the small but horrendous gash across its neck. The copper scent of its lifeblood. Peppa had clenched the cigar with her bone-white canine teeth and studied him through thick clouds of smoke. The fat cigar made it look like Peppa was smiling—but Ignacio knew this was not the case. And if she was not smiling, she was angry—or sad. Maybe both. Either way, he was left feeling as if he'd been gutted.

Señora Peppa had probably not placed a curse on him, though she'd made it very clear to him that Santeria left room for the practice. She told him of a man whose mother-in-law had cursed him after he'd murdered his young wife. She said this man's testicles had shriveled until they were nothing, and he'd ended up throwing himself into the sea. Surely Ignacio's behavior did not rise to the level of murder—though Señora Peppa said the American was now in prison, and in Cuba, that could lead to the same thing. She'd been extremely clear that if her niece was arrested, Ignacio would not have to wait for his testicles to shrivel. She would cut them off herself. Even with the reprieve, Peppa's patron goddess, Oyá herself, might take a very dark view of the way he had betrayed his teacher. The gods could be that way—protective, vindictive.

The ash on the cigar Peppa burned on the night the Americans arrived had foretold a death. Ignacio was certain that the death was his. Either Alacrón would kill him for refusing to cooperate anymore or Peppa would kill him for the cooperation he'd already given. Ignacio bit the pillow, screaming into the cloth. He could not betray Señora Peppa again. But there was no holding back from Señor Alacrón. The man could make him talk with a simple stare. Ignacio was simply no good at this business. His choices were limited. Tomorrow morning, he would either leave Señora Peppa's place and run away—or he would sit down with Señor Alacrón and tell him the American's real name.

Chapter 26

Violeta Cruz was smarter than most anyone she'd ever met—certainly smart enough to know she didn't have much experience with life outside the lab or classroom. The debilitating fear for her mother's safety had unlocked a new kind of hatred that she'd never felt before. She kept it to herself, plodding along behind General de la Guardia, all the while thinking of him as General Penguin. The minions followed as well, no doubt making sure Violeta didn't strangle the little man with the lock of her mother's hair.

The light was fading by the time Penguin's driver, Fuentes, turned off the narrow goat track that the Cubans called a road and brought the Lada to a stop in front of the dilapidated barn. Had she not been a genius, Violeta would have been in her sophomore year of college. She had a difficult time controlling her smart-ass attitude under the best of times, and stress only made it worse.

She nodded toward the barn. "I know it's bad here in Cuba," she said in English. "But your house smells like shit."

De la Guardia screwed up his face—like he was about to sneeze or say something hateful. Seeming to think better of it, he gave Fuentes a look and then hustled toward the front door.

Fuentes grabbed her arm and dragged her forward before she could start walking on her own. "You would be wise to keep your tongue in your mouth."

"He needs me," Violeta sneered. "He already said so."

"Yes," Fuentes said, letting go of her arm. "But he does not need you to have a tongue. I do not speak figuratively. Keep talking, and he will have me cut it out with a pair of tinsnips. I have done it before."

Violeta swallowed hard, wondering if these maniacs stayed up all night thinking of creepy things to say. She ached to be able to talk to her mother. Even now, Violeta could picture her face, warning her to be smart. *When the time comes, fight like hell*, her mother always said. *But wait until it is time.* She'd often recounted how Violeta's father had agreed to send her off to a state school—until the authorities had driven away and he could sneak the family to the United States. Violeta knew one thing: Either her father had been gone when General Penguin's men came for her mother—or he was now dead.

Deep in thought, Violeta wandered to the left instead of straight toward the double doors of the big barn. Fuentes grabbed her arm again. "Careful!" he barked. "That is the lagoon."

She saw the burbling lake of sludge a few feet in front of her about the same time a waft of acrid gas hit her full in the face. The ammonia smell of rotting manure had been strong before, but now it threatened to choke her to death. The hum of generators and pumps came from inside the barn.

She threw a forearm across her nose, squinting at the terrible smell. "Lagoon?"

"Sewage," Fuentes said, arm across his own nose.

He'd obviously been here before, but there was no way to get used to the stinking, stinging ammonia that filled the night air. "This place was a poultry farm for decades before the revolution. Years of chicken shit must go somewhere."

De la Guardia turned at the doors and glared. "Take her for a swim if she's so interested," he said.

Fuentes pushed her toward the door. "Go."

The smell inside was only a little better. Violeta wanted to feel sorry for the pimply kid standing guard duty. Maybe he was here against his will too. She estimated the old barn to be roughly fifty by one hundred and fifty feet. The bulk of the wall to her left was taken up by a series of generators and pumps. Black hoses, four inches in diameter, came through the wall from the sewage lagoon below, slurping a toxic mix of rainwater and chicken crap.

General de la Guardia led the way past the bleary-eyed sentry, all the way to the back of the enclosure. There was a trapdoor in the floor to the right, leading underground. A plywood closet nearby was perhaps twenty feet wide and half as deep. Inside were a long wooden bench and a half dozen orange protective suits, each with a self-contained breathing apparatus.

A munchkin-sized suit was at the end of the row. General Penguin took this one, stepping into it as he nodded to the line of others that hung like flayed orange skins from wooden pegs set in the plywood wall.

"Change quickly," he said. "Fuentes will check the seals after you are dressed."

Violeta looked around as she slipped off her shoes and stepped into the suit. She'd been in plenty of clean rooms, but she had never worn a chem-bio suit before.

There were no airlocks, as far as she could tell, which meant she wasn't dealing with anything biological. Chemical? Probably. Hell, a good whiff of the gases coming off that sewage lagoon outside would probably kill a horse. Anything stuck down below was likely to eat right through one of these flimsy suits. The more she thought about it, the more she realized there was no way of knowing what kind of microbes and diseases were hiding in fifty years of chicken crap. Maybe she *was* dealing with something biological. These morons just didn't have the sophistication to know that the outsides of their suits were probably toxic. The manure lagoon probably contained enough deadly stuff to kill Havana three times over.

De la Guardia led the way once they were dressed. He lifted the wooden trapdoor—which looked much too flimsy to keep whatever bugbears were lurking below trapped there. A beam of white light poured upward into the gloom, as if ready to transport the general into some other dimension. Violeta followed him down a heavy wooden ladder to a chamber fifteen feet below. The valves on her breathing apparatus clicked and whirred overtime from exertion and fear.

The heavy rubberized boots of her protective suit made a hollow thump when she hopped off the bottom rung of the ladder and onto perforated wooden floorboards like some sort of astronaut stepping onto the surface of an alien planet. Her eyes traveled back up the ladder—which looked to be the only way out—and watched as the trapdoor closed.

The ceiling, the subfloor of the barn above, was comprised of a crosshatch of heavy timbers, overlaid with felt and plywood. Most of it was ancient, decades old, but installed well after the barn had been built, probably during or shortly after the revolution with the help of the Soviets. The enclosure was smaller than the footprint of the barn above, with heavy battenboards creating a false wall along the far side of the room, directly under the pumps. No doubt this held back the sludge from the sewage lagoon. The same hum and slurp of generators and pumps that she'd heard above was doubly loud down here. They'd have a hard time keeping up once the rains from the approaching hurricane hit. It was no wonder they had to wear these cumbersome suits.

Seven others in similar gear crowded like ants around a crumb of food, surrounding what looked like a scale-model Soviet MiG at the center of the brightly lit enclosure. One of them looked up and noticed the general, announcing his arrival on the intercom in his suit. His electronic voice was accompanied by the same click-whir, click-whir that Violeta heard inside her own hood.

The others stepped away, giving her a clear view of the mini MiG. It took her a full minute to figure out what it was, and another thirty seconds to understand what this maniac would want her to do.

A bitter sob caught hard in her chest at the sudden realization. There was no way she was getting out of this alive.

Chapter 27

Odesa was buttoning up her boat for the night when Ronnie walked down Pier 2 at Marina Hemingway. A humid wind caused the palms to chatter overhead. Dock lines groaned and bumpers squeaked. Odesa looked up and heaved a sigh of annoyance, as if she'd narrowly missed her chance to escape. She unlocked the two padlocks at the top and bottom of the door and stepped back, allowing Ronnie to enter so they wouldn't have to talk outside among the mosquitos and the bothersome neighbors on the vintage Chris-Craft cruiser that had tied up in the next slip to the east, stern to stern with *Danotria*.

"Have you returned for another *cafécito*, my sister?" Odesa said, half sneering.

Ronnie shook her head, arms crossed, hugging herself.

"I need your help," she said.

"*Cafécito* it is," Odesa said.

"I'm serious," Ronnie said. "My friend is in trouble."

Odesa raised a brow. "Your boyfriend, Jim Shield?"

Ronnie nodded. Her cell phone buzzed before she could answer. She looked at Odesa. "Sorry," she said. "This might be my auntie."

Odesa waved away her apology and busied herself with the coffee press while Ronnie answered her phone.

It was Peppa, her voice at once jubilant and guarded.

"I know where they are holding him."

Ronnie put her phone on speaker. "Odesa is on the line as well," she said. "Where is he?"

"Valle Grande," Peppa sighed. "It is a prison, but authorities sometimes use it for detention before a trial. It is a blessing that they did not take him to the Villa." The shudder of relief was evident in her voice. "Apparently, they think of him as a common criminal."

"A common criminal?" Odesa lit a gas burner under her coffeepot. She shook out the match and held the smoking stick in her hand. "And that is a good thing?"

"It means they do not see him as a political prisoner," Peppa said. "Tomorrow is visiting day. There is a chance we will be able to see him."

Odesa shook her head as she measured out her coffee from the sack she kept in a plastic tub above the stove. "I do not think it will be possible to see him so soon," she said. "I had to get on the visitor list fifteen days early to see my friend. He is not at Valle Grande, but I imagine the rules are the same." She brushed a lock of blond hair out of her eyes and flopped down next to Ronnie on the settee, interested now in the situation. "They will make you kick the ball around and around before they let you score."

"I imagine so," Peppa said. "But I have, shall we say, greased the way. We are on the list for tomorrow."

Relief flooded over Ronnie at the notion of seeing Jericho in person. "How did you get us on the list?"

"It is best you do not know," Peppa said. "Visiting hours are at ten, but I understand we should arrive three hours before that."

"True," Odesa said. "And you should take him a rice sack full of cigarettes, crackers, that sort of thing. He can trade them if he doesn't smoke—and the crackers will make the shitty food go down a little easier. I'll make you a list. You probably won't be able to find most of it at this late hour, but you can try."

"You are on the list as well," Peppa said.

Odesa cocked her head. "Me?"

"I got us on the list," Peppa said. "But I know little of the bureaucracy and rules once we walk through the front gate."

"You expect me to waste my entire day going to a filthy jail where I have never been with a sister I do not know to help a man I do not care about."

"Exactly," Peppa said. "It is what families do. As I said. You know the rules. Will three hours be early enough?"

Odesa groaned. Even on the phone it was impossible to say no to Peppa Garcia. "There will be a long line, but that should be plenty of time."

"What else?" Ronnie asked. "What else should we know?"

"Well," Odesa said. "When I went, the jailer warned everyone that the prisoners were animals, especially those who had been locked away from women for some time. He told us not to wear anything low cut or tight. Evidently, the prisoners are certain to become inflamed with passion at the sight of a woman in clothing that accentuates her breasts or hips."

Peppa gave a tight chuckle. "If that is the case, my dear muchachas, then we are all very much doomed."

Chapter 28

The hurricane was predicted to make landfall in the next day and a half, but no one had told the wind. Instead of blowing in advance of the storm, it had died off completely, throwing the island into muggy doldrums of heat and humidity and leaving Ronnie Garcia feeling like a melted lump of goo.

Peppa hired a driver to pick up Odesa in front of Marina Hemingway at a quarter to seven in the morning. They'd been waiting five minutes now. It was still dark, and she'd still not shown. Garcia sat with her auntie in the back seat of the old Chevy, each woman leaning out of their respective window, hoping for a breath of cooler air. Thankfully, neither of them were the type to wear much makeup. That would have made it unbearable. A bank of wicked gunmetal clouds boiled over the ocean east of Havana, blocking any hope of seeing one of the sunrises Garcia remembered from her childhood.

On Odesa's advice, Garcia wore her loosest pair of jeans and most modest shirt—a red polo, fastened up to the second button. The prisoners would just have to deal with the little bit of cleavage that peeked above. It was just too hot to button it all the way. She couldn't decide if it would be more modest to wear her hair down or pulled back in a ponytail. Peppa had taken one look at her and said it would not matter. Few of the prisoners would be looking at her hair.

"I feel like a *jinetera*," Peppa said. She tucked the strap of her bra back inside the shoulder of her white cotton blouse, less revealing in the neckline, but much tighter across the bust than her customary off-the-shoulder peasant blouses.

This drew a sideways look in the rearview mirror from the cabbie. Literally, *jinetera* meant "jockey," but in Cuba, the term was interchangeable with "prostitute." The edict from the jail that women needed to wear pants seemed counterintuitive to Garcia. Peppa's multicolored skirts were much less suggestive than the formfitting jeans she now wore.

Odesa whistled from the walkway under the Marina Hemingway sign, hustling along in the early morning shadows as one did when running late. She carried a large white rice sack, much like the one Garcia had stashed between her feet. Her navy blue T-shirt was one size too large, but her tan slacks were not.

She opened the door on Ronnie's side, forcing her to scoot over, and climbed in.

Garcia started to say something about sweating to death in the middle, but she realized Odesa had brought the extra sack of goodies for Quinn. She endured the heat in silence, Peppa on one side and Odesa on the other, arm pressed against fleshy arm. Neither woman had anything close to air-conditioning. Like a myriad of other discomforts they endured, being crammed in the back of a taxi with other sweating bodies was just a fact of life.

The cabdriver turned back toward Havana proper on the Panamericana, meandering until he got on Avenida 23, which eventually turned into Highway 101

and took them almost due south into Valle Grande—
a neighborhood named for the place in Bolivia where
Che Guevara had been killed by Bolivian troops as
advised by officers from the CIA. The Agency arguably
had much to be ashamed of in Central and South America, but from what Garcia knew of Che Guevara, his
death was not one of those things.

Princess palms, the kind that looked like they belonged around a golf course or hotel, lined the patched
macadam road up to the prison gates. As in prisons and
military bases everywhere, a captive labor force kept
the grounds well maintained. A line of visitors, mostly
women and children, snaked out of the double doors
from the prison lobby. Garcia counted at least sixty
people that she could see, each carrying a white rice
sack full of supplies. Odesa had dumped the contents
of her bag—a carton of Cohiba cigarettes, some fruit
drink powders, crackers, canned fish, and two small
jars of mayonnaise (which Quinn would never eat,
but Ronnie didn't have the heart to tell her that)—into
Ronnie's. Odesa reasoned that the guards would have
fewer chances to say no if they brought only one bag.
According to her, the moment they walked through the
gate, they would hear "no" more than anything but
crying. Ronnie counted five women standing next to a
side door, each of them heavily made up and dressed to
the nines. They too carried the obligatory rice sack.

"What's with them?" Ronnie whispered. "I thought we
were supposed to keep from inflaming the prisoners."

"Conjugal visits," Odesa said, matter-of-factly. "The
jailer explained it all to me when I went to visit Higinino, but ours is not that kind of relationship. You must

get on that list a month in advance and be tested for AIDS, hepatitis, and—"

"That's okay," Garcia said, imagining the nasty conditions where the conjugal visits took place. "I was just asking."

It took over an hour of standing in line before they reached the front desk. Peppa did the talking, handing over all three sets of identification, including Garcia's passport. There was always a chance that Quinn's record had been flagged and someone would come out and arrest Garcia as soon as they read her name. Thibodaux had warned her against pulling a boneheaded move like walking into a prison, but she'd reasoned that the authorities knew where she was staying. If they wanted to arrest her, they would have done it already. As it turned out, Peppa slid her card to the guard at the desk, and he let them through. He told Garcia to inform the guard at the metal detectors that Sergeant Hernandez had approved her visit.

The rest of the process was much like airport security, only agonizingly slower. There was no one to complain to. You either put up with the system—or you went home, and your loved one went without his crackers and mayonnaise. Everything and everyone was x-rayed or run through a metal detector. Peppa's hair comb had enough metal to set off the magnetometer, earning her a once-over with a wand by a leering male guard. His face fell when he didn't get to pat her down.

An hour and forty-five minutes after the driver dropped them off in front of the prison, Ronnie was given back her rice sack with a blue plastic zip tie showing it had been properly screened, and the three women were seated on the same side of a concrete table. They were surrounded by dozens of identical tables and rice sacks. Prisoners began filing in one at a time. Women cried, children shied away from fathers and boyfriends. A partition under each table went all the way to the floor, presumably to keep anything from being passed by foot, but it was evidently alright to hold hands on the top side. After an unbearably long wait, the officious guard standing beside the door that led back into the bowels of the prison called the name Jim Shield, and Jericho walked out, stopping long enough to open his mouth and lift his tongue to show he wasn't smuggling anything into the visitation room. Garcia figured it was just another way to screw with the inmates, but Peppa reminded her that prisoners were constantly trying to get the stories of their abuse to the outside world.

Quinn smiled when he saw them, nearly sending Ronnie into a meltdown. He looked like he'd been run over by a train—his head shaved, eyes black, limping from other unknown injuries. It wasn't possible, but he looked ten pounds lighter than the day before. She'd never seen his hair so short and was surprised at all the white scars on his head—old injuries.

Quinn sat across from them at the table, looking dazed enough that Garcia wanted to cry. As bad as he looked, he smiled when she took his hand, putting on his brave face—which, Garcia knew, was the only face he had. Two nasty-looking guards strode up and down the aisles, peering down at the prisoners and their guests as if to remind all present that every last soul in the room was under their control. One of them, a pale guy with a belly that lopped over a black radio belt, carried a length of hose that he slapped against his fat thigh as he waddled by.

"That's my new friend, Blanco," Quinn whispered.

"Seriously," Ronnie said. "That guy is your friend?"

"Nope," Quinn said, still forcing a smile, talking through his teeth. "I plan to beat him to death with an axe handle if I ever see him outside." He released a pent-up sigh. "So anyway, this is a surprise. I'd love to hear how you pulled it off, but we only have a few minutes."

"It was Peppa's magic," Garcia said.

Her auntie laughed. "If Peppa had magic, you would not be in here."

Quinn looked at the rice sack. "What's this?"

Odesa explained, gushing a little, looking at her fidgeting hands as Ronnie gave her the credit. It was obvious that she had a little crush on Quinn, making Garcia wonder if she should feel proud or ask to borrow Quinn's axe handle when he was done with Blanco.

Quinn seemed more interested in solving the mystery of his friend's death in Florida than getting out of jail. "So fill me in," he said. He open a packet of crackers while he spoke,

Garcia gave his hand a squeeze and looked back and forth at the other two women.

Quinn shrugged. "They're here," he said. "They might as well be brought in on the conspiracy."

Odesa pulled her hands off the table as if it were hot. "Conspiracy?"

"Or you can wait outside," Garcia said.

Odesa gave a resigned sigh. "Nothing interesting ever happens to me. I may as well see what the inside of a prison cell looks like."

"You would not like it, child," Peppa said, completely serious. "I promise you that. But I, too, am ready to listen."

"Good," Quinn said. "You're both smart ladies. Maybe you can help us figure out our next move. An aeronautical engineer named Alejandro Placensia fled Cuba a few days ago with his wife and child. He landed in Florida, where he told my friend he had information vital to United States."

"Perhaps he was exaggerating his claim in order to gain asylum."

Quinn shook his head. "Maybe, but someone murdered him, his wife, and my friend, minutes after he made landfall. The cause of death makes us think Intelligence Directorate might be behind the killing. If that's the case, then this guy knew something important enough that the Cuban government wanted to shut him up."

Blanco waddled by, causing everyone at that row of tables to fall quiet. Tapping the rubber hose against his thigh was meant to intimidate, but Garcia found herself happy for the warning of the guard's approach.

"It gets worse," Garcia said, looking at Quinn. "Palmer sent a message after your arrest. According to him, an aeronautical engineer working at Cape Canaveral went missing, night before last."

Quinn brightened at the new development. Anything new meant a possible trail that he—or someone on the outside—could follow.

"Just disappeared, or foul play?" he asked.

Garcia shrugged. "Looks like a kidnapping. A neighbor was found shot to death yesterday morning. The scientist's name is Violeta Cruz. Local PD went to make contact with her parents. Their cars are in the driveway, but they've vanished as well."

Quinn nibbled on a cracker. "That can't be a coincidence." He gave a slow nod. Ronnie could tell he was chewing on more than the cracker. "Violeta Cruz . . . I'm guessing she's Cuban?"

"She was," Garcia said. "Her father brought them out in a raft when she was a kid. Palmer has some Bureau guys running down the rest of it now."

"I keep thinking about how Placensia's mother told you he smelled like chicken manure," Quinn said. "The need for an aeronautical engineer very likely equates to some kind of weapon."

"But what kind of weapon?" Ronnie asked. "Would we know if Cuba had nukes?"

"There is no doubt," Odesa said. "You would know because Fidel or Raúl would have used them against you by now."

"True enough," Quinn said.

A painfully loud buzzer sounded, signifying the end of visitation. Ronnie's heart sank, and she grabbed Quinn's hands, squeezing them harder. She was a kick-ass woman, but leaving Quinn in this place was worse than staying here herself. The guard in the raised booth tapped his microphone twice, as if everyone hadn't already heard the buzzer, and ordered the visitors to stay seated as the prisoners filed back out the way they'd come.

Quinn grabbed his rice sack and got to his feet. He leaned across the table as if to kiss Ronnie goodbye. "The Soviets had some short-range nukes in various places around the island in the 1960s. Check and see if any were near Santiago."

Chapter 29

Luckily, Peppa left early so Ignacio did not have to sneak out. Señor Alacrón had made it abundantly clear that he wanted to meet early and go over a few things regarding his report.

Ignacio nearly bounced off the walls during the ride over on the humpbacked camel bus. He found it even worse than he thought when he arrived. Not content to keep the report among the Committee for the Defense of the Revolution, Alacrón had decided to bump it up to the Department of State Security.

The CDR was terrifying enough, but even Ignacio knew Alacrón was basically incompetent. He certainly would have been easier for Señora Peppa to intimidate. SDE operatives were animals. Heartless, sadistic. Worse yet, they were extremely competent.

The man in Alacrón's cramped office looked like a professional athlete—trim and confident, with a focused eye that already knew the answers to every question he asked. He introduced himself as Morales, though Ignacio knew this was likely an alias. State Security men hardly ever used their real names. The old guard— well before Ignacio's time—had been trained by the Soviet KGB, and they, in turn, had trained their young protégés in the ways of assassination, dirty tricks, and the interrogation of young Cubans who might have something to hide.

Morales took Ignacio's mobile phone so he could not record their meeting, then motioned to the only other empty seat. Alacrón's office was covered in baseball memorabilia and photos. On Ignacio's last visit, he'd seen photographs of players like Jose Canseco and Rafael Palmeiro. But they were gone now that the State Security man was here. The only remaining photos were of Cubans who had not betrayed their country and defected to play for the *Yanqui* dollar—Antonio Pacheco, Orestes "Minnie" Miñoso, Omar Linares.

Alacrón sat with his wooden chair tipped back against the wall, fidgeting with a baseball that had been autographed by someone whose name Ignacio didn't recognize. He must not have stayed in Cuba, because Alacrón was about to rub the name off with his thumb. He, too, seemed to regret having the SDE man in attendance.

Morales asked only a few questions, scribbling notes in favor of looking up. Why had Ignacio noticed the American in the first place? Had he overheard some conversation? Who was the woman with the American? Ignacio stammered and coughed at every question. The American was up to no good. He had felt it. No, he had not heard much of a conversation, just a few negative things about the revolution. He could not remember what exactly, but they were capitalist ideas, he remembered that much. The woman? He had no idea who she was. None at all. No, absolutely not. But the man's nickname was Jericho—or something like that. He couldn't be sure. His leg bounced out of control, and he felt the overwhelming urge to scratch himself all over. He chewed on his lip, willing himself not to cry, and hoped the name wouldn't mean much in the long run. He'd not implicated Señora Peppa or her niece—who'd obviously been born in Cuba but was pretending this wasn't so. She would be in danger of imprisonment if this were discovered, so Ignacio guarded that little tidbit of information as if his testicles depended on it.

It was over less than half an hour after it began. Morales stared at him for a long time, unblinking. It was inhuman. How could a man go so long without blinking his eyes? Did he know something? Of course he did. State Security made it their business to know everything. Any minute someone would come in and slap Ignacio in handcuffs, and he would never see his mother again. Sweat pooled at the small of his back. He wished Alacrón would say something. He wished Morales would blink

Finally, Morales slid his notes across to Alacrón, who reached behind the desk. Ignacio's reward for betraying his mentor: a cellophane package of three stinking cigars. They were cheap—not nearly as good as the Cohibas Peppa used in her ceremonies—but Ignacio accepted them with a twitchy smile.

"I will see you next week," Alacrón said, pressing the cigars into his hand and shoving him out the door. There were three others in the hallway, shoulders stooped under the burden of terrible secrets.

"I thought he was going to piss his pants," Ignacio heard Alacrón say as the door shut behind him. He picked up his pace and was down the hall before he could hear if Morales answered.

* * *

Alacrón disliked the word *chivato*, since, as a CDR area supervisor, he was the chief of the rats. He preferred to call his informants "auxiliaries" or "civilian collaborators." No one liked a snitch, not even State Security. They were nothing more than a necessary evil. There was no getting around that. It was not Alacrón's fault that he'd not been able to pass the stringent background check to become a high-and-mighty SDE operative.

Actually, it was entirely his fault. Background interviews revealed that he'd slept with the daughter of an influential army general, a daughter of the Minister of the Interior, and the wife of the superintendent of his university—among other daughters and wives. Some might think these exploits heroic, even laudable— Alacrón certainly did—but the *apparatchiks* at State Security felt he "lacked certain vital decision-making skills" and possessed an "out-of-control libido."

Alacrón knew his chief sin was being caught. In the world of intelligence and counterintelligence, one had to be smart enough to remain discreet—and Alacrón had always been one to follow his manhood places where others would not go with a loaded shotgun. Out of control, indeed. What good was libido if one had to control it?

Morales surely looked down on him. He was sure of that. That's why it came as such a surprise when the DI interrogator pushed the stack of paperwork to him and asked if he minded dropping them off at his head-quarters offices. Morales offered to conduct the last three interviews and suggested Alacrón avail himself of the Ministry of the Interior canteen. They were serving beef today—something that was generally reserved for rich tourists and state elite. Killing a cow in Cuba garnered more prison time than murdering a human being.

Alacrón stuffed Ignacio's report into a manila envelope, tucked it under his arm, and set off to eat some beef. The SDE man would search his office for "capitalistic items of dubious origin" while he was gone. It was a crime warranting a lengthy term in prison. Morales would be looking for the autographed Jose Conseco photo, not so much so he could lock up Alacrón— though he certainly would do that, if only to keep him quiet. No, Morales too was a baseball fan. *Too bad for you, Señor Security Man.* Alacrón thought. *I have hidden all the photos where you will never find them, but I am happy to go and eat beef while you look for them.* He laughed to himself. Perhaps State Security were not so smart after all.

Alacrón loved visiting State Security headquarters— and not just for the food. The hallways smelled of furniture polish and success—none of the pervasive stink of mildew as in his CDR hovel. And they were air-conditioned, which made life so much more bearable. More important, SDE women were extremely attractive, and some of them had proven to be quite willing in the past. Alacrón could not shake the feeling that this was going to be his lucky day.

He bounded up the steps, stopping just long enough to show his identification card to the squinting guard and explain that he was on an errand for Morales. The guard looked back and forth from the identity card to Alacrón, going so far as to hold it up to compare it side by side with his face—as if anyone would sneak into the bastion of state security. Cubans walked on the other side of the street to avoid this place. Alacrón swallowed his words. It was better to be silent and eat a little beefsteak than cause trouble just to make a point.

The guard finally waved him through.

Alacrón took the files straight to Morales's office and gave them to his secretary, a black woman who was curvaceous and beautiful, and probably willing, but much too close to his age. He would not waste this trip on a woman over forty with so many younger willing, beautiful, curvaceous women walking these halls. He smiled at her anyway, taking a moment to flirt a little. She kept working at her computer as he spoke—probably trying to finish some important assignment for Morales. Curvaceous and dedicated. Anyway, Morales could have her.

Alacrón followed his nose down the polished marble stairs to the canteen, again showing his ID card and throwing around Morales's name as if it were the key to the kingdom. It worked, and the fat woman at the door let him in without so much as a second look. What did she care? From the looks of her, she did not often miss any beefsteak or fish pie, which was the other meal choice in the canteen. For the life of him, Alacrón could not figure out why anyone would eat fish pie when there was beef to be had.

He walked down the serving line with his tray, looking at the food items as if they were exhibits in a museum. The salad greens were not wilted, the carrots orange instead of bleached yellow, and there was even some of that miniature corn that he'd seen in movies. The beefsteak was covered in mushroom gravy, and so tender it fell apart when the young man in the hairnet slid a piece onto his plate. Alacrón thought he might shed tears of joy when the server offered to give him a second piece because the other one broke.

With more food on his plate than he usually ate in three days, he carried his tray across the large lunchroom, avoiding the tables of superspies who looked at him with disdain. He searched the chattering crowd until he saw the familiar faces of two interrogators who had been with CDR until they'd made the move to State Security. One of them, a man named Cordero, was more of a player than Alacrón. He just had enough sense to know which women to leave alone. He had the most fabulous mustache, much better than Alacrón's. Cordero waved him over, motioning to the empty chair across the long table. In fact, there were several empty chairs, a testament to the fact that no one really wanted to eat their lunch sitting next to these men and their filthy stories. They were Alacrón's kind of people, and he was shoveling down beef and gravy in no time, listening to the other men laugh and telling stories of his own.

". . . like a little girl," Alacrón said, sucking a bit of lettuce and salad dressing off his fork. "I was sure he was going to break down and piss himself at any moment."

"Pitiful," one of the men said. "The Cuban male today has been emasculated by the West."

"Don't forget Cuban women," Cordero chuckled.

"Yes." Alacrón smiled. "They too have been emasculated. Your wife is not half the man she used to be."

The men at the table roared.

Cordero pretended to be mad, giving Alacrón a stiff punch in the shoulder. "Is this pissy little man-girl in prison now?"

Alacrón shook his head. "He is apprenticed to the

Santeria priestess, Josefina Garcia." He fanned his face with the fork. "Aie, aie, aie, I am no believer, but that woman certainly has the ass of a goddess."

Cordero laughed. "So you will leave the boy alone, and he can make you a date with your Santeria priestess."

Alacrón spit a piece of beef gristle into his hand and set it on the corner of his plate so it didn't get lost in the gravy. "He is useless anyway. He gave me some information on an American who is up to no good, though I am not sure what. I don't think the boy does, either."

"Americans," Cordero said, smoothing his mustache with a thumb and forefinger. "They are always up to no good. What have you done with this one?"

"He is cooling his heels in jail," Alacrón said. "Until we can figure out what else there is to know."

"Or until you can make something up," a man beside Cordero said.

"If needed," Alacrón said. "But I doubt we'll have to. We have established he has an alias. I will go and visit him tomorrow."

"An alias?" Cordero said.

Alacrón scraped the last of his beefsteak into a single bite. "Jericho," he said. "If you can believe it. An odd name. Biblical, I think." Fork to mouth, he turned, noticing for the first time a bright young woman sitting at the end of his table. She was perhaps five feet tall, proportioned as a woman should be—or at least as Alacrón preferred them—and she was looking straight at him.

Chapter 30

Serafina drank down the last of her coconut water, thinking she would soon need all the energy she could muster, and dabbed her lips with a paper napkin. She tossed a smile to the babbling man with gravy on his mustache and slid down the bench as if she could not wait to hear more of his absurd jokes. The men at the table disgusted her, but they were outcasts among their own coworkers, so there had been plenty of seats at their table.

It was a fluke she was in the building at all, sent here to pick up a file for Colonel Mirabal. He'd not asked her to. He was not that sort of boss. He picked up his own files and bought his own cigars. She'd volunteered. She lived nearby, and anyway, the SDE canteen had fish pie on Thursday. And carrots. Her mother loved the fresh carrots. Serafina planned to take her some, wrapped in a bit of wax paper—then she'd heard the word.

Jericho.

Intelligence work was often as much about containment as gathering new information. This disgusting *jamonero*, Alacrón, had no idea that he had anything important.

Serafina's mind raced as she sat there surrounded by

these cackling hyenas. She needed to contact Colonel Mirabal, let him know there was a problem, a link to the Placensia job right here in Havana. Not yet. *Slow was fast*, the colonel often said. She must take her time and do this right. A hasty move would scare the prey. The colonel said that, too. First, she would get Alacrón alone, find out where he'd come upon the word. No one at the table could know she was interested in something or someone called Jericho.

General de la Guardia would quash any investigation, but no point in making more loose ends she would eventually have to clean up.

It took less than thirty seconds to learn that Alacrón fancied himself an expert on baseball. He argued statistics with the bald one beside him and the one across the table with a weedy mustache.

The men may have seen Serafina around, but they did not know who she was or what part of the Ministry of the Interior she worked for. She mentioned the latest roundup of "dirty heads"—Cuban professional ballplayers who had tried to defect so they could play for Major League teams in the U.S. Alacrón boasted of his prowess at bat, so she egged him on, going so far as to feel the muscles in his arm, cooing a little as if mightily impressed, all the while trying to keep from vomiting in her mouth. He probably could have played professionally, Alacrón said, had he not chosen a life of service to the revolution. Serafina laughed at that— inside anyway. Men like this did not *decide* on a life of service to the revolution. They latched on tight to the government tit because they had absolutely no idea how to do anything else. They were what was wrong with the revolution.

Why were there no more men like Colonel Mirabal? He was not so sickeningly easy to manipulate.

Serafina had always been fascinated by the game of baseball, she said—and the extremely macho men who played it. It took her all of four minutes to steer Alacrón into taking her someplace where they might talk in private during the remainder of their lunch break. Face flushing a deep red, he leaned in closer to his mustached friend, whispering urgently, nodding as if listening to directions. The man with the big mustache dug in his pocket and produced a key, which he passed on to Alacrón.

Serafina had thought at first he had an office here, but he led her instead to a storage closet off a deserted side hall on the other side of the building. Serafina smiled within herself when she saw all the offices along the hall were vacant, apparently used as storage. They were absolutely alone.

Alacrón was so excited he dropped the key twice while trying to unlock the door. That was a good sign. Victims focused on something else were much easier to deal with. He pushed the door opened with his hip, dragging her in with all the finesse of a rutting goat. Understandable, she supposed. Women who followed men into storage closets sought something other than romance.

Though it suited her purposes perfectly, Serafina was sickened by the little room. Boxes of mildewing files filled four rows of wooden shelving, older than the revolution. The place was probably long forgotten by everyone in the security service but for the select club of men who used it as their private bedding chamber.

Alacrón went straight to the back wall, brightening

when he found the mattress his friend must have told him about. He pulled it out from behind the shelving and lay it flat on the floor, leaving zero doubt about why he'd brought her to the room. He tried to pull her down immediately, but she pushed him away, playfully but forcefully, using the point of a knuckle against the top of his sternum. She smiled as if she did not mean to hurt him, but raked down enough to cause him to jump in pain.

His face fell, confused, until she began to unbutton her shirt. It was a dance women had been playing for millennia when dealing with brutish men, men who they detested, but from whom they needed something valuable.

She let the shirt hang open, pulling him to her for a quick kiss. He tasted of flour and grease. She pulled back, allowing him to touch her breast, if only to stop the kissing.

"I heard you mention Jericho," she said. "My grandmother read the Bible."

Alacrón tried to pull her toward the filthy mattress. She pushed him away again.

"It's hot," she said, tugging the tail of her shirt. "Let me take this off. Jericho is a place in the Bible, yes?"

He nodded, coughing when he spoke, his voice husky like he needed a drink of water. "I think so," he said. "In this case it is a nickname, I think."

She stopped just short of taking off the blouse. "Someone you arrested?"

He took her hand again, nodding.

"I have never made an arrest before," she said. "Was this man very dangerous?"

"He damaged two of my men," Alacrón said.

"Were you hurt?"

"No," Alacrón said. "I am much too smart for that."

He was lying. She could see it in his vacuous eyes. He was not the sort of man to put himself in danger.

"I wish I could have been there," Serafina said. "May I come with you on the next one?"

"I suppose you can come along," Alacrón said. "But it is very dangerous."

This man had no idea what danger was. Serafina gushed anyway. "What was it like? Did you have to shoot him? Where is this man? Can I see him?"

Alacrón gave a husky chuckle. He stepped out of his trousers, hopping on one foot. "Mr. Jim Shield is not much to look at. At least not now."

"But I can see him," Serafina said, making a mental note of the name. She stepped closer to toy with the hair on Alacrón's chest.

He draped the slacks over a box, oblivious to all the dust. "I suppose that would be possible," he said. "I'll work it out with the jail."

"Which jail?" Serafina asked coyly, reaching up to the collar of her open blouse.

"Valle Grande," he said. Taking her by the hand again. "Now come, let us discuss something more interesting than dangerous traitors."

Serafina slipped the tiny dagger from the plastic sheath in her collar. Made of stainless steel and razor sharp, it was not much larger than the arrowheads Colonel Mirabal used for hunting. He had, in fact, designed this highly concealable weapon. She pinched it between her thumb and forefinger, cupping it behind her palm to keep it out of sight. It hardly mattered. At this point, Alacrón would not have noticed a dead dog in the middle of the mattress.

Careful to keep the sharp edge away from her skin, she stepped forward, following Alacrón to the mattress. Naked from the waist down, it was an easy matter to find a convenient target. She stabbed him five times before he even knew what she was doing, sticking the steel into the blood-rich area where his thigh met his groin. He pushed away in pain, drawing back as if to slap her. He opened his mouth to scream, but the poison on the blade was too quick. Ironically, it was a shellfish toxin developed by the American CIA in one of their many plots to try to assassinate Fidel Castro—back in the days of the Kennedy administration.

Serafina gave the croaking man a shove, pushing him over so he landed on the mattress, his pale legs hanging off, splaying obscenely onto the chipped tile floor.

"*Jericho*," Serafina said, turning the word over on her tongue as she punched Mirabal's number into her mobile phone. She left her blouse unbuttoned, finding it exhilarating to talk to him while only half dressed, though he would never know.

"Colonel," she said as soon as he picked up. "There is a situation that requires immediate attention."

Chapter 31

Though Joaquin Mirabal was employed by the *Dirección de Inteligencia*, he was not, in the strictest sense of the term, an intelligence officer. More akin to what the American CIA called the Special Activities Division, he engaged in the paramilitary side of the equation—what the Russians, and now his own government, called "active measures."

He was a hunter.

This was one of the rare moments he was not out hunting. He'd been enjoying a game of cribbage with his wife and nine-year-old son when Serafina called. He took the call in his trophy room, as he did all calls from work, sinking into a leather swivel chair. Rich cherry paneling threw the room into shadows. An oscillating fan fluttered the papers on a simple mahogany desk, swirling the odors of cigar smoke and naptha, used to preserve the animal mounts. A Purdey double rifle in 450/400 nitro express hung above the mantel across the room, below an angry-looking Cape buffalo mount. The rifle—a gift from a grateful Angolan warlord—was probably taken off some unfortunate white hunter. Wherever the gun came from, it was worth as much as most Cubans could hope to earn in a lifetime. There were many other mounts as well—kudu, springbok,

Thomson's gazelle, a zebra, a wildebeest—each with a tale of a hunt to go with it—but the Cape buffalo was his prize. It was *the* bull, the one that had given him the scar on his face—and a certain clarity that would stay with him for the rest of his life. It had very nearly stomped him to death. Looking at it helped him focus—and he looked at it often when he was home.

Serafina's call was brief. Like anyone he allowed on his team would, she'd called with a possible solution to the problem. He made a few suggestions and left the details to her.

He tossed the mobile on the desk when he was done, leaning back in the chair with his hands behind his head. De la Guardia would need to be informed, but Mirabal decided to wait a few moments and allow time for Serafina to implement her plan. This way he could tell the general everything in a single call, obviating the need to talk to the vile little man any more than necessary.

Paulo, his son, poked his head through the study door. He had his mother's dark skin and curly hair, as well as her broad smile.

Mirabal gave a flick of his hand, motioning for him to come in. He'd never been a rough disciplinarian, but the boy had always been a little flinchy. Perhaps, Mirabal thought, he could sense what his father did for a living.

Paulo walked to the desk, mouth opening in awe as it always did when he came into the study. The boy sidled up next to Mirabal and looped his arm over his neck. It was the most natural gesture in the world, and Mirabal wondered how long it would be before Paulo thought such actions unmanly. All too soon, Mirabal thought, hugging his son close.

"Tell me again about the old Dagga boy, Papa," Paulo said, nodding his curly head and using the term for an old bachelor Cape buffalo bull. *Dagga* meant "mud" in Swahili—or sometimes "crazy." Both were fitting descriptions of the old bulls.

"Again?" Mirabal said. "You have heard that story a thousand times."

"A thousand and one, if you please," Paulo said, sober, contemplative. Yes, he was very much like his mother.

"This is the story of how I killed the bull that killed my best friend—and that very nearly killed me." Joaquin Mirabal began the tale as he always did, raising his crooked brow to highlight the white scar than ran diagonally from his forehead and across his nose to end at the corner of his chin. "I learned much of what I know of hunting from my good friend Kondo. He was the finest tracker I have ever seen—in Africa or anywhere. He spotted the spoor belonging to the bull that would kill him early in the morning. We tracked it through the mopane thickets all that day—"

"Papa," Paulo said. "Do you think Kondo knew he was going to die?"

Mirabal touched his son tenderly on the shoulder. "We rarely know which bull will get us," he said.

"But Kondo was smart," Paulo said. "He might have known."

"Perhaps," Mirabal said, smiling. Nine-year-olds had to be the most difficult audiences on earth.

Paulo nodded, absolutely certain of his logic. "I think he knew which bull would get him."

"Perhaps," Mirabal said again. "Do you want to hear the story or not?"

"Please," Paulo said.

"The day was dangerously hot," Mirabal continued. "We heard the roar of lions in the brush, the chiding of baboons, even the periodic cough of a leopard, but no Dagga boys. I had run completely out of water by the time I saw black ears flicking through the tall grass. Dagga boys are old and mean and often alone, but this one was with a small herd of six other bulls." Mirabal nodded to the mounted head on his wall, remembering the heat on his neck, the fluttering tick of grasshoppers as they flew up in his path. "This one was the best of the lot, with a thick boss and sharp horns that shone black as the devil's eyes. None of the bulls had seen us, and it seemed that there was no wind—"

"But there is always wind," Paulo said, reciting the story by heart.

Mirabal smiled. "But there is always wind," he repeated. "The bulls caught our scent immediately. Instead of running away, they ducked their massive heads and charged straight for us. The three other men with us fled—"

"Like dickey birds," Paulo said.

Mirabal nodded, even now picturing, *smelling* the scene. "My dear friend Kondo, a man of much courage, was just two meters to my right when the bull hit him, hooking him in the belly and throwing him high into the air. I put a bullet through the beast's lungs, but—"

Paulo shook his head, brown eyes glistening, wide. "But the damage was done. Poor Kondo was dead."

"He was a good man, Kondo." Mirabal gave a solemn nod but kept talking, his voice building toward a crescendo with each word. "The bull dropped to both knees, but he sprang back to his feet and turned toward me as the rest of the herd vanished into the bush. I shot him again, and again he fell, this time giving his death bellow."

Paulo trembled now. He always grew emotional at this point in the story.

Mirabal drew him closer for support. "I loaded my rifle with two fresh rounds of ammunition and went to check on Kondo, turning my back on the dead bull—"

Paulo gasped, as though hearing the story for the very first time. "But the bull was not dead!"

"He was not." Mirabal smiled, patting his little boy on the head. "The old Dagga boy sprang to his feet when I was only two meters away. I shot again, hitting him in the center of his chest, but not before he ran straight over me, one of his hooves stomping directly on my face. His lifeless body skidded to a heap, close enough for me to reach out and touch."

"Seventy-five stitches." Paulo traced the jagged scar with his finger. "Lucky you reloaded your rifle."

"That is true," Mirabal said. "There was some luck involved. But a hunter must never underestimate his prey—especially if that prey is capable of killing him."

Mirabal's wife coughed in the doorway, eyes narrow, head cocked to the side.

The colonel gave his boy's shoulder a firm squeeze. "Your mother does not approve of so much talk of death. Perhaps she is right. We should wait until you are nine."

"But I am nine, Papa!"

"You are?" Mirabal shrugged at his exasperated wife. "I suppose we are okay then."

The mobile on his desk buzzed again, and the colonel shooed his son out of the trophy room with a quick kiss to the top of his head. It was Serafina, letting him know the team was ready to move. Again, the call was short. As distasteful as it was, he now needed to pass the information to General de la Guardia.

This Jericho fellow was in Cuba, so he must know something of the incident with Placensia. He needed to be contained, dealt with, before things got completely out of hand. As a hunter, Mirabal knew that not all problems could be hunted down and killed—but most of them could.

Chapter 32

It took some time, but Auntie Peppa found an attorney willing to look at Quinn's case. Señor Guzman's father had assisted her in her previous issues with the government, and she trusted him completely. Unfortunately, the father had recently passed away, leaving the legal practice to his son, who Peppa admitted she did not know at all. Still, Guzman the younger was all they had, and according to the sign in the dusty lobby of his office, he specialized in lost causes. Peppa reasoned, all too seriously, that if one was in jail in Cuba for anything at all, it was most definitely a lost cause. Ronnie paid Guzman a five-hundred-dollar retainer—the rate for representing American lost causes, apparently.

He spoke English and seemed competent enough, if a little rumpled. Most important, he'd agreed to talk to the police and interview Quinn—who he thought was an American real estate agent, James Shield.

Garcia felt as if she might crawl out of her skin by the time the taxi dropped her and Peppa in the almost vacant parking lot of Valle Grande Prison for the second time. Drops of rain dotted the gray asphalt.

Guzman hustled out of the door as they walked up. He was a short man, evidently accustomed to rich food from the size of his girth. His wrinkled suit was hopelessly stained, and he seemed to have a difficult time keeping his shirt tucked in. He shook his head when Ronnie tried to speak with him, motioning back toward the parking lot. His face was red, as if he'd been running. Sweat beaded under his baggy eyes.

"Follow me," he snapped, moving faster than his bulk suggested he could. "It is better that you don't go near that place."

"But what about my friend?" Ronnie said.

"Your friend is the very reason you should not go in there."

Ronnie glanced at her auntie. "What?"

"Señor Jim Shield is not someone with whom you want to associate," Guzman said. "He is a drowning man who will drag you down with him." The attorney stuffed a wad of sweaty bills into Garcia's hand. "I will not charge you for my time spent thus far. I do not want his name or anyone connected with him written in my ledgers. In fact, you should step away from me at once."

Peppa moved closer, crowding the startled Guzman against his dented car. "Tell us what has happened, you spineless cockroach."

He shot a furtive look over his shoulder at the jail doors. "Your friend has been taken."

"Taken?" Ronnie said. "Taken where?"

"This—this I do not know," he stammered. "He could be in any of a hundred different secret facilities by now. All I know is that they came and got him."

Garcia grit her teeth. "Who are *they*?"

The lawyer gave a little shiver. "If you absolutely must know, then go in and ask for Señor Shield by name. You will find out for yourselves, because they will probably arrest you and take you to the same place. Whatever you do, leave me out of it."

Ronnie glowered, ready to knock the little creep's head down between his shoulders. "Who. Took. Him?"

"SDE," he hissed under his breath. "State Security." He turned to Peppa, sneering a little, gaining back a measure of courage. "You remember them, don't you? I read my father's file on you—"

Peppa spat in his face, her lips trembling.

Guzman wiped it away and took a deep breath. "Please," he said. "Let us sever this relationship once and for all. I will thank you not to contact me again. If you choose to do so, I will be forced to report you to the CDR." He got into his dented car without another word and drove away, looking over his shoulder as if he feared the women might run after him.

Peppa put her arm around Garcia, each woman providing support for the other. Peppa groaned, deep within her body.

"This son of a whore causes me to rethink my stance on curses," she said.

The coarse cloth of the hood made it difficult for Quinn to breathe and impossible for him to get his bearings. Blanco had come to the cellblock to get him in the early afternoon, saying he had a visitor. Jorge Santana looked down from his bunk and shook his head as a warning, but there was nothing Quinn could do but comply. The fat guard had shoved him down the hall, past the trustee's cell to the infirmary, where he'd been met by a swift blow to the side of his head as soon as he walked through the door. Hands cuffed behind his back, he'd been unable to catch himself when he fell. He vaguely remembered the back of a wooden chair coming up to meet his face, a muffled female voice—and then nothing.

When he came to, he was hooded and in a swaying vehicle. He thought of trying to keep track of turns and stops, but with no starting reference point, it would do him little good.

The vehicle squeaked to a stop about a half hour from the time he woke up. A sliding door opened, making him think he was in the back of a van—though that detail didn't help, either. Gulls cried overhead, and he could hear the lap of water against something hollow. Judging from the smell of low tide, it was the hull of a boat.

The air was heavy with the approaching storm, and the slosh of choppy waves was impossible to miss. They'd driven too far to be at Marina Hemingway. The wind was coming from his left as he faced the ocean, so it was possible that they were now on the south side of the island.

A hand prodded him forward, much too gently to be Blanco. Quinn heard the clomp of wood, probably a boarding plank, and then felt the sway of a boat beneath him.

"Hey, fellas," Quinn said, shuffling his feet to keep from tripping on the swaying deck. He hoped to engage his captors, as a terrified tourist might try to do. "Can someone tell me where we're going?"

A youthful male voice that sounded pleasant enough started to speak, but a female voice shushed him with a flurry of Spanish.

Quinn heard the usual zip of dock lines casting off and the familiar grumble of revving engines. He felt the boat begin to move. Two minutes later, the wind freshened and the boat began to heave. Quinn imagined that they'd rounded a breakwater and were now in the open ocean. But why? Where could they be taking him?

The blind uncertainty of the hood began to do its work. Handcuffed and heading out to sea, Quinn felt worry rise in his chest. Were they taking him out to kill him? Were Jacques and Emiko compromised? Had Odesa talked? If so, then Ronnie and Peppa were in grave danger of arrest—maybe in custody already. People did drastic things when coerced—and the Cuban Intelligence were experts at coercion.

Quinn had performed enough interrogations himself to know they would keep everyone separated. No, Odesa would not have talked yet. It would take them a long time to break her. Quinn braced himself against a bulkhead, turning his head in the dark hood and working to slow his breath. She would eventually break—everyone did. Even him.

Chapter 33

Wind thrashed the palm crowns in front of the Hotel Sevilla, threatening to rip the trees out of the earth at any moment. The face of the hurricane loomed just offshore now, only a few hours out according to the radio, and the leader of the people-to-people tour had left five messages with the front desk, warning Garcia to get off the island.

Thibodaux and Miyagi sat in the lobby, watching the wind toss garbage around in the trees outside the windows. Ronnie was in a wicker chair across from them, legs crossed, nervously bouncing her knee. She could handle danger to herself, but danger to Quinn made her want to pull her hair out. It had started to rain, and the fat letch from the front desk stood at the door, taking a perverse pleasure in watching people lose their umbrellas to the hurricane winds. Ronnie was severely tempted to go find an umbrella and drive it through the idiot's ear.

Jacques, who had some experience with Cuban intelligence from his time stationed at Guantanamo, bore out Peppa's warning that there were countless secret detention facilities and black sites around the island.

"Sons of bitches coulda taken Chair Force to any one of them," he said.

"We can't just give up," Ronnie said, choking back tears of frustration.

The big Cajun grimaced, incredulous. The cable-like tendons on his thick neck flexed as he clenched his jaw. He turned a little so he could look directly at Ronnie with his good eye. "Who said a thing about givin' up, *cher*? I plan to find those two goons who were following y'all at the marina and have a little laying-on of hands with them. Crawl back up the rope, so to speak. They'll know something."

Miyagi gave a contemplative nod. She too was upset by Quinn's sudden disappearance, but she manifested her worry with a quiet simmer instead of a rolling boil. When the time came, she would be more than happy to cut someone's heart out—quite literally—if it meant saving her friend, or even finding out where he was.

"I wonder what changed in his circumstances," she said, softly, in deep thought. "How he was compromised . . ."

"There's a good chance it was my *lingua larga* sister," Ronnie whispered.

"You really think that?" Thibodaux said, shaking his head.

"Probably not," Ronnie admitted. "But she's a place to start. Anyway, I have to do something. You two follow at a distance, and I'll find out what she knows. If nothing else, there's a good chance the goons will come by the marina to talk to her at some point. You can have your little talk with them then."

Less than ten miles to the east, near the seaside resort of Villa Islazul, a caretaker dragged the last of the plastic beach furniture into the concrete storage building at the far end of the property. His back to the sea, he felt a creeping tickle on his neck and turned to find the body of a young man bobbing facedown in the surf, some twenty meters away. The caretaker trotted over, knowing before he even turned the body over that he would find a bullet hole in the forehead. The resort was located at the end of a curving road, on a semi-secluded bay. The tourists did not know it, but because of the land formation, the sea often washed bodies ashore on this spot—bodies that someone had dumped into the ocean on the outskirts of Havana. The caretaker looked up and down the beach, but it was deserted, the hurricane having driven everyone either inside or off the island. He dragged the body out of the water and checked the pockets for identification—and anything of value. *La lucha,* getting by in life, meant using the things that fate placed before you.

There was no money, but a plastic identity card said the young man was Ignacio Baca. He looked very sad, the caretaker thought, as someone might who knew he was about to receive a bullet in the forehead. He would call the police since there was no money, but before he could turn to walk to the office, the surf spit a second body onto the shore. The caretaker groaned. He hoped this was the last one. Far from a young man, he was in no shape to be dragging bloated corpses out of the ocean all evening long. The second man, this one shot in the back of the head, had no money or identification, but it would probably be easy for the police to identify him. His ears were badly damaged from fighting. Probably some kind of boxer, the caretaker thought.

Chapter 34

The boat sailed for well over an hour, engine lugging, rolling in the heavy swells. The wind came from the left for the entire trip, and with the hurricane coming in from the east, Quinn felt reasonably sure they were heading south, away from the main island. He imagined a map of Cuba in his head and saw the Isle of Youth across the Gulf of Batabanó. Formerly the Isle of Pines, Castro had spent time there in the monstrous Presidio Modelo. After the revolution, El Comandante had ordered many surviving Batista soldiers incarcerated in the awful prison and built boarding schools on the island to lure young people from other socialist countries around the world, particularly those in Africa.

The prison was long since closed, but the facilities still stood, making Quinn think Presidio Modelo, or someplace near it, was a likely destination.

Dragged off the boat as soon as they reached the docks, Quinn found himself shoved into the back of another van. This time, the ride took less than twenty minutes. Blind and confused, it seemed interminable to Quinn. That was exactly the point of the hood. He couldn't help but think of his little girl, of Ronnie, and even his ex-wife, Kim. None of them deserved the worry he put them through on a near-daily basis.

His world now was nothing but rough hands and a series of sounds—made more grating against his nerves by the fact that they were his main form of stimulus. Gears grinding—the vehicle stopped. Footsteps slapping on pavement, and the van door slid open. No one spoke, but hands grabbed him and pulled him outside. Spits of rain hit his arms. Treetops swished in a humid wind as if they were in the middle of a clearing, away from the sea where the wind from the storm would have been more direct. A heavy door opened, and Quinn stepped gingerly into nothingness, barely catching himself as he made his way down steep stairs. There were hollow echoes when the stairs leveled out. Then Quinn was pushed against a wall, a strong hand on his shoulder shoving him down on a bench, skinning his knuckles on hands cuffed behind him.

Footsteps grew quieter as someone—probably a few someones—walked away, but the telltale growls and gurgles of a stomach told Quinn someone had been left to guard him.

Quinn thought it was probably late evening, but he couldn't be sure. He couldn't use hunger as a timer. Stress suppressed the appetite. He was exhausted—another effect of imprisonment—and kept nodding off. Each time his chin sagged, loud music blared from a speaker in front of him. It was close enough for him to feel the bass woofers, thumping his chest with every beat.

It wasn't long before the footsteps came back down the hallway. Rough hands hauled him to his feet by the arms and dragged him down the hall, this time without giving him time to get his feet underneath him.

This was no longer a transport. The interrogation had begun. The echoes widened out, probably an effect of leaving a relatively narrow hall for a wider room. His flimsy prison uniform was cut and ripped away, leaving him naked but for the hood as he was pushed backward into a cold metal chair. Metal leg irons clanged at his feet. Heavy straps secured his wrists to the chair's arm.

Quinn willed himself to sit completely still, straining to hear any kind of clue for what would happen next. He didn't have to wait long.

Metal scraped against the concrete floor as something was dragged closer from across the room. A clammy hand touched his wrist, as if examining it, then a constriction bandage was wrapped around his upper arm. A moment later, he felt the sting of a needle and then the lingering sensation of a catheter as someone started an IV line.

An instant later, the hood was yanked from his head.

Chapter 35

Quinn blinked rapidly to clear his vision, turning his head back and forth to take in as much information as he could before the hood was replaced. He'd been through SERE School—Survival, Escape, Resistance, and Evasion—and he knew that the hoods often went back on as soon as they came off in an effort to disorient the prisoner. There was no need for that. He was as disoriented as he'd ever been in his life.

Compared to Valle Grande Prison, this place was like a hospital—a third-world hospital, but still a hospital. The floors and walls were sealed concrete that gleamed like a freshly waxed airplane hangar under powerful incandescent lights. The wall to Quinn's right was blank, nothing but concrete. When he craned his neck around he could just see a door in the wall behind him, some thirty feet away. A long mirror—obviously an observation window—took up fifteen feet of the wall directly in front of him. To the left, he could see a toilet through a half-open door. Just to the left of the door was a cot, neatly made, with a blanket folded on a green military footlocker.

A balding man with a small, well-groomed mustache that ended at the corners of a pinched mouth moved between Quinn and a long metal table, five or six feet away. His movements were precise and fluid, his long white lab coat flowing behind him like a cape and trailing a strong, fruity cologne in the wake of every turn.

Quinn kicked against the chains, acting appropriately terrified—like a private citizen stripped and chained to a chair would act. The table next to him contained bone saws, scalpels, tooth pliers, and even an elastrator banding device used to castrate cattle, so acting terrified wasn't exactly a big leap. A pointed rock pick, like the one that had been buried in Placencia's mouth, rounded out the collection. Under normal circumstances Quinn would have been happy to see that kind of clue—but not now.

"Has anyone heard back from my embassy?" he asked, adding a shaky chirp to his voice.

The bald man in the lab coat—Quinn began to think of him as "Doc"—ignored him, continuing to putter around the steel table. He filled two syringes from two separate amber bottles, humming softly to himself as he worked. Quinn felt as if he were an insect pinned to a piece of Styrofoam under the lights of a biology lab. The vials were labeled, but sudden exposure to the light after the hours of darkness in the hood caused Quinn's eyes to water and blur, making it impossible for him to read.

A clear liquid, probably saline, dripped from a clear plastic bag hanging from a rack above his chair, feeding the line in his vein. Quinn blinked his eyes to clear them, fighting the panic that rose in his belly.

Quinn envisioned himself planting the rock pick in the creepy Doc's ear.

"Please," he whispered, making certain he didn't sound as menacing as he wanted to. "Can I have something to drink?"

He was under no mistaken notion that Doc was going to run and grab him a Coke, but he wanted to check the man's mood—and his humanity. This guy appeared to have none.

He cocked his balding head and regarded Quinn for a long moment, holding a syringe in either hand. At length, he returned to his work and went on with his humming. Pig eyes, Quinn thought. I'm not even human to him.

Doc searched the table of medieval torture devices until he found a small plastic T valve. It allowed medical personnel to push two kinds of liquid into an IV line in rapid succession. Quinn recognized it from his days as a Combat Rescue Officer with Air Force Special Operations.

Chin pressed to his chest, Quinn resumed his combat breathing while he watched Doc attach the valve to a port in the IV line near Quinn's arm. He screwed a syringe to each port on the valve.

"Maybe you don't speak English," Quinn said, his breath erratic now in spite of his training. He needed to be thought of as something other than a lab rat to this man. In truth, the incessant humming grated against his nerves like sandpaper, and he hoped a little conversation might get him to stop. "Sorry. I don't speak Spanish. Guess I should have learned it before I came to Cuba on vacation."

Doc scoffed at this and turned back to do something on the table. Quinn kept babbling, but he used the moment of privacy to try and dislodge the syringes. It was no use. His ankles were secured to the chair with leg irons, giving him a few inches of play in the chain, but the heavy rubberized straps, like those used to secure mental patients, held his wrists and upper arms in place. He could flex his hands and fingers, but just barely.

"I know some Spanish," Quinn said. "But nothing very useful under the circumstances. Where's the bathroom, I'll have a beer. You know, stuff like tha—"

Doc wheeled on him now. "I speak English well enough, Mr. Shield. Do you suppose you are on an island populated by fools?"

"No—I mean, not at all," Quinn said. At least the guy was asking questions now—and not humming.

"Why are you in Cuba?"

"Vacation," Quinn said.

"Lie!" the man spat. "You arrived just before the hurricane. No one comes to Cuba in advance of a major storm."

"It changed course," Quinn said, incredulous. "It was supposed to miss us. Everyone knows that."

Doc stared at him. For the first time, Quinn's vision cleared enough to see that the man wore a flesh-tone earpiece. The pauses in his speech made more sense now. Someone on the other side of the two-way glass was feeding him questions to ask.

He gave an almost imperceptible nod. "What is Jericho?"

Quinn remained motionless, repeating his own name as if it was a new word to him. "Jericho?"

Doc closed his eyes, listening to his earpiece. "How do you know a man named Theodore Schoonover?"

"Ted Schoonover?" Quinn said, doing his best to give a passive shrug while chained to the chair. "He's in real estate. I bought a house from him in Florida a few weeks ago."

"And Alejandro Placensia?"

Quinn shook his head. "No idea."

The fact that this guy was laying all his cards on the table was a bad sign. Whoever was behind the glass didn't care what Quinn knew about them. They didn't plan to let him leave. The cold truth of it chased away his panic. The unknown was frightening. With knowledge, Quinn found new focus.

"Placensio, is it?" Quinn didn't have to work very hard to affect a hoarse throat. He broke into a coughing fit, whispering through the spasms and making Doc think he was missing some juicy intel. The man stepped closer, leaning in to pick up what was being said, getting just close enough that Quinn was able to kick out with his foot and catch the man on the shin, knocking his feet out from under him.

Physics did the rest. Doc fell forward, allowing Quinn to sink his teeth into one of the bald man's ears. Holding Doc in his lap with nothing but his teeth, he was able to reach up with his fingers to the ink pens the man kept his shirt pocket. Quinn slipped his prize under his palm as Doc screamed in pain and surprise, clutching what was left of his ear and cursing in his native tongue. Glowering over Quinn, he regained enough of his composure to stop screaming. He hit Quinn in the face with a fist, but there was little power in the blow. Judging from the way he winced, it hurt Doc much more than Quinn's jaw.

"I am going to enjoy this, Señor Jim Shield," Doc fumed.

Quinn spit the bloody ear at the man, blood running down his chin as he nodded to the IV. "Shouldn't you give me the truth serum before you ask me any questions?"

The bald man scoffed, hand to the side of his head. He spoke through clenched teeth. "Oh, señor." He smiled now, putting his hands on the syringes. "This is not truth serum. I am afraid you operate under a mistaken understanding of the situation. I was merely curious. This is not an interrogation. This is your execution."

Chapter 36

Peppa had not seen Ignacio since he'd confessed, ruining one of her best scarves with his tears and snot. Had she not read the cards and thrown the cowrie shells, she might have thought he'd run off to sulk—but the shells did not lie. Something bad had happened. She did not know what, but the idea that he'd been arrested filled her heart with dread. He was too weak. He would not survive an hour in such a place. Peppa knew all too well.

Still, Ignacio had made his own bed, blackmail or not, and Peppa had to focus on other things—principally, keeping her favorite niece out of prison. Neither the cards nor shells nor a fat cigar blown over the blood of a freshly killed rooster were enough for her to divine where Veronica's friend was. She knew his name was Jericho Quinn, but she dared not even think the words, let alone say them out loud. Her months in the Villa had convinced her that the government could pry most anything from her brain.

Though no ceremony told her where Quinn was being held, they did inspire her to start working her phone. She began by calling every one of her female friends, acquaintances, and past clients who had any connection to the police or intelligence apparatus, either personally or through their children. She talked to the women as a spiritual leader and friend, checking on their welfare and the welfare of their children in advance of the hurricane. Even patriotic mothers who were devoted to the revolutionary cause worried about their children. Though, Peppa noted, as time under Castro's yoke dragged on, it had become more and more possible for mothers to be fiercely loyal to Cuba but spitting angry at the regime—at least as angry as they were at the United States for all the painful sanctions.

It took her seventeen calls to find something worthwhile. This mother was concerned because her son who was in the army had to ship out that very afternoon for Isle de la Juventud along with several of his friends, directly into the path of the storm.

"Can you imagine?" the woman said. "Who will look after me? Whatever there is on that cursed island can look after itself. Do you agree, Señora Peppa?"

"Hmm," Peppa said.

"There is not a single thing on that island worth guarding," the woman added.

Peppa warned the woman that it was probably safer to keep such thoughts to herself.

"Of course you are right, dear Peppa," the woman said. Her voice grew quieter, as if someone had walked into the room and she did not want them to hear. "I should not tell you this, but my son is very important."

"Hmm," Peppa said again. "If they sent an important soldier to the Isle of Youth, then perhaps there is something very important going on there."

"Perhaps," the woman said. "I am not supposed to say who he works for." She was whispering again. "But I can tell you this much. It is not the army."

"You are a lucky woman," Peppa said, changing the subject before the woman decided she had to confess the conversation to her son. "Please be careful during the storm. Have you got candles and water?"

"You are so kind to look after me . . ."

Peppa ended the call as the wind picked up outside, rattling the wooden shutters. She tried to call Veronica, but got no answer. This information was not something she wanted to leave in a voicemail.

She checked her watch and flipped through her address book until she found the number for Odesa Dombrovski. Odesa answered on the second ring.

"Child," Peppa said. "Your sister is coming to see you. You must give her a message."

"Okay," Odesa said warily.

Both women knew there was a high likelihood that the line was tapped. It couldn't be helped, but Peppa spoke in broad terms.

"Your sister will explain the problem," she said. "Her friend is not where we left him—"

Odesa gasped. "Really? Where—"

"Your sister will explain," Peppa said. She said the next in quick English, hopefully making it a little more difficult for any listener. "Ithinkhemayhavegonetothe-islandofyouth."

There was silence on the line.

"Do you understand," Peppa asked, still in English.

"I think so," Odesa said. "I will pass on the message. Should I help?"

"I do not know," Peppa said. She knew Odesa would ask the question, and she dreaded having to answer it. "I have asked Oyá this."

"What do the shells say?"

"You must choose your own path," Peppa said. "I am not certain if you would survive—"

There was loud crackling on the line. "You cut out, auntie," Odesa said. "Did you say I would not survive?"

"Again, child, I do not know," Peppa said. "What I do know is—"

A rash of static filled the line, followed by a loud pop and nothing but dead air.

Peppa set the phone on her table next to the bloody machete and tried to imagine what Veronica was going to do when Odesa gave her the message.

Huge raindrops bounced off the pavement, giving the impression of as much water going up as was coming down. What little traffic there was had to slow to a crawl. Waves crashed into the Malecón, shooting skyward like so many geysers all along the seawall. The young man driving Garcia to Marina Hemingway turned off the main road to hunt a faster route.

"Are you certain you want to go to the marina?" the cabbie said, craning his head around to look over a skinny shoulder. He was a kid really, with a little flap of hair across his forehead like someone from a grunge band. "The sea is a monster tonight."

Garcia smiled. "Sorry," she said. "I have to meet someone." She held her breath, suddenly grateful for the good windshield-wiper blades on her Impala back in the U.S. The ones on this cab looked as if they'd been carved out of old pieces of tire—and they did about as much good.

She fought the urge to look over her shoulder. Jacques

and Miyagi were somewhere behind her in another cab. She'd tried to send a text, but cell service was down—not unexpected, given the storm now slamming the island and the sketchy state of Cuban cell service even when the weather was bluebird clear.

The cabbie muttered something under his breath. Though Garcia could hardly see past the rivulets of water on the windshield and the reflection of oncoming headlights, the kid's white knuckles on the giant vintage steering wheel were impossible to miss.

"I need you to wait five minutes when we get to the marina," she said.

He shot her an "are you crazy?" look in the rearview mirror. His shoulders went up and down as he sighed, no doubt coming up with an excuse. He wanted to drop this insane *Yuma* woman as quickly as possible so he could get out of the storm. Ronnie considered forcing him out and stealing his car. He probably would have been relieved.

In the end, the decision was made for her when the cabbie took a corner too quickly and hydroplaned into a curb. There was a sickening pop like the report of a distant gun as the front tire blew. The cabbie cursed in earnest now, no longer bothering to mutter under his breath. He didn't care if Garcia knew what he thought of her.

She tried to call Thibodaux again while the cabbie got out to check the tire. Still no signal. They were supposed to be somewhere behind her, if things were going as planned—which they never did. Stuffing the phone into the pocket of her jeans in a hopeless attempt to keep it dry, she bailed out into the rain, careful to exit on the curbside to avoid being smeared across some other blind driver's windshield like a drenched bug. It was like stepping in front of a firehose. Rain, surprisingly cool considering the warm air, pelted every inch of exposed skin, stinging like BBs.

Garcia faced the oncoming traffic, standing just close enough to the road that she hoped Jacques or Miyagi would see her. Several cars careened by, throwing up rooster tails of spray, but none of them slowed. Garcia gave up after three minutes, and turned to see if she could give the cabbie a hand with the tire.

She was surprised to find him still standing by the right front fender, hands in his pockets, staring down at the damaged tire.

"Let me guess," she yelled over the moaning wind and rain. "You don't have a spare?"

The cabbie nodded. He seemed calmer now, as if the rain had cooled his temper. "I have a spare," he said. "It is bald, but it even has a little air."

"That's a relief," Garcia said. "I'll help you put in on."

Water ran from the flap of hair over the kid's face as he hung his head. "I have a spare, but I have no jack."

"That's just great," Garcia said, kicking a divot in the roadside mud.

"I had one," the kid said. "But it was stolen. My uncle always tells me I will miss the old donkey cart he once used as a taxi. Donkeys do not have flat tires . . . though sometimes they are afraid of the lightning . . ."

An old pickup truck splashed past the taxi, wisely pulling over in front of it so as not to bear the brunt of any accident if someone ran off the road coming around the bend.

Ronnie insanely hoped that the old guy who stopped to help might want to hurry and get out of the rain as bad as she did. No such luck. The two men just stood there talking. The kid thought the tire could be repaired, but the old man assured him it would have to be replaced.

Garcia could take it no longer. "How far is it to Marina Hemingway?"

"Three miles," the old man said, squatting to run a hand over the damaged tire.

"I'll walk then," she said.

Both men looked up at that. "In this?"

"I have an important appointment," she said. She pointed to the right. Then looked at the older man. "Unless you want to give me a ride. I can pay."

He shook his head and pointed into the darkness to their left. "I am almost home. My wife will be worried."

Ronnie bowed her head and began to walk west, stinging rain pushing against her back and the thought of doing something to find Quinn pulling her forward. He was in trouble. She had to help him, even if everyone driving by thought she was insane. She brushed a lock of hair out of her eyes, sinking up to her calves in a deep puddle. Maybe she was insane. Quinn had that effect on people.

Chapter 37

Doc continued to hum his executioner's song as he puttered over to the table, preparing Quinn.

"Before this is over," he said, turning with a wide smile. "You should know that I have seen photographs of your girlfriend. She looks quite delicious." He began to scrape away silver dollar–sized patches of the dark hair on Quinn's chest with a disposable razor, leaning in slightly as if he didn't want to be heard by the people on the other side of the glass. It made Quinn wonder where the microphones were.

"It is beyond the scope of my duties," Doc continued, "but I have decided to pay the lovely woman a visit."

"That might be a little more difficult than you imagine," Quinn said.

"Oh." Doc shrugged, tossing the razor onto the steel table with his other instruments. "I have you in my chair. I don't suppose it will be much trouble to get your little whore in my bed."

"A little closer, Doc," Quinn said, "and I can take care of your other ear."

Unfazed, the executioner pressed two adhesive pads to the bare spots on Quinn's chest, one directly over his heart and the other slightly below and back, over his ribs. To these, he attached the electric leads of a heart monitor that he rolled up from the other side of the steel table. Still careful to keep his distance, he turned the monitor toward Quinn, presumably so he would be able to witness the last few blips of his own heart. It was the modern—but no less barbaric—equivalent of an Aztec priest ripping out a beating heart and holding it before the victim's eyes.

Quinn had faced impossible situations before— fights against much larger and stronger opponents, the deaths of good friends, assassination attempts, torture, pitched firefights when all seemed lost—but the finality of the bald man's actions robbed him of his last shred of hope. Quinn was a realist, preferring to see things as they were, not as he wished them to be. He was in a dungeon of some forgotten prison on an island a hundred miles from his nearest friend—and no one even knew he was here. It would be a straightforward endeavor to defeat the locks on his wrist with the pen he'd snatched, but he'd need a moment of privacy to accomplish that. He'd be dead before he had the opportunity.

There was zero chance for escape—but he had to try. His heart rate rose on the monitor, climbing above his customary sixty beats per minute to well over ninety as he cast his eyes around the room for something, anything that he could use or do to stall for time. Something to keep him alive long enough to form a plan. He could tell everything he knew—which was essentially nothing but a string of educated guesses hinging on sketchy intelligence information and the murder of Ted Schoonover.

He thought back to when Winfield Palmer had first recruited him and Thibodaux, how he'd explained the nature of the work he wanted them to do. It seemed so long ago now, sitting in the back of the armored limo in Miyagi's driveway. He'd not even met the strangely beautiful woman yet. Jacques, with his usual eloquence, had observed that it would be extremely easy for Palmer and the president to "drop them in the grease." Palmer had only smiled and said he thought they would both jump in the grease willingly if the need arose.

Quinn had mulled over the conversation many times in the ensuing years. His study of Eastern philosophy and the Japanese samurai mind-set called for him to come to grips with his own death. Death was something he would face alone, no matter who he was with. But that was not true. His mother, his father, Kim, Ronnie, Thib, Miyagi, and his little girl were right here with him. They always were . . .

Doc gave him a shove on the point of his shoulder, bringing him out of his thoughts.

Quinn scoffed. "Sorry," he said. "I forgot you were here."

"Why are you smiling?"

"Thinking about my friends," Quinn said. "Something you could not possibly understand."

Doc glared. "Americans," he said. "Arrogant to the last."

"One-eared turtles," Quinn said. "Ugly to the last."

Doc pushed the contents of one syringe into the IV line, following immediately with the second. He turned to glance at the heart monitor. "Your arrogance will be gone soon enough."

A rush of warmth spread up Quinn's arm and then down both legs, followed by a tremendous pressure in his lungs, as if an elephant had climbed onto his chest. An overwhelming sense of doom followed the cool liquid up his vein from the IV site. His heart rate, over a hundred during the lead-up to getting the drugs, began to slow at once, ticking down the last few seconds of his life.

"What?" Doc sneered, leaning in closer now, no longer afraid of getting bitten. "Nothing smart to say?"

Quinn was vaguely aware of a tear running down his cheek. His heart rate fell rapidly as the feeling of inescapable despair rose, flooding his body. The count slowed to thirty beats per minute, then twenty, then eight—then blipped once before the pulsing line went flat. The pressure in his chest excruciating now, Quinn watched the final beat of his heart. Though groggy, he was still conscious enough to watch himself die.

Chapter 38

General de la Guardia was ready for this operation to be done. The United States would suspect Cuba; he was smart enough to know that. But the *Yanquis* were much too civilized to follow through on any act of retribution without substantive proof, and a sixty-year-old rocket with nuclear material from a Soviet warhead would be problematic to track—not impossible, but problematic, which would be enough to muddy the waters. And anyway, de la Guardia thought, there was enough hatred focused on the U.S. to suspect a dozen or more actors. Suspicion would, of course, be focused on Cuba, but that was exactly what the general wanted. Suspicion would be enough to destabilize talks. The U.S. did not seem to mind if civilians were killed tangentially, but they were never considered a primary target for bombing runs or drone attacks. An invasion was always possible. The American president was an ex-Navy man who was probably spoiling for war. But few other politicians would have the balls to do anything but heap on more sanctions and march forward with the status quo.

At least, that was the hope. The general would fire the missile and then sail on to Nassau, where he would melt into the population to lay low for a few months before traveling back to Cuba. He was a good boy, trustworthy and committed to the revolution. Not to mention his station in life as a de la Guardia.

The only fly in the ointment was this Operation Jericho—whatever that was. The word had come up too many times to be a coincidence. Mirabal had seen it on a mobile phone after he'd dealt with the traitor, Placensia, and then heard it again, right here on the island. What on earth could it mean? The general was not versed in matters of God and religion, swearing off such ridiculous notions as idiotic under the leadership of Comrade Fidel. But his mother was a different story. It took time to eradicate years of religious faith, even from an island as small as Cuba. She and her own mother before her were devout Catholics. No one, not even the *comandante* himself, could dissuade them from their scripture. Some of it must have rubbed off for the general to remember that Jericho was the name of a city in the Bible. But that knowledge did not help him at all. One thing was certain: De la Guardia did not believe in coincidence, especially when it came to matters of state security.

This Shield fellow knew something. Perhaps he was connected to Placensia. His handler, perhaps. Maybe Placensia had been working with the Americans for some time, and Jericho was his code name. But if that were the case, why had he not given up the information earlier? De la Guardia was under no mistaken notions that the U.S. would not send over a team of highly trained operatives if they thought for one second that there was a nuclear missile being prepped to head their way. The general stifled a tense laugh. Hell, if they knew that, they would have just carpet-bombed the entire island

and apologized later for all the women and children they'd been forced to murder. But according to Colonel Mirabal, the traitor and his family were still soaked from staggering out of the sea when they were intercepted. De la Guardia doubted there had been enough time for any information to be passed, but if the traitor had already been in touch with someone off island . . .

De la Guardia looked at his watch—a nice G-SHOCK he'd picked up on a recent trip to Japan. It was worth perhaps a hundred dollars, but here in Cuba a hundred-dollar watch might as well have been a Rolex. It was getting late. He wanted to phone the prison and check on the situation, but the telephones were down. He hadn't spoken with Mirabal since shortly after his team had arrived on Isla de la Juventud, and he could not help but wonder if the strange little bald man at the prison had done his work. If he had, the problem of Señor Shield would be behind them.

Chapter 39

Odesa Dombrovsky paced back and forth in the pitch-black night on the deck of her boat, dressed in an olive drab military rain poncho she'd gotten during her compulsory service with the Cuban army. She'd never done any fighting, and she didn't really like guns—unlike her half sister, who appeared to be some sort of superspy. Or at least her very handsome boyfriend was.

Odesa had triple-checked the dock lines and chafe guards, set the bumpers in the optimum spots, done everything she could imagine to take care of her boat. It would have been better to haul it out—but who had that kind of money? She had weathered hurricanes before, so she would rely on the breakwaters of Marina Hemingway to protect the vessel from the storm.

The power was already out on this side of the island—a bad sign, since the hurricane proper still hadn't actually made landfall. Well over an hour had passed since Peppa had called with the message, plenty of time for Veronica to make the trip, even in this weather—and yet she was nowhere to be seen. There was a distinct possibility that the same people who had picked up her boyfriend had gotten Veronica as well. But someone needed to lay eyes on Jim Shield to see if he was really on the Island of Youth. Political prisoners had a much better rate of survival if someone knew where they were. Once they disappeared, it was all too easy to make their disappearance permanent.

Odesa wondered if she'd feel so bent on going to save him if he were not so handsome, so . . . smoldering. Yes. That was it. This was a man off whom rain would sizzle. Perhaps she wanted to rescue him to punish Veronica. Maybe. Probably. But the man would not likely care about her motives, so long as his life was saved.

She looked at her watch for the fifth time. Ninety minutes gone, and still no Veronica. The storm was only getting stronger, so if she was going, it would have to be now. Peppa's warning about the danger played in her head as she scrawled out a note for her half sister and left it on the salon table in the cabin of her boat— which she would leave unlocked. "Call your auntie," the note said.

If anything, the element of danger only made this all the more appealing.

Odesa's 1981 Ural MT11 sidecar motorcycle was manufactured years before she was born. It had been passed on to her after her maternal grandfather's death, grudgingly, since her grandmother knew the true circumstances of Odesa's bastard conception. Odesa always assumed that the bitter old woman hoped she killed herself on the thing.

Odesa had gotten the bike when she was seventeen and, much to her grandmother's disappointment, had ridden it safely for almost a decade. She always wore the equestrian helmet when she rode—though, as her grandmother observed, such a helmet would only serve to keep her brains in one place if she were to have an accident, making it easier for the road crews to scrape them up.

Odesa had fastened a belt around the waist of her poncho, turning it into a semi-waterproof smock that she hoped might keep out a little more of the storm. She looked ridiculous in the poncho, riding helmet, and goggles, but she didn't care. Hardly anyone would be able to see her anyway in this downpour—an additional problem for a motorcyclist at night.

She was a sturdy woman—at least that's what her father had called her—but she was not particularly heavy. Starting the old, Soviet-era motorcycle required her to stand up on the foot peg so she could get all her weight over the kick lever. She was not so tall that she had to lean over much to keep one hand on the throttle as she transferred her weight, kicking the 750cc engine to sputtering life. She gave it a scant minute to warm up, threw a leg over the soaking wet seat, and after situating the poncho so it didn't fly up in her face at speed, shifted the bike into gear with a loud clunk and rolled into a sheet of solid rain.

The trip south across the island was not incredibly far—just over thirty miles—but the roads were poor in the best weather. Havana traffic sent up a heavy stream of spray, covering Odesa's goggles in muck and, worse yet, blinding all the other vehicles on the road. She'd be glad to get clear of Havana, though the dangers would only be different outside of the city. Torrential rain would turn streams into rivers and rivers into lakes, covering the road in spots and hiding dangerous potholes that waited to tear down the bike. Any advantage the Ural might have over a car at negotiating the narrowing roads was obviated by the driving rain that obscured Odesa's fogging goggles and threatened to send her careening off the road in the soupy red muck.

She had only a vague notion of a plan for what she might do when she reached the other side of the island. She'd get a boat for the ninety-kilometer journey across the bay to the Island of Youth. Her friend, Higinino, had told her about a secret facility at the old Presidio Modelo. She'd try that first because it was the only place she knew to try.

She toyed with the idea of a quick side trip to check in with Peppa Garcia. Odesa had never been a great believer in Santeria—or any religion, for that matter— but perhaps a small ceremony to consult whatever god one consulted about an insane plot to save a man she hardly knew might prove helpful. But the detour would cost her more than an hour, and the storm was going to get worse before it got better. She needed to get to the water as soon as humanly possible if she wanted to cross the bay at all.

In the end, she decided that the Lord of the Crossroads would only tell her to hurry or not to go at all—an answer she was unwilling to accept.

She rode on, leaving blacked-out Havana, which at least had a few candles and lanterns in the windows, for the utter darkness of the deserted southbound road. If she crashed now, no one would find her until after the storm blew through—if even then. Mudholes made convenient graves for the foolish.

Chapter 40

Quinn's eyes fluttered, unable to look away from the train wreck that was his own death. He'd spent years preparing for this moment, studying ancient Eastern texts, training long hours with Emiko Miyagi, the closest person he'd ever heard of to a living Japanese samurai, meditating, breathing, readying himself for the moment of acceptance.

And still, he could not escape the swirling pit of doom and dread. Was this what death was like? Would he linger here for some time, conscious of the blood settling in his extremities?

The doctor stepped back and grinned, gloating at his handiwork.

Quinn gasped, fighting the pressure in his chest and neck. He heard a noise from somewhere in front of him—a thousand miles away. Someone else had entered the room. A door slammed. There was muffled yelling, like a man screaming inside a metal can. He was vaguely aware of a person next to him, tugging at the IV in his arm . . . no, not tugging at it, but injecting something else into the port.

A single blip sounded on the monitor. Quinn forced himself to look, watching in dismay as the numbers began to climb. Beat by agonizing beat, his heart began to reanimate, and the oppressive weight lifted from his chest. Someone barked out orders in Spanish, angry, in charge. Quinn's vision was too blurry to make out more than dark forms, but there was more than one. He thought the one beside him was female.

Quinn fought to stay conscious, wondering if he was dreaming, if his heart hadn't actually restarted. A man he didn't recognize stood in front of him, patting him on the cheek to keep him awake. Even through the foggy, drug-induced haze, Quinn could see the large diagonal scar running across the man's face.

"This was a mistake, señor," the man said, heavily enunciating each word in perfect English. "You have been treated badly. You must accept my apologies."

Quinn tried to speak but his mouth felt full of cotton. His head was too heavy for his neck. He coughed, jerking feebly at the straps on his wrists. Mistake or not, they weren't taking off the cuffs, but that didn't matter right now. Finally, he was able to get his mind and tongue to work well enough to form a single word. It was hoarse, and barely audible, but it was sincere.

"Thank . . . you," Quinn croaked, before his eyes rolled back in his head and his shoulders sagged in the chair.

It took Ronnie Garcia forty minutes to walk, jog, and slosh through the storm from the broken taxi to Marina Hemingway. She was soaked to the skin before she'd gone ten meters. The wind, which should have come from her back, pelted her from all directions, slapping her in the face with a mask of sopping wet hair. She had to stop in the middle of the downpour and tear off a strip of cloth from the hem of her T-shirt to tie it back so she could see. She never saw the cabbie again and assumed he'd written off any fare he was owed in favor of escaping the storm.

She was surprised at how dark it was as soon as she turned into the marina proper and left behind the headlights and passing cars. Some of the boats surely had battery power, but no one appeared to be foolish enough to remain on board during a hurricane. The hotel must have had a generator. There were a few lights in the windows, but the blackness of the storm seemed to press back any feeble glow. It was nearly impossible to see where the wet pavement of the pier ended and the void of water began. The boats themselves were black holes against a blacker ocean, groaning against their lines. Palm trees chattered above the piers, periodically flinging heavy fronds to the sodden ground with a slithering crash. Garcia was not the type to get creeped out by nature, but the skeletal look of the palm fronds made her pick up her pace.

The telltale scrape of a shoe above the wind caused her to freeze as she reached Odesa's boat. Her hand swept her waistband for the pistol that was not there.

"Hey, *cher*, it's us." Thibodaux's comforting voice carried out from the darkness aboard *Danotria*.

Garcia shot a glance over her shoulder, back the way she'd come, just in case any of the palm fronds had turned into CDR goons.

Thibodaux spoke again. He was barely visible now, standing there on the back deck like one-eyed Odin. "Our cabbie took so many turns to miss traffic I swear he was trying to shake a tail for us. Anyhow, I'm thinkin' all the Committee for the Defense of the Revolution snitches have gone to hunt their holes in this shit. We should be good to go for a short meeting."

Miyagi moved forward a little. Garcia could just make out her silhouette under the eaves of the boat cabin. "We arrived half an hour ago," she said. "We have seen no one but you."

Garcia climbed over the gunwale and stepped down onto the deck. Odesa had secured the boat snugly to the cleats on the pier, but it swayed and rocked, almost as if the harbor waters were breathing.

"Come here, kiddo." Thibodaux gathered Garcia in a wet bear hug. "Looks like you had to walk?"

Garcia filled them in on her problems with the taxi while staying safely enveloped in the hug, taking refuge, but feeling guilty since Quinn was out there somewhere enduring God knew what kind of treatment. She wanted to cry. But that was ludicrous. Crying wouldn't help. Much. She was worried sick about the man she loved. Worried sick—that was the truth. Her head throbbed, her gut churned, hell, even her groin ached with the same tension she got when she stepped too near the edge of a steep cliff. Knowing that Jericho was in danger was awful, but not knowing where he was and, worse yet, being unable to do anything about it threatened to grind her into the mud.

Emiko nodded toward the window at the dark and empty cabin. "Your sister is not here. Do you know where she lives?"

Ronnie smoothed the wet bangs out of her eyes and

gave a half-hearted shrug. "I just assumed she lived on the boat."

Thibodaux tried the door and found it open. "Looks like a note on the chart table." He stepped aside so Garcia and Miyagi could get in out of the storm ahead of him.

Garcia used a small Streamlight flashlight to scan the single sheet of paper on the table, reading it aloud. "Call your auntie." Quickly scrawled in pencil, there wasn't much to it. Garcia had to admit that the message was brilliant in its simplicity insofar as tradecraft was concerned. It gave everyone concerned deniability. No one was named, but Ronnie had no doubt that the note was meant for her.

"There is no sign of struggle," Miyagi said, looking around the room. "Your sister apparently left of her own accord after securing her vessel." She lifted the lid to the chart table, looking through the storage underneath the wooden desk for any clue as to where Odesa Dombrovski might be. There was a compass, a couple of folded paper charts, and a pair of navigational dividers. She moved the charts and found a wooden frame containing a five-by-seven photograph of a petite, auburn-haired woman. The facial features were a near perfect match to Odesa. Miyagi held up the photograph. "Do you know where her mother lives?"

Garcia raised a hand as if to ward off the sight of the photo. It was one thing to meet her father's love child. Seeing the woman who he'd cheated with was beyond the pale.

"I have no idea," she said. "But I wouldn't go over there even if I did."

Thibodaux held his mobile away from his ear. He'd tried again, just to be sure. "Still no signal," he said.

Garcia leaned into the small V-berth up front and rummaged around until she found a towel that smelled clean enough to pat her hair dry. "Then there's nothing to do but trudge back to Peppa's and see what she knows."

"We'll come, too," Thibodaux said. "I wouldn't mind going back to the hotel and having a little talk with that creepy desk clerk dude. He thinks this little ol' hurricane is bad, he's about to meet a storm of another form."

"Good idea," Ronnie said. She pitched the wet towel back into the V-berth. Borrowing stuff and not taking care of it was what sisters did.

"You think Odesa is at your auntie's?" Thibodaux asked.

"She'd better be," Ronnie said.

"She did leave you a note," Miyagi said. "That has to be worth something."

"I guess," Ronnie said, mouth set in a glum frown. "But for all we know, she's the one that turned us in in the first place."

"You really believe that?" Thibodaux asked.

"You keep asking me that," Ronnie said.

Thibodaux raised the brow over his good eye.

"You keep sayin' it. Now look here. If she did turn us in, we're all hosed for certain. I think the gal deserves a break."

"And why is that?" Ronnie asked.

Thibodaux put an arm around her shoulders and drew her in for another hug, like she suspected he did with his own children when they needed counsel. "None of that business with your daddy is her fault."

"I know that." Ronnie scuffed her foot on the deck.

"Then how about you cut the girl some slack," Thibodaux said. "For all we know, she's bustin' Chair Force outta some Cuban prison as we speak."

Ronnie smirked. "Fat chance of that. She hates me too much to help any of us."

Chapter 41

Odesa rode south, throwing up a heavy spray behind the wheels of the Ural sidecar, squinting reflexively inside her goggles. During a normal rain, she could turn her head to the side and let the wind blow away the drops, but this came in buckets—no, barrels—and nothing helped to keep her vision clear.

She eventually caught Highway 101. In good weather, she would have had to dodge people crowding in from the roadside, hawking braided bundles of garlic or lumps of homemade cheese. The hurricane had chased all but the most dedicated vehicles off the road. The cars that did see her didn't give her a second look. Cubans did what needed to be done. If she was riding her motorcycle on the ragged front edge of a hurricane, then she must have a good reason.

She continued to work her way southeast as she left Havana proper, keeping to the larger roads. They were not exactly well maintained, but they were marginally better than the more rural routes—especially on a motorcycle. A soupy right-hand turn loomed up from the darkness before her. She felt the sidecar begin to rise and gave the bike a little throttle to bring it back down, slithering through the corner before she tapped her brake to bleed off the speed to something a little more survivable.

Moving toward her goal, she formed the bones of her plan as she rode. There were several small villages on the southern coast that would offer her a place from which to launch some vessel for the Island of Youth. She had an old boyfriend in Guanimar who owned a fishing boat. He still had a thing for her and would have probably offered to lend her the boat if the seas had not been so rough—and she promised to spend some time with him in Guanimar. But she had no way of contacting him now, and chances were he'd moved the boat anyway, out of the path of the storm.

The state ferry left from Sudiero de Batabanó farther east from Guanimar. A small neck of land jutted into the sea from the tired little town, protecting the harbor from easterly winds. There would be several boats there, Odesa thought, dodging an enormous pothole and giving the Ural gas so it would veer quickly to the right toward the sidecar and narrowly avoid a black cow that was trotting down the center of the flooded road. Driving a Ural was a science, but it was also an art. The cow bawled as she rode by, protesting the spray from the back tire—as if she could possibly get any wetter.

Hopefully, at least one of the boats in Sudiero de Batabanó would be fast. With any luck, the keys would be on board. One thing was a virtual certainty. The vessels would not be guarded.

Only a fool would steal a boat and set off in the middle of a hurricane.

* * *

Peppa gave Ronnie, Jacques, and Miyagi towels that smelled like cigar smoke and coconut oil when they arrived at her house looking like drowned rats. Her altar room was surreal enough when there was electricity, but the dozens of candles she now relied on for light gave it the otherworldly feel of a crypt. Jacques, who'd grown up in New Orleans with a grandmother who read the Good Book every morning and every night and taught her grandson how to keep from "gettin' got with a voodoo hex," seemed not to know where to settle his good eye. In the end, he put his back to the nearest wall while he faced Peppa, who he did not appear to trust, no matter whose aunt she was.

Peppa briefed them about her findings regarding Isla de la Juventud and the distraught mother whose military son had been dispatched there on special assignment that very afternoon.

"I have heard of panopticon prisons," Miyagi said, nodding slightly as she sipped a cup of tea from the tray Ramón brought in. "Large round buildings."

"Correct," Peppa said. "Presidio Modelo was modeled after one of yours in the United States."

"Joliet, Illinois." Miyagi nodded again. "Five buildings, four of them built around a larger center structure, each five stories tall."

"Exactly," Peppa said. "The Castro brothers were imprisoned on the island when they were younger. After the revolution, Fidel imprisoned soldiers from Batista's army there—at least, the ones he did not shoot. The guards had very little contact with the prisoners, watching them instead from a five-story tower, somewhat like a lighthouse, in the center of each unit. The guards accessed these towers through underground tunnels beneath the prison. My mother used to joke about sending me to Presidio Modelo when I misbehaved as a child."

Ronnie ran her fingers through her wet hair, holding a handful of bangs as she spoke, and squinting like she had a headache. "What does this have to do with Quinn? That prison closed before I was born."

"The prison closed before *I* was born," Peppa said. The ignition of a flame from a match illuminated her face as she prepared to light a small cigar. "But such a small detail did not stop your grandmother from threatening me. There is a museum there now, but few people visit."

Once it was lit, she stuck the cigar in the lips of a clay statue in front of her altar table, beside the bowl of eggplant. The statue was obviously an orisha, but Ronnie had no idea which one, and she was in no mood for a lesson on Santeria.

"So," she prodded. "What about Quinn?"

"Ahh," Peppa said. "There are rumors, too many to discount, actually. Some say special prisoners are taken to cells within the tunnels that run underneath Presidio Modelo."

"And you think Quinn was taken there?"

"The timing suggests so," Peppa said. She lit a cigar of her own and blew a geyser of smoke straight up into the air in front of her face. "Members of a specialized army intelligence unit are deployed to the Isle of Youth on the same day—almost within the same hour—that your friend is removed from his prison cell and taken to a secret location. On a day without a storm, I *might* call that a coincidence. But probably not even then."

She puffed the cigar until the end glowed orange,

pondering something. "I could do a ceremony and ask the ancestors—"

Ronnie threw up her hands, causing Peppa to jump, knocking the ash off her cigar. "I don't want a ceremony, Auntie. And I don't want to talk to a bunch of dead people. What I want to do is get to that island and check on my friend. Can we just do that?"

"Ordinarily, yes," Peppa said, pointing the cigar toward the window. "But not now. Even if you were not arrested, the seas are just too bad between here and the island."

Miyagi leaned forward, resting her arms on her knees. She'd spoken little since they arrived at Peppa's house. Normally one to sit ramrod straight, even in a soft chair, now she seemed bent under the weight of the world. She looked back and forth from Jacques to Garcia, her flawless skin glowing amber in the light of a dozen candles.

"There is something else we must consider," she said.

The big Cajun gave a solemn nod. He turned to Garcia, but closed his good eye, as if he couldn't bring himself to face her. "There is at that," he said, agreeing with Miyagi. He took Garcia's hand. "It kills me to even think about it, *cher*, but we've got—"

Garcia jerked her hand away. "Dammit!" she shrieked. "No. No!"

She knew exactly what they were talking about, and there was no way she was going to let that happen.

Peppa too seemed to know what was not being said. She continued to smoke her cigar while the others sat in silence. "Whichever path you decide to take, it will be my honor to assist you. But remember this. Any attempt to cross the Gulf of Batabanó tonight would be suicide."

Less than an hour after she left Marina Hemingway, Odesa found herself in Sudiero de Batabanó on the southern coast, within spitting distance of the Isle of Youth—provided one could spit sixty miles. Ten minutes after that, she was at the helm of a relatively new go-fast boat, probably one the police had seized from some Caribbean drug runner and then used to run drugs themselves. It did not matter. The keys were conveniently located in a locker next to the steering wheel, and as she'd suspected, there were no guards but for the monstrous green waves that threatened her outside the breakwater. She'd hid her motorcycle behind a dilapidated storage shed, half a block from the marina. She wondered if she'd ever see it again. For that matter, she wondered if she'd ever see anything beyond the bottom of the ocean again.

The seas were angry and building, to be sure, but the shape of Cuba herself offered some protection to these inner waters of the Gulf of Batabanó from the much heavier weather of the open Atlantic. Six-foot seas and a howling wind made the crossing uncomfortable but marginally possible—for now. In another hour, the sea state would double.

An accomplished sailor, Odesa quartered away from the waves, in the air as much as she was in the water as she bounced and flew almost due west, staying clear of the fringing islands of Cayo Grande that guarded the eastern approach to the Isle of Youth like a snaking fortress wall. She would skirt around the Isla Mangle at the northern edge of these keys, then cut back to the southeast toward Nueva Gerona, the only notable city on the island and the location of Presidio Modelo. The prison was east of town, but she would need to steal a car to get there, and the cars were in Nueva Gerona. One of the beautiful things about the vintage cars in Cuba was that they were easy to steal. Of course, if she were caught, she would certainly go to prison—if the owner didn't get to her first and give her a *machetazo* to the neck.

Cold rain poured down her collar, salty spray stung her face. The poncho, in tatters now from the ride in the Ural, flogged her sides in the wind. Odesa wiped her face enough to see the dial of her watch, then checked the speed of her boat. She estimated she'd reach the island in a little over two hours. There would still be some darkness to play with, to help hide her—so long as the little boat held together and the howling wind didn't drive her onto a reef.

Chapter 42

The man with the diagonal scar bisecting his face introduced himself as Colonel Joaquin Mirabal. He was obviously in charge, or at least had enough juice to stop an execution. Quinn cheered inside as he watched Mirabal berate the balding doctor and order him out of the room, taking note that the doctor's name was Ibarra. Mirabal told a much younger man to unlock the restraints at Quinn's wrists and ankles.

"We should leave the IV in place." Mirabal gave Quinn a pat on the shoulder as if he truly cared. "For your own safety, you understand. I can't be sure of your long-term reactions to the drugs. We may need to medicate you quickly—"

Quinn ripped out the IV line anyway, ignoring the blood that spilled from his arm. He didn't want the thing in him for another millisecond.

The young woman with short black hair moved to stop him, but Mirabal waved her back.

Quinn tried to rise but felt his knees go wobbly as he put weight on them, forcing him to lean on the chair. One of the first rules of surviving an interrogation was to accentuate any injuries, appeal to the better angels of the interrogator. Quinn didn't have to do much acting. The drugs Ibarra had given him, combined with the massive adrenaline dump from watching himself die, fogged his brain and made it nearly impossible to stand.

The ballpoint pen fell from his hand, clattering to the concrete floor at his bare feet as he tried to catch himself.

Instead of getting angry, Colonel Mirabal gave a serene smile and nodded at the younger man, who stooped warily to pick up the pen.

"I do not blame you," the colonel said. "If I found myself in your shoes, I would have done anything to escape." He raised his head slightly, looking up and down at Quinn's body. "My friend," he said, "your scars have many stories to tell."

Regaining enough balance to stand upright, Quinn held both hands over his groin. He'd spent enough time in Japan and Europe that he was not embarrassed by his own nudity. But an innocent American being held in a Cuban dungeon would be particularly aware of such things.

"Speaking of shoes . . ."

"Of course," Mirabal said, nodding to the young woman. "Serafina, please find our guest his clothing."

Serafina retrieved Quinn's prison slacks and vest from a chair in the corner. The T-shirt had somehow disappeared. She searched the pockets, then handed them to Quinn, who stumbled as he took them. Again, there was little acting involved. Sitting back in the metal chair, he pulled up the slacks, amazed at how heavy his legs felt. The adrenaline was already ebbing, allowing the pulsing pain in his ribs to light him up every time he breathed—or tried to put on pants. Somehow, he managed to shrug into the vest.

Colonel Mirabal waited for him to dress, then nodded to the far corner of the room, adjacent to the long observation window, where two chairs were set around a small table—a break area for those exhausting moments between executions.

Quinn took a moment to look around. The windowless room was perhaps twenty by thirty feet. Much more cluttered than the typical interrogation room—which was meant to give the subject nothing on which to focus but the interrogator. This place was a cross between a hospital emergency room and a torture chamber.

"Come," Colonel Mirabal said. "I can imagine you would want to put some distance between you and that disgusting chair." He pointed an open hand at the table. There was a Cadbury chocolate bar and a bottle of water, cool enough that the outside of it was sweating moisture. "Please."

Still on his feet, Quinn threw back the water in one gulp, but took his time to let the chocolate bar melt slowly in his mouth. He'd not realized how hungry he was.

The resulting jolt of energy gave Quinn a new clarity. He blinked sleepily as if completely relaxed, trusting in his apparent savior, Colonel Mirabal. Suddenly opening his eyes, he appeared to brighten.

"Please, tell me you're from the embassy?"

The colonel shook his head, motioning again to one of the chairs at the table, making sure Quinn's back was to the door. "Sadly no, señor," he said. "I am with the Cuban government. Please do not misunderstand. Your situation remains extremely grave, but contrary to what your politicians in America might tell you, we are not monsters here. Dr. Ibarra grossly exceeded his authority. For that, you have my most sincere apology."

Quinn licked chocolate off his lips. He looked back and forth at the young man and woman who flanked the guy with the scar. "Okay." His chest fell in a deflated sigh. "What . . . what do I need to do to fix this?" He waved his hands around the room. "Whatever *this* is. You have to believe that I'm just an investment guy on holiday with my girlfriend. I have money—or my company does, if it's a matter of—"

Mirabal put up his hand. "Please," he said, looking pained. "Let us start fresh before we are both embarrassed." He put the flat of his palm to his chest. "I am Joaquin Mirabal, a colonel in the Cuban Revolutionary Armed Forces. These are my associates, Lieutenants Duran and Lopez.

"Jim Shield." Quinn said. "James, if you want to get technical."

"We do." Mirabal raised a skeptical brow. "Please be as technical as possible. James Shield, *investment guy*?"

"That's right," Quinn said, forcing an emphatic nod.

A broad smile crept over Mirabal's face, made slightly uneven by the scar than crossed it at the corner of his mouth. "So, they teach *investment guys* in the United States how to utilize a ballpoint pen to escape? Do they teach investment guys how to best two highly trained police officers in physical combat? I must tell you that one of the men serving the lawful arrest warrant in the hotel stairwell suffered three broken ribs at your hand. This man also happens to be Dr. Ibarra's cousin. That could account for the doctor's hasty behavior." Mirabal leaned forward. "Tell me, Señor Shield. Where does an *investment guy* learn tradecraft and fighting?"

"I boxed a little in school," Quinn said, ignoring the part about the pen. There was no way to explain it away, so he wouldn't try unless pressed.

Mirabal leaned back in his chair, drumming his fingers on the table, studying Quinn through narrow eyes. He sat quietly for a time, letting silence seep into the room.

"To be honest," he finally said, appearing to change tack. "I am not a professional interrogator. I was on my way here on another matter, so my commander asked that I accompany you."

Quinn allowed his voice to quiver slightly. Too much would have been unconvincing. "I don't understand why they couldn't just question me in the regular jail. Or why I was arrested in the first place. They accused me of robbery . . . but I never robbed anyone." He stared hard at Mirabal's scar, imagining a red laser dot from a rifle. It was a trick he'd learned at the Air Force Academy when some heavy-handed upperclassmen decided to get in his face for instruction. Mirabal might act friendly, but Quinn had no mistaken notions about whose side the man was on.

Mirabal saw him looking and touched the scar with a forefinger. "Courtesy of an angry Cape buffalo bull when I was deployed to Angola."

Quinn finished off the chocolate and carefully folded the wrapper, smoothing the creases against the tabletop, giving his mind something concrete to focus on. Mirabal let him. Maybe he really wasn't a professional interrogator.

"You're a hunter?" Quinn asked.

"I am," the Cuban said. "Do you do a little hunting along with a little boxing?"

Quinn chuckled, waving off the comment, though it was overflowing with veiled challenge—*I wonder who's the better man . . .*

"I hunt," Quinn said. "We fill our freezers with wild game where I come from. Never been to Africa. I read a lot of books about it as a kid."

"You must go," Mirabal said. "It is the most amazing place. Once this business is over and you have told me the truth, I will tell you my favorite spots. I have been many times. Have you hunted in Alaska?"

Quinn nodded, wondering how much this man knew.

"I have not had the pleasure," Mirabal said. "But I would imagine it is one of the few places on earth that could match Africa for game that will hunt the hunter."

"Indeed," Quinn said. Mirabal didn't know anything. He genuinely hoped to hunt in Alaska one day.

Mirabal continued to drum his fingers on the table. "It gets in your blood, don't you think?"

"Africa?"

Mirabal smiled thoughtfully, touching his scar again. "No," he said. "I meant hunting things that hunt you back."

Quinn heaved a long sigh. "Yeah, I guess no matter how good you think you are, something like your big Dagga boy can stomp you to death after you think the danger is past."

"That is more true than you know," the Cuban said. His finger traced the puckered white flesh above his brow. "This bull certainly stomped me. Gored my tracker to death. I had to tie a filthy rag around my injured scalp to keep the flap of skin in place while I hiked out back to the jeep, all the while avoiding a pride of lions that obviously smelled blood."

Quinn whistled under his breath. "That sounds like some of the stories I read. Good thing for me that bull didn't kill you."

Mirabal chuckled at that. "Yes," he said. "Good thing. The bull's head now resides in a place of honor in my personal study. I suppose you could say I have two trophies to remind me of the hunt." He eyed Quinn contemplatively. "It is rare that such a worthy adversary comes along."

"I'll bet it is," Quinn said. "It must have been a terrifying ordeal."

Mirabal shrugged. "As I said, it gets in one's blood." He lay both hands flat on the table and stared down at the backs of them, as if to change the subject. "I have to tell you, the authorities who arrested you report that you beat them soundly—not once, but twice, at one point getting away when you were near the National Art Schools."

"Were those the same guys?"

Mirabal scoffed, not buying a word Quinn spoke. "Indeed they were," he said. "And I remind you, they said you were quite formidable in your skill. In fact, they describe your actions as smooth and efficient—as one might find in someone trained in espionage or military matters. That does not sound like someone who boxed some in school."

"Or," Quinn said, "maybe they just said I was extra good so they wouldn't look extra bad."

Mirabal considered this for a moment, then said, "Perhaps. Or perhaps you are not the person you say you are.

"I'm just me," Quinn said. "Plain old Jim Shield. You have my passport."

"You must give me something to work with," Mirabal said. "Or I will not be able to help."

The lights flickered, the way they did in movies when someone was being electrocuted. Quinn tried to ignore them. "Look. I'm telling you the truth—"

The door behind him gave an electronic hum as the lock activated. Quinn turned to see a baby-faced corporal with shaggy hair and an olive green Cuban military uniform enter the room. He walked up tentatively and whispered something in Duran's ear. The lieutenant, in turn, stepped forward to whisper something to Mirabal. As if on cue, the colonel pushed back from the table and shook his head. The consternation on his face was evident.

"Apparently, the hurricane has caused some communication issues. I must find a way to report my discussion with you to my command using an archaic, unsecured radio system. General officers are such a pain, wouldn't you agree?"

Quinn grimaced. "How am I supposed to know that?"

"Touché," Mirabal said. He stood and gestured to the baby-faced soldier. "The corporal will see you back to your cell." Mirabal's eyes narrowed as the soldier replaced the handcuffs behind Quinn's back. "I would use the remaining hours of this night to think long and hard on the matters we have discussed. Eventually, I will have to leave. Dr. Ibarra will then be the ranking official in this facility. I do not believe he would actually kill you now, but he is certainly capable of making your life exceedingly unpleasant."

The electronic lock actuated again, and Mirabal filed out with his two lieutenants. The twitchy corporal replaced the black hood over Quinn's head, prodding him forward with the brutal force of someone who was new to the job and terrified that he didn't know exactly what to do.

Quinn counted twenty-two steps before they made a left, then another seventeen before they turned left again. They stopped, and the corporal shoved Quinn's face against a wall, cursing to himself. The hood was thin enough that Quinn could tell the lights had gone out completely. The corporal said something in Spanish that Quinn took for "don't move or I'll wet myself," and they waited. Eventually, more footsteps came from Quinn's right. He heard the metallic clank of keys as someone new came to the corporal's aid. The blackout had rendered not only the lights but the electric lock on Quinn's cell door inoperable. Hopefully, any surveillance cameras would be out as well. A sliver of hope grew as the door swung shut—and the beginnings of a plan began to form in Quinn's mind.

Chapter 43

Odesa's fingers were wrought into iron claws from gripping the wheel for two solid hours by the time she rounded the Mangle Island. Her shoulders shook with fear and exhaustion. Water crashed over the gunnels as she turned back south, broadside to the face of the storm. Luckily, the waves were smaller by this point, paltry four-footers that would still have sent her rushing for Marina Hemingway had she been out in her own boat.

She slowed the boat to a more manageable ten knots and turned again into the more protected waters, working her way upriver to the boat docks in Nuevo Gerona proper. Hurricane winds whipped the surface of the river to a froth, but it was nothing compared to what she'd just been through. The sudden lull in terror gave her time to think—a dangerous thing, under the circumstances. Her mind began to dwell not on moving forward, but on the hundred ways that this night could end. And none of them were good.

Like Havana, the entire island was in darkness. The small marina on the river was completely deserted. Even the three large police patrol vessels bobbed at their slips, abandoned and dark. There was probably a night watch, either hiding in the shadows or cowering in fear in his bunk. Odesa motored past, secure in the knowledge that the howling wind covered the sound of her arrival.

She tied up on the lee of an old fishing boat, using it to block the view of the patrol boats and break the wind. There was no way anyone even knew the go-fast was stolen yet, and even if they did, phone service was down all over the island. Radios might work, though, so she took nothing for granted.

Rain and flying debris pelted Odesa as she tied up the boat, forcing her to work by feel more than sight. The poncho was nothing but rags now, so she peeled it off and let it fly away with the storm. Accepting the wind and rain made the storm much easier to deal with. She'd long since given up any hope of staying dry.

It took her less than ten minutes of sloshing from shed to shed along the river to find an ancient German MZ motorcycle. Everything in Cuba was old, but it was a great irony that things on the Island of Youth were even older.

The muddy street was more river than road—and she saw no one else as foolish as she was. The wind was so strong that she could barely keep her feet. The bike would be more maneuverable and more convenient to hide than a larger vehicle if she could keep it upright, but she wondered if it might just slam the bike into the mud as soon as she started to ride. But the MZ was heavy, and the tires seemed to have relatively good tread. More important, it was straightforward to hotwire, so she took it anyway. If she made it only half a kilometer, that was half a kilometer she wouldn't have to walk in soaking wet boots.

Lightbulbs for motorcycle headlamps were expensive

in Cuba, and often nonexistent, so the lights did not come on automatically when the engine was switched on. Economy took priority over the safety of being seen by other vehicles. Odesa left the light off, risking potholes and road litter in favor of stealth.

She headed east out of Nuevo Gerona, wrestling more than riding the fishtailing bike. She should have been riding into the wind, but the gusts—sustained howls of some angry creature—came from all directions, pelting her with stinging rain.

Lightning split the sky, giving her periodic glimpses of the ghostly, circular panopticon-style buildings in the distance. Then suddenly Presidio Modelo was looming just before her, severe and imposing. Stripped of vegetation when the prison was open to discourage escape, the grounds surrounding the buildings remained barren, as if blighted by the events of the past. Four round housing units, each containing five stories of cells, surrounded a fifth, slightly larger building of the same shape and design—like the five spots on dice. After the revolution, Castro had stuffed over six thousand prisoners into spaces meant for some twenty-five hundred—political opponents, homosexuals, counterrevolutionaries, Jehovah's Witnesses, anyone the *comandante* deemed disagreeable, but not quite bad enough to shoot. The sinister buildings were easy to discern against the lighter grounds.

Even now, in the almost complete darkness, Odesa could tell the things were rotting with decay and disgusting history. It was only a matter of time before the walls became so weak that a strong storm like this one would topple them one by one. It seemed that every storm brought down more old buildings. *Hard to blame that on the Americans, my comandante*, Odesa thought.

Several smaller structures of a more common size formed the cluster of a dilapidated neighborhood around what was once the prison administration building, but was now a school and museum to the national monument of where the Castro brothers were imprisoned for their part in the bloody raid of the Moncada Barracks. History was indeed written by the victors. Who else in the world would erect a monument to murderous criminals?

Odesa rode the outer limits of the prison grounds, keeping well away from this neighborhood. If there were any military personnel onsite, this is where she would find them. Crossing the bay in the storm had seen her chilled and exhausted when she'd arrived on the island. The wild ride on the MZ should have made it worse, but she felt more alive than ever before— liberated, doing what she wished instead of what she had to do. She had hoped to approach under cover of darkness and use any existing lights coming from the prison to help her formulate a plan. At least she'd know where to look. But if they had a generator, they'd not turned it on. A few candles glowed in the houses beside the school, but everything else was in complete darkness. She could feel that there were people here, but she saw no way forward in finding out where they were.

By the third time around, the chill and exhaustion returned, this time accompanied by despair. What had she been thinking, anyway? If Veronica's boyfriend had been taken by the authorities, then he was gone. If he was here, then he was certainly underground—if not dead already. There was nothing she could do about it.

Now she would have to find someplace in which to crawl and spend the night out of the storm. She knew no one on the island, had no relatives here, no reason for visiting. Eventually, she'd have to explain how she got here and why a stolen boat was tied up at the docks on the very night of her arrival. The Cuban police were authoritarian bullies, but they were not stupid. It would not take them long to put two and two together.

What had she been thinking? Making Veronica jealous was one thing, dying while doing it was just stupid. She would have to come up with another plan, one that would keep her out of prison—an ironic thought, since she was slouching on a motorcycle in the middle of a hurricane, under the shadow of what was once the biggest one in the country.

She would have to go back—tonight, before it got light. The waves would be worse, but if she left now, she could stay ahead of the teeth of the thing, perhaps making it back before the seas grew so high they would chew her to pieces.

She looked back to the west the way she'd come, debating one more round just in case she'd missed something. She'd come this far. If Quinn was here, she could not just abandon him because she was frightened. One more turn around the block, she decided, slower this time.

There was still nothing to be found.

She'd just reached the intersection where she would retreat like a coward back to Nuevo Gerona or keep looking when headlights flicked on from beside one of the small outbuildings. The brilliant pool of light flooded the night, hitting her broadside, temporarily blinding her. She squeezed her hand around clutch and brakes, skidding to a stop to keep from careening off the road. Rain streaked through the beam like silver bullets—but, so far, no bullets of the lead kind.

At least three men piled out of the truck. Judging from their silhouettes, all of them carried rifles. Conflicting orders carried on the shrieking wind as black shadows advanced in front of the lights.

"Get off the motorcycle!"

"Don't move!"

"On the ground!"

"Raise your hands!"

Odesa's heart sank as she lifted her arms high above her head. Cool rain stung her open hands. If there was a secret prison here, she was about to see the inside of it—if these jittery fools didn't shoot her to pieces.

Chapter 44

Quinn suspected that no prison guard in the history of guarding prisons had ever quietly closed a cell door.

The heavy clank-clunk of frame colliding with door, the finality of sturdy bolts sliding into place, were all part of the psychology of control. The sounds might have filled Quinn with despair, but he was grateful for the privacy.

Still hooded, he took a few moments to focus on his breathing while he got his physical and emotional legs underneath him. He'd figured out late in the game that Ibarra didn't actually intend to execute him. The doc wanted to make Quinn think he was going to kill him— so Colonel Mirabal could swoop in and save the day. But being *fairly* sure he wasn't going to die offered very little solace when bound to a chair with heart-stopping drugs pumping into his veins.

It was probably adenosine, judging from the broken darkness that rushed into his body like a fast-moving cancer of the soul. Quinn had logged hundreds of emergency room hours as part of his training as a Combat Rescue Officer with Air Force Special Operations. More than once, he'd seen men and women come in with acute tachycardia. He'd watched the ER docs order adenosine, pushed with saline through a three-way stopcock identical to the one Ibarra had used on him. Adenosine slowed the runaway heart, often stopping it completely for a few seconds, all the while causing the feeling of tremendous pressure on the patient's chest and an over-whelming sense of dread. It was easy to believe you were dying, even if you knew you were not.

The whole thing was a sophisticated version of good cop, bad cop, sometimes called "Mutt and Jeff" in the interrogation world. People confided in a person who showed them kindness. And what could be kinder than saving a person's life?

The guard's footsteps had long since faded down the concrete hall. Quinn gave him another slow fifteen-count anyway before shuffling forward along the concrete floor until he hit the far wall. He walked the walls next, moving slowly to keep from tripping over a low mattress, the only furnishing but for a single drain hole in the center of the room. Exploration didn't take long. The cell was three paces by two—barely six by ten feet. Reasonably sure he was alone, Quinn felt his way back along the wall, dragging his shoulder against the rough concrete blocks for reference until he reached the door. He faced inward toward the drain hole and the center of the cell, his hands on the heavy steel plating. He didn't think his actions would be on camera, even on the off chance the system was operational during the blackout.

He was still wobbly and a little dazed from his ordeal in the chair under the hand of Dr. Ibarra. He'd take care of that one on the way out, one way or another—and not just for pretending to kill him. Quinn had been around more than his share of evil people, and Ibarra wasn't bluffing when he'd threatened Ronnie Garcia. As long as she was on the island, this maniac was a danger to her.

The time out of the cuffs talking to Mirabal had given the circulation time to return to his hands, allowing a little more dexterity in his fingers. He reached into the waistband of his prison slacks at the small of his back and removed the second of the two ballpoint pens he'd taken from Dr. Ibarra's pocket. The first he'd given up as a sacrifice, drawing everyone's attention away from the other one as he hid it in the pants. It was a straight-forward matter to break the metal pocket clip off the pen and slip it between the ratchet teeth and the single bar of the cuffs, allowing the bar to rotate away. It took some contortion, and he would have some bad bruises on his wrists, but his hands were free in less than two minutes.

The interrogation told Quinn much more about his captors than they'd learned about him—and certainly more than they realized they were giving away. Ibarra wasn't some angry man acting alone. He'd been wearing an earpiece, fed information from someone—probably Colonel Mirabal—from behind the observation window. With Mirabal, the good cop, gone for the night, bad-cop Ibarra would eventually visit the cell. Quinn smiled at the thought. Win or lose, he would get a great deal of satisfaction from that meeting.

It took almost three hours, but Quinn finally heard the scrape of footsteps outside his cell. He suspected it was sometime around two in the morning. He'd taken a chance and removed the hood so he could get his bearings and take a better look around the room, but it didn't make much of a difference. Scant light filtered in from a horizontal slit high on the far wall.

That wasn't such a bad thing. The nervous corporal had ushered Quinn to his cell alone, but one-eared Dr. Ibarra would likely be a little more cautious. Rays from a flashlight played underneath the door said whoever was out there wasn't paying attention to their night vision.

Quinn draped the hood, still closed like a single piece of cloth, over the side of his head, leaving his vision clear but providing the guards with the image they would expect to see when they opened the door—a prisoner with his hands behind his back and a black cloth on his head.

Quinn moved as soon as the lead guard broke the threshold of the door, giving him just enough of a sideways shove to cause him to push back. Quinn reversed the direction of his attack immediately, snaking his arm behind the startled man's neck and helping him in the direction he was trying to move, slamming him face-first into the inner wall of the cell. Quinn held nothing back, aiming to drive the poor kid's face right through the bricks.

Ibarra was next in line, his eyes following the flashlight the young guard had dropped. Something long and silver glinted in his hand. A cattle prod. Highly effective at eliciting fear and excruciating pain, the device was a favorite of sadistic interrogators the world over.

Ibarra realized Quinn's hands were free a fraction of a second too late. The doctor shoved the business end of the prod forward like a spear in an effort to fend off an attack. The twin copper prongs arced and sizzled against Quinn's forearm as he parried upward with his left wrist. Squatting low to steady himself and rally the power of his legs, he grabbed the base of the prod with his right hand and the end with his left, push-pulling as he drove upward, turning the device back on Ibarra. Quinn spun, taking the lead in the dance that put the doctor's back to the cell, grateful there were no more guards.

Quinn gave Ibarra two long shocks to the chest, driving him down to the concrete floor, feeling more than a little guilty pleasure as he watched the man's face contort in agony in the orange glow of the fallen flashlight.

Unlike what the movies made people think, an electric shock device rarely knocked anyone out. If the amperage was strong enough, it might kill you, but strong voltage incapacitated by causing the muscles to convulse. Victims were left exhausted if the shock was applied long enough, and with a few chipped teeth, but they were rarely rendered unconscious.

Quinn followed up the shock with a solid stomp to the solar plexus, not caring at all if he snapped off the end of Ibarra's breastbone in the process.

Any guards that were up the hallway would expect to hear screaming. Ibarra did have the cattle prod after all. Quinn gave him another shock, then scooped up the flashlight so he could check the unconscious turnkey. There was blood running from the young man's ear. Couldn't be helped. These guards were surely conscripts, soldiers just doing their job, but Quinn didn't have the luxury of playing nice. They surely wouldn't.

With the turnkey no longer a problem, Quinn turned his attention to Ibarra.

"You will never escape!" the man spat, lapsing into rapid Spanish, then back to English again. He sounded like Ricky Ricardo when he was mad at Lucy.

Quinn ignored the bravado. "What are Mirabal's plans for me?"

Ibarra coughed, whistling through the gap in his teeth. "You son of a—"

Quinn slapped him hard. "Listen to me," he hissed, his face inches from Ibarra's. "What are Mirabal's plans?"

Ibarra laughed, saliva drooling from the corner of his mouth. He scooted himself up straighter, pressing against the floor with both hands. "He is a hunter, that one," he said. "It would be impossible for you to get away from him."

"I don't know," Quinn whispered. "I got you in my cell."

Ibarra sneered. "You think because you have me that your woman is safe?"

Quinn stood, half looking away as if considering the threat. He turned quickly, kicking sideways to plant a foot directly in the middle of Ibarra's right forearm. Elbow against the wall and hands on the floor, there was nowhere for the bone to go. Ibarra howled as both his radius and ulna snapped. Quinn chambered his kick quickly, allowing the doctor the split second he needed to transfer his weight to his good arm, similarly placed on the other side of his body. Quinn repeated the procedure, destroying that arm as well.

Ibarra shrieked, jerking both flopping arms to the center of his body to protect them from further assault. Shattered bone ripped and tore muscles and connective tissue, doing even more damage. Out of his mind with pain, the man listed to his right, sliding sideways against the rough wall.

"The execution . . ." he groaned, pleading for mercy

now. "It . . . it was only a ruse. I only pretended to administer a lethal drug—"

"Wish you had told me sooner," Quinn whispered, his voice grim and breathy. "I would have only pretended to break your arms."

Quinn heard a voice call out from down the hall. Ibarra heard it too and changed his tune. Smiling as if he was back in control, he opened his mouth to call out—until Quinn gave him a hammer fist in the Adam's apple. He tried to clutch his throat, but his useless arms could do nothing but flail. Instead, he fell sideways on the filthy concrete floor and gurgled for air. If he lived, it wouldn't be Quinn's fault.

A quick pat down revealed that neither Ibarra nor the guard had any weapons beyond the prod. Ibarra had a mobile phone, and the guard had a ring of keys. Quinn took them both, stuffing the keys down his waistband since the prison slacks had no pockets. He locked both men in the cell and retraced the steps he'd counted back around to Ibarra's dungeon, hoping with each step forward that at least one of the keys he'd taken off the corporal would get him outside. For all he knew he was in the center of a military base or, worse yet, a larger prison. Just one in a long list of things that couldn't be helped.

One problem at a time.

Quinn passed several cells along the way, each quiet and dark, making him wonder if he was the only prisoner in this place. A light glowed from the end of the hallway when he rounded the first corner, brighter than a flashlight, but not as bright as the operating theater he'd been in before. An emergency generator, he thought, and prayed that someone wasn't watching him on a security camera at that very moment. He switched off the flashlight and stuffed it in his waistband opposite the keys, grasping the cattle prod like a club in his right hand.

More voices now, speaking Spanish. One of them was female, and oddly familiar.

Chapter 45

The three soldiers who'd captured Odesa were ignorant of what they had. She was just a woman poking around where she should not have been. They'd watched her go around twice, thinking at first that she was lost. On the third time, the sergeant in charge decided she was suspicious enough for them to leave the dry interior of their truck. He'd tried to call for advice first, but their only radio was not working in the storm. After a short conference amongst themselves, they'd left her bike along the roadside and frog-marched her to a set of stairs that led under the ghostly prison building nearest the museum and school—and, Odesa presumed, their barracks.

The sergeant, the oldest at all of nineteen, from the looks of them, led the way down while the other two brought up the rear, prodding Odesa nervously if she so much as paused to look where to step. The callow sergeant tried his radio again, got the same result, and ended up banging on the door with his fist. They waited for what seemed like an eternity, with rain blowing down the steps on top of them, until the leader slung his rifle and dug through his pockets and found the key.

The outer reception area was illuminated with emergency lighting but completely deserted. One of the soldiers gave her a rough shove, speeding her up when she tried to look through a long observation window. The sergeant handed his rifle off to one of his comrades, who opened a heavy steel gun cabinet and locked all the weapons inside.

Odesa stopped breathing when they shoved her through the door beside the observation window and stopped long enough for her to look around. A metal chair with leather straps and horrific medical devices left no doubt about the purpose of the room.

Muttering under his breath now, angry at not being able to find anyone to tell him what to do, the sergeant sneered, shoving Odesa face-first against the wall beside the observation window. He leaned in close, lips to her ear, running his hands down both sides of her body, warming up to a more thorough pat down.

Odesa was handcuffed in front, a drastic underestimation on the part of the soldiers. They'd been scared, but not scared enough. She pushed off the wall with both hands, turning at the same time and reaching up to grab a handful of the hapless letch's collar. Yanking him to her, as if to plant a kiss, she jumped upward to give him a vicious headbutt. She missed his nose, giving herself a goose egg on the forehead, but managed to split his lip. The real damage was to his ego.

Embarrassed in front of his fellows, he bellowed, hitting her hard across the face with the back of his hand and knocking her to the ground.

The other soldiers laughed now, little dogs caught up in the moment of attack. The sergeant knelt beside her, grabbing her breast.

"You are supposed to hit the nose," he sneered.

The two other men shouted something unintelligible, cheering their buddy on, no doubt anticipating their turn.

Odesa cursed vehemently, spitting in his face as she twisted out of his grasp. He moved to hit her again, but one of his comrades fell on top of him, a rock pick protruding from the socket of a lifeless eye.

The leader saw it too and panicked. He scrabbled as if someone had just dumped a bucket of spiders on his head, trying to back away, but Odesa and the wall were in his way.

A shrill whistle came from above them and a second soldier fell into the mix, this one with something metal—a scalpel, maybe—sticking from the side of his neck. Hand to his throat, his bright arterial blood arced between his fingers.

The leader flipped all the way over, lying on top of Odesa now, pressing her against the floor with his back.

Odesa's heart lodged in her throat when she recognized Quinn, dark eyes locked on the man in front of him. His shorn head and the spray of blood across his cheek simultaneously terrified and thrilled her.

The sergeant saw him, too, and shouted for help—screamed, really, a babbling, infantile cry like Odesa had never heard. The other two soldiers were long past being able to assist. Quinn lunged, shoving the point of a silver pipe like a sword straight at the guard's face, shattering teeth and driving it into his broken mouth. The soldier shrank backward, writhing to escape the attack, but Quinn pressed forward. The soldier's body went rigid, allowing Odesa to scramble out from underneath. She looked back in time to see blue lines of electricity arc from his open mouth, crackling amid his muffled screams. The man clawed sideways, groping for anything to use as a weapon, but Quinn simply leaned in. Odesa heard a loud pop, like a dowel snapping, and the screams fell off, leaving only the crackle of electricity and the scrape of teeth against metal.

Odesa folded her arms across her chest, shaking and suddenly sick to her stomach. She bent to dry heave on the floor but nearly collided with the rock pick in the dead soldier's eye.

Quinn put a steadying hand on her shoulder, though he himself looked ready to topple over.

"We should go," he said.

Odesa nodded, but just sat there, stunned.

"Right now," he whispered. "I've already met more of these guys, and there's one I don't want to meet again."

Chapter 46

Violeta Cruz held her breath, taking a break from the stale air of the respirator. She'd never considered herself claustrophobic, but the moist confines of the stinking suit and the constant *click-whir* of the apparatus made her want to rip off the hood and live with the consequences. Of course, her rational brain told her she wouldn't have to live with them very long. Ventilation fans worked overtime to get rid of the toxic sewage fumes, but the bunker was literally carved out of ground that was mostly chicken manure. Percolating rain turned the whole thing into a massive methane generator, filling the pit with poison gas as quickly as the fans could get rid of it. The lagoon outside was even worse. She found herself mildly surprised that flocks of birds didn't drop out of the sky when they flew over.

That was probably where they would dump her body when they were done with her. Because they certainly didn't intend to let her live—not after what she'd seen.

She'd worked in enough labs to recognize a dosimeter. Every technician working on the device had one attached to the collar or pocket of his shirt inside the protective suit—but not her. They expected her to do her job and expire, no need to check her exposure to the warhead.

As old as it was, they might as well be holding the raw plutonium in their hands.

Violeta had long since given up on trying to survive. She picked at the guidance system, working complex math problems on her computer and running diagnostics so she'd look like she was doing something constructive. She considered rigging the coordinates so the missile would turn around and hit Havana, just for spite. But that was like signing her parents' death warrant. Someone was bound to know enough trigonometry to check her work, and though they apparently didn't know enough to rig a guidance system, they would know enough to recognize it if she got it wrong.

General de la Guardia had assured her that they had no idea why they were being held, and if they did not know, then there was no reason to silence them. *Silence* was his way of saying *murder*, and he said it a lot, either threatening her or her parents. It made sense, didn't it? But it also made sense that he would just silence everyone involved. That's what the math said, anyway. Her body would end up at the bottom of the sewage lagoon, but she had to try. She had to do something, even if it didn't make sense.

Logically, she knew she should blow up the rocket and turn this place into a smoking crater of chicken shit. General Penguin and his minions would die. She would die, but there was a chance that if the boss was dead, the men holding her parents captive would just fade away.

She thought of her mother's kind face, her papa's serene eyes. Both of them risked everything to get her out of Cuba. Maybe she should just do as she was told—rig the guidance system to de la Guardia's target.

The small warhead would devastate central Miami, killing thousands, but her parents were north. The only danger to them from the bomb would be having to watch the carnage on the news. A hundred percent chance of killing ten thousand, and perhaps a thirty percent chance that her parents would survive. What made ten thousand lives more important than two?

Years before, right after her parents had gotten her out, a Sunday school teacher in Hialeah had told a story about a railroad switchman who had to make a choice between saving all the people on an oncoming train or his little son who was playing on the tracks. In the story, the switchman had sacrificed his son—and then carried the broken body home to his wife. Ten-year-old Violeta informed the class that if her husband ever did such a thing, she would stab him in the heart with a kitchen knife. The teacher explained the story was meant to illustrate God's love for all his children, but Violeta suspected the little boy on the tracks would have had something else to say on the matter.

Now she held the switch. Blow Miami to hell and maybe save her parents, or save Miami and know that she'd killed her parents—or . . .

Her shoulders slumped under the weight of it, but there was really only one decision to be made. The math said so.

Chapter 47

Ronnie Garcia woke with a start from a vivid dream. Quinn was drowning, calling to her as he was carried away by a powerful rip current along the seawall. Her dreams were always more intense when she was worrying about him—which wasn't uncommon. She blinked, momentarily relieved to see she was crammed in the backseat next to Thibodaux and not standing on the edge of the sea. The big Marine was still asleep, his impossibly wide shoulders smashing her against the door of the ancient but serviceable Ford Falcon, like the kind used by the Argentine secret police. Peppa had borrowed it to take them from Havana to Santiago de Cuba. The first third of the five-hundred-sixty-mile trip had been on a monotonous, six-lane highway. Wipers thwacked back and forth. Hissing rain and thumping tar snakes under the tires worked as good as an Ambien, and she'd conked out less than half an hour out of Havana.

Thibodaux, who, like Jericho, had learned over the years to grab a few winks during times of stress, snored beside her, his neck craned back as if he were staring at the Falcon's sagging headliner. Peppa was at the wheel, with Miyagi in front with her, chatting to keep her awake. No small feat for a woman who was customarily silent unless there was something imperative to say.

Garcia yawned, and tried to stretch the kinks out of her spine without waking Jacques, but she finally gave up. The road had narrowed now. Pelting rain cut through the headlight beams as if the little Argentinian Ford were making the jump into hyperspace. Scrubby trees bent to the west under a howling wind that shoved the little car around like a toy. They'd been driving for hours, but it was still dark outside, and it would be for several hours with heavy storm clouds and torrential rain. Garcia stared out the window anyway, past her own reflection. She vaguely remembered the shadowed buildings of at least two towns, made even harder to see because of the blackout. At times, Peppa slowed periodically for a swollen stream, slammed into a hidden pothole, or thumped across a rickety suspension bridge— but, mostly, there'd been a hell of a lot of nothing.

Thibodaux, in keeping with his notion that the island resembled a vacuum cleaner, called the Carretera Central, the shoulderless, two-lane road that ran up its spine, the "Suck Highway." It was a good description of the road and, at the moment, Garcia's disposition.

Jericho was out there, alone and in trouble—and she had cut him loose to fend for himself. Friendship was fine and love might be lasting, but the mission came first in this business. It was one of the first things they taught you at "The Farm."

To that end, Ronnie had grudgingly agreed that there were just too many coincidences surrounding Alejandro Placensia. They had to check out the abandoned poultry farms near Santiago de Cuba—look at the old tactical nuke sites and gather intelligence. Quinn would have. It was the reason they were on the island.

Leave no man behind, Ronnie though, beating her head against the window. *Until you do—*

Reality, it turned out, was worse than her nightmares. With a riptide, at least Quinn stood a chance.

Peppa hit the brakes, causing the car to hydroplane and Ronnie to slide forward on the seat. Garcia had gotten used to bracing herself for these emergency evasions, even in her sleep. Peppa drove as fast as her headlights would let her, faster really, and sometimes she had to swerve around a downed tree. Once, there had been a boulder the size of a horse, inexplicably sitting in the center of the road where there were no other cliffs or stones of any size.

Peppa cursed, and the car continued to slow. Ronnie glanced up, tensing at what she saw. This was no tree or rock.

Fifty meters ahead, a military truck blocked their lane. It wasn't large, just a full-size pickup truck with a shell on the back for carrying equipment. Feeble amber hazard lights flashed on their last legs, barely visible though the heavy rain. Three men in drenched green uniforms stood in the middle of the oncoming lane, leaning into the wind. One of them waved a flashlight at the Falcon, motioning them forward.

Peppa slowed to a crawl.

"Roadblock," Miyagi whispered. She had a hat pulled down over her face and was peering from underneath the large brim. At first glance, it was easy to miss the fact that she was Asian. Ronnie knew she had Peppa's machete at her feet.

Jacques shifted just enough to get a view of the scene without causing suspicion. "How many?"

"Three working the road," Ronnie said.

"Their truck has a back seat," Miyagi said.

"At least one more, then," Jacques said. "Sure as shit, the officer will have the troops standing in the rain while he stays dry."

Peppa was almost stopped now, still twenty yards from the truck. "I do not think this is a roadblock."

The soldier waved more emphatically.

Peppa continued. "I think they are broken down. They are probably looking for a ride."

Ronnie felt Jacques shift beside her. "Well, they ain't gettin' ours. Punch it."

Peppa turned to look over her shoulder, dark eyes wide in the scant green glow of the dash lights. "I'm not sure what that even means. But if you want me to run them over . . ." She shook her head. "They are just boys."

Jacques exhaled through his mouth, focusing his energy. "A teenage boy will kill us as quick as a grown man, Peppa." He nodded, as if considering his point. "Sometimes quicker."

They were too close now to argue.

Jacques rested his fist on the door handle, preparing to fling it open if he had to, but still pretending to be asleep. "Emiko—"

"I will see to anyone in the truck," Miyagi said. There was no question in anyone's mind that she'd employ Peppa's machete with deadly effect.

"Gun situation?" Jacques asked.

Ronnie shook her head. She was smiling now, just in case the kid with the flashlight could see her as they approached.

"Two of them have rifles slung," she said through

clenched teeth. "The guy waving us over is wearing a poncho, but I think he's got a pistol on his belt."

"But he is so very young," Peppa whispered.

"He's Cuban Revolutionary Army," Jacques said. "He will follow orders, and then we're—"

"I was in the army," Peppa said. "Most young Cubans are at some point in their lives. Veronica would have been, had she stayed."

Jacques shifted his weight toward Garcia, freeing up his left to move once he opened the door. "As a matter of fact—"

Ronnie put a hand on his leg. "Peppa," she said. "Listen to me. We are good at what we do. Jacques and Emi will pretend to sleep. But if these guys demand to see identification, or try to take our car, then you must drive, even if it means running them over."

Peppa slumped, nodding. One hand on the wheel, she cranked down the window to talk to the earnest-looking young man who stood in the rain.

Three minutes later, the Falcon was on its way again, careening wildly into a wind that seemed bent on blasting away what little paint remained on its rusted body.

The *young* soldier turned out to be a thirtysomething *capitán* who waved them through as soon as Peppa offered to tell the police in the next town of their predicament.

"You don't really intend to stop at a police station?" Thibodaux asked from the back seat when they were well away from the soldiers.

"Of course not," Peppa scoffed. "But one small lie is

better than running them down in cold blood. Is it your preference that we kill every Cuban we encounter?"

"The ones who aim to kill me, yes," Jacques said, as if it was obvious.

"I am Cuban," Peppa fumed. "Veronica is Cuban. Do not lump us all into the same box as the idiot Castro brothers." Ronnie saw her glance in the rearview mirror at the last, making sure the soldiers did not hear her—though they were three miles behind them now.

Garcia shook her head. "I am *from* Cuba," she said. "I am American. And honestly, auntie, considering what's at stake, I'm okay erring on the side of caution here. We have to think of this like war. It isn't fair, but that's the way it is."

Peppa's eyes locked on the road ahead. "I know." Everyone was silent for a time, and then she said, "And anyway, Jacques was wrong. The officer was out in the rain, working alongside his men."

Jacques wagged his head back and forth. "He was still a *capitán*. Anything above major woulda stayed in the dry."

Garcia offered to take a turn behind the wheel. Five hundred miles was much too far for any one of them drive and still have the energy they'd need at the end of the trip. Peppa pulled over long enough for everyone but Jacques to switch places, with Miyagi sliding into the back while Peppa took her spot in the front passenger seat. Garcia was in the weather for less than ten seconds, but she looked as if she'd just stepped out of the shower when she climbed in behind the wheel. She pulled back onto the road as soon as she heard Miyagi slam the back door.

The trip took over ten hours in good weather. It would be midmorning before they arrived at the target location, forcing them to approach in the light of day—another reason to be grateful for the sound and fury of the storm. It would offer them some semblance of cover, if it didn't kill them.

Chapter 48

Joaquin Mirabal squatted beside Dr. Ibarra's body, hands on knees, breathing slowly through his nose, thinking. Mirabal felt no sadness at Ibarra's death. Quite the opposite, in fact. This man who had tied so many to his chair and mutilated them now found himself bruised and broken. Mirabal pulled back the dead man's eyelid with his thumb and clucked to himself. Ruptured blood vessels had turned the whites red. He'd choked to death. Gentle pressure against the throat showed his larynx had been crushed. And the arms . . . both so badly damaged it was difficult to tell elbow from forearm. Corporal Aleman was alive, but his jaw was broken in two places, causing him to babble incoherently. The three soldiers in the front had gotten it as bad as Ibarra. Duran's rock pick had been put to efficient use, as had one of the doctor's scalpels and his cattle prod.

A wide swath of destruction for a real estate salesman who had boxed in high school.

The colonel rose with a groan. "I want to take a look at the dead soldiers up front."

Serafina gave him an anxious nod, always excited to watch him work.

"What does the scene tell you?" Mirabal asked a few moments later, after they'd made their way back around from the cellblock.

"They're all piled on top of each other," Duran said. "Killed three different ways. More than one assailant?"

"Could be," Mirabal said. "There was more than one prisoner here." He leaned forward and picked up a white plastic watch, small like a woman's.

Duran shrugged, thinking it a test and speaking openly—as Mirabal encouraged. "That does not mean much. It could have come from a pocket. Or even been taken from an earlier prisoner."

"It could have," Mirabal prodded. "But I do not believe that to be the case. Keep looking."

"His trousers," Serafina said, pointing to the soldier lying faceup on the concrete. "They are unfastened. His belt as well. The woman who had the watch could have been their prisoner."

"Very good," Mirabal said. "It is a shame the surveillance cameras are inoperable. We might have seen who came for our friend Mr. Jim Shield."

Duran looked at the puddles on the ground, counted four large ones, then pointed them out to Mirabal, attempting to redeem himself. "No tracks, but four individuals stood here prior to the fight—"

Mirabal raised his eyebrows. "When?" he asked. "What about the puddles tells you they were created prior to the fight?"

Duran shook his head. "I . . . I am not certain, Colonel."

"It is always possible that a team of four *Yanqui*

commandos broke in and killed everyone, freeing our prisoner." He patted the young lieutenant on the back. "I think you were right the first time, but it is important to differentiate between conjecture and fact when one is hunting."

"I understand," Duran said. "One thing is certain. The storm will have scoured away all his tracks. He will be impossible to follow in the wind and rain."

Mirabal smiled. "You know me better than that," he said. "Of course we will follow him. This man has killed four of our men and severely wounded another. We cannot merely let him go."

"I do not suggest—"

"I know you don't, Duran," Mirabal said. "Remember, tracks on the ground aren't the only kind of spoor someone leaves behind. People under stress make mistakes. We must press this Jim Shield to make sure that he does. There are two kinds of tracking dogs— sight dogs and scent dogs. We may have lost sight of our quarry, but we can certainly smell him—be aware of the things he does and where he is trying to go. Where would you go if you were trapped on an island with me?"

"I would attempt to get off the island," Duran said. "As soon as possible."

"He should be easy to capture," Serafina offered. "He has nothing in the way of supplies or food—and no other weapon beyond perhaps a knife, or a stick."

"Maybe," Mirabal said. "But it is just as dangerous to underestimate our quarry as it is to overestimate him. This man has left behind him a path of blood and carnage. I feel quite sure he is capable of leaving a great deal more if we are not careful."

Mirabal squatted beside the dead soldiers, making certain not to miss anything. He touched the scar on his forehead as he thought. *This one will be a worthy challenge—whoever he is.*

Chapter 49

Quinn sat at the handlebars of the little bike, wringing every ounce of speed he dared from the throttle. He spent more time fishtailing than he did riding in a straight line, and he began to wonder if the tires had any tread left on them at all. Odesa navigated from the almost nonexistent pillion seat, hanging on behind him and shivering from shock, arms wrapped tightly around his waist. She tried yelling directions over the storm, but the wind ripped any words away as soon as they left her mouth. They eventually made do with pointing, allowing Quinn to concentrate on keeping the bike on two wheels instead of constantly looking back to try and make out what she was saying.

Quinn wished for a gun—but that couldn't be helped. The soldiers hadn't been particularly disciplined, but they'd been smart enough to lock up their weapons before they came into the cellblock. He and Odesa had already passed through the heavy steel doors by the time he found the lockbox out in the foyer. The locker keys were probably inside on the dead soldiers, but he wasn't about to venture back and risk getting trapped if the power came back on. Better to keep moving.

There would be weapons when he needed them. There always were.

They passed no other vehicles—everyone in Nuevo Gerona was too smart to be out in this mess—and made it to the docks along the river in less than ten minutes. The plan was to wait in the boat until the first break in the weather that made the bay passable enough.

The storm surge pushed the river well over its banks, spreading out on a floodplain and forcing Quinn and Odesa to trudge through calf-deep water to get to the go-fast boat. Odesa got to the boarding plank and froze.

"What's wrong?" Quinn yelled above the shriek of wind.

"I just realized," Odesa screamed back. "They took the keys."

Quinn looked up and down the docks. There weren't many other vessels, and most of those were old fishing boats, decrepit, hardly safe enough to go out in fair weather, let alone a blow like this. The most seaworthy were the military boats, belonging either to the police or the coastguard. Quinn picked the smallest of the three, a thirty-five-foot rigid-hull with an enclosed cabin and a stabilizing foam ring around the gunnels that made it look like a large inflatable.

Odesa slowed as they got ready to board. "What if there is a guard?"

"I'll take care of it," Quinn said.

"You mean kill him?"

"Or we can sit here and let them catch us," Quinn said. "Anyway, it looks dark on board. Odds are, any night watch will be on one of the larger boats."

Odesa pulled a strand of wet hair out of her mouth and nodded, shivering.

Quinn used a knife he'd taken from Ibarra's torture table to jimmy the back door into the boat's cabin. It took him all of twenty seconds, Odesa watching with rapt interest and making him promise to show her how he'd done it. The boat strained at its moorings like a horse in the starting gates, but the wheelhouse offered some protection from the noise.

"Look over there for the keys," Quinn said, nodding toward a chart table while he rifled quickly through the glovebox and under the captain's seat.

A metallic rattle grabbed his attention.

"Find it?" he asked.

"I'm not sure," Odesa said. She knelt at the base of a small dinette, shining the flashlight in an open cabinet door that was set back in the bulkhead, careful to keep the light pointed down. The windows had blackout curtains to protect the boat's interior from the sun, but the light would still be visible to anyone on watch who happened to take his job seriously enough to be out walking the docks. She held a brass lock away from a heavy steel hasp. "There is something important in here. Weapons, maybe—or the key."

Quinn knelt beside her.

It was an old combination lock with a five-digit code on spinning tumblers at the bottom. The Cyrillic stamping on the back told him it was in Russian. Hammer marks were still visible on the brass body, giving the impression that the thing had been made on an anvil instead of a factory machine. Like many products from Russia, what it lacked in fit and finish, it made up for with brute strength. Quinn couldn't help but think it would make a fine slock, an improvised weapon made from a lock slung inside of a sock. If he had any socks.

"Can you use the knife?" Odesa asked.

"I don't think so," Quinn said. "I can pick it, but I need a thin piece of metal." He turned the lock upward and pointed to the space beside the dials with the point of his blade. "Small enough to fit in here."

"The clip of a ballpoint pen?"

"Almost," Quinn said. "But that's probably going to be too thick."

Odesa though for a moment, then gave a slow nod. "A very thin piece of metal? About the size of a pen clip, but much thinner? Like a tiny leaf spring?"

"Exactly," Quinn said. It was easy to forget that Odesa and thousands like her manufactured replacement parts for virtually every machine and tool on the island from old tires and sardine cans. He tapped the base of the lock again. "It has to fit in here so I can use it as a feeler key."

"Here. Hold this." She passed him the flashlight, then pulled her arms inside her T-shirt, turtle-like. A few contortions later, her bra dropped into her lap and her arms popped back out through the sleeves.

"*Ajustador*," she said, holding up the bra. It was off-white and, though Quinn would never mention it, leaned a little on the industrial side, meant for the heavy lifting that women like Odesa and her sister required.

"It is not as sexy as the American brassieres," Odesa continued. "I have seen them in magazines and even here in shops, but I cannot afford such luxuries. And anyway, why would a woman spend so much money on something that her husband is only going to take off?"

Quinn hoped this was a rhetorical question. Thibodaux

could have written a ten-page treatise on the subject, but luckily, Odesa didn't seem to require an answer.

She turned the bra upside down and picked at the bottom seam, borrowing the knife from Quinn to cut a few threads. Then, using her thumb and the edge of the bladelike pliers, she slid out an eight-inch sliver of spring steel, less than a quarter inch wide and only slightly thicker than a piece of paper. "Underwire," she proclaimed, smiling as she held up the trophy. "Will it work?"

"I think so," Quinn said with a look of admiration that made her blush. He slipped the wire in the gap between the first wheel and the brass body of the lock, then pressed the corner of the shim against the axle, turning the wheel slowly, number by number, until he felt it land on a flat spot.

"Remember these numbers," he said. "Three." He worked the next wheel until he reached the flat spot, moving from wheel to wheel. ". . . three . . . seven . . . one . . . six."

Odesa leaned closer, impressed. "The combination is three, three, seven, one, six?"

"Not quite," Quinn said. He moved the lock slightly so it caught the full beam of the flashlight, then began spinning the dials again. "These are ten-numeral wheels, so the numerals we want are five digits off, on the direct opposite side of the wheel—eight, eight, two, six, one."

Odesa's eyebrows shot upward when the lock clicked open. "I will remember this the next time I am running from the army."

The lock defeated, Quinn handed the thin metal shim back to Odesa.

"Keep it," she said, long lashes fluttering with mock drama. "To remember me by." She was definitely related to Ronnie.

He smiled, pushing the shim back to her. "We might need it again, and I have no pockets."

She looked at him through narrowed eyes for a moment, waiting to see if he'd respond to her flirting. When he didn't, she took the piece of metal and stuffed it in the front pocket of her pants.

The keys inside the safe had a bright orange fob from the Miami boat show—capitalist, but convenient for making sure they didn't get lost overboard. There was no weapon, but Quinn hadn't expected to find one. Salt water had a way of chewing through gun parts and turning them to a chalky mess, especially when mixed with the shoddy maintenance procedures of conscripted soldiers and coastguardsmen.

Quinn tossed Odesa the keys. Mirabal and his minions were probably out there now, creeping up on the boat. If the colonel was truly a hunter, he'd know Quinn would want to get off the island. The storm made sneaking up on someone as easy as if they were inside a carwash.

Odesa scrambled into the seat behind the wheel, playing the light across the console to familiarize herself with the controls.

"We have plenty of fuel," she said. "You release the lines and I will take us out. I know a place around the point to the east where we can wait out the storm. We will be able to—"

"If you know a place," Quinn said, "then they will

know of the same place. I have a plan, but in order for it to work, we have to get back across to the main island."

Odesa stared at him, dumbfounded. "If your plan involves us being swallowed up by the sea, then that will work." She closed her eyes, explaining the realities of life to a very small child. "I know these rocks, these reefs. They are like teeth, a lot of teeth, just waiting out there to chew an unwary boat to splinters and spit it into the sea. This is a good boat, but once we leave the river, I will only have the illusion of control. If we go out in this, we will drown. It is almost certain."

"Odesa," Quinn said, taking firmly her by both shoulders. "You know who I am. What I am. If we stay here, these men will kill me—and, I'm sorry to say, they will kill you as well because you are associated with me. That is one hundred percent certain. Zero doubt. When given a choice between certain death and almost certain death . . . there isn't much of a choice."

Odesa pulled away. "You Americans," she scoffed, shaking her head as she turned the key in the ignition. "You're always thinking . . ."

Quinn felt the tug and sway of the boat as he watched the water bash the surrounding windows and listened to the deafening roar of rain and wind. He'd learned to ignore it, but the moment he lost focus, the banshee-like screaming closed in around him. The residual drugs and lingering feelings of doom only added to the storm's dizzying effects.

"I'll cast off," he said, hand on the door.

Odesa turned the key and coaxed first the starboard, then the port engine to life. She rested long fingers on the throttles and gave him a nod along with a forced, tight-lipped smile. "Go, then," she said. "If we are to die, we should get on with it."

Quinn worked quickly, bowing his head against the wind. He was already drenched, so he didn't have to worry about trying to stay dry. He had just tossed the last line when he heard a sharp crack above the hissing rain—like thunder, but not quite. He ducked, scanning the shoreline. His heart sank when he saw flashlight beams playing back and forth.

Another crack split the air, this one just feet from his head. Two more slapped the aluminum hull in quick succession. Quinn sucked in a quick breath, counting the shots, instinctively figuring the angles. Probably more than one shooter.

He crouched low, duckwalking toward the pilot-house, willing the thin metal to provide him cover rather than just the concealment it actually did. He pounded on the window, barely able to make out Odesa's face through the running water on the windscreen.

"Go!" he yelled, knowing she couldn't hear him or the shots, but hoping she could discern the intensity in his face.

A bullet shattered the glass, making his point for him. Quinn didn't hear the engines, but he felt the boat lurch as Odesa threw it into gear and headed out into the river, catching the current and letting it swing the bow around. She gunned it as soon as they were pointing north. Now Quinn heard the engines.

More shots came, along with frenzied shouts and a flurry of more lights. Everyone was running except one man. The rain made it impossible to make out his face, but Quinn was certain it was Colonel Mirabal, the hunter. He'd figured out exactly where they had gone—outguessed them, followed without tracks. He'd get his own boat now, somehow, and sail into the jaws of a hurricane after Quinn, even if it killed him—exactly as Quinn himself would have done, had the roles been reversed.

Chapter 50

As smart as she was, Violeta had zero sense of direction. Her father often spoke in unintelligible gobbledygook, like "head east and then turn north" instead of saying "turn right at the Walmart" like a normal person. But she could reason, and deduct, and her deductions told her that since the storm was coming from the east, the sewage lagoon was probably on the bunker's north wall.

Brown water oozed from a long vertical seam that ran from floor to ceiling in the timbers, dripping down to form a growing puddle at the base of the wall. General Penguin cursed when he saw it. He ordered two of the men to clean it up with towels and a third to adjust the pumps. Violeta turned slightly at her work, allowing the hood to mask the direction of her gaze so she could get a better look. The bright work lights revealed a slight bulge in the retaining wall—a weakness in the shoring that held back the tide. The pumps that kept the moat of crap at a given level were beginning to fall behind. If they failed, the sewage lagoon would overflow and flood the bunker. The thought of it made her knees wobble. Dying in a nuclear fireball would be quick and painless. Drowning in chicken shit would not be an easy death.

The general's disembodied voice clicked in the speaker inside her hood. "Are you finished?"

She answered automatically. "Almost."

"Hurry," he snapped. "I want to be ready to move when the storm passes."

"Hurry?" Violeta parroted, anger rising in her belly. "You gave me four hours to rest last night in the corner of a stinking barn, and then you want me to rush through programming a very delicate guidance system? Sure. I'll get right on that for you. I'll be done in a jiffy. Of course, your precious missile might hit Havana, or Nassau, or some rogue wave in the middle of the Gulf of Mexico, but hey, if you want me to hurry, then I'll cut a few corners and we can wrap this right up right damned now."

De la Guardia turned her so she was facing him— two orange monsters, hood to hood. "You would do well to show a little respect, if only to protect your parents."

Violeta closed her eyes and took a slow, deliberate breath.

"I'm sorry," she said, choking back honest tears. "This hardware you've brought in looks like something out of an old Nintendo. I'm having a hard time getting the computer to talk to the software. It's taking some time to work out the bugs. We should be ready to go in a couple of hours."

"Outstanding," the general said. "Was that so difficult?"

She shook her head, but the hood remained in place. "I'm just scared," she said. "And, honestly, I would be more productive if I could rest my eyes for about five minutes and get some water."

De la Guardia let his eyes play up and down, as if

there was much to look at in the suit. At length, he flicked his hand, and then ordered one of the guards to accompany her up the ladder. "Your parents will be fine," he said, almost as an afterthought, "if you do exactly as I tell you. You have my word."

Violeta turned toward the ladder, antsy to make the climb that would take her out of this poisonous atmosphere—and get her away from The Penguin. He gave his word. What a joke. Her parents would soon be dead, if they weren't already. But it would do no good to let this maniac know she'd lost hope. As long as he thought he had control, de la Guardia would continue to allow her a little latitude—which she would give her the space for what she had to do.

Less than a hundred feet from the rear of the barn and just inside the tree line, Thibodaux gave Garcia a solid nudge in the ribs. The forest thrashed back and forth in the wind as if some giant beast were about to emerge from the foliage. Rain pelted the red slurry of mud that was more of a lake than a forest floor.

"What?" Ronnie yelled above the storm. The row of skeletal old barns was close enough to hit with a rock, but she didn't worry about being heard, not in this mess.

Jacques rubbed rain out of his good eye and nodded toward the tree line perpendicular to their hiding spot, off the end of the nearest barn. "I think Emiko took out the sentry!"

Ronnie yelled the information in Peppa's ear. Her auntie lay in the mud on the other side of her, and both women squinted through the haze of rain and flying debris at a shadowed form, almost hidden in the trees.

The figure had been standing, but now slumped at the base of a tall pine.

They had used Palmer's coordinates to locate the area believed to have housed the Soviet missiles almost sixty years before, driving as far as they dared on mud-choked roads before continuing on foot. They checked three different complexes of abandoned poultry barns before almost stumbling into this one—the first one they'd seen with any sign of human activity. There appeared to be only one sentry hidden in the trees. Unfortunately for him, he was more worried about keeping his flimsy rain gear buttoned shut than lurking threats.

There were five barns in all, set side by side about a hundred feet apart. Ronnie estimated each long, slender building to be roughly fifty by two hundred feet. All but the nearest one looked to be abandoned. Large earthen mounds, some almost as tall as the buildings, sat off the ends of each structure. Manure, Garcia thought. Pushed out by tractors—or, more likely, with shovel and wheelbarrow, in this part of the world. Her Auntie Madonna had raised chickens in a backyard coop in Hialeah. It was nothing short of amazing how much crap a dozen birds could manufacture in a year. During its heyday, this place must have housed thousands of birds to make these mountains.

Miyagi ghosted through the trees a moment later, seeming to materialize from the sheets of rain. She fell on her stomach and wormed her way in between Thibodaux and Garcia, shoulder to shoulder.

"This is the place," she said, facing the barn so both of them could hear. "There is a small gap in the grating along the outside wall, so I was able to get a look inside. The device looks to be an FKR—a Soviet short-range nuclear missile. A probable yield of eight to fifteen kilotons. Nine people down below—six working on the device, two acting as guards, and one standing around shouting at everyone. I could not get a clear shot or I would have—"

"Wait," Thibodaux shouted. "A clear shot?"

Miyagi's lips perked in an uncharacteristic smile. She passed a black Makarov pistol to Jacques before pulling another from her waistband and handing it to Garcia. "The two sentries I met won't need them anymore."

Garcia pulled the slide back a hair, press checking to make sure there was a round in the chamber before popping the magazine out to see that it was topped off as well.

Peppa nudged her, pointing at the barn.

Two figures in orange protective suits came out the door at the end of the building. Both of them unzipped their suits and threw back the hoods, seemingly grateful to get some fresh air even if it meant getting drenched. One of the newcomers was a young man in his mid-twenties. A rifle was slung over his shoulder. He lit a cigarette and kept his hand cupped in front of his face to protect it from the rain.

The second figure proved to be a young woman with short blue hair. She threw her head back as soon as she'd removed the hood, gazing up at the sky, hands down by her sides. It was difficult to tell with the baggy suit, but Garcia guessed her to be on the plump side.

"Violeta Cruz," she said under her breath, recognizing the missing engineer from the photo Palmer had sent with his last message.

"Fancy that," Thibodaux said, almost inaudible.

Peppa leaned in, lips to Ronnie's ear. "Could she be working with them?"

"Not likely," Garcia said. "They have a guard on her."

Miyagi was already scuttling backward, out from between them. "I'll be right back," she said.

"Don't forget to grab the rifle," Thibodaux said, tipping his head toward the sentry.

Miyagi rolled her eyes. "What an outstanding idea, Jacques-san," she said, before disappearing into the trees.

Ronnie lost sight of Miyagi but had the advantage of knowing where she would next turn up. She felt Peppa catch her breath when Miyagi loomed up behind the smoking sentry and used her short blade to kill him quickly. Violeta wheeled at the noise, backpedaled in horror as the young man writhed in the mud. Miyagi put up her hands, but the bloody knife didn't exactly make her look like a friendly. She must have said something because Violeta looked toward Garcia, peering through the rain but obviously seeing nothing. She shot a glance over her shoulder at the barn, then back at Miyagi. A moment later they trotted back into the tree line. Two minutes later, Violeta Cruz stood in the relative protection of the forest, shaking in disbelief.

"Where did you guys come from? How did you find me? Are my parents okay?"

Miyagi held up her hand, careful now to keep the knife out of sight. "We did not know you were here," she said.

"I'm sorry," Thibodaux added. "But we don't have any info on your parents."

Miyagi kept one eye on the barn as she talked. "Do you know what you're working on?"

"I do," Violeta said. She was shaking now, her eyes glazing in shock "A tactical nuke."

Peppa noticed, too, and squeezed the young woman's hand through the cumbersome rubber glove.

Miyagi nodded. "Is there a way to disarm it?"

The young woman rapidly briefed them on her situation, then said, "He'll kill my parents if I don't cooperate. That guy named Fuentes knows where they are. I have to find them."

"We'll do our best," Thibodaux said, rubbing his face. He stooped some, making himself look smaller to tone down his hulking size and try and put the girl at ease. "Who's Fuentes?"

"The general's main thug. He's still down there."

"Okay," Thibodaux said, nodding, taking it all in. "What do they have you working on?"

"Guidance," Violeta said, lips trembling.

"FKRs have a short range," Thibodaux said. "Less than a hundred miles."

"This one has been revamped." Violeta's her eyes glazed, staring blankly a thousand yards away. "I'm sure it could reach Miami." Her head suddenly snapped up. "I wasn't going to let that happen, you know."

Thibodaux put a hand on her shoulder and smiled. "I believe you."

"What would you have done?" Garcia asked.

Violeta chewed on her bottom lip, then took a deep breath. "See that big lagoon there beside the building? It's full of sewage, probably ten or fifteen feet of water and old chicken manure. The bunker has a false floor built above even more of the stuff. They're pumping it out from below into this lagoon and using secondary pumps to keep that from overflowing—but the rain is getting ahead of the pumps. The lagoon is filling up and weeping through back into the bunker."

"Okay . . ." Thibodaux said.

"See that foam on top?" Violeta said, on a roll now. Everyone nodded.

"I took a look at it during my last pee break. I'm pretty sure it's made up mostly of methane."

"Methane?" Garcia mused. "From the chicken manure breaking down?"

"Exactly," Violeta said. "And I plan to blow it up."

"Blow it up?" Peppa said.

"The foam is usually stable, but if it's agitated, the bubbles pop, and a spark can set it off. I read about a pig barn in the Midwest that got blown two feet in the air when some guy was welding a gate—the entire barn. This rain is agitating the foam, popping the bubbles, and letting the methane escape. I'm not a structural engineer, or an expert on poop, but I think the pressure from the resulting explosion would shatter the retaining wall and flood the bunker—"

A smile crept over Thibodaux's face. "Drowning everyone down there in chicken shit," he said. "I like it."

Ronnie held up her hand. "Hang on," she said. "Why not just damage the vents, let everyone inside die like mice in a jar of alcohol?"

Thibodaux smirked. "What kind of kid were you?"

"Seriously," Garcia said. "The vents will be easier than counting on an iffy detonation."

Violeta shook her head. "I thought of that. The vents appear to be made of a concrete conduit. Old school and simple, but very heavy duty. It would take a couple of strong men an hour to damage them enough to make a difference."

"We don't have to damage them," Garcia said. "Couldn't we achieve the same result by just turning off the fans?"

"Everyone is wearing respirators," Violeta said. "They would just come topside until the fans were fixed."

Ronnie threw up her hands. "Okay," she said. "If that's our only option."

"We will need to buy some time," Emiko said. "Quickly, step out of your suit. I'll take your place inside the bunker."

"Hang on, now," Thibodaux said, his face falling dark. "Nobody has to go back down there. We'll just put a bullet through the foam. That should set it off. Right?"

Violeta shook her head. "Maybe," she said. "But the odds are very low."

Peppa stepped forward. "Let me go."

"Not a chance," Garcia said. "If anyone goes, it's me."

Miyagi snapped her fingers, hurrying the girl along. "No," she said. "We are approximately the same height—"

"Yeah," Violeta said. "But you're seventy pounds lighter."

"The suit will cover that," Miyagi said. "Do what you need to do."

Thibodaux paced back and forth in the rain, hand on top of his head, looking like he might punch a tree. "Emiko, this is suicide."

"I don't wish to die," Miyagi said. "Ignite the foam in ten minutes. I will come out in nine and a half."

The big Cajun clenched his teeth, unconvinced, but he began work on the plan.

Violeta gave Miyagi the suit. "There is a soldier stationed inside the building reading a porn magazine. His job is to watch the generators. Go straight to the ladder, and he won't pay you any attention. I was working out of a white plastic toolbox on a table next to an open laptop computer. The oval metal plate to the guidance system is in the toolbox, giving you access to the hardware on the left side of the nose. Someone did some modifications on it before I got here. Your mask will fog right after you go back in, but it will clear quickly because of the filters. If you go directly to the nose of the missile, they might not be able to see your face." Her lips trembled. "Listen, I know it's not the priority, but if you can get Fuentes's phone while you're down there . . . maybe it would help me figure out how to find my parents."

"I will try," Miyagi said. She stepped into the suit, looked at her watch, and zipped herself in quickly.

"How will you know when nine and a half minutes have passed?" Peppa asked.

"I will know," Miyagi said. She leaned closer to Garcia. "You must detonate the foam, even if I am not out."

"Emiko, I—"

Miyagi raised her hand. "Jacques will not do it. It has to be you."

Chapter 51

"Are they still back there?" Odesa asked, fingers tight and white on the wheel.

Quinn glanced over his shoulder at the mixture of gray sky and green water, waiting for a wave to lift them up so he could see. It was like trying to find a specific sock at the bottom of a washing machine during the spin cycle. His stomach fell as they surfed down the back of a fifteen-foot wave, forcing him to gulp to keep from getting sick.

Mirabal was too far back to tell what kind of boat he was in, but Quinn suspected it was one of the smaller patrol vessels—a SAFE boat like the one they were in. Had it not been, they would never have survived this long, let along been able to gain ground. Red and green navigation lights flickered in the distance beyond the endless train of waves that rose like monsters behind them. The lights vanished in the troughs, only to bob to the top and show themselves a moment later—over and over, taunting, hounding.

"Yep," Quinn said.

"Shit!" Odesa peppered her frustration with a string of Spanish curses. Quinn recognized the ones commonly employed by Garcia when she was particularly angry, but he got the gist of even those that he'd never heard before.

Odesa had crossed the bay from the Isle of Youth and at an angle, keeping the SAFE boat inside the southern lee of the main island of Cuba, tucking in as close as she dared without running onto the boat-eating rocks and cays that littered the southern coast. They'd passed Fidel's private island, fearing an interception party, but it had apparently been evacuated during the storm. She'd considered venturing closer to land in an attempt to lose Mirabal, but gave up that idea for fear of running aground in the unpredictable surge.

"Why is he doing this?" she fumed. "This is so crazy. We have to go out in order to escape. He does not."

"The colonel is a hunter," Quinn said. "We run. He chases. It really is just that simple."

"So we stop, he stops," Odesa said.

Quinn shook his head. "We stop, he kills us."

"You are both insane."

"Maybe," Quinn said. "But you and I will still be dead."

Odesa gave an exasperated groan and flicked her hand to ward away any further conversation. She had to concentrate on keeping the boat from being thrown broadside by the screaming wind.

Waves loomed around the speeding craft like living mountains, often making it impossible to see anything but walls of savage green water on every side. Just when it seemed as if they would be swallowed whole, a wave beneath would drive them upward, leaving them to hang there for an agonizing moment, motionless on the top of a windswept peak.

Odesa drove with two parts skill and one part cursing, keeping them pointed into the wind whether climbing up the face of an impossibly tall wave or skating down the back side of it to crash bow-first into the streaked green water. The boat was built for ocean rescue, with extra flotation around the gunwales and large scuppers to drain the decks, but Quinn wondered how many direct hits from massive waves the windscreen could take when it was partially shattered by bullet holes.

If the glass came out, the cabin would fill with water on their next trip down—and if that happened, they were doomed.

Quinn took shallow breaths, trying to focus on the distant shore during the rare moments it showed itself. He'd always been at home in or on the water, working summers on his old man's commercial fishing boat from the time he was old enough to pull nets and pick fish. The Bering Sea was a fickle place, prone to nasty storms and freak waves, and not once had he ever been seasick. But his time in Dr. Ibarra's chair and the after-effects of adrenaline and adenosine closed around his stomach like a clenched fist. He hadn't had anything to eat since the chocolate bar Mirabal had given him, and he was beginning to wonder if that too hadn't contained some kind of drug. He swallowed hard and gutted it out. There was no time to be sick. Not with Mirabal behind them.

Quinn reached above the console and turned the marine radio to channel twenty-two, immediately gratified to hear a string of numbers read by a female voice. He listened until the string had run completely through three times to make certain he had it correct before turning the radio back to scan.

"What was that all about?" Odesa asked.

"A numbers station," Quinn said. "It's broadcasting a code about the location of our extraction point. My friends must have gone to Santiago because our pickup is at this end of the island. They have no idea we're here, so Ronnie must have set it up."

"How can you tell from the numbers?"

"It's a coded grid," Quinn said. "It covers prearranged points all around the island that we all memorized. The numbers we just heard correspond to a place called Playa Las Coloradas. It's relatively protected from the storm."

"I know the Playa," Odesa said. "It is essentially dead ahead—"

The radio crackled and Colonel Mirabal's static-filled voice ordered, then implored them to go ashore before everyone drowned. Quinn clutched the handrail above Odesa's head, his hip pressing against her shoulder for support as he grabbed the radio mic clipped to the console. He thought for a minute about what to say, then hung up the mic without speaking.

Odesa hunched forward in her seat, peering through the rain and swishing wiper blades. "Why do you not answer?"

"I don't want to give him anything," Quinn said. "My voice might give away that I'm still sick from what they gave me. He needs to believe we are strong."

Odesa glanced up at him, then quickly back at the windscreen. "Strong?" she spat. "You are about to pass out. I am so scared my hands can hardly grip the wheel.

Even if we get away from these people, I can never return to my boat. I have committed so many crimes that I will spend the rest of my life in prison if I am not put against the wall. My insides feel like they are coming unmoored. Drifting away. No, that is not right. Blown away." She shook her head in disgust. "You and I are very far from strong."

Quinn used the railing overhead to make his way to the back door, peering out the window. "I think they're getting closer. How far are we from Cape Cruz?"

Odesa consulted the color screen of the GPS chart-plotter on her console. "It is ten miles to our southeast. I thought we were going to Playa Las Coloradas."

Quinn put a finger on GPS. "That's about here. Right?"

She nodded. "Yes. South of the village of Belic."

"It's just before two p.m.," Quinn said. "Our window for pickup is in thirteen hours. We don't want to lead him directly to our extraction point, and he's likely to catch us if we don't do something drastic. Can you take us around the cape?"

Odesa gave a maniacal laugh. They were both yelling above the roar and crash of the storm. "My sister must like her men crazy. You think these seas are tall? I will show you tall if we round Cabo Cruz."

Quinn worked his way forward, standing next to her while he studied the GPS screen. It was a mass of small islets and cays near shore, but to the south was open water. "We could make a run for Haiti. There's a chance the island would blunt the force of the hurricane. Maybe we could even get to Jamaica. That's relatively close."

"The bottom of the sea is relatively close, my friend," Odesa said. "The waves on the lee side of Haiti might not be as bad as the open ocean, but they will be worse than this—and we will not survive worse than this. We are already running low on fuel. Without fuel . . ." Her voice trailed off.

One hand on the boat, the other flat on top of his head, Quinn stared at the bouncing image on the GPS, running through their options. He squinted hard in an effort to clear the cobwebs that coated his thoughts. He tapped the screen in the area around the cape, away from the muddy marshes and lagoons that lay directly ahead. "Have you ever been to this area?"

"I have not," she said. "It is a national park. I know there are caves there. Many cliffs and thick vegetation. The Castros hid out in the mountains to the east for years. But I already told you, if we go around we are as good as dead."

Quinn used the buttons to zoom in, checking the soundings along the shore, his mind working a million miles an hour to cut through the haze.

"Just do it," he said. "It's our only chance. If I re-member right, Fidel and his revolutionaries were almost shot to pieces because they were trapped in the marshes when they landed near here. Mirabal will not hesitate to do the same to us unless we go around. I'm going to look around and see what kind of gear I can scrounge up." He tapped a spot on the screen. "See this area here?"

She nodded, shooting him a doubtful glance. "What about it?"

"Run us aground somewhere close to this where we

can make for the woods. The colonel fancies himself a hunter. We'll give him something to hunt."

"If we live," Odesa said.

Quinn gave her a reassuring pat on the shoulder. "We'll live. So long as you take us around the cape."

Chapter 52

Garcia stood at the edge of the sewage lagoon with her forearm pressed across her nose. Noxious fumes brought a cascade of tears to mix with the rain that pelted her cheeks. Shirt collar pulled up in a makeshift gas mask, Jacques stopped in the mud beside the generator powering the two pumps that pulled sewage out of the lagoon and into a narrow ditch that led into the trees behind the nearest manure mountain. Snotty foam, beaten by the wind and rain, bubbled and jiggled in the wide pool just feet away. Peppa and Violeta waited a few feet back. The younger woman pointed to what she believed to be the weakest point in the retaining wall along the edge of the poultry barn. The fumes didn't appear to bother her as badly as they did everyone else. Ronnie decided the poor girl was in shock or had gone noseblind. Probably both.

"The fluid pressure against the wall would be intense," Violeta said. "I don't think it matters where the explosion happens. There's enough methane in the foam to set off the gases in the subfloor. We'll want to be well back when it goes off."

Jacques squinted up through the rain with his good eye, then pulled the collar down from his mouth to give a nod at the chugging generator. "And the guy inside is gonna know when this thing quits?"

"There's a board with red and green lights," Violeta said. "It's right in front of him so he can see how all the pumps and generators are operating. If he looks up from his porno magazine, he'll be able to tell if one of them is out."

Ronnie glanced at the barn. "And the backfire spark when he restarts the generator will be enough to set off the methane fumes?"

Violeta shrugged. "It should be."

Peppa stared at the lagoon, entranced. "Such an explosion will not detonate the nuclear bomb?"

Violeta wiped rain off her nose. "I don't think so," she said. "I'm guessing the whole thing will just get covered up in sludge." She gave a tired sigh. "But that missile is old, so I can't promise anything."

Garcia shooed them back toward the tree line. "We'll be right there." She stepped closer to Jacques after they'd gone.

His jaw tensed, lips set in a grim line.

"Ready?" she asked.

"Four and a half minutes gone," he said.

"She'll make it out."

"Yeah." Thibodaux's hand hovered above the generator's kill switch. "I can't quite believe we're the ones saving the day here. That's usually a Chair Force thing."

"I know," Garcia said, blinking back tears when she thought of Quinn, grateful for the rain that streaked her face.

"Okay," Thibodaux groaned. He checked his watch for the tenth time. "I figure we got at least couple of minutes before the soldier inside notices the generator is out and gets off his ass to come check it. I'll pull off the spark plug lead after I kill it so we can get a good arc when he tries to start it. If that girl knows her shit, we should get a big boom."

"Kill it," Garcia said. Thibodaux complied.

The generator fell silent. Thibodaux pulled the spark plug wire, making certain he was close enough to the plug to arc, and then they ran for the trees.

Emiko Miyagi kept her head down as she walked past the soldier with the magazine, focusing on the wooden trapdoor that led to the underground bunker. Years of training and actual battle had taught her the futility of pondering her own death. She would observe, strategize, fight if need be—then either die, or not. There was nothing she could do beyond her best.

The ladder down was simple enough, though she took her time, reasoning that a fatigued and frightened young woman of Violeta's build would come down haltingly.

Miyagi found the bunker just as Cruz had described it. No one challenged her as she made her way to the nose of the missile. A quick scan of the room told her there were nine people, all of them wearing the same type of orange protective suit. Most huddled around the winged missile, working on one component or another. One stood back against the far wall, farthest from the weeping sewage lagoon wall, hands folded at his waist. He wore a wide leather belt around his safety suit and carried a wooden club. Security. This had to be the one called Fuentes. Another man, this one even shorter than

Miyagi, stood talking to two others off the far wing of the missile. He looked up and gave her a sneering nod. The speaker inside her hood clicked as he ordered her back to work in dismissive Spanish.

General de la Guardia. If anyone had a gun down in the bunker, it would be him. The scientists would all be smart enough to worry about sparks setting off the gas, and he would placate them by making his security man carry a stick—but he would at least have a pistol tucked inside his protective suit. If things went bad, he would be the first one she killed, cutting the head off the snake.

Miyagi gave a submissive dip of her head, rounding her shoulders to appear more like Violeta Cruz. She climbed the three wooden steps quickly to the scaffolding alongside the missile's fuselage, locating the plastic toolbox where Violeta said it would be. A flat cable ran from a multi-pronged connecter in what was presumably the aircraft's guidance system to a port in an open laptop computer.

Miyagi rifled through the tools, choosing a Phillips-head screwdriver with a hefty ten-inch shaft. She surveyed the electronics inside the open nose hatch and was contemplating where the screwdriver might do the most damage when de la Guardia gave a flick of his hand and told one of the men beside him to keep an eye on her.

The tallest of the two gave a crisp response, obviously accustomed to kowtowing to the general. He wheeled immediately toward Miyagi. She palmed the screwdriver and leaned closer to the nose of the missile, reaching in to destroy four small circuit boards before he could make it up the steps. She clucked to herself as if working through some problem as he came up beside her onto the two boards that comprised the scaffolding.

Time could speed by like lightning when a task had to be completed. But in an underground bunker surrounded by people who would happily kill her, Miyagi found the minutes barely oozed by. Her internal clock told her no more than half her allotted time had elapsed. Her phone alarm was set to vibrate at eight minutes. She'd thought to tinker around until it did, then feign some issue with her respirator, giving herself a full two minutes to fight her way to the exit.

The guy beside her was obviously a scientist, and now he was checking her work—throwing a wrinkle into her timetable.

The man clicked on a small plastic penlight and peered inside the open hatch. Miyagi could hear his breathing speed up ever so slightly when he found the damage she'd done with the screwdriver.

"*Que*?" she whispered, imitating Violeta's raspy voice. She moved closer, bringing the screwdriver up and backward in a flash, driving the tip of it into the unsuspecting man's throat, just below his chin. She was careful not to hit him with her fist, allowing the pointed steel to do the work, puncturing his trachea and snapping the hyoid bone. The rubberized material of the protective hood concealed the injury, along with any telltale bleeding. Miyagi reached down with her left hand and popped the door off the battery compartment off the man's intercom, letting the six AA batteries spill onto the ground and roll out of sight under the missile.

The wounded man teetered for a moment, trying to call out, but managing only a gurgle that Miyagi alone was close enough to hear. She turned her back on him the moment before he toppled off the scaffold so it would look as though she was oblivious—and uninvolved in what was going on.

Chattering voices erupted over the intercom as soon as the body hit. Miyagi looked up at the sound, recoiling a bit as she imagined the Cruz girl would under such circumstances.

Everyone but Fuentes and de la Guardia rushed to assist the fallen man. The general turned to look at Miyagi, standing tiptoe as if the scant few inches would give him a better look at her. He waved his thug forward, instantly realizing something about her was different.

Miyagi's phone began to vibrate at her belly inside the suit at the same moment the security man's lead foot hit the steps to the scaffold. The shaft of the screwdriver ran alongside the back of her wrist, out of sight, ready to meet him. Instead of coming up, he gave the scaffold a rough shake, trying to knock her off balance. Incredible genetics and years of practice had given Miyagi near-catlike balance. The movement itself didn't cause her to fall, but the fraction of a second it took for her to find her feet gave Fuentes a chance to swing the wooden club. The blow caught her hard across the calf, stunning the nerves and causing both of her legs to buckle. She hit the ground in a roll, on her feet in an instant and narrowly avoiding what would have been a devastating strike to the head.

The bulky suit robbed her of her usual fluid movement. Worse, it made it difficult to see and impossible to hear anything but the intercom.

Fuentes got a look at her face now and shouted something in Spanish about an intruder.

A strong hand gripped her shoulder from behind.

Instead of fighting, Miyagi melted with the touch, trapping and flowing with the direction of the applied energy, then spinning rapidly to turn the wrist back on itself. She felt bones snap, heard a muffled cry over the intercom, then pushed the wounded man away as she continued her spin. It was not Fuentes.

He and two other men now blocked her path to the exit.

Miyagi's phone buzzed again inside the suit at her belly, indicating a full minute had passed since the alarm went off the first time. Time, it seemed, had sped up exponentially now that there wasn't much of it left.

If Jacques was doing his job topside, she now had sixty seconds to keep the five men behind her off her back while she fought her way past three men in front of her and up the ladder.

She kept the screwdriver hidden along her wrist. Contrary to many knife-fighting tutorials on the Internet, she didn't intend to use it to threaten her opponents, or even display it at all. Anyone who got in her way would feel it soon enough.

It took the soldier almost three minutes to venture into the storm and check on the generator after Thibodaux hit the kill switch. He was just a kid— twenty-one, if that. The collar of his jacket was turned up against the rain as he walked to each pump, for some reason checking them instead of the generator itself. Then, inexplicably, he stared off into the forest and took out a cigar.

Garcia and Thibodaux lay belly down in a slurry of manure and mud around the corner, less than fifteen meters away. Peppa and Violeta had retreated into the trees. Violeta had warned Garcia and Thibodaux to get farther away, but neither of them wanted to leave until Miyagi made it out.

Garcia held her breath as the soldier stuck the fat cigar in his mouth.

"Maybe he'll just light a match," she said. "Take care of our problem."

"Maybe," Jacques said. "Nasty-ass place to have a smoke."

He started to move, but Garcia grabbed his arm.

"Where are you going?"

"Emiko hasn't made it out yet," he said.

"Jacques . . ."

"You'd want me to get you, wouldn't you?"

She nodded. "Of course. Go. But one of us has to make sure this thing blows."

"Understood, *cher*." He winked with his good eye. "Back in a flash."

"Careful," Garcia said, sure the wind and rain covered her words. Jacques would be brash. He would be bold. But to get Emiko Miyagi back, he'd have to be anything but careful.

Garcia watched him duck into the barn before she turned her attention back to the sewage lagoon and the soldier beside it.

The kid was squatting now, unlit cigar clenched in his teeth as he looked over the generator. Garcia worried for a moment that he might have noticed the loose wire, but he stood, one hand on the starter rope, and made ready to pull.

Garcia pressed herself into the muck, ducking her head behind the manure mountain. She didn't want to be staring at the lake of shit if this plan worked.

"Jacques," she whispered. "If you're going to get her, now's the time."

Miyagi crouched like a fencer, knowing she was far from imposing in the oversized orange suit. That was fine. The more ridiculous she looked, the more they would underestimate her, and the deadlier she could actually be. She feinted left, drawing the nearest man in close enough to stab him twice in the ribs as she rushed by, oblique to the group and away from the retaining wall. The man likely thought he'd just been hit, but the screwdriver had punctured a lung. It wouldn't be long before he felt the effects.

Miyagi kept moving, taking advantage of the men's inability to see any better than she could in the rubberized suits. She tried to draw in Fuentes, hoping to get his three-foot wooden club. But he was cagey, experienced enough to stay back and bide his time, waiting for the others to wear her down or for her to make a misstep. Someone rushed in from behind, attempting to grab her in a choke. She felt them coming and squatted low, sweeping with one leg as she spun, knocking the attacker off balance. She let this one fall without stabbing him, not wanting to tie up her only weapon with so many other threats around her. The man beside Fuentes rushed her now, earning a snap kick to the groin.

Striding quickly, she bounded to the far corner. This put her closer to the exit and funneled any would-be attackers, narrowing the area she had to control. The remaining men bunched together now, prodded forward by Fuentes. None of them were fighters, and she could have killed them all easily if she'd had the time. Even

Fuentes led with his head, leaning slightly forward, completely uncentered. He was a large man and made the mistake of relying on muscle. It was a mistake Miyagi intended to make him pay for in short order.

Her phone buzzed again.

Ten minutes gone.

Jacques would be blowing the methane fumes now . . . or, more likely, Garcia would. Miyagi shook her head slightly to clear it. She did not want to die, but if it was to be, these men would kill her, not some lake of rotten sewage.

She held her shoulder and pretended to stumble, this time drawing another man and Fuentes forward. She drove the screwdriver straight through the oncoming man's face shield. Fuentes pushed him aside, eager to end the fight. The big security man realized too late that Miyagi wasn't as weak as she appeared. His momentum carried him—and his club—right to her, knocking everyone else out of the way.

Miyagi grabbed the wooden stick with both hands, one at the end, the other down at the base where Fuentes held it like a sword. She pulled low and pushed high, smashing the security man in the face with his own club. The rubber hood of his suit protected him from serious injury, but he pedaled backward, losing his grip on the weapon, throwing up an arm to fend off another blow.

Miyagi used the long club like a pool cue, driving another man backward before swinging it hard and low, hearing it crack against Fuentes's knee. He went down hard, giving her the opening she needed to bound up the ladder. She dropped the club when she reached the top rung, needing both hands to hang on and push open the hatch.

A grunting boom shook the entire building. The whole floor buckled, lifting the wooden ladder upward. Miyagi flung the trapdoor open, catching a glimpse of frothy brown sewage rushing in as if shot from a fire-hose through the two-foot fissure in the retaining wall. The missile fell off its stand, splashing wing up into the rapidly rising sludge. De la Guardia screamed commands, ordering the others to see to the missile.

Miyagi had almost made it out when Fuentes grabbed both of her legs from below. Air rushed past her out the trapdoor, displaced by the gushing sewage that filled the bunker. She could smell it now even through the suit, although that had probably torn against the ladder. Gripping the top rung with all her might, she kicked blindly backward, trying to rid herself of the man who wanted to pull her back down—and get her out of his way so he could escape the horrific death below.

The rubberized gloves were snot-slick from splashed sewage, making it almost impossible to hang on even without Fuentes's added weight. Miyagi groaned, straining to stay on the ladder, feeling herself slipping backward.

And then two strong hands reached down through the trapdoor and grabbed her under each arm.

"You've gained weight, *cher*," Thibodaux said, sitting back to haul both her and Fuentes up and out of the flooding bunker.

The trapdoor fell shut behind them. Miyagi rolled away to stomp Fuentes twice in the groin. He tried to crawfish away, putting his back over the door just as two shots slammed up from below—no doubt from a panicked General de la Guardia. The first took Fuentes in the hip, the second through the chest, nicking a lung.

The entire west wall of the building was gone, blown away by the methane explosion. Miyagi threw back her hood so she could chide Jacques. Amid the roar of the storm, she was greeted by a horrible slurping sound as thousands of gallons of sewage drained from the lagoon through the broken retaining wall below.

Thibodaux grabbed her by the elbow. "We should haul ass," he yelled. "I don't want to be here when this floor gives out."

She nodded, sodden hair whipped across her face by the wind. "Bring Fuentes," she shouted. "He can tell us where Violeta's parents are. You had no business risking your life."

Thibodaux grinned. "Glad to see you too, Emiko."

She shuddered, swaying from the ebbing adrenaline, then leaned forward to kiss him on the cheek.

He grimaced, his good eye flying wide. "That was . . . I mean to say . . . How about we go back to you hatin' my guts?"

"Do not worry, Jacques," she said, giving the slightest of nods. "I have never stopped."

Chapter 53

Odesa rounded Cabo Cruz to find the seas even angrier than she'd expected they would be. In the relatively protected lee of the island's horn, she'd been able to drive the boat with some difficulty. Now, she merely kept it pointed into the wind and held on. After twenty minutes with the throttles shoved all the way forward, she found herself dangerously low on fuel.

"Now or never!" she yelled back at Quinn.

"You're the skipper," he said, still rummaging through the holds in search of supplies.

"I wish you would have told me that an hour ago."

She did her best to aim the SAFE Boat towards the imposing black cliffs that loomed above the shores of Parque Nacional Desembarco del Granma. Fidel and eighty-one of his revolutionaries had landed here in 1956 after sailing their sixty-foot yacht, *Granma*, from Mexico. Che Guevara had been there then, along with Camilo Cienfuegos, Fidel's brother Raúl, and many of the other notables who'd fought Batista's soldiers—and eventually won.

Odesa picked a dense line of forest less than a hundred meters up from a narrow crescent of beach. It was difficult to tell for sure through the rain and spray, but there looked to be a cut in the cliffs, a narrow valley that, with any luck, would provide them a route off the beach and into the trees.

Both had long since donned life jackets, weighing certain death by drowning against a possible death of getting shot while bobbing on the mountainous waves. The bright orange vests each had a flare, a flashlight, a folding knife, a signal mirror, and a compass. The most significant find was the packaged meal replacement bars—one in each vest. The labels were written in German, but they'd been able to figure out that each bar provided a whopping seven hundred calories. Quinn had eaten his immediately and advised her to do the same. One of the coastguardsmen had left a one-liter bottle of water on board. It was opened but almost full, and they took turns drinking most of it down. Eight-plus hours of near-constant adrenaline burn had left them both running on fumes. The water and energy bars gave them an immediate boost and pushed back the fog of fatigue. It also allowed them to see the danger of their situation with much greater clarity.

Quinn lurched forward and stood to her left, one hand on the dash, the other on a grab rail above his head. He'd told her about the drugs they'd given him, but she couldn't tell if he was still wobbly from that or if he didn't quite have his sea legs. She spent almost every day on the water, and this constant heaving threat of drowning was making even her sick.

It was an easy thing to see why Veronica was attracted to this man. He had a sort of feral scent about him. Dangerous. She'd seen that firsthand. But there was more to him than that. There were plenty of dangerous men in this world. Jericho Quinn seemed the kind of man who would, if he lived to tell the story of tonight, speak of how she'd sailed across rough waters to save him from the Presidio Modelo while conveniently leaving out that he had pulled the awful guards from on top of her as they prepared to rape her. All the men she'd ever known lived off stories of their own escapades. Quinn had many such stories. She was sure of that. But he was content to keep some of them to himself—only adding to his air of mystery.

Instead of wasting time telling her how to drive the boat, he'd found a rice sack in the forward locker and filled it with what meager supplies he could scrounge. He dropped in what was left of the water, along with a fifty-foot coil of line about the size of parachute cord but with a twisted paper core instead of seven strands of immensely stronger nylon; two more hand-pull aerial flares; a tin of waterproof matches; and a sugarcane knife that resembled a half-bladed machete, flat instead of pointed at the tip.

Odesa shot a glance behind them. Mirabal's boat was at the peak of a wave, about to slide down the face and gain a precious hundred feet.

"I was hoping we would find a gun," she said.

Quinn held up the sack. "I think we'll be good," he said.

She eyed him warily. "As long as you don't fall over."

"Don't worry about me," Quinn said. "I'm a fast healer."

"Well," she said. "I am not."

Quinn winked. "Me, neither," he said. "But it sounded good. Seriously, though. The meds are wearing off by the minute."

"If you say so," she said. "I would tell you if I was sick."

"I'm fine," Quinn said, but the pale hollows in his cheeks said he was far from it.

Odesa began to make out dozens of waterfalls, silver lines against a black rock, appearing then vanishing, off and on and off again through the melee of rain and cloud and spume. The small crescent of beach was less than a hundred meters ahead now. She suspected it would have been much larger had it not been for the storm surge. The hurricane whipped the waters into a frothy mess that made it impossible for Odesa to judge depths. Mirabal and his team were less than half a mile back, but she had to slow to keep from hitting one of the many hidden rocks while they were still too far offshore to swim.

They rode in on a monster wave, surf shoving the boat sideways and causing her to wallow until Odesa nudged up the throttle.

"Brace yourself," she said. "We'll run aground at any time."

As if on cue, the boat gave a shudder, spinning violently as the aluminum bow slid over a gravel bar with a sickening screech and the waves slammed into the beam.

Quinn made his way to the rear of the cabin, bracing himself against the doorframe to get a better look behind them. "I count four," he said over his shoulder. "Colonel Mirabal is out front." He turned, stumbling forward in a vain attempt to time his steps with the cresting waves. "This boat draws less than theirs by a couple of feet," he said. "So we can go shallower. Keep driving until you can't go any farther, even if you rip the bottom off of her. We need to stay out of their range until we make it to the trees."

"We are already there," she said, gunning the engines one last time to no avail. "Now what?"

Quinn started for the door and Odesa followed.

"Now," he said, "we bring them in close."

"Colonel!" Duran had to shout above the wail of wind and gunning engines. "Any closer and we risk running her aground."

Mirabal glared at him. "Then run her aground. This is not my boat." Rain and sea spray soaked him to the skin. The chilly water turned the jagged scar on his face a pale blue, giving him a ghoulish appearance.

Joaquin Mirabal's SAFE boat scraped against the rocks offshore and listed to the side a scant six minutes after Jericho and the woman had abandoned their own vessel. Six minutes was too much of a head start. He watched his prey disappear into a tree-choked cut in the limestone cliffs that loomed above the beach.

Estrada, ever one to charge into danger, scrambled off the boat first, leaping from the bow to keep from getting crushed by the SAFE boat as it was driven back and forth by surging waves. The water was to his knees one moment, then over his waist and carrying him toward the shore the next. He was able to get behind a rock outcropping before the rip took him back out, then pressed on quickly, shoving his way to the beach. He'd nearly reached the shore by the time Mirabal was ready to get in the water. Rain fell in sheets, and the danger of losing any tracks forever was a real possibility.

"Run ahead!" the colonel shouted, his words ripped

away by the wind. He yelled again, and this time Estrada turned, one foot on the beach, the other still in the surf.

"Find their tracks!" Mirabal shouted. "The rain will quickly wash them away. But do not go far alone!"

Estrada raised his rock hammer in salute to show he understood, then spun in the sand to trot toward the cliffs, less than a hundred meters away.

"Hurry!" Mirabal motioned Duran and Serafina forward like a cavalryman leading a charge. "We must press them. Force them to make a mistake."

It took them less than three minutes to clear the surf and run to the tree line, but in that time, Estrada had disappeared into the dense thicket that spilled down to choke the narrow gut between the cliffs.

"Dammit!" Mirabal spat. "I told the fool to wait."

Duran pointed at the sloppy trail that led into the thatch of tangled stalks and vines.

Serafina squatted beside the footprints. "Here are Estrada's," she said. "And look at this, Colonel. See how the American drags his toe? He is limping." She smiled. Water dripped off the tip of her nose. "We will capture him soon enough. He is injured."

He put a hand on the girl's shoulder and scanned the track before looking again to the wood ahead where the threat was. "Perhaps," he said. "But I remind you again, do not underestimate your prey. Especially prey you believe is wounded."

Duran stood at the mouth of the trail and pulled down a branch the size of his wrist from the thatch above, pointing at the razor-sharp thorns. "*El marabú*," he said. "The place is choked with it. They will be forced to go only one way."

Mirabal wiped the rain from his eyes and put a hand to his forehead, shaking his head like a disappointed father. "I know this," he said. "But do you not see the problem?"

Serafina understood first, as he'd expected.

"Estrada will be forced down one path as well," she said.

Quinn and Odesa hit the gap in the thicket at a dead run, slipping and clawing their way up the muddy incline. A dense tangle of thorny *marabú* weed formed a wall on either side. Someone, likely a corps of prison labor, had hacked their way through, forming a trail into the interior of this portion of the national park. The fact that anyone had spent the time cutting through the nasty stuff led Quinn to believe there was something worth seeing at the top of the cliff—a monument, the headwaters of an important stream, something Fidel or Che had written about in their journals. Sometimes called sicklebush or Kalahari Christmas tree, *marabú* weed was an invasive species native to Africa and Australia. Densely grained, it was covered in hard, awl-like thorns.

They were both wheezing for air by the time they clamored over the lip and reached the top. The trail had turned into what was essentially a muddy waterfall. Odesa slipped, slamming a knee hard against the ground, but was up again in an instant. The tangled forest thinned to form a clearing of grass and scrub approximately thirty feet across. Protected from the worst of the wind, almost still, it was still as a cathedral compared to the violence they'd endured out on the water.

Quinn tugged on Odesa's arm, urging her forward. She took three steps before she noticed he did not follow.

"Keep going!" he said, waving her on.

She slogged back to him, her blond hair dark from rain and mud, plastered across her face.

"You can't fight them all by yourself."

"I don't intend to," Quinn said, finding a piece of *marabú* as big around as his wrist. He cut off a length of about four feet with the sugarcane knife and trimmed away the thorns to make a handle. "Before we made it to the trees, I saw one of them strike out ahead of the others to scout. He's going to come right through that gap in three or four minutes." Quinn wiped the rain and sweat from his eyes with the shoulder of his prison vest. "He needs to see you when he does. Go to the far edge of the clearing, but be ready to run as soon as he notices you. Understand?"

"I suppose," she said. "Why a club? Why not kill him with the blade?"

"Odesa, please!" Quinn took her by the shoulder. "I know what I'm doing. I'll be right behind you. Don't forget to run. Do you hear me?"

"There are caves here," she said, turning to go. "Many caves. You do not have to fight. We can hide."

"No time. If we don't make it out of here and get to the pickup site, we are as good as dead."

"But—"

"Go!"

Odesa turned and trudged up the trail.

Quinn stepped to the side of the gap and buried the blade of sugarcane knife into a thick branch of *marabú* so it would be within easy reach if he needed it. Odesa was right. There were caves here. Limestone caverns that pocked the land, known as *karst*, and ran beneath the cliffs in a system of sinkholes and caverns, some of them all the way to the sea. They might be able to use them to their advantage, but they could not survive underground forever. Mirabal would never stop looking until he found them or their bones. They had to make it to the evac site tonight or risk being left behind for good. The only way to do that was for Quinn to do what he did best.

He did not have long to wait.

Estrada came through the gap, head up, hunting. The rock pick hung from his belt. A black pistol was clutched in his hand. He moved tentatively at first but bolted forward the moment he caught sight of Odesa loitering among the sparse trees at the far edge of the clearing. The proverbial ass magnet kicked in, and he was pulled forward by the chase, blind to any threat until it was too late.

Quinn swung the *marabú* staff like a katana, his hands slightly apart so he could use the last few inches of wood like a lever, causing it to whip as it impacted the bridge of the other man's nose and splitting it with a loud crack. The combination of forward momentum and swinging club caused Estrada to flail out with both hands. The pistol flew from his grasp toward the tangle of brush. Quinn's heart sank. He'd hoped to get the weapon, but he had no time to look for it. The initial attack had stunned Estrada, but he was simply too mean for one blow to the head to stop him. His hand dropped immediately to the rock pick. Quinn pressed in, suddenly dizzy, unsteady on his feet, but still able to tut-tut Estrada's wrist with the tip of the staff, shooing it away from the other hammer. For all he knew, the man knew how to throw the thing. Seeing double now, Quinn ran the risk of dodging the wrong pick if it came at him.

He kept up the parry until his head cleared, knowing he didn't have all day. He prayed Odesa had listened to him and was now long gone. Mirabal and the others would be along any minute. The feeling passed, and he upped his attack, pressing in and driving the other man back on his heels.

Estrada proved incredibly quick and agile, even with blood streaming from the wound between his eyes. Quinn feinted left, causing the other man to slip in the mud at the same moment he committed to grabbing the hammer. Focused on what he would do with the cruel weapon, Estrada didn't fade back quite far enough. Quinn caught him in the point of the chin with the tip of his staff, slamming his teeth together. Estrada's chin snapped up, letting the staff continue skyward. Reversing direction before Estrada could shake off the blow, Quinn brought the staff down on top of the other man's head, again using both hands in a levered chop, multiplying the force at the moment of impact. Had it been a sword, it would have cut the man in half down the center. Quinn spun with the flow of the staff, allowing it to come around quickly for a follow-up strike as Estrada slumped to his knees. Dizzied from the movement, Quinn had to lunge forward to keep from falling. He struck Estrada twice more, but he needn't have bothered. The first blow on to the top of the head had likely killed him. It just took a while for his body to figure it out.

Quinn shot a glance over his shoulder. He expected to see Odesa running toward him, but to her credit she'd disappeared. He turned back to Estrada's prostrate body and rolled it faceup in the driving rain. There was one thing left to do before he followed Odesa up the trail.

He did it quickly—then ran.

Overflowing streams of mud and debris obscured much of the trail once he reached the trees, and Quinn found himself following periodic divots in the mud and gravel in his attempt to keep following Odesa. Rain, and fatigue, and the drugs Mirabal had given him blurred his vision and made him doubt his tracking abilities. He'd expected to find her waiting for him, but she was nowhere to be found. Two hundred meters into the brush, he found out why.

Chapter 54

Ronnie Garcia shivered, despite being crammed into the back seat of the car with Miyagi and Violeta. The reflection of her mud-streaked face stared back at her from the side window, angry enough to bite the head off one of her auntie's live chickens. Wind moaned like a banshee outside, buffeting the car and thrashing the trees beyond the abandoned poultry houses. Arm along the headrest, Thibodaux craned around from the passenger seat. Peppa, who sat behind the wheel, turned as well.

Ronnie wiped her nose with a forearm, attempting to hide the sniffles that went hand in hand with tears— even angry ones. Hell, especially angry ones.

"Look," she said, almost shouting. "I don't give a shit what the rest of you do. I'm not leaving him."

Thibodaux's chin jutted forward, chewing on the decision they all had to make. "Listen to me, *cher*," he said. "This is a shit sandwich, no two ways about it. But we need help. And we won't do him any good if we're in a Cuban prison. It's up to us to get Violeta back home and pass on the information Fuentes gave us to the FBI so they can free her parents."

Beside her, Miyagi gave a quiet sigh. She did not

chastise or even offer advice. She simply said, "Veronica," and let the look in her eyes carry the rest of her thought.

"I know what we have to do," Ronnie said, no longer even trying to hide her tears. "But we're abandoning him. He would never leave us."

"No," Thibodaux said. "He would not. And we're not, either. I swear to you, *cher*, we'll get Ms. Cruz safely back home, report the exact whereabouts of this missile, and then we scoot right back and find our little buddy. If he's on that island where Peppa thinks he is, then we'll get him out—or die trying."

Emiko nodded. "Yes," she said. "We will,"

Peppa drummed long fingers on the steering wheel. "I am with you either way. But we should leave this place. Someone might have heard the explosion, even in this hurricane. Tell me which way. It is two hundred miles to the pickup site you have described. The road follows the coast for much of the way, so there will be many downed trees and mudslides in our path." She tapped the dash. "And we need fuel."

Thibodaux raised the brow of his good eye and looked at Garcia. "*Mon ami?*"

Ronnie banged her head against the glass. "Just go," she said.

Jacques and Emiko were right, of course. They couldn't help Quinn if they were locked up or dead, but she couldn't shake the knowledge that he would walk barefoot across broken glass into gunfire to save her.

He had, in fact, done just that.

Quinn pulled up short in the mud, sliding to a stop inches away from the crumbling lip of the sinkhole. The broken stump of a wooden post was all that remained of the warning sign that had marked the danger. The sign itself was nowhere to be found, having been blown away by the storm. Closer inspection revealed a length of sisal rope lying flat in the mud and limestone gravel. Skid marks in the mud, similar to his own, were rapidly disappearing in the rain.

They were new.

The sickening realization that Odesa had fallen into the hole hit him like a brutal slap. He fell to his knees, hands on the crumbling edge, and called out. He couldn't see the bottom and, without a flashlight, had no idea how deep it was. Flat on his belly in the mud, he leaned over and dropped a small stone. He thought he heard water, but couldn't be sure over the incessant wind.

Quinn clamored to his feet, covered with mud. Mirabal would reach Estrada's body any minute. He might pause for a short time, but if Quinn judged the man correctly, he'd quickly head up the trail, going even faster after having lost a man.

Pushing back the despair at Odesa's disappearance, Quinn worked to control his breathing. She could be down there, her leg broken, or unconscious, waiting for him to come to her. The sisal rope in the mud was too short to lower himself into the hole, and surely weakened by exposure to sunlight. He had the line he'd taken from the coastguard boat. A South African rappel might work. He needed nothing but a rope for that. The thin line would burn him badly, cut through him like a saw, if it didn't break outright—but he had to try, and he had to do it quickly.

A wheezing sound like the woof of a doe drew his attention back toward the clearing. He looked up to see

Odesa running toward him from back down the trail the way they'd already come. Quinn shook his head, assuring himself he wasn't seeing things. He couldn't have passed her.

Her face was ashen when she reached him. her eyes wide in terror. She threw herself at Quinn, nearly taking him to the ground.

He took her by both shoulders and pushed her to arm's length. "What happened?" he said over the wind. "Are you alright?"

She spoke in rapid Spanish until she realized Quinn was only getting a tiny percentage of what she was saying. "I thought I was dead." She nodded to the hole. "Luckily, the pool at the bottom is deep enough it broke my fall."

"How deep?" Quinn asked.

"The water?" Odesa shrugged. "I don't know. Deep, I think. I did not go all the way to the bottom."

"How about the fall?"

"Twenty feet, maybe," Odesa said. "It seemed like I fell forever."

Quinn glanced back the way she'd come, expecting to see Mirabal at any time. "But how did you get behind me?"

"The pool drains into an underground stream, a river now with all this rain. It flows toward the sea, but comes out in a little cave just before you get to the clearing off to the right of the trail, about . . . fifty yards or so. I did not know where I was. It was only by accident that I found the trail." Her eyes brightened. "Hey, we could jump in the hole and get behind them."

Quinn nodded slowly, thinking. "That might work," he said. "With a one little tweak." He looked from Odesa to the sinkhole and then back to Odesa again. "Do you trust me?"

Odesa pushed the hair out of her face. "Yes." Her shoulders trembled in his hands—not fear, like a bird, but rage. "What would you do if it was my sister here with you?"

"The same thing we're going to do now," Quinn said. "Can you fight?"

She nodded, but gave no other explanation.

"Okay," Quinn said, looking behind them again. "Listen carefully, because we don't have much time. Mirabal earned that scar on his face chasing dangerous game. He is a hunter. I am a hunter. I believe I know what he will do in these circumstances—and I'm certain he thinks he knows what I will do."

"So what does that mean for us?"

"It means," Quinn said, "that we have to do something he does not expect. Be the most dangerous game he has ever encountered."

Colonel Mirabal led the way out of the *marabú* thicket. He was relieved to catch sight of Estrada, who knelt beside the trail some twenty feet away, head down, studying the ground. It was foolish to stay out in the open like that, but the boy was eager to show off his tracking skills for his boss. Mirabal had given the order to wait, but he was surprised to see the young hothead had not run off half-cocked after their quarry. He'd warned all his team never to underestimate their prey— that held doubly true for this man called Jericho. And still, Estrada could be arrogant about his own abilities.

As he approached the scout, Duran and Serafina

spread out, flanking the colonel to watch outbound while Estrada gave his report.

Mirabal put a hand on Estrada's shoulder. "What have y—"

The young man toppled sideways into the muddy slop, revealing the short stick against his chest that propped him up from the ground. The rock pick stuck out from between shattered teeth, leaving zero doubt that he was dead.

Mirabal checked his pulse anyway. A thorough hunter, he examined the wounds. The method one man used to kill another said a great deal. He almost put a thumb through the top of the man's head. The skull was demolished, the flesh beneath it jelly. The pick in the mouth had not killed him. Jericho had beaten him to death.

"Colonel," Serafina said from a bare spot of mud just off the trail. It was eerily calm here inside the clearing, with relatively little wind. She did not have to shout. "Look at this."

Mirabal rose from Estrada's body with a groan and went to see what she was talking about.

She pointed to divots in the mud and grass. He could make out the outline where someone had lain prone, complete with toe-digs and footprints. One elbow divot was well behind the other. Normally, he would have used this as a teaching moment, asked the lieutenant what she saw, but there was no time for that now.

"Come," he said.

"Do you not think he has a gun?" Serafina asked. "The impressions left by his elbows indicate he was looking through a scope. His legs are splayed, his feet on their sides, quiet, as a sniper would lay."

"He does not have a gun," Mirabal said, already moving up the trail.

Serafina trotted to catch up, in no way questioning his assessment, merely eager to learn. "How can you be sure?"

Mirabal paused for a scant moment to turn and look at her. "If he had a gun, we would already be dead."

Chapter 55

The *marabú* thicket remained sparse beyond the clearing, leaving the flooded trail wide enough that Duran and Serafina could fan out slightly ahead, allowing Mirabal to keep his eyes on the ground while they provided oversight and watched for any deviation in direction of travel. The storm robbed Mirabal of his ability to hear signs of danger, so he ordered the others to draw their pistols and remain alert to a possible ambush. Rain turned any tracks into puddles. Details he customarily looked for were obscured, but stride distance remained visible, allowing the colonel to see the changes in gait. Jim Shield—Jericho—had been limping when he ran from the boat, but his stride was more even now. This man was anything but a simple real estate salesman.

A shout from Duran jerked Mirabal's attention upward. His grip tightened around his pistol when he saw the woman standing frozen in the middle of the trail less than thirty feet away. Mud and rain plastered her hair to her face. Her shirt was in tatters. She turned to run but slipped in the mud as she did, falling flat on her face.

Jericho was nowhere to be seen.

This was all wrong. He was not the sort of man to leave the woman behind. Mirabal took a reflexive step backward, sensing a trap at the same moment Duran moved forward to grab the floundering woman. He shouted a warning, but it was too late.

Mirabal spun, firing at but missing the flash of movement to Duran's right. Jericho exploded from the trees and crashed into an unsuspecting Serafina. Both fell, then inexplicably vanished.

Mirabal rushed forward, pistol trained on the spot where the pair had vanished. He saw the sinkhole before he'd gone five steps. Duran was too busy with the sputtering woman to notice.

"Be still!" Mirabal barked.

The woman continued to spit and claw at Duran's face.

"I said be still," Mirabal repeated. "Or I will shoot you myself."

Mirabal resisted the urge to peek over the edge of the hole. Serafina's gun was unaccounted for, and there was too much of a risk Jericho was sitting below, waiting to shoot him in the face. He tossed a large rock in instead, waiting as close to the lip as he could without exposing himself. He strained his ears, thought he heard a splash. He threw another stone, then waited two full minutes before motioning for Duran to bring the woman closer.

Duran hauled her to her feet and dragged her to Mirabal.

He stared hard at her for a long moment. Then he grabbed a handful of her hair and the waistband of her slacks and shoved her toward the edge of the sinkhole. He leaned back against her weight, holding tight so she didn't fall in. There was no shot, and he chanced a quick peek himself. Nothing but blackness. He got down on his hands and knees, threw another rock, then waited. This time he heard a definite splash.

"Lieutenant Lopez!" he shouted. "Are you alright?"

Nothing.

He called again. "Serafina! Talk to me!"

Anger welled in his chest when he got no answer. He pushed himself to his feet and gave a flick of his hand, motioning Duran to bring the woman forward again.

"What is your name?"

She looked mutely at him, so he slapped her. "You are right," he said. "Your name does not really matter. What is your plan here?"

Her chin came up, eyes blazing, defiant.

Mirabal hit her again, this time with his fist. She let her head snap sideways, obviously having been hit before, but he was certain he'd caused her great pain. He hoped so. This woman was part of the trap that had taken Serafina, and for that she would pay with her life.

"I asked you a question," he spat, chest heaving, working to steady his breath.

The woman squinted hard, shaking her head. He'd blurred her vision. That was good. He struck her a third time, holding back ever so slightly so he didn't knock her unconscious—yet.

She sagged in Duran's grasp, fighting back tears. Mirabal pressed the pistol to her forehead. "For the final time—"

"He was supposed to cause a diversion," she said quickly. The pistol had the desired effect, and she began to sob. "He told me you would follow him and I could get away."

"Who is this man?"

"Jim Sh—"

Mirabal pressed the pistol harder against her skull, thinking seriously about shooting her then and there.

"Jericho," she said. "His name is Jericho. I don't know his last name."

"Quinn."

The voice came from behind them, in the trees. The wind and rain made it impossible to tell an exact location.

Mirabal jumped to his right, scrambling over gravel and narrowly avoiding the sinkhole.

"Jericho Quinn," the voice said.

"You need to come out," Mirabal shouted. He snapped his fingers, and Duran moved in closer with the girl. "We can discuss this like men."

"I don't think so, Colonel," Quinn said.

Mirabal took the girl and grabbed a handful of hair, cranking her head backward. "I'm afraid you have no choice." He nodded toward the voice, motioning Duran forward.

"Your thug should stay where he is," Quinn said.

"You are not giving the orders," Mirabal said, astounded at this man's audacity.

"And yet," Quinn said, "he should stay put."

Duran turned to start for the trees, but Mirabal stopped him, whispering under his breath. "Wait a moment." He turned his attention back to Quinn. "Where is Lieutenant Lopez?"

"The woman?" Quinn said. "She did not survive the fall."

"Is that so?" Mirabal choked back rage.

"I should say, she did not survive long after the fall."

Mirabal could feel the muscles in his face begin to twitch. "Go," he whispered to Duran. "Kill him."

"With pleasure, Colonel." Duran stepped to the tree line. A single shot cracked over the sound of the storm and Duran staggered back into the clearing, spinning to pitch facedown in the mud.

Three down, Quinn thought, moving as soon as he shot Duran. The bullet had caught the Cuban under the left eye, leaving little reason for a follow-up shot—and Quinn needed to conserve ammo. He had no extra mags. He was lucky to have the pistol at all. The woman had been holding it when they'd gone into the sinkhole, and she'd tried to bring it around as they fell, but a vicious headbutt to the nose had stunned her before they hit the water. He'd been able to grab the pistol just as it had slipped out of her grasp. She'd fought hard, but Quinn had the advantage of knowing he'd need to hold his breath. Gun in hand, he'd wrapped both arms around the girl and kicked downward, driving her deeper as he pushed the air out of her lungs. She managed to scratch at his face, but he held fast. He felt her reach for something with her dominant hand, then draw back as if to stab him. He'd fired once, the shot taking her between the ribs at point-blank range. She'd fallen away, and he'd swum for the cavern opening. It was right where Odesa had said it would be, and he made it out and back to the trail in less than five minutes from the time he'd gone over the edge.

He'd wanted Duran to come after him, and making Mirabal angry had done the trick, getting him to send the lieutenant straight to his death. But now he had no clean shot.

Mirabal spoke through clenched teeth. He was not afraid, but furious—which was almost as good at clouding the brain. "I was mistaken about you," he said.

"And how is that?" Quinn moved through the trees as quickly as possible, avoiding thorns when he could, bearing the wounds when he could not.

Mirabal turned slightly, keeping Odesa between them. "I thought you to be a Cape buffalo."

"Is that right?" Quinn said, taunting. "Seems like you thought me a piece of meat. The Adenosine was on your orders?"

"Correct," Mirabal said. "If I had it to do over, I would use something that permanently stopped your heart."

"I'll bet," Quinn said. He jockeyed for a clear shot, but each time he moved, Mirabal sensed it and brought Odesa around to shield him.

"No," Mirabal continued. "You are definitely not a Cape buffalo. You are a leopard. Smart, elusive, and your claws infect whatever they scratch. Have you ever hunted leopard, Mr. Quinn?"

"I have not."

"Instruments of destruction, they are," Mirabal said. "Like you. They are also very secretive, difficult to catch, impossible to stalk." He yanked harder on Odesa's hair.

"They sound dangerous," Quinn said.

"They are, indeed," Mirabal said. "Fair chase is impossible with a leopard. You must hunt them over bait."

"You want to discuss this like men?" Quinn said. Odesa's eyes fluttered. She gave a slight nod.

"I do not think so," Mirabal said. "I have learned not to underestimate my quarry."

"Unfortunately," Quinn said. "You should have also learned not to underestimate your bait."

Odesa threw her feet out from under her, letting her body sag and throwing Mirabal off balance. She'd kept a small blade doubled in her fist from the first moment Duran had grabbed her, and now she plunged it over and over again into Mirabal's unprotected groin. He screamed, shoving her away as if she were on fire.

Quinn shot as soon as Odesa was clear, emptying the magazine into Mirabal's chest.

Odesa backpedaled. The gun slipped from Mirabal's hand as he sank to his knees. Blood bathed his teeth. He tried to speak, but managed only a long, rasping groan. Quinn ran forward to scoop up the dropped pistol and train it on the colonel. Many a mortally wounded man had killed the one who'd killed him.

There was no need. Mirabal raised his hand in defeat. "A leopard . . . indeed . . ." He toppled sideways, still.

Quinn checked his pulse and then, seeing he was no longer a threat, turned his attention to Odesa.

"Are you alright?"

She nodded, a little too emphatically. "He was going to kill me."

"I know," Quinn said.

She fell against him, and for a time they just stood there, holding each other up in the wind and rain.

"We have to go," Quinn finally said. He knelt beside Mirabal, taking his watch, phone, and the money in his wallet. "I hate to steal from the dead."

"He no longer needs it," Odesa said.

Quinn checked the time. "We have roughly eight hours to make it to the pickup site at Playa Las Coloradas.

Odesa brightened. "The tip of this island is only five or six miles wide. We could walk it in eight hours."

Quinn shook his head. "But the trail goes north, and we need to go northwest. I know it's not all *marabú* weed, but five miles bushwhacking through this stuff might as well be a hundred."

"Highway 4 must be directly west of us," she said. "It's not the right direction, but there are some cabanas at Cabo Cruz. There will surely be a car there we can . . . borrow. Vehicles in Cuba are easy to hotwire. We are not likely to encounter anyone on the drive north to the Playa in the middle of this storm."

Quinn smiled, feeling a glimmer of hope for the first time in . . . he didn't know how long. "It'll be dark by the time we get there, but that's even better if we're going to borrow a car. This could actually work."

"Of course it could work," Odesa scoffed. "We will get off this island." She stopped, stricken by a sudden thought. "You are taking me with you? Do you think they will let me stay in the United States?"

Quinn put a hand on her shoulder. "Odesa," he said. "You saved my life. I happen to have a couple of friends in government who will make certain you can stay."

She looked at the phone in his hand. "Should we call your friends and let them know you are alright?"

"No signal," Quinn said. "But even if there were, I wouldn't want to risk giving away the location of the extraction site. We're too close to it. We know where they're going to be. Now we just have to get there before they leave."

Chapter 56

Carretera Nacional 20, the coastal highway from Santiago, required nerves of steel to drive in the best of weather. Attempting it during a hurricane was insanity. Peppa admitted that she'd never driven the route before but suggested they try, believing they would make better time than taking the more inland route through San Luis and Yara. No one would be stupid enough to drive the 20 during this storm, which meant there would be much less risk of running into any authorities. She was right. There were no military or police checkpoints—or traffic of any kind. Just a crumbling excuse for a road and monstrous waves chewing away at what had once been pavement. Thibodaux called it the sidewalk of death, saying it didn't even deserve the status of dirt road. With a white-knuckled grip on the steering wheel, Peppa observed that if there was a bright side, it was that the ocean was only thirty feet below, so they would not have far to fall before they drowned. Sheer walls of the Sierra Maestra mountains rose on the other side. There was no shoulder—just mountain, cracked roadway, and the edge. The wind came from behind them, but the ocean didn't seem to know that. Spray from confused waves shot meters into the air and then broke across the highway, obscuring Peppa's view and slowing the car to a crawl. At times, the wind seemed to come straight out of the mountain and threatened to blow them off the road. It was lucky that no one else was stupid enough to brave the route, because there were many places where the road was only wide enough for one car. Ronnie was sure Peppa had to hang a wheel off the edge at least once.

"Wouldn't that be somethin'?" Thibodaux said, staring out the side window at some spot where gray sky met gray ocean. "We survive an explosion of atomic chicken shit, only to die in a car wreck. I'll tell you one thing, Cuba sure as hell ain't boring."

By the time the group came to a consensus that it would be better to turn around and chance a run-in with State Security, they'd already gone more than halfway.

It took the better part of five hours to go a hundred and fifty kilometers. Everyone in the little car heaved a collective sigh of relief when the road turned inland. Rain still fell is sheets, and the wind shoved them around, but the mountains provided just enough relief to make it bearable. Peppa found a secluded spot and pulled in behind a copse of tall pines to wait until it was closer to the extraction time. In the United States, the place would have been turned into a campground, but few in this country had time or inclination to leave what meager comforts they had to brave the elements in a tent.

A little rest was good for everyone's frayed nerves—except Garcia. Eyes open or shut, she could think of nothing but Quinn. Thibodaux appeared to read her mind and turned slightly in the front seat so he could look at her with his good eye.

"I know, *cher*," he said, simply. "Me too."

Miyagi sighed and gave a quiet nod.

They reached the area near the extraction point of Playa Las Coloradas at one in the morning—two hours before the appointed pickup time. Arriving too early risked discovery, but they didn't want to miss the window, either. Two hours gave them time to survey the area. None of them expected to find any police or military out on patrol looking for errant U.S. submarines, but there was always a chance that some Cuban coastguard or Army unit might inadvertently happen on the extraction while out on a rescue mission of their own.

So far, the entire beach was black, with periodic flashes of silver from low breaking waves. A brutal wind carried leaves, twigs, sand, even bits of trash, scourging any exposed skin. The storm stirred up the water, but this location had been chosen specifically because it was relatively protected. The four-foot waves were small relative to the monsters on the south side of the island—but still plenty large enough to swamp the inflatable tender that would ferry them out to the extraction vessel. Playa Las Coloradas—the red beach—was not red at all, at least not normally. It was, however, choked with red mangroves. The storm surge raised the water level and provided an acceptable place for the inflatable to approach without risking being upended by the violent surf.

Peppa parked off the road at the edge of the trees, and the little group huddled in the car and waited.

There were cabanas in the area, plush resort properties and a few smaller, humbler homes belonging to the people who worked at the resorts. The power was out over much of the island, and most of the cabanas had likely been evacuated due to the storm, but Ronnie thought she saw the glow of candles in at least two.

Peppa had been the picture of calm through the entire ordeal, but now, on the verge of rescue, she seemed ready to crumble. Arms folded tight across her chest, she bounced on her feet and craned her neck to stare into the black melee.

"We underestimate the Cuban security apparatus," she said. "There is some sort of boat out there. I feel sure of it."

Ronnie had never known her aunt as anything but solid rock, but now her entire body shook as if it might fly apart and be carried off in the wind.

"Or a truck," Peppa continued. "There are soldiers garrisoned in Niquero. Surely the sensors have picked up your rescue ship and they are all out searching for us, even now."

Thibodaux shook his head, somehow making himself look smaller, less imposing. "We got this, *cher*," he said. "No way we're snatching defeat from the jaws of victory. Honestly, this hurricane is giving us top cover. But they'll have a diversion set up to the north to keep any soldiers from Niquero out of our hair. They're sending a robot out into the no-man's-land between the fences at Guantanamo to blow a few mines. The local garrison will think people might be running the gauntlet to escape, and they always get their panties in a wad—or try to figure out a way to escape themselves."

"And if they think we are trying to escape?" Peppa said, developing the head of steam that Ronnie remembered. "What then? Our regime does not let people just walk away. I have seen things, Jacques, terrible things. They will kill me before they allow me leave this island."

The Cajun gathered Peppa up in powerful arms, the way Ronnie imagined he did when he was consoling one of his children. "That ain't happenin'" he said.

Miyagi cut him off, calm but firm. "Five minutes," she said, her voice cutting the wind as surely as a sword.

Five minutes before the appointed pickup time. Thibodaux pointed a flashlight out to sea and turned it on and off three times. Miyagi watched for threats to the north while Ronnie faced south. Violeta had moved in behind Peppa so they could huddle together. Adrenaline was ebbing, and they were not off the island yet. Jacques's pep talk notwithstanding, it would be all too easy for some passing fisherman or security guard to see the flashing light and walk up on them while everyone's attention was focused out at sea.

Ronnie leaned in. "Anything?"

"Nope," Thibodaux said. "I'll try again in three minutes."

Surf crashed and hissed and chattered, just a few feet away in the blackness.

Violeta breathed out suddenly, like she'd been hit in the stomach.

"What is it?" Ronnie asked.

"Did you see that?"

"See what?"

"Another light."

Ronnie took a half step sideways so she was shoulder to shoulder with Violeta. "How far out?"

"Not out there," Violeta said. "Among the mangroves south of us. Someone else is flashing a signal, just like ours."

* * *

A good place to hide was a good place to hide. Jericho and Odessa had picked a spot in the mangroves some fifty meters from the others. Quinn couldn't see Garcia or the others, but he knew they were out there. He also knew she, Thibodaux, and Miyagi were familiar with Morse code and began to flash his initials with a flashlight as soon as he saw them signaling to extraction craft.

Ronnie was the first one to reach them, running into him so hard in the darkness that she almost knocked him over. She ran a hand across his shaven head, then let go long enough to embrace Odesa. Both were crying, though they assured Quinn the tears were from nerves, not because they were weak. Of that, he had no doubt.

Thibodaux had gotten a return signal from the extraction craft and was busy guiding in the rescue boat with periodic flashes of light. Garcia guided Quinn and Odesa back to the others, reaching them about the same time two men wearing black drysuits maneuvered a fourteen-foot inflatable into the mangrove canals. The one on the bow threw Thibodaux a line.

"Somebody ring for the United States Navy?" the coxswain said from his position at the electric motor at the stern.

"You have no idea how glad we are to see you guys," Ronnie said, stepping from the shadows, still arm in arm with Quinn.

The sailor on the bow hook nodded politely. "Good chance we're popping hot on somebody's radar, so we should get moving." He shot a glance toward the back of the inflatable, then turned back with a tight grimace. "Who's in charge?"

Everyone looked at Miyagi, who pointed to Quinn. "The major," she said.

The sailor turned to address him. "We were only expecting four, sir," he said. "I'm sorry, but there's not enough room onboard for all of you this trip."

"Understood," Quinn said. "How many can you take?"

"In these seas," the sailor said. "I can squeeze in six, tops."

"I'll stay back," Quinn said.

"Forget it, mango," Ronnie said. "I'll stay."

Thibodaux scoffed. "Let me ask you a question, Chair Force. Stop being such a dumbass."

Quinn chuckled in spite of the situation. "Good to see you, too, my friend. But that's not a question."

"No shit?" Thibodaux said. "How about, 'What is stop bein' such a dumbass?' for five hundred, Alex. Now get in the damned boat. I got friends outside the wire near Guantanamo who can help me."

Peppa said, "I will stay. No one even knows I have been involved."

"Not a chance," Ronnie said. "State Security knows enough to connect you to me, which will get you in plenty of trouble. You already sacrificed everything for my benefit. I won't let you do it again."

"Quinn-san," Miyagi said. "I am sorry to say it, but you look ill. Perhaps you should not be the one to stay. Thibodaux, Ronnie, and I will stay behind until we arrange—"

"Excuse me, sir," the sailor at the bow said. He shot a nervous look up and down the coast, eager to be on his way. "I don't think I made myself clear. Transfer's a bitch in these seas, but there's room on the dry submersible for all of you. We're just going to have to make two trips in the inflatable."

Ronnie reached up and rubbed Quinn's shaved head again. "Who loves you, mango?"

Quinn closed his eyes and sighed, his knees nearly buckling with relief as he stepped into the boat.

"Honestly," he said. "I'm pretty sure you all do."

Epilogue

Two weeks later

It was early in the morning when Quinn, Garcia, and Thibodaux made their way down the docks outside Fort Lauderdale. The hurricane had blown over, and the air was incredibly clean.

Miyagi had returned to D.C., much to Jacques's relief.

In spite of angry demonstrations in Miami, Alejandro Placensia's two-year-old daughter, Umbelina, had been returned to her nearest relative, her grandmother, back in Cuba.

Peppa had gotten a small apartment near her sister Madonna. Santeria was alive and well in Hialeah—and she was already building up a sizable clientele.

FBI Hostage Rescue located Violeta Cruz's parents and took them without incident—if rupturing eardrums with flashbangs and dislocating the shoulder of one of the kidnappers was not considered an incident. Violeta decided to move back home for a time but had already returned to work.

Odesa had invited her sister for some *cafécito* on her new boat. Quinn and Thibodaux had come along as moral support.

The big Cajun was engrossed in his phone, reading a text from his wife, and Garcia kept nudging him back on course to make sure he didn't walk off the pier.

He beamed. "Looks like my bride has decided to come down to Florida for a little R and R."

"Taking the kids to Disney World?" Quinn asked.

"I don't think she's up for another theme park vacation," Thibodaux said. "Listen here, what do you think this means?"

Quinn braced himself.

Thibodaux held up the phone so Ronnie could see: *On the six p.m. flight to Miami. It's been too long. A woman has knees.*

Quinn shrugged. "Knees?"

"It's been too long," Ronnie repeated. She threw back her head, eyes clenched in glee. "A woman has knees . . . *needs*."

A grin spread across the Marine's face. "I do love that woman."

"Seems like you and Miyagi are getting along a little better," Quinn said, hoping to steer the subject away from Camille before it went any further than her knees.

Jacques shoved the phone in his pocket. "She's not so bad," he said. "But I'm pretty sure we won't be exchanging Christmas presents or anything." He snatched the phone out again to have another look at Camille's text. "I'm gonna have to tell her to send a pic—"

"So," Ronnie said, cutting him off. "Sounds like the U.S. envoy to Cuba is making some headway."

"Palmer plans to brief us this afternoon," Quinn said. "It took some time, but the decision was made not to pussyfoot around the fact that the device exists. The official story is that a Cuban agent who is now safely outside the country let us know about the missile, and we're just making the Cubans aware of it, like the good neighbors we are. Too much of a danger it might fall into the wrong hands unless governments take control of it. Cuba has agreed to turn it over to Russia—what's left of it."

"You think they even know we were there?" Garcia asked.

"Not a chance," Thibodaux said, returning the phone to his pocket for the second time. "Their general and his coconspirators are buried up to their eyeballs in chicken shit. Far as the Cubans know, the hit man colonel and his squad are all cooling their heels in a bar in West Palm Beach."

"Hey!" Odesa shouted from the end of the dock. She wore khaki shorts and a yellow T-shirt that Ronnie had given her.

She was on her boat, scrubbing the deck of her new thirty-four-foot Boston Whaler. Win Palmer used P.L. 110, the public law that intelligence agencies used to set up cooperating individuals who came to the United States, to give Odesa training and assistance toward getting her Coast Guard six-pack license so she could take out fishing charters. Quinn had offered to cosign for the boat, but Ronnie insisted she be the one to do it.

"Hello," Odesa said. She held up a tube of white paper about two feet long. "You are just in time to help me put the decal of her name on the transom."

"What are you calling her?" Quinn asked.

Odesa handed Ronnie one end of the paper.

"The same thing as my old boat in Havana," she said, unrolling the word *FREEDOM* in three-inch block letters along the transom so it lined up with pencil marks she'd already measured and put in place. "Only here, I can spell it out."

ACKNOWLEDGMENTS

As with any novel, there were a lot of hands involved in writing *Active Measures*.

First and foremost, I want to thank my wife, who listens patiently to dozens of possible story and character ideas for each book, doing her best to keep me straight when they overlap. She's the greatest.

My friends at Northern Knives in Anchorage gave me space to talk weaponry and be inspired.

I didn't meet fellow Alaskan Jill Flanders-Crosby until my wife and I were on a trip to the South Pacific, but she's become a good friend and valuable resource on Cuba.

Lt. Colonel Rip Rawlings USMC provided color commentary about the Marine Corps, Cuba, and life around Guantanamo Bay.

Dr. Erin Felger was incredibly patient, letting me bounce crazy ideas off her for the drugs used during Quinn's interrogation.

My barber, Linda, continues to be one of the best cheerleaders for Jericho Quinn on the planet. And big thanks to fellow retired lawman Scott Hogberg, a superfan, who has become something of a Jericho Quinn and Arliss Cutter evangelist.

Retired CIA officers Jim and Gary assisted with insider lingo.

Ben O, formerly of AF OSI, never seems to get mad that I pepper him with questions about his agency. I'm grateful to him and his fellow OSI agents who help me with the details.

Dan O and his buds at Anchorage PD for their willingness to continue to discuss tactics with a former action guy.

I've worked with the team at Kensington Publishing for over fifteen years now, and it remains a pleasure. My editor, Gary Goldstein, and literary agent, Robin Rue, of Writers House, have stuck with me through a lot more thin than thick. I am fortunate to count them both as friends.

Keep reading for the special bonus novella

DEAD DROP

by bestselling author Marc Cameron!

DEAD IN THE WATER

Every summer, thousands of families head to the nation's largest water park, famous for its 21-story waterslide, the "Dead Drop." This year, one visitor didn't pack his bathing suit. He packed explosives. When the bomb goes off, dozens of people are instantly killed. The rest are herded into the park's massive pool by the bomber's accomplices. An organized team of fanatical terrorists, they seal off the entrances, turn the waterslide into a watchtower, and train their sights on the families below.

But one hostage isn't playing along.

He's special agent Jericho Quinn.

He's on vacation with his daughter.

And he's about to turn this terrorist pool party into one righteous bloodbath . . .

I have a high art, I hurt with cruelty those who would damage me.
    —ARCHILOCHUS, 650 B.C.

Prologue

The line to nineteen-year-old Mukhtar Tahir's concession stand grew longer with each passing minute, as if someone had leaked an awful rumor that the world was running out of shaved ice. Buccaneer Beach Thrill Park was pirate themed, and like most of the other buildings, the ice stand was built to look like the hull of a wooden ship, with cartoonish lines and white sails of carefully tattered canvas. Handing two drippy paper cones through the large cannon port in the side of the ship's hull, Mukhtar used his forearm to push the stupid black tricorne hat out of his eyes for the tenth time in as many minutes and caught a glimpse of a pretty twentysomething named Fadila. She must have been on a break, because she loitered on the oak-lined path behind the funnel cake shack. Her long hair hung loose around smallish shoulders and even from half a block away he could see it shimmering blue-black in what was left of the evening sun.

Like Mukhtar, Fadila wore the black uniform polo shirt and khaki shorts of a park employee. She was also from Iraq—from Fallujah, the scene of some of the most intense fighting. Mukhtar thought she must have been very brave to make it out of such a horrible place alive. He was sure she was a virtuous girl, despite the fact that she exposed so **much of her** body wearing the park uniform. But her family was poor, just like Mukhtar's, and this was a different world. They both needed this job.

She kept looking over her shoulder, then up the path, as if planning a secret rendezvous. Fadila was assigned to work the smallest roller coaster on the amusements side of the park, which was always much less busy than the water park side. This was lucky, because that roller coaster was a lame ride anyway, with short lines that allowed her frequent breaks and time to loiter in the shadows.

Mukhtar barely had time to use the restroom, much less attend any clandestine meetings. A shaved ice was included in the cost of each admission to Buccaneer Beach—and the roughly fifteen thousand patrons who showed up each day seemed determined to get their money's worth. There were three stands that sold the sickeningly sweet treats, located strategically around the park. With so many customers, there was rarely a moment when Mukhtar wasn't refilling syrups, ripping open supplies with his box cutter, or shaving ice. Like soldiers holding a beachhead in a video game, it was all he and the two girls he worked with could do to keep from getting overrun.

His turn on the machine, Mukhtar held a flimsy paper cone under the ice chute and shoved back his pirate hat again, wishing he could throw the stupid thing into the bushes. His two coworkers, college girls from Virginia, actually looked good in their hats. But for Mukhtar, even the purple grackle hopping along the sidewalk with a French fry in its beak seemed to mock his cockeyed pirate hat with a hateful black glare.

Mukhtar handed off the cone and craned his head out the cannon port so he could see behind the funnel cake shack. Fadila still stood there, alone. Mukhtar continued to fill paper cones with ice and began to fantasize that she was waiting to see him when he took a break. They'd spoken before, only briefly, but she had seemed nice, if a little intense. They had much in common, and it seemed destiny that they would connect sooner or later.

Groaning, Mukhtar looked out the gunport at the endless line and shook his head. Some laughed among themselves, some chatted on mobile phones, others stood, drenched from their latest ride, swaying to the park's swashbuckling music that had sounded cool the first two hours Mukhtar had worked there, but wore thin soon after that. He would gladly have paid ten times the cost of a shaved ice not to have to stand with so many people in wet bathing suits. He'd been exposed to more pallid, sweaty flesh over the last two weeks than any nineteen-year-old boy should have to witness in ten lifetimes.

One eye on Fadila, he shaved up another cone of ice and handed it to a little girl in a dripping green swimsuit, giving her his best smile. He always took the time to smile at the customers. A few smiled back, some looked as if he had just threatened to hijack their airplane. Most ignored him completely.

A wrinkled raisin of an older woman, tan as a mud brick, stomped and cursed when she got bubble gum instead of cotton candy flavoring on her shaved ice. Mukhtar forced another smile and tried to explain that those two flavors were exactly the same; only the colors differed. The woman screamed as if she'd just lost an appendage, demanding blue syrup as well as a full refund of the shaved ice portion of her admission ticket. Mukhtar gritted his teeth and gave her a blue ice, hoping it gave her a particularly bad brain freeze.

He peeled off the clear plastic gloves and pitched them in an empty box at his feet. "I have to use the rest-room," he said. The two college girls rolled their eyes but didn't say anything. Each of them had already been to the bathroom three times this shift.

Mukhtar left his hat below the counter and made his way through the milling tourists toward the restrooms— by way of the path behind the funnel cake shop.

The sun sank rapidly toward the top of the oak trees along the western wall, beyond the towering, twenty-one-story waterslide that drew tourists like flies to the two-hundred-acre park an hour from Washington, D.C.

Mukhtar was still fifty feet from Fadila when he saw the other boy approaching her through the crowd. It was Saleem, the new guy. His cheeks were hollow and pale and sweat beaded across his high forehead. Even in the late evening, the temperatures still hung above eighty degrees, but Saleem didn't look hot. He looked ill. Dressed in the same black shirt and khaki shorts as every other park employee, Saleem got to wear the tool vest of someone assigned to maintenance and repair. It was certainly more of a manly job than shaving ice. No wonder Fadila had chosen to meet him.

Mukhtar ducked his head, pushing the aching thoughts of this stupid girl out of his mind and heading for the restroom. Committed with the flow of the crowd, his neck burned with shame that he'd ever considered the thought that this beautiful creature would want to talk with him. He had to pass within yards of the clandestine couple, who now chatted intensely in hushed Arabic under the shade. Mukhtar slowed a half step when he heard the first snippet of their words.

". . . if I fail?" Saleem said. "What if I hesitate when the moment arrives?"

". . . hinges on you . . . we depend on you," Fadila said. ". . . infidels . . . death . . . *fi sabilillah* . . ."

Mukhtar could see a series of bulges around Saleem's waist as he walked by. They were partially hidden under the vest, but he recognized them at once for what they were. He hadn't been able to hear much, but what he did hear was enough to fill him with a sinking dread. He broke into a sprint to find his supervisor as soon as he rounded the corner and made it out of Fadila's sight. Infidels, death—he'd heard such talk in Iraq, but it was the mysterious belt under Saleem's vest combined with Fadila's last phrase that made him double his pace: *fi sabilillah.*

"To fight in the cause of Allah."

Chapter 1

Come now, and follow me, and no hurt shall
*   happen to you from the lions.*
            —John Bunyan, *The Pilgrim's Progress*

Fifteen minutes earlier

Jericho Quinn threw the Impala into park and took a
deep breath, reminding himself that everywhere on
earth was not a war zone—despite his experiences to
the contrary. Still, a nagging sense that something
was wrong gnawed at his gut—the Japanese called it
haragei, the "art of the belly"—and Quinn had learned
not to ignore it. Even under the best of circumstances,
he was not the sort of man to leave his guns in the car,
but this evening he had, in fact, gone against every
ounce of his better judgment and left his Kimber 10mm
and his Japanese killing dagger locked in the safe back
at his apartment in Alexandria. The "baby" Glock 27 was
locked in a small metal vault in the vehicle's console—
where he knew it would do him absolutely no good.
The usual complement of weapons that had driven his
ex-wife to divorce him had been reduced to a thin
Benchmade 943 pocketknife that he'd tucked discreetly
into the inside pocket of his swimsuit. The huge summer

crowds at Buccaneer Beach Thrill Park and the fact that Quinn was with his eight-year-old daughter only added to the helpless angst of being unarmed.

"What time do they close?" Mattie said, unbuckling her seat belt and leaning forward to stick her head between Quinn and his girlfriend, Veronica "Ronnie" Garcia, who sat in the passenger seat. The two wore matching canary yellow one-piece swimsuits, but, mercifully for Quinn, his little girl still had a few years before she would be able to wear it even close to the way Garcia did.

Mattie had the park's website memorized, and Quinn knew full well that her question was not a question at all, but a jab at him for having to work late. Even the fact that he'd been in a meeting with the president of the United States was no excuse for cutting short their promised day at the amusement park.

"We still have four hours," he said, eyeing the colossal waterslide that loomed in the dusky evening beyond the park gates like a skyscraper, with its looping, twisted guts hanging out. "Looks like we'll make it in before the sun goes down."

"Just barely," Mattie said, falling—no, throwing herself—backward into her seat. The words came on the heels of an exasperated sigh that reminded Quinn of his ex-wife when she was angry.

"Don't know if you've heard," Quinn turned to look between the bucket seats at his daughter. "But they have this cool new invention called the electric light. Makes it so you can actually have fun after the sun goes down."

Mattie ignored him. She had the passive-aggressive thing down to level-ten expert. But she couldn't stay mad for long. The sight of the waterslide known as Dead

Drop—so named for its trapdoor beginning—made it impossible for the little girl to even sit still. Pressing her face against the window to stare, her voice fell to a reverent whisper, as if she'd just discovered the golden idol in an Indiana Jones movie. "There she is . . . Shawn Thibodaux says she has a hundred and eighty-nine steps to the top."

Ronnie Garcia turned to give Quinn a sultry wink, touching one of the many pale shotgun-pellet scars visible below the hem of his board shorts on his otherwise copper-colored thigh. "You didn't tell me that freaky, ginormous slide was a she." Thick black hair cascaded over her broad shoulders and fell across the leather upholstery. She reached out and ran the tip of her index finger across the stubble of his dark beard. Quinn had shaved for the Oval Office meeting but had, as usual, grown a healthy five o'clock shadow by noon. Thankfully, Garcia didn't seem to mind that even in a suit, he typically leaned toward the shaggy side.

Quinn shrugged. "I didn't know it was female, either, until just now." He threw a glance back at Mattie, who was now up on her knees staring out the window. She had his dark hair and copper skin but, thankfully, her mother's oval face.

Garcia's head lolled against the seat. Her full lips perked into a smile. "I guess it makes sense," she said, hints of her Russian and Cuban heritage seeping out in her accent. "Mattie's been hanging out with the Thibodaux boys over the last couple of weeks. To hear their dad talk, all the scariest things in the world are female."

Quinn smiled while he chewed on that for a minute but was too smart to agree out loud.

Garcia was attached to the same working group—she from the CIA, he from Air Force Office of Special Investigations, or OSI. Both fell under the immediate supervision of the President's National Security Advisor. She'd been present in the Oval Office meeting earlier that day. Quinn had known her long enough to be able to tell by the way she hummed softly under her breath that she was busy processing all the new information. Garcia was always more contemplative after intelligence briefings, as if she took terrorist threats personally. Quinn couldn't blame her—not considering the things she'd been through, the way she'd been hurt.

"Well, we got here, anyway," Quinn said, banging the flat of his hand on the top of the Impala's steering wheel like a judge imposing a sentence. "Now remember, we have to stay together."

Garcia smiled at him again and opened the door, gathering her gauzy cover-up and small handbag in her lap before climbing out into the sticky evening heat. Quinn didn't like crowds, but as he sat and watched her exit the Impala, he couldn't help but look forward to an evening with his buxom girlfriend and her yellow swimsuit. He wasn't artistically or musically inclined, but if he were, she was the sort of woman who would inspire great works from him.

Marine Gunnery Sergeant Jacques Thibodaux, Quinn's friend and partner, wheeled the black fifteen-passenger van he called the TAV—Thibodaux Assault Vehicle—into the vacant spot beside the Impala. Quinn counted four round faces pressed against the side windows. He knew there were three more somewhere in the van. The Thibodaux boys ranged in age from twelve to one—no small feat considering the gunny had spent much of the last eight years deployed to various hot spots around the Middle East.

Shawn, the oldest, shot a glance at the setting sun as he jumped out of the van, followed by five of his younger brothers. A frown turned down on his freckled face. All of them wore matching white T-shirts and blue board shorts like their dad, but Shawn had taken a pocketknife and cut the sleeves off his shirt.

"Marlin Shawn Thibodaux!" his mother bellowed as soon as she saw him. "That was a brand-new shirt, mister!" A dark and brooding South Carolinian of Italian heritage, Camille Thibodaux seemed to get pregnant every time Jacques walked by her. Seven energetic sons had made her an expert bellower. A sheer white cover-up hung to her hips, revealing her black one-piece swimsuit that showed off her full figure. She gave one of her patented glares.

The boy shrugged, flashing her a grin. "Sun's out, guns out, Mama," he said, flexing his newly discovered biceps. He'd spent much of his life in the northeastern United States, but there was a definite Cajun drawl to his voice. Five minutes around the kid and it was apparent he took after his daddy in physique and irreverent demeanor. He was only twelve, but he was already taller than his mother. Mattie thought it was a secret, but Quinn was well aware that she had a crush on the boy.

One of the other boys, a sensitive eight-year-old named Denny, bent over the pavement beside the open door of the van.

"I need a Band-Aid, Mama," he said. Blood dripped from his nose.

"You can't bandage a bloody nose, son," Jacques said.

"It's for his wart," Camille said. "He's been pickin' at it." She turned her attention to Denny and left Shawn alone to show off his "guns."

"Warty toes and bloody noses," Thibodaux winked at Quinn. "See what you're missin' havin' just the one kid?"

Quinn was sure all the Thibodaux boys were just as grouchy as Mattie at having their day at the amusement park postponed while their daddy met with a bunch of men in suits. Jacques sauntered around the corner of the van and gave Quinn a high five with a hand that looked like it could palm a bowling ball. He was a mountain of a man with an iron jaw and a Marine Corps–regulation high and tight. A black eye patch, courtesy of a gunfight in Bolivia while on a mission with Quinn, made him look even more severe than the haircut did.

"Well, we made it, Chair Force," he said, never missing the chance to take a jab at Quinn's branch of the service. "And that ain't no small feat. Getting all my boys here without someone throwin' up or one bitin' a hunk out of another is a minor miracle. Know what I'm sayin'?"

Mattie ran up and tugged on Quinn's arm. "Come on, Dad. Shawn says the line to Dead Drop probably gets even longer after the sun goes down."

"He does, does he?" Quinn shot a glance at Thibodaux. "Do I need to worry about your boy there, partner?"

Jacques gave a solemn sigh. "I would," he said. "Poor kid's just like I was at his age."

Mattie ran ahead with the two oldest boys so they could stare together in awe at the distant waterslide. All three had carefully measured themselves several times over the last week to make certain they would meet the fifty-inch height requirement to step on the trapdoor that would take them down the Dead Drop. Now, even Shawn looked a little shaken by the sheer height of the monstrosity.

Camille stooped beside the van to blot Denny's bloody nose with a tissue that she dug out of the pocket of the sheer nylon cover-up.

"You sure you don't want to put on more clothes, Cornmeal?" Jacques called his wife by her pet name, throwing a diaper bag over his shoulder. "I ain't gripin' about the peek at your legs, mind you, but it's liable to get chilly after the sun goes down."

Camille shot him an impatient glare. "I shaved those legs in great anticipation of this trip," she said. "And I'm not about to waste a wax by covering everything up." Leaving Denny pressing the crumpled tissue to his nose, she leaned into the van to drag the baby out of the car seat and then nodded to the diaper bag in Thibodaux's hand. Quinn had seen the big man in so many firefights and bloody brawls that it was odd to witness him acting like the big teddy bear that he was.

"Don't forget to put a half dozen more diapers in there," Camille said, strapping the baby into the stroller she expertly unfolded with one foot. "I just put a new bag behind the seats."

Quinn walked with his friend to the twin ambulance doors at the back of the van. He shook his head as Jacques stuffed diaper after diaper into the pack. "The park closes in less than four hours. How many do you think he'll go through?"

Thibodaux gave a long, low whistle while he mashed in more diapers. "I swear my Henry's like some baby alchemist. He can manufacture a half gallon of poop from two tablespoons of strained peas."

Quinn grinned, then turned more sober, nodding toward the park gates. "What do you think about all this?"

"I'm with you, l'ami," Thibodaux said. The big Cajun looked sideways at the high walls and constant flow of people coming in and out of the park. "My first instinct is to keep 'em all stashed away behind the safe walls of my home. But I guess there's risk in everything. There's sure enough risk in makin' our little ones grow up locked inside a fortress, that's for certain." A wide smile spread across the Marine's face as his wife walked up beside him, pushing the stroller. "As it is," he said, "I get to spend the next few hours looking at the best pirate booty around."

Camille punched him in the arm, but the glow on her face said she never got tired of the attention he heaped on her.

Ronnie sidled up next to Quinn, holding one of the younger Thibodaux boys by the hand. Mothering suited her, but Quinn didn't dare point it out. Apparently able to read Quinn's worries from the look on his face, she fell easily into the conversation. "I have to admit I don't like being unarmed, either," she said. "I thought about putting a gun in my bag, but then I wouldn't be able to leave it anywhere. There's just no way to carry in a water park."

"Speak for yourself," Jacques said as the group began to walk toward the gates. Mattie and the three eldest boys took the lead, scampering ahead. Camille pushed the stroller while Jacques threw one boy up on his wide shoulders and took another by the hand. Quinn was the only one not watching out for a Thibodaux boy, which was all right with him. It allowed him to keep an eye on his daughter. He knew she felt like he watched over her with the intensity of a thousand suns—but he didn't care.

"Wait a minute," Quinn said, picking up his pace so Mattie didn't get too far ahead. "You're armed?"

"Damned right I'm armed," Thibodaux said. "Got a little Ruger .380 under my board shorts." He shrugged. "It ain't much, but it'll do for a gun-gettin' gun. I figure if it ever hits the proverbial fan, there's liable to be guns aplenty. I can use this to get me something bigger." He gave the crotch of his shorts a tap. "Crossways, right here."

"Looks like a way to shoot yourself in the femoral artery," Garcia chuckled.

"Well," Thibodaux raised the brow over his good eye and wagged his head. "I ain't pointin' it at anything important."

Mattie drifted back, falling in beside Quinn as they neared the gate. "Dad," she said, apparently having forgiven him for their late arrival. "Shawn says he'll save me a place in line, but I'm so excited I have to go to the bathroom."

"We'll find one as soon as we get inside," Quinn said. He tried to give Shawn Thibodaux a fatherly glare, but Ronnie punched him in the arm.

"That's okay," Mattie said. "I memorized the map. We turn left and walk through the food court. Restrooms are right on the way to Dead Drop."

"Good job on the map, kiddo," Quinn said. "But are you sure you want to start with the biggest slide in the park?"

"Daddy!" she said, lowering her voice so Shawn Thibodaux couldn't hear. "Don't act like I'm a baby. I'm almost nine, you know. We've been waiting all week to do this." She blushed. "Anyway, Shawn said he'd go before me so I can see what it's like."

Quinn sighed. Maybe the nagging feeling in his gut had to do with Mattie discovering boys. If Shawn hadn't been Jacques Thibodaux's son, he might have taken the Dead Drop together with the boy and had a little man-to-man talk—even if he was only twelve.

Chapter 2

8:00 P.M.

Mukhtar paced back and forth in the outer waiting area of the park offices. He'd demanded to see the manager, Mr. Cunningham, but Ms. Tiffany, the two-hundred-pound ball of rules and regulations who was his personal assistant, had decided any meeting would just have to wait. Before now, Mukhtar had never known the sun to sink at such an alarming rate. It was well below the trees, and he could picture his father joining other neighborhood men at the mosque down the street from their apartment for Maghrib, or sunset prayer. The stone in the boy's chest grew heavier at each passing moment.

Mr. Cunningham made it a point to tell all of his employees when they were hired that while he did not want to interfere with any religious practices, park rules forbade them from praying in public and frightening the guests. Mukhtar knew this was probably against some law, but decided he needed the job. Fadila did not argue with the boss, but made it clear to anyone who would listen that Buccaneer Beach was an evil place and Mr. Cunningham was little more than a dog. If she and Saleem were going to do something violent tonight, it would happen during Maghrib.

Mukhtar wheeled from the window and stood directly in front of Ms. Tiffany's desk. "He is coming back soon?"

Ms. Tiffany was high enough up the park pecking order that she didn't have to wear one of the stupid pirate costumes. Her green blouse and round figure made her look like an unripe tomato. A pair of white earbuds hung beneath frizzed red hair.

"I told you, hon," she said, popping out one of the earbuds. "I do not know. Tell me what it is you need and I will pass it on to Mr. Cunningham."

"You have to listen to me," Mukhtar said. He leaned across the desk, talking through clenched teeth. "This is a matter of life and death."

"I see." The woman's jowly face blanched white. She picked up the desk phone with one hand and her cell with the other. "Are you threatening me? Because I will not hesitate to call the police."

"By all means," Mukhtar said, looking over his shoulder to stare out the window at the orange glow to the west. He looked back at the woman who sat frozen at her desk, then slammed his fist down in front of her, knocking a pile of papers to the floor. "Tell them the threat is to all of us!" Spittle flew from his teeth. "Have you ever seen what explosives can do to a crowd of innocent children? Please, call the police at once!"

He punched in 911 himself on the desk phone before turning to shoot a frantic glance out the window again. The last rays of golden light flickered out in the tops of the oak trees.

The call to prayer would begin any moment.

It did not matter now. The police would never arrive in time.

The gathering darkness of late evening did nothing to thin the huge crowds. Strings of electric lights illuminated the concrete pathways between grass huts and wooden stands selling corn dogs, shaved ice, and pork chops on a stick. The smell of fried grease and chlorine filled the humid air, and Quinn could not help but think there wasn't enough oxygen to go around.

Immediately to their right, off the main path and next to a large wading pool, sat the hulk of a wooden pirate ship, complete with miniature slides coming off the deck. It was hollow inside with places for families to get out of the sun during the heat of the day.

"Listen up, powder monkeys!" Thibodaux bellowed. "If anybody gets separated, we meet back at this here pirate ship." He raised his brow and looked from son to son. *"To konprann?"*

All the boys nodded to show they understood. When their daddy broke into Cajun, he meant business.

Mattie sprinted ahead as soon as she saw the long stockade-like building where the restrooms were located. Thick oaks that gave welcome shade during the day provided far too many dark places for bad things to hide to Quinn's way of thinking.

Garcia stood next to him, patting his shoulder. "I'll keep an eye on her," she said, starting for the restrooms.

Quinn stifled a gasp when she walked past him. He'd been right about the yellow swimsuit. Theoretically a modest one-piece, there was little that was modest about it. With her build ever so slightly on the zaftig side of athletic, there was really no piece of clothing beyond a loose flour sack that could be considered anything close to modest on Veronica Garcia. She wore a black swimming wrap tied around her waist and a light shawl jacket much like Camille's over her shoulders. Neither did much to cover anything up. The suit certainly offered no place to hide a weapon, even one as small as Jacques's gun-gettin' gun.

"I'll go with them," Camille said. "After seven kids, I know better than to pass up a chance to use the little girls' room." She took the baby out of the stroller. "It's been fifteen minutes. I know this one will need a change anyhow."

"I'll wait here with the kids," Thibodaux said, nodding to a bored-looking kid standing beside the high-striker attraction. "When you come back I'll ring the bell with that big freakin' hammer and win you a teddy bear or something." He shook his head and winked at Quinn before staring back at his wife. "I hate to see her leave, but I sure like watchin' her walk away." He nodded to the milk can game next to the high-striker but kept his good eye focused on his wife's back end. "You're a hell of a pitcher. You should try and win Ronnie somethin'."

Brad, the three-year-old, suddenly decided he needed to go to try out his new potty training. Jacques told Shawn to take him, but Dan, the second oldest at ten, volunteered. He was quiet, more reserved than any of his brothers.

"Go now or forever hold your pee," Thibodaux said, rounding up the remaining sons. "The rest of you men stick with me." Quinn appreciated the way Jacques expected even his youngest boys to act like men—though Shawn might consider himself a bit too much of one.

Streetlights blinked on up and down the park pathways in the gathering darkness. The last feeble rays of the sun finally winked out behind the trees as Quinn looked at his watch.

A fiberglass log splashed into the pool at the end of the log flume fifty meters away, sending up a chorus of giddy screams along with a huge spray of water.

A moment later and the entire park shook with the sound of an explosion.

Quinn and Thibodaux exchanged worried looks. A hot wind, the kind that came on the heels of a blast, blew in the men's faces, bringing with it the smell of concrete dust and hot metal. Both had been downrange enough times to know the sound of a bomb when they heard it—and both knew full well that the smell of charred flesh would come later.

The Cajun scooped his boys closer in big arms, nodding back toward the gate where they'd entered the park. "It came from that way," he said to Quinn, his face set in a grim line.

Terrified screams punctuated by sporadic gunfire filled the night air. People fled in every direction, disoriented and panicked from the blast and the ensuing gunfire. A woman ran past holding the limp body of a toddler that looked as if it had been dipped in blood. A man dragging what was left of a shredded leg pulled a woman much older than himself to a nearby patch of grass, where they both collapsed.

Camille ran from the restrooms. She pressed baby Henry tight against her chest with one hand and dragged little Brad along by a chubby arm with the other.

Jacques gave an audible sigh of relief at the sight of his wife. "Thank the Lord," he said.

"Mattie and Ronnie?" Quinn shouted above the panicked crowd that ran in all directions.

"I thought they were behind me," Camille said. She did a quick head count and shot a terrified look at Jacques. "Where's Dan?"

Quinn nodded toward the pirate ship at the end of the kiddie pool. Rifle fire popped in front and behind them, bringing more terrified screams. The hulk of the wooden ship appeared to be the only safe direction to go.

Thibodaux put a hand on his wife's shoulder. "Take the boys and hide in the boat. I'll go get Danny."

The acrid smell of smoke drifted on a wind from the initial blast. Thibodaux was already moving. Quinn ran beside him against the flow of a fleeing crowd, toward the sound of screams, gunfire—and his little girl.

Chapter 3

Mukhtar was standing over Ms. Tiffany with both hands flat on her desk when the explosion rocked the building. The windows nearest the front gate shattered, showering the room with tiny shards of glass. Large white tiles fell from the suspended ceiling. Bits of fiberglass insulation drifted down onto the desk like snow. He'd spent his younger years in war-torn Iraq and knew the bomb was close when it went off. Ms. Tiffany clutched the phone to her ear with white knuckles. "What was that?"

The flat crack of semiautomatic gunfire and the screams of the dying answered her question.

A rampant twitch spread from the corners of her mouth to her round cheeks, her chin, and then her eyes— as if she'd lost all control over the muscles in her face.

"P-p-please don't hurt me," she stammered. "Only Mr. Cunningham and the security guys have the combination to the safe. It's impossible for me to get to the money."

Ms. Tiffany obviously thought he was there to rob her.

Mukhtar threw up his hands in disgust, causing her

to hold up the desk phone receiver like a shield between them.

"I do not want the money," he said. "I am here to help."

"I have two kids," Ms. Tiffany babbled, breaking down in earnest. "Please . . ."

Mukhtar pushed away the fear knotting in his belly and looked down at the pitiful thing. "What must I do to show you I am not your enemy?"

The woman stared at him, blinking back tears, her brain playing some perverse loop of what she thought he was saying. "I don't have the combination—"

"Ms. Tiffany," he said, affecting what he hoped was a soft and calming tone. "We need to call the police." Perhaps a task would calm her down.

She pressed the phone against her ear in a shaking hand. "The line is d-d-dead," she said, dropping the phone and cowering lower behind the desk. "Please, I am a mother, for heaven's sake. I beg—"

The office door flew open, causing both Mukhtar and Ms. Tiffany to flinch. Mukhtar felt certain he was about to be shot. Instead, the park manager, Mr. Cunningham, stumbled across the threshold clutching a wide-eyed little boy tight in his arms. Wearing only a bathing suit, the child was maybe two or three years old and covered from head to toe in gray soot. He blinked, staring at nothing with huge brown eyes, likely deafened from the initial blast and too frightened to utter even a whimper. Mukhtar heaved a sigh of relief when he saw it was the man he'd originally come to see. Mr. Cunningham was smart. He would know what to do.

"I believe Fadila and her friends are responsible,"

Mukhtar said, spilling all his information at once. He felt a pressing need to explain everything he knew to someone one in authority. "I came to tell you I saw Saleem had an explosive belt—"

Mr. Cunningham's eyes fluttered. He pushed the child at arm's length as if he wanted someone to take him. His shoulders sagged, and it was obvious he would not be able to hold the position long. Only then did Mukhtar see the jagged shard of wood sticking from his boss's bloody shirt just below his ribs. Mr. Cunningham's face grew more ashen by the moment. He gave the boy a final shove, pressing him into Mukhtar's arms before staggering over to push Ms. Tiffany out of the way and collapse in her chair.

"Park . . . lights," he gasped, his breath barely strong enough to propel the words. Sooty, bloodstained hands trembled over the computer keys. "Have to . . . turn off lights. Make it . . . easier . . . for everyone . . . to hide . . ."

Cunningham gave a final click of his mouse and the office fell dark. Mukhtar peeked out through the mini-blinds to watch as the main lighting all over the park flicked off, leaving the concrete pathways, the concessions, and the water attractions bathed in the eerie yellow glow of the small number of emergency bulbs. It would indeed be much easier now for people to hide in the shadows. This simple act had saved countless lives. His mission complete, Mr. Cunningham slid out of the chair and pitched face-first onto the carpet. Mukhtar had been around death often enough to know it when he saw it, and this man was dead.

Now completely unhinged, Ms. Tiffany threw her jowly face back toward the ceiling and let go a burbling howl. Her head bobbed in time with the intermittent rattle of gunfire outside, as if she were absorbing the bullets with her body and not just her ears.

"Be quiet!" the Iraqi boy hissed. "You'll bring them down on top of us!"

The woman leaped over her dead boss and ran to the corner as if she thought she'd find a door there. She bounced when she hit the wall and collapsed there in a heap, screaming as if she'd been set on fire. Mukhtar had seen such a thing and she sounded exactly like that. Some people went catatonic at the death of a friend— or the prospect of dying themselves—others went immediately and completely crazy, as if their last shred of sanity had been whisked away in the awful cyclone of violence.

Mukhtar had no idea where to go, but he knew that to stay here in this place with this babbling woman meant eventual and certain death. He pressed the little child to his chest and then ducked out the door into the vague and inky blackness of the water park—and ran.

Chapter 4

"**C**ontact right!" Quinn hissed. The lights blinked out and the music fell silent over the entire park, leaving nothing but gunfire and screams to fill the sudden void. Still twenty meters from the restrooms, Quinn ducked as he ran, digging in to gain more speed to get him to cover before the approaching gunman spotted him. His stomach rose into his throat at the thought of his missing daughter, but his instinct fell to immediate action over hand-wringing worry. His loose deck shoes slapped the pavement as he ran, and he chided himself for not wearing something more secure. It was hard enough to run, let alone fight, when you were worried about shoes flying off your feet. Both he and Thibodaux slowed, cutting around a group of oak trees and ducking behind the wooden hut for the high-striker carnival game. A Middle Eastern man, probably in his late teens, worked his way down the adjacent pathway, firing an automatic shotgun randomly at fleeing patrons, cutting some down as they ran, letting others pass unharmed. He wore the black polo shirt and khaki shorts of a park employee. Quinn scanned left while Thibodaux, who was closer, focused on the on-coming threat.

Seemingly oblivious that anyone might actually fight him back, the young shooter focused only on whoever happened to be in front of his shotgun. He laughed when he blasted an older couple in their tracks before turning to stalk directly toward the children's wading pool—and the pirate ship where Thibodaux's family was hiding.

The Cajun's huge fists opened and closed, clenching until his knuckles turned white. A quiet roar welled up from his barrel chest. Rather than drawing the .380 pistol, the furious Marine grabbed the huge wooden mallet from the high-striker machine, gripping it at his side like a war hammer.

"You get the kids out of the outhouse, *l'ami,*" he whispered. "I'm about to go all Gallagher on this guy's brain housing group before he gets to my family."

Thibodaux ghosted into the trees without another word. Incessant gunfire peppered the terrified screams of children, flooding Quinn's brain with horrific images of his little girl. He shook his head in a futile effort to clear it, forcing himself to look past the falling bodies and focus on a second gunman who worked his way toward the long wooden building that housed the restrooms. Tongues of flame burst from the muzzle of what looked like a large-caliber handgun, periodically illuminating the man's park uniform as he stalked along the sidewalk between the cotton candy shop and arcade games. An elderly couple shielded three small boys, giving them time to run, and then fell, mortally wounded.

Naturally wired to run toward the sound of gunfire, Quinn moved obliquely, staying out of the man's line of sight, while he worked his way closer. For all his years of training and actual downrange experience, thoughts of his daughter out there among these killers made it nearly impossible to control his breath and keep from getting tunnel vision himself.

Using the faded plywood of a mini-doughnut stand as cover, he came up perpendicular to the pistol-wielding gunman and crouched, waiting for him to approach. The shooter was close enough that Quinn could hear the clatter of an empty magazine as it hit the pavement.

A young family struggling with a baby stroller and dragging a toddler tried to make a run toward the emergency exit. The gunman scoffed and swung the pistol at the same moment he reached the edge of the doughnut stand. Quinn sprang up behind him, close enough now to smell gun smoke and the stench of the man's body odor.

Still crouching, Quinn swept the back of the shooter's right leg with his forearm, bending the knee and causing him to fall backward. The pistol shot went wild, missing the young family and zinging off the concrete walk. Quinn's hand closed around the startled jihadi's hand, turning his wrist and the pistol back on itself. The young man's momentum worked with the odd angle to snap the small bones in his wrist, allowing Quinn to snatch the handgun away before the man hit the ground. Wasting no time on negotiation, Quinn put two quick rounds into the jihadi's chest and a third in his forehead, just in case he was wearing a vest. Quinn groaned inside when the slide locked back on the last round, signifying the gun was empty. It was an FN Five-seveN, a gun that Quinn was familiar with but had never carried. Quinn stooped to search for another magazine but found the kid had run dry—and with the relatively uncommon cartridge, Quinn wasn't likely to trip over any more unless one of the other shooters carried a similar weapon. It seemed odd that anyone would mount a terrorist attack armed with only a pistol and a handful of magazines, but Quinn had seen people try to kill him with nothing more than a broken broom handle. Cursing that he still lacked a functioning weapon beyond his pocketknife, he stuffed the empty pistol in the waistband of his shorts and then took a quick moment to snap a photo of the dead shooter with his cell phone. He tried to call 911 but got nothing but a fast busy signal.

Expecting he'd be shot at any moment amid near-constant gunfire, Quinn sprinted across the open ground. He met Ronnie Garcia as she stumbled out of the women's restroom. She'd lost her gauzy cover-up, and the strap of her yellow swimsuit hung off her left shoulder. Even in the feeble amber light of the emergency bulbs, Quinn could clearly see her knees and knuckles were badly skinned as if she'd had an up-close-and-personal meeting with the concrete. A streak of blood across the swell of her breasts stood out in stark contrast to her caffè-latte complexion and the yellow swimsuit. She held what looked like a STEN submachine gun, straight from a British World War II movie.

"Where's Mattie?" Garcia asked, scanning.

"What?" Quinn clutched her arm, as much to steady himself at the news as to check on Garcia. "She was with you."

"Oh, Jericho," she whispered. Her eyes met Quinn's, and then flicked away toward the trees. "People ran in right after the first explosion," she said. "You know, try-ing to hide anywhere they could. I'd just grabbed Mattie to get out of there when this guy walked in and started shooting through the stall doors, executing everyone. He was a big kid, like a football player, but he had a knife on his belt and he didn't expect me. I was able to use it on him from behind . . ."

"Mattie?" Quinn took Garcia by both shoulders and stopped just short of shaking her. "Tell me the truth! What happened to Mattie?" His knees threatened to buckle at any moment.

"I . . . don't know," Garcia said slowly, looking at the ground. "She must have gotten away." The guilt of losing Quinn's daughter was bright in the timbre of her voice. "She had to have run right past you." Garcia held up the STEN gun. Well worn and gray, it looked like a piece of pipe. The magazine jutted out the side instead of the bottom.

"I thought we might be able to use the bastard's gun, but I tried to shoot him with it and it's in-op."

"Broken spring or a jam?" Quinn asked.

"I'm not sure," Garcia said, tugging at the bolt on the side of the metal tube. It didn't budge. "I'll bring it with and see if I can get it to work."

Quinn cursed under his breath. A working firearm would have come in awfully handy. "What about Dan Thibodaux?"

"I never saw him." Ronnie bit her lip.

More gunfire sent Quinn and Garcia diving for the shadows behind a doughnut shack. They stopped, back-to-back, peering through the thick foliage before going any farther. Quinn could feel the heat of Garcia's torso against him as she heaved with each deep breath. He worked to control his own breathing, centering his thoughts. Images of Mattie's tearful face, the imagined sound of her plaintive cries, threatened to flood his mind and undo him completely. Bits of his soul felt as if they were being ripped away like shingles off a shaky building in a terrible wind.

He nodded at the STEN gun in Ronnie's hand. "The guy you took that from is dead?"

"Oh yeah," Garcia said. "Very dead."

More shots stitched the night—flashes in the trees, whirring ricochets—sending them deeper into the shadows. Quinn put his arm around Garcia's bare shoulder as they ran. The acrid smell of gun smoke carried on the back of screams. Families and hastily formed groups of complete strangers darted this way and that in the darkness. They moved with no real destination in mind, only running away from the last shot they'd heard. With gunmen closing in from every direction, running, hiding, anything at all seemed a futile game. Some were lucky and spilled around the shooters. Others were cut down as they ran.

"We have to get to the kids' pool," Quinn said, taking Garcia by the hand.

She looked up at him with stricken eyes. "Jericho, I'm so sorry."

Quinn gave her hand a pat, hoping to offer more comfort than he felt himself. He gritted his teeth in an effort to block out the screams of the wounded and dying.

"It's not your fault," he said. "Jacques told his boys to meet back there at the pirate ship if they got separated. If Mattie and Dan got past us we should find them back there."

8:10 P.M.

Quinn's heart sank when he ducked back into the dark belly of the ship with Garcia and found over thirty terrified people crammed inside—but no Mattie.

In the daylight the place was a playground, a place for families. Now, in the scant yellow glow of emergency lights, with the shadowed tables and hidden ladders, it was a hulking black monstrosity. The smell of urine and fear hung heavy in the air, thick enough to cut. Terrified parents clutched their children close, struggling to keep them quiet. Chattering teeth and ragged breathing seemed loud enough to alert any passing shooter. Camille worked her way through the trembling mass of bodies, stopping in her tracks when she saw Quinn.

"Where is my Daniel?" she asked, sniffing back tears. It did not matter that six of her children were safe if one was still out there.

"I'm sure he's hiding out somewhere safe," Quinn said, before the poor woman could jump to the same awful conclusions that already filled his mind. "I'm hoping he and Mattie are together."

Quinn was certain the strain on his face did little to console the Thibodauxs. His mind racing, he glanced at the glowing dial of the TAG Heuer Aquaracer on his wrist—eight minutes since the initial explosion. Time sped by at an alarming rate—and wasn't likely to slow down anytime soon. A lot of terrible things could happen in eight minutes. He fought the natural urge of a father to run into the darkness, screaming Mattie's name. It would do her no good if he were dead—assuming she was even still alive.

Both Quinn and Garcia maneuvered through a knot of sweating and terrified bodies until they stood next to

Thibodaux, who stood by a small porthole in the ship's hull, keeping a lookout with a shotgun.

Quinn eyed the gun. Thibodaux had obviously been successful with the high-striker mallet.

"Hell of a thing, Chair Force" his friend muttered, still gazing out the porthole with his good eye. "Having to decide whether your kids would be slightly less screwed up if they saw some dude get beat to smithereens with a wooden hammer instead of getting his skull blown across the concrete with this blunderbuss . . ."

Quinn knew it was a dangerous endeavor to engage in his friend's battlefield philosophy. Everyone dealt with the vagaries and meanness of mankind differently. Quinn threw himself into the conflict, expecting some shrink would untie his war knots at some later date—if he survived. Jacques Thibodaux philosophized, often while the bullets were still flying.

"I have an empty FN," Quinn said, nodding toward the submachine gun in Ronnie's hands. "She took out a shooter in the ladies' room but he was armed with a vintage STEN that looked like it hasn't been cleaned since the Korean War. As far as working guns, we have the Remington and your .380 pistol." Quinn looked back and forth between his two friends, seeking refuge from his thoughts in the formulation of a strategy. "Anybody have a best guess on the number of bandits?"

Camille Thibodaux stepped up, full lips set white in a grim line. She held baby Henry tight to her chest with one hand and grabbed her husband by the shirt collar with the other. Her grip was none too gentle. "Jacques," she said, squeezing the baby hard enough to make him whimper. "You better go and bring back my Daniel right damn now. You hear?"

The Cajun put a monstrous arm around his wife and gathered her and the baby in close. She looked like a child against his barrel chest. "You can count on us, Boo." He kissed the top of her head, his chin beginning to quiver. "I guarantee it. But we gotta make us a plan first or we can't do Dan nor Mattie any good at all."

Camille closed her eyes, pressing tears from clenched lashes, but said nothing.

"How many?" Thibodaux mused, turning back to Quinn, gulping back his emotions. "Hard to say for certain, but I'd guess at least six more. There's gunfire and screamin' all over the damn place, *l'ami*. Could even be double that."

"Our cell phones aren't working," a man in a pirate hat and lacy white shirt said. He held his iPhone out in a trembling hand as if to offer proof.

"What's your name?" Quinn asked, checking his phone again. He too found it impossible to get through.

"Larue," the man said.

"Well, Mr. Larue," Quinn said. "It could be that everyone is trying to call out at once. Or there's a chance these terrorists are using some kind of swamper to jam our signal."

"Do you think the police even know we're in trouble?" a voice from the shadows said.

Quinn glanced up at Larue. The man looked ridiculous in his frilly shirt and pirate hat but he seemed squared away enough under the circumstances. "You work here?"

The man nodded.

"Does the park have security?" Quinn asked.

"Just two," Larue said.

"Armed?"

"Yes." Larue nodded. "But they're only here to call

the police . . . and to stand by when the armored car guys come for the daily deposit. My guess is they both ran off to save their own skins at the first sign of danger."

"Fair enough," Quinn said. "How many visitors come through the park each day?"

"Fifteen thousand, maybe, if we have a good day."

"Okay, we'll go with that," Quinn said. "Let's say a quarter of those were in the park this evening . . ."

Thibodaux gave a low whistle. "Hard to contain three or four thousand people. A shitload of 'em had to have gotten out."

"Then where are the police?" a woman from the back said. "The people who got out must surely be talking to police, telling them what we're up against. I mean, people are dying . . ."

"I'm sure they're passing that information on," Quinn said, trying to ignore the nervous banter. "Sometimes law enforcement will jump and run toward the sound of gunfire as soon as they arrive if they think it might stop an active shooter. But with so much gunfire and hundreds of potential witnesses pouring out toward them . . ." Quinn shook his head, imagining what he'd do. "Some of the departments around here use drones with remote cameras—but they'll take time to get into the air and, frankly, it's time we don't have." He looked at Garcia. "Let's hear your best guess on numbers. How many do you think we're dealing with?"

Garcia ran a hand through thick hair, pushing it out of her eyes. Though she was dressed in nothing but the yellow one-piece, the blood of the man she'd recently killed smeared across her front said she was all business. "I'm thinking at least eight or nine shooters from the various directions of the shots—but that's not counting the three we've already taken down." She paused. "And, of course, any sleepers."

Quinn nodded at that. His mantra of "see one, think two" reminded him to take into account the unseen threats. There was the very real possibility that some terrorists had yet to identify themselves, but hid among the park visitors, waiting for the right time to step into the light and assist with the killing spree.

Nervous coughs and the scrape of shuffling feet suddenly ran through the belly of the pirate ship like a wave of some contagion. The group of people huddled near the door shrank back from a shadowed figure that stepped into view, backlit by the feeble emergency bulbs along the concrete pathway outside. He stepped forward, as if to highlight the particular worry over an unidentified killer.

"My name is Mukhtar," he said.

Chapter 5

The Middle Eastern newcomer, a teenager really, held a small boy of two or three in his arms. He looked to be protecting the child, but the thought occurred to Quinn that the young man could just as easily be using the small body to conceal a suicide vest. Just like the shooters he and Jacques had taken out, the newcomer wore the uniform of a park employee. A woman with gray hair, frizzed and tightly curled from the humidity, snatched the child away, nearly falling backward into the crowd in an effort to get away. She looked to be in her late fifties. Her last name was Hatch, but she'd been as stingy with her first name as she was with kind words.

"I'm afraid we're full, dear," Ms. Hatch said, through a tight, pasted-on smile. More gunfire and broken screams underscored the thinly masked hatred. "You should just move along."

"My name is Mukhtar Tahir," the boy said again, dipping his head slightly. "I only wish to help—"

"Well, Mukhtar," a skinny man in a Toronto Blue Jays ball cap sneered, eyeing the boy up and down. "How about you tell us what you use that box cutter hanging off your belt for?"

"Opening boxes." The boy held up his hands. "You must believe me. I am in no way a part of this madness."

Quinn stepped forward. "You said you want to help?"

"I believe I know the people responsible for the shooting," Mukhtar said.

"Oh, I'm certain you do, my dear," Ms. Hatch said through a clenched jaw that made her sound like a transatlantic snob. Quinn was sure he could hear her teeth cracking. "But we really are full to capacity here. You run along now—"

Thibodaux pointed at the woman, glaring at her with all the intensity of his good eye to shush her. "I'd prefer honest mean to insincere sweetness," he said. "How about you shut up and let the boy say his piece?"

The man in the Blue Jays hat pushed his way through the milling crowd. He wore only a pair of white board shorts, which contrasted sharply with his deeply tanned chest. His teeth and darting eyes stood out clearly in the scant light from the emergency bulbs outside the ship. The man looked at Thibodaux and grunted, as if he wasn't having any of it. "You're big as a house," he said. "I'll give you that, but being big don't make you the one in charge." He rested a hand on top of his ball cap and looked directly at the boy. "Innocent bystander or not, the needs of the many outweigh being politically correct at the moment. This haji puts us all in danger just by being here."

Mukhtar's shoulders fell. He sighed and turned to leave. "I am sorry. I meant no ha—"

A rapid string of shots cut him off. Quinn held up his hand to keep everyone quiet. Thibodaux kept the shotgun but passed Quinn the little .380. They took up positions on either side of the door. The pirate ship itself was little more than a façade of plastic and wood that offered concealment but not real protective cover. Lead bullets would punch through without so much as slowing down. Thibodaux shot a glance at his wife, who put all her boys flat on the ground without being told, as if they'd practiced this very scenario. Garcia stood off Quinn's right shoulder, far enough away to allow him freedom of movement, close enough to pick up the gun and defend should he become unable to fight.

On the sidewalk just thirty feet away a group of kids in blue and orange University of Virginia T-shirts had run headlong into one of the killers. Had they not, the shooter would certainly have discovered the pirate ship full of stowaways.

The jihadi was partially hidden from view by a grove of trees, but Quinn could tell from the size of his exposed arm that he was tall and well-muscled. He barked orders in heavily accented English. The UVA students raised their hands, the three boys attempting to shield the two girls.

Mukhtar's mouth fell open. "I know that one," he whispered. "His name is Kaliq."

"Please!" one of the girls sobbed, an audible catch in her throat.

"Have you got a clear shot?" Quinn hissed, glancing at Thibodaux.

"Neg-a-tive," the Cajun said under his breath, the shotgun pressed to his cheek. "Bastard's behind a tree. Buckshot pattern will spread from this distance and I'm liable to pop one of the kids. I could maybe get him in the knee but if he falls the wrong way and starts to spray us, we're hosed."

Outside on the sidewalk, one of the girls whimpered again. "You don't have to do this—"

Her plea fell on deaf ears. Kaliq, who looked as if he could have played football at the same university, mowed the cowering youths down with a derisive chuckle as if he didn't consider them worthy of taking the time to aim.

Quinn forced himself to watch the massacre, fearing he'd miss valuable intelligence if he looked away in disgust. All five of the youths collapsed under the gunfire. Mercifully, most died quickly, but one of the boys continued to struggle, attempting to put his body between the jihadi and one of the girls, even after he'd been shot. The gunman finished him off with a shot to the head. They were close enough that Quinn could hear the familiar thump of lead on bone, smell the acrid odor of gunpowder and blood on the night air.

Thibodaux cursed under his breath. "If he'd take half a step more to the right I could wax his ass—"

"Wait!" Quinn held up his fist when he caught movement through the trees. Even under the emergency lighting he could tell from the affected swagger that this was another gunman. "Second shooter at one o'clock, fifty meters out, coming this way."

"Shit!" Thibodaux said through clenched teeth.

"Can you take them both?" Garcia said.

"Maybe." The big Cajun shook his head. "But maybe ain't good enough. They'll have to get some closer to make it clean with the buckshot. If I only wing 'em . . ." He shook his head. "Well, you know what that would mean."

Instead of waiting for his partner to approach, the first gunman walked through the trees to join him.

"Remind me to feed this Kaliq guy his guts when I see him next," Thibodaux whispered so his sons couldn't hear.

The man in the Blue Jays hat staggered back a few steps once the immediate danger passed, vomiting on his own flip-flops. His queasiness turned to rage when he looked up at Mukhtar.

"You . . . you get your ass outta here," he said, stifling a sob as he stepped forward with a piece of concrete, intent on taking out his fear and frustration on the Iraqi boy.

Quinn slapped the chunk of concrete out of his hand. "Listen to me," he said. "Everybody's scared. But we have got to work together if we want to live through this."

Thibodaux put a hand on Blue Jay's shoulder. "Look, brother, it won't do any good to be goin' all *Lord of the Flies* on us."

"I get it." The man shrugged off Thibodaux's hand. "You have the gun, so you make the rules?"

"Didn't you hear what my little buddy said about working together?" Thibodaux said.

The man stooped to pick up the chunk of concrete again, homing in on Mukhtar. His voice was much louder than it should have been. "I don't give a shit what either of you say. I got as much say as you do, and this guy is outta here."

Thibodaux's face fell dark as he leveled the muzzle of the shotgun at Blue Jay's temple. "I just beat a man to death with a wooden mallet, dumbass," he said. "I will not hesitate to end you right now."

The man froze, eyes rolling toward the gun barrel.

He choked back a frustrated sob. "Who put you guys in charge?"

Quinn shot a glance toward the door. "Seriously, you need to be quiet."

Blue Jays shook his head. "You're not the boss. I'm telling you, that haji's gonna cry out to his own kind and get us all killed, slaughtered like fish in a damned barrel."

"I said shut up," Quinn hissed, fearing the man's blubbering would draw the shooters back.

"I don't want to die." The man sobbed in earnest now, out of his head. "But when I do, I want to die with some dignity—"

"Then wipe the snot off your lip and live with some." Thibodaux cuffed him in the ear, rattling his teeth and knocking his hat to the ground. "In the meantime, shut the hell up."

A young mother with tears streaming down her face stepped up from the mass of huddled bodies clutching her little girl. Blood from the wounded child smeared the belly of the poor woman's swimsuit. "My daughter needs an ambulance. I heard you say the police are on the way . . ."

Quinn nodded. "I'm sure they are, ma'am," he said. "But I have to be honest. The first responders will come in fast once they think they know what's going on. These walls and fences will funnel them into a death trap."

A high school kid in an open Hawaiian shirt shook his head in sophomoric disgust. "Way to keep everybody positive, mister," he said.

Quinn stared at the kid hard enough to send him shrinking back into the shadows. "I prefer to see things as they really are," he said. "Painting a rosy picture of how I wish they would be will just get us killed. I'm afraid we have to save ourselves. The police aren't going to be much help right now."

"They better help," another woman said. "That's what we pay them to do. You guys look like you're planning something that will just get us all shot. I say we work our way to the gate. The police are probably already there."

"Ordinarily I'd say that was a good idea," Quinn said.

"Well, I think it's a good idea now," the woman said.

Quinn shrugged. "Do whatever you want. So long as you're quiet and don't get in my way. But I was just out there and saw a couple of shooters hiding near the gate." It wasn't in Quinn's nature to try and convince people of anything. He looked around the room, working out the rudiments of a plan as he spoke. "Anybody in here have medical training?"

A young woman flanked by two teenage boys raised her hand.

Quinn didn't even ask what sort of training. "You're in charge of medical needs," he said. "See if you can stop the bleeding on this one and then triage anyone else who's hurt."

"Run, hide, fight," another man said. "I read online that's what they say to do?"

"Yeah," Ronnie said, "But who's 'they'? Every instance is different. 'They' don't know shit about what's going on here and now."

"Maybe," the man said. "But these guys have guns and we don't. We can't very well fight them off. Running might be our best option."

"It may come to that," Quinn said, holding up his hand at the sound of more gunfire as it illustrated his point. "But these shooters are moving around in ones and twos. The shotgun will hold off an immediate threat."

"Excuse me for saying this," Larue said, pushing the pirate hat back on his head. "But I heard you say you're going out to find your kid. What are we supposed to do without the shotgun?"

Quinn shot a glance at Thibodaux, then looked back at Larue. "The shotgun stays here. We'll take what we need from the terrorists. If you do have to run and it comes to a fight, swarm the bad guy. Everyone go at him at once. Attack back, so to speak. These guys are young. They won't be expecting that."

"A lot of people will die if we do it that way," Larue whispered.

"They might," Quinn said. "But it's a certainty if you don't. This can't be handled with some easy checklist you read on the Internet. You have to be fluid, willing to change your strategy."

"What about the police?" Larue asked. "Surely—"

"Look," Quinn cut him off. He looked from face to face in the terrified group. "We have to rely on ourselves for the time being. These terrorists picked this park for a reason. High walls, limited access points. If the police that get here first make it inside without getting killed—and that's a big if—they'll move directly toward the sound of gunfire, working to stop the threat before more people are killed. They will step over the wounded—even children—and keep going, in an effort to get to the shooters as quickly as possible."

"And you know this how?" the gray-haired woman asked, turning her glare on Quinn.

"Because that's what I would do," he said.

"We're staying here," Camille Thibodaux said. She gathered her remaining sons to her like bear cubs around a very protective mama. The desperate look in her eyes was clear, even in the dim belly of the ship. She seemed to force herself to look out the porthole, peering across the deserted walkway at the bodies of the murdered students.

"Jacques," she said, her eyes still locked on the horrific scene outside. "You go bring back my Daniel. You hear me?"

"I'm sure he's with Mattie," Garcia said, the guilty catch still in her voice. "They probably ran together while I was busy fighting the guy in the restrooms."

The Iraqi boy stepped forward, holding up both hands to show he was not a threat. He tipped his head to Ronnie, averting his eyes as he did. "A small girl wearing a yellow swimsuit much like yours and a boy with a very short haircut?" He turned quickly toward Quinn, as if gazing for too long on Garcia's voluptuous figure might turn him to stone. "I saw these two little children on my way here. They ran toward the mechanical room above the log ride."

Quinn's head swam at the news. This boy had actually seen his daughter alive.

Garcia put a hand on his arm, seeming to read his mind. "Go," she said. "I'll stay here and look out for Camille and the others."

Quinn opened his mouth to object, but she shut him down.

"I'd just split your focus—and we can't have that." She kissed him fiercely on the lips, something she rarely ever did in public.

"Boys," Jacques said. "You protect your mama while I go and retrieve your brother. You hear me?" All six of them nodded. Even baby Henry.

Thibodaux passed Ronnie Garcia the shotgun,

patting the wooden stock with the flat of his hand. "I'm much obliged, *chérie*," he said. "Plug's out of the tube so you got ten rounds of big mamma jamma buckshot in here. That's ninety little lead chances to send some of these bastards to hell before you even have to reload. Don't you let anyone near this place. Got me?"

Garcia nodded. "I'll use them wisely," she said.

"And some extras if you need them," Jacques said. He gave her a handful of loose shells he'd got from the dead shooter's pocket.

Quinn eyed the Iraqi boy. "You said you want to help?"

"I do," Mukhtar said. "Very much so."

"Then you're with us."

The boy gave an emphatic nod. "What are we going to do?"

Thibodaux scoffed as if the answer was all so clear. "We're gonna go save our kids, and then hunt these sons of bitches down and kill every last one of 'em."

Chapter 6

The park was eerily still as Quinn and Thibodaux ran with the Iraqi boy through the darkness, past the restrooms. They kept to the cover of now-deserted snack stands and carnival games, working their way toward the fort-like wooden structure that housed the workings of the log ride. Gunfire popped and cracked at various points around the park, but the broken cries of victims seemed to pour in from every direction. Here and there, dark shadows crept and scurried through the trees like terrified rats—surviving patrons and park employees, all desperate to stay hidden but unable to find a way outside the high park walls. Any of them foolish enough to try the gates were cut down on the spot. Quinn kept Mukhtar between him and Thibodaux as they ran. He shot a glance at the boy. "When we run into any of the shooters, you stay out of the way and let us handle it. Hear me?"

"Obviously," Mukhtar said, trotting easily beside the men. "You appear to know what you are doing. I assume you were both in the U.S. military. Did you ever go to Iraq?"

Both men nodded.

"My father," the boys said, "he was interpreter for the United States Marine Corps in Fallujah."

"Well, ain't that somethin'," Thibodaux said, sounding unconvinced.

Mukhtar's shoulders slumped. "It does not matter what I do," he whispered. "No one here will trust me . . ."

"Well, son," Thibodaux said, still jogging, "you gotta admit, these murdering sons of bitches who happen to all dress and sound and look just like you have put us in a tough spot. Makes it hard to tell the difference between the good guys and the bad guys. Sometimes profiling is the only thing between a bullet in the brain and makin' it home to see your kids."

"But they do not all look like me," the boy said, his hands up and open, pleading to be understood. All three slowed to a stop, thirty meters from the hulking shadow of the log ride. "Tariq," the Iraqi boy continued, "the one who I believe to be in charge, he is American."

"A convert?" Thibodaux mused. "Are his parents refugees?"

"You do not understand." Mukhtar shook his head, then shrugged, hands still up, and moving to emphasize each and every word. "His real name is Terry, Terry . . . Spencer, I think, but everyone calls him Tariq. He says his father is some kind of lawyer in Washington, D.C. He is as white as you."

Chapter 7

Fadila stood at the base of the Dead Drop waterslide and turned away from the young couple she'd just cut down at point-blank range with her pistol. They had tried to help her, believing that because she was a female, she was also a victim. Fools. Weak, incompetent fools. Pistol still in hand, she used her forearm to wipe a spatter of blood from her cheek. She shot a triumphant glance at her boyfriend, a sly smile spreading across her angular face. The killing—all of it—was even more exhilarating than she had imagined it would be.

"It is working," she said. "Just as you said."

The boy with a mop of blond hair grinned back at her, brandishing a stubby black semiautomatic H&K MP5 that made him look even handsomer than she already thought him to be. He'd taken up the war name Abu Tariq—the Night Visitor. He was no longer boring Terry Spencer, only son of a mindless pawn for wealthy American pigs. Abu Tariq assured everyone that Terry Spencer was a disappointment to his father, but Abu Tariq did not care. Abu Tariq had left Terry Spencer behind and now wanted nothing more than to submit himself to Allah, to make a difference, and to eventually die a martyr alongside his new friends—especially Fadila.

"Of course it is working," Tariq said. "It is also entertaining. These dogs will do anything to postpone even certain death, even if it's just for a minute or two." He raised a blond brow and cocked his head slightly in the way that made Fadila's heart beat in her throat. "Who do we have guarding the wave pool now?" he asked.

"Abu Fahad and Abu Nasser," Fadila said, hoping he did not see her blush.

Tariq gave a thoughtful nod, running his fingers through his golden hair. "Good. Tell them to shoot anyone who tries to get out of the water. A couple of bloody bodies at either end of the pool should convince most of them to stay in place." Abu Tariq stared into the distance, thinking of some bit of strategy, no doubt. Fadila had never seen an American boy so good at strategy. "Long enough for our purposes, at least."

Fadila bowed her head. "Of course," she said, beaming with gratitude and knowing that she was fortunate to be associated with a man so dedicated to the cause of jihad. It was Tariq who had first shown her the Islamic State videos on the Internet. It had been he who made first contact with the recruiter in Arlington, he who had worked with Islamic State operatives to supply their group with weapons, ammunition, and the belt bomb for Saleem. Every member of their group was pious as well as eager, but they were also young and inexperienced. Tariq had worked with the I.S. contact to devise the perfect plan. Members of the group had pledged their loyalty on a video forum earlier that day, before coming to the park—one by one, ensuring with their violent rhetoric that they could never go back to their former lives. Even the name of their little group of lions, Feesabilillah—"in the cause of Allah"—had been Tariq's idea. Fadila had never met the Islamic State operative, but Tariq told her the man had heartily approved of the name.

More shooting broke out behind Tariq as he stooped to pick up the black duffel he used to carry his extra ammunition. His blue eyes flashed when he stood up, narrow, with an intensity that sent a warm shiver down Fadila's legs. She chided herself for the unholy thoughts.

"It's coming from beyond the tube slides." Tariq looked at his watch. "That would be the police trying the side gate. They have finally gotten off their fat asses and decided to come to our party."

More screams filled the humid night. Tariq lifted a yellow handheld radio to his lips as he threw the duffel over his shoulder. "Brothers," he said. "Listen to me. Conserve your ammunition for when we really need it."

He clipped the radio to his belt and then held his free hand out toward Fadila. "This will be over soon," he said, pulling her closer. "The news helicopters will be overhead before long. I'll watch from the top of Dead Drop, then send word when I see they've started to film. Then they can open up on the pool." He gave her a wink. "I guarantee you it will go viral."

Fadila squeezed his hand, looking deep into his blue eyes for any sign of resignation or second thoughts. She found none. "And then?" she asked, though she knew what his answer would be. "After you have sent word down to us?"

"Then . . ." he nodded slowly. "Then, I will come down and kill as many policemen as I can before I die beside you, Fadila."

Chapter 8

Mattie Quinn knelt next to Dan Thibodaux behind a fiberglass log that was as big as a car and made to look like a fat dugout canoe. Larger than life, it was fixed on a stand made of two more fake logs as if in the process of being hollowed out by the animatronic pirates that surrounded it. Riders boarded the log ride on the floor below, going up and around several turns and splashing into a small pond before making the long, clicking climb up to the second story of the same long building. Once inside, they floated on the man-made river between a motorized scene of fierce-looking pirate mannequins, each armed to the teeth with boarding axes, cutlasses, and blunderbusses, while they worked to bury their treasure and make boats.

A single emergency light cast an eerie yellow glow around the room, throwing huge shadows of the mannequins onto the wooden slat wall. All the pirates had frozen in place when the lights had gone off, but whatever powered the emergency bulbs must have run the water pump and conveyor gears, too, because empty fiberglass logs continued to float into the dim building, bumping the sides of the deep trough with hollow thuds as they moved along the man-made river and disappeared out the far doorway fifteen feet away. Mattie could hear each log as it careened down the flume to splash into the waiting pool below. There was still screaming in the park—a lot of screaming—and gunshots. But sometimes, in between shots, if the screams and the splashes were timed just right, Mattie could imagine someone outside was having fun and not scared out of their minds.

The room was full of motors, rubber belts, and iron wheels—all meant to move the mannequins back and forth to provide a show. The smell of gear oil and dust filled the air. The water had to be deep in the flume in order to float the big fiberglass logs. Mattie had first thought they should try and swim out but decided against it when she thought about the huge drop just outside the door.

Hiding, trying to make herself as small as possible, Mattie found it difficult to breathe, as if she'd been caught in an invisible bear hug. She clenched her mouth shut in an effort to keep her teeth from chattering.

Heavy footsteps clomped around on the wooden floor below. Mattie had caught a glimpse of one of the terrorists when she and Dan ran up the stairs. The man hadn't seen them yet, but was looking all over the place. Every so often, he called out to anyone who might be hiding, promising he wouldn't shoot if they came out.

Mattie was only eight, but she was old enough to figure out what her daddy did for a living, and had listened to him enough to know there was no use talking to someone already pointing a gun at you. She'd been close to death before, so close as to sink her teeth into the hand of a man trying to kill her, to give her dad a chance to kill him. She knew her dad would be looking for her. There was no doubt in her mind. So would

Ronnie Garcia, but neither of them was here now—and besides, it was a big park, and they wouldn't even know where to look.

A foot away, kneeling behind the same giant fake log, Dan Thibodaux held a piece of white PVC he'd found outside on one of the fences. He'd first thought to try and use one of the axes or swords from the pirate mannequins, but they all turned out to be plastic. In the end, he'd bent the flexible PVC pipe into a bow with a length of twine he got in the mechanical room. A broken piece of thin bamboo fencing became a makeshift arrow. The top end was notched enough that it fit nicely against the bowstring. The pointy end, where Dan had snapped it off from the ground, looked sharp enough to Mattie that her mom would have taken it away—which made Mattie think it might actually be dangerous enough to work.

Dan had already loaded the arrow and stared intently in the direction of the stairs. Mattie was sure you didn't say it that way—"loaded the arrow"—but she didn't know how else to think of it. The rough wooden floor made her knees hurt, but it also creaked and she didn't want to let the man below know they were there, so she kept still. Dan seemed weirdly calm, even when the footsteps began to clomp up the stairs to get them. It was like he shot terrorists with a homemade bow and arrow every day.

"Think you can hit him before he shoots?" she whispered, her nerves making her talk even when she knew she should be silent. "It might give us time to run."

Ten-year-old Dan Thibodaux kept his eyes on the stairwell and nodded. Next to her dad, he was the coolest person Mattie Quinn had ever seen.

* * *

Quinn and Thibodaux stopped in a small stand of trees whose branches were decorated with life-size models of pirate corpses hanging in metal gibbets. In a morbid juxtaposition, the bodies of five shooting victims, one of them a little girl about Mattie's age, lay sprawled in the grass among the same trees where they'd fallen in the process of fleeing their killers.

Quinn motioned for Mukhtar to get behind him when he saw one of the shooters enter the four-story wood-sided building that housed the log ride. A second, taller shooter disappeared around the corner.

"Tell me about the inside of that place," Quinn said, nodding toward the log ride.

"It is tall," the Iraqi boy whispered. "But apart from where people board the logs to begin their ride, most of the lower interior is scaffolding of wooden beams. There are only two floors. The second floor is at the very top." He went on to describe the pirate scene inside while peering into the darkness at the building. Finished, he looked back and forth from Quinn to Thibodaux. "There is another door in the back but it is also on the first floor. If they are inside, your children have nowhere to run."

"I got the tall son of a bitch around the corner," Thibodaux hissed. "You take care of the one going in the side door. I'll join you shortly."

Quinn gave a grim nod, experiencing the white-hot rush he felt in his chest prior to any deadly conflict. These two surely murdered the little girl at his feet. "Wait here," he said to Mukhtar, before moving out at a steady, silent trot. He had no weapon, but Mattie was in danger. If he had to, he would use his teeth.

* * *

Jacques Thibodaux was a very large man, large enough to kill one of these teenage pukes with his bare hands if the opportunity arose. But Hollywood movies notwithstanding, killing was rarely a quiet occurrence. People had a tendency to gurgle or squeak before they actually expired. Sometimes it took a brain a while to come to grips with the fact that it was already dead.

Sporadic gunshots popped and rattled around the park—killers, stalking and slaughtering their prey. A few more shots wouldn't raise any suspicion. What Jacques couldn't afford was for the kid to get a word out on his radio that someone had decided to fight back—or worse yet, to tip off the shooter inside and screw up Quinn's approach.

This had to happen quickly.

As big a man as he was, the Marine could be a feather on the wind when he moved. He made a mental note to thank his sweet bride for making him wear the Sperry Top-Siders instead of his favorite pair of squeaky runners.

A giant paw dwarfed the minuscule Ruger .380 pistol. Standing in the shadows of the dark wood at the edge of the building, he cocked his head to one side, listening intently to try and pinpoint the location of his target. He could hear the idiot humming just around the corner, as if the guy was certain he was at the top of the food chain, with nothing to fear in the world. Thibodaux had gathered himself up to pounce when a flurry of movement in the bushes less than ten feet away caught his eye. At first Thibodaux thought it was Dan and Mattie, but it turned out to be three boys huddled together in the manicured shrubs. They looked to be about the age of his middle sons—somewhere between six and nine. Terrified and obviously separated from their parents, they were caught out in the open, in plain view of the shooter.

Still hidden by the corner of the building, Thibodaux raised his arms to try and get the boys' attention and warn them without giving away his position. Around the corner the humming stopped.

"Hey little children," a sneering voice called, thickly accented. "Do you think the shadows hide you? I can smell your piss and see the leaves shaking from here. Come out and maybe I will not hurt you."

Spellbound, the little boys stared, frozen in place. For a moment Thibodaux feared they might actually comply. He reckoned from the sound of the voice and the scrape of a boot on gravel that the shooter was just around the corner—maybe five feet away and certainly close enough to hit the kids with no problem if he shot.

Thibodaux scoured the ground around him with his good eye, looking for a rock, but found none. With nothing else to throw, he kicked off one of the Top-Siders and threw it at the bushes, startling the kids out of their stupor.

Thibodaux heard another telltale scrape of a shoe as the shooter moved closer to the corner, no doubt trying to set up for a shot. Thibodaux heard him chuckle under his breath as the boys broke from the bushes like frightened rabbits.

The big Marine rolled around the corner with the .380 in his hand, coming face-to-face with the startled shooter. Surprised that anyone had the audacity to fight back, the tall jihadi attempted to backpedal. He held the rifle out with both hands, attempting to use the wooden stock to fend off what must have looked like an oncoming freight train barreling down on top of him in the darkness. Thibodaux swatted the rifle barrel out of the way with one hand as he brought the little pistol up directly under the shooter's chin, depositing three of its seven rounds in rapid succession.

The terrorist's eyes flew wide open as the bullets tore through his tongue. Three copper-jacketed lead slugs punched through his soft palate and sinuses to lodge in the slurry of bone fragment, blood, and gray matter that had moments before been his brain. Thibodaux grabbed the action of the little M1 carbine as the dead jihadi toppled straight backward like a felled tree.

"And that," the Marine said to the lifeless body as he tucked the little .380 back in the pocket of his board shorts and shouldered the carbine, "is why I call it my gun-gettin' gun."

Chapter 9

"**H**e's coming," Dan Thibodaux whispered. Mattie could see sweat beading on her friend's forehead, but his breathing was steady, still oddly calm. He raised the white PVC bow and aimed the bamboo arrow at the open doorway. The footsteps grew louder on the stairs. "Get ready to run," he whispered. A new log came through the black opening at the far edge of the building, splashing with a loud whoosh into the water, bumping and clunking along the side of the flume as it bobbed by between the kids and the opposite door.

Mattie tried to squish herself into a ball, getting as low as possible while keeping both feet flat on the floor. She had already decided she was going to run no matter what happened. One of her earliest memories was of her dad giving her the "Stranger Danger" talk—warning her about what to do if someone tried to kidnap her. Her dad said she should always run. There was a chance the bad guy wouldn't even hit you if he did decide to shoot. And if he did actually hit you, it wouldn't be like the movies. The chances you wouldn't die were a lot better than if you just stood there like a helpless target.

Sometimes, though, it was hard to be anything else. Mattie clenched her eyes as the steps got closer.

Water in the flume sloshed, bringing the log closer with a series of hollow thuds.

"Anybody home?" a voice said. It was almost playful. "Time to come down with all your friends . . ."

The emergency light in the stairwell threw the lopsided shadow of a man with a gun into the room, sending it creeping across the pirate mannequins a moment before the terrorist actually entered. Dan pushed the PVC bow out in front of him. He drew the string all the way back to his cheek, letting the arrow fly the instant the man turned to face them.

The bamboo shaft zipped through shadows, sticking the terrorist in the belly. Instead of falling dead, the man looked up, eyes wide in surprise. He put a hand on his stomach, but left the arrow in place, as if afraid to touch it. His face twisted into a dark grimace.

Mattie felt a shiver run through her body. She gathered herself up to run.

"You little shit!" The wounded man screamed, the protruding arrow bouncing as he glared at Dan Thibodaux. He dabbed at the spot with his fingers in disbelief and came up with blood. "You think you are brave man to save your little bitch." He threw the rifle to his shoulder, but a series of quick pops outside the building caused him to stop and look toward the door.

Mattie dove for the passing log, feeling Dan jump behind her. From the corner of her eye, she caught a flurry of movement in the flume by the far door. A silver flash rose from the water behind the terrorist, an instant before Mattie and Dan floated out to plunge into the darkness below.

The movement was so fast and fierce that Mattie was gone before she had the chance to realize it was her dad.

* * *

Unable to move directly up the wooden stairs without alerting the shooter, Quinn elected to scramble up the underside of the log ride. The pungent odor of creosote hung in the humid shadows as he worked his way up the scaffolding. The heavy timber beams were spaced just far enough apart that he had to jump to reach each one as he climbed. He had plenty of incentive with Mattie at the wrong end of a gun and made it up to the crosspieces supporting the flume in a matter of seconds. Water dripped from the leaking trough in a steady stream, slicking the timbers and causing Quinn to slip twice, narrowly missing a four-story plunge to the concrete below. Feet dangling, and hanging by his armpit just outside the entrance to the building, he was finally able to pull himself over the side of the flume and slip into the water. He moved belly down in the man-made river, grabbing the side of a floating log and letting it pull him along unseen. Over the lip of the log, he could just see the image of the shooter as he came through the door. Floating steadily forward, Quinn was almost close enough to make his move. His heart skipped a beat when he saw Mattie hiding in the darkness, and he was happily surprised when Danny Thibodaux shot the arrow from his homemade bow. The shot was minimally effective, but bought him a fraction of a second to make his move against the gunman.

Quinn exploded out of the water at the same moment the young jihadi raised his rifle to cut down Mattie and Dan. He saw the children move, but was too focused on the would-be killer to know where they went.

A low growl escaped his teeth as he brought his left

elbow across in a devastating strike that all but tore the shooter's nose off his face. Following through with the same elbow on the way back across, Quinn snaked his arm over his stunned opponent's throat, snapping the man's head backward in a reverse guillotine choke that arched his entire body backward over his heels. Probably still in his teens, the kid had no idea what was even happening.

Trapping the shooter in tight next to his armpit, Quinn drove the thin stiletto-like blade of the Benchmade over and over again into his exposed chest in a rapid series of hammer-fists, letting go to rage at the man who had killed so many—and would have murdered his little girl.

"He's gone, *l'ami*." Thibodaux's thick Cajun whisper worked its way through the angry red mist of Quinn's brain.

He drove the blood-slicked knife into the dead man's chest for the final time. Panting, his face spattered in blood, Quinn let the dead man slide from his grasp.

Chapter 10

Quinn spun, knife still clutched in his hand, thinking he'd find Mattie hiding in the corner. He stood panting, thinking, trying to make sense of things when he saw she wasn't there. He wiped the blood off the Benchmade on the leg of his wet shorts and returned the knife to his waistband before stooping to pick up the fallen jihadi's rifle. Water and blood ran in rivulets off his body, forming a dark puddle on the wooden floor. Thibodaux stood by the door to the stairwell, the wooden stock of an M1 carbine in one hand, while he studied the dead terrorist with his good eye. He looked up at Quinn to give him a sober nod.

"You okay, Chair Force?" the Cajun said. "You got a lot of blood on your face."

"Good," Quinn said. He jumped across the log flume to search the area around the pirate mannequins where he'd last seen Mattie and Dan.

"I figured you'd done what you needed to do when I didn't hear any gunfire. Mukhtar is right behind me." He looked over his shoulder. "Come on up, kid."

The Iraqi boy stepped hesitantly into the room and gave a wan smile. He looked down at the dead jihadi. "That is Ibrahim," he whispered. "He is a bully."

"Was a bully," Thibodaux said, looking from the dead man to Quinn. "You shoot him with a piece of bamboo?"

"Not me." Quinn held up the white PVC bow. "Mattie and Dan were here," he said. "They must have run as soon as Danny shot." Quinn went to the opening where the logs exited the building and peered out, making sure not to silhouette himself. He saw nothing but the dark outlines of trees and the empty splash pool at the base of the log ride.

Thibodaux came up beside him and took the bow. "My Danny shot that guy with this?"

Quinn nodded. "Looks that way."

Thibodaux pulled the bowstring and sighed. "Clever boy," he said. "Takes after his mama." He dropped the bow and turned toward the door. "Come on, *l'ami*. If they just left they're likely still down below. We can catch up to 'em before these shitheads do."

Both men froze when the radio on the dead jihadi's belt broke squelch. Quinn picked it up and held it in an open palm between them as they listened.

"Everyone needs to slow down," a voice on the radio said, this one absent the Middle Eastern accent of the others. "Keep the prisoners moving but save your ammo."

"That one," Mukhtar said. "That is Terry Spencer—Tariq, the one I told you about."

Another voice came across the radio. "Two cops tried again to breach the eastern gate," the voice said. "I shot them before they could get inside, praise Allah, glory to Him."

"Excellent," Terry/Tariq said. "The news choppers will arrive soon and then we can make our demands. Everyone wait for my signal."

"Wahib, copy."

"Saqr, copy."

"Al Riyad, copy."

"Yasir, copy."

A garbled mix of sounds came next, as several people "bonked" each other, all trying to speak at the same time. Terry/Tariq's tense voice cut them all off.

"Shut up! Shut up! All of you!" He all but screamed over the radio. "The police have radios, too, you idiots! Anyone who happens to be listening in on this will be able to count us."

The radio fell silent for a long moment before the lone reply.

"Sorry . . ."

Thibodaux rolled his good eye. "I think we got us a bunch of highly trained professionals," he muttered. He tapped an identical radio clipped to the waist of his board shorts. "Which reminds me. I took this off the tall goober I met outside. Turned it off so it didn't give me away when I was sneakin' up on another one."

Quinn sighed, thinking. "Amateurs can be difficult to figure."

Thibodaux stepped to the threshold and did a quick peek around the corner, checking for more gunmen. "I'm goin' to find my boy," he said. "You comin'?"

In his darkest moments, Quinn had always seen some glimmer of a way forward, a way out, but by the time he'd scoured the area around the base of the log ride and found no sign of Mattie, he was as close to hopeless as he'd ever been in his life. Thibodaux kicked the body of the shooter he'd killed earlier, cursing at the frustration of not being able to find his son.

Normally a picture of calm, even during the heat and fog of battle, Quinn peered into the darkness from the shadows of the scaffolding and willed himself not to scream. His chest heaved, his face twisted with worry. "They're out there somewhere," he whispered, "trusting us to come save them."

Thibodaux stood beside him, shoulder to shoulder, facing the opposite direction. The whimpering cries of the wounded threatened to snap Quinn's last nerve. Mukhtar seemed to know enough to stay well back and out of the way.

Sirens blared in the distance but offered little hope of rescue. The terrorists' conversation on the radio showed a police presence was part of their plan—whatever that was.

"You know these guys are just waiting for the police," Quinn said. "It's up to us to stop them."

Thibodaux gave a slow nod, like a wolf deciding which member of the herd to cut out and kill. "Wouldn't have it any other way, *l'ami.*" He looked at the rifle in Quinn's hands. "A Mini 14?"

"It is," Quinn said, holding up the Ruger. "I have two magazines with a grand total of thirty-one rounds left."

Thibodaux scrunched his nose and tapped the carbine's wooden stock. "Don't this seem odd to you, Chair Force?"

"How's that?"

"This hodgepodge assortment of guns," Thibodaux said. "Seems like it came out of some grandpa's gun safe instead of an ISIS arms supplier. I mean a World War II STEN, an auto-loading duck gun, an M1, and a Mini 14." He shook his head. "And that one dude had nothin' but a pistol. What sort of terrorist uses a handgun to launch a terror attack on a park this big? Somethin' don't fit. Know what I'm sayin'?"

Quinn gave a slow nod, chewing on the idea and knowing Thibodaux was right. Still, killers used what they had at hand.

Wherever the guns came from, the shooters were using them to great effect. There was no way to know how many people had already been murdered, but Quinn had stepped over and around dozens of bodies.

He turned to Mukhtar. "I counted five separate voices on the radio," he said. "Even if they're down to one mag each . . ." His voice trailed off.

"Translates to a hell of a lot more dead kids," Thibodaux said. "Any idea how many there are, not countin' the five we've already put under?"

The boy shook his head. "I am not certain, but it is possible there are as many as seven more. I have seen at least a dozen gathered around Terry . . . Tariq, listening to his stories. I once saw him talking to one of the security guards—"

"The guards that watch when the armored car comes in?" Quinn asked. This was new information. Quinn had been hoping to run across one of the armed guards and enlist their help.

"Yes," Mukhtar said. "An older man, much older than you, maybe in his late fifties. It is difficult for me to tell with you Americans. You all look old to me."

"Could the security guy have been talking to him about his rhetoric?" Quinn asked. "Giving him a warning maybe?"

"Maybe," Mukhtar said. "But they seemed to be on friendly terms."

"Maybe one of the guards is involved . . ." Thibodaux rubbed his broad jaw, pondering. "And twelve of these bloodthirsty kids."

"Perhaps more," Mukhtar said. "Fadila would make at least thirteen." His face turned down into a hangdog pout. "Fadila has always been friendly with Tariq, though I was blind to it in the beginning.

"Fadila?" Quinn mused, thinking that it made sense. At some level, there always seemed to be a woman involved.

"She works on one of the roller coasters," Mukhtar said. "I used to like her, but I do not want to have anything to do with her if she is involved in this."

"Good thinkin', that," Thibodaux said. He took out his cell phone and tried 911 again, then stuffed it back in the pocket of his shorts. "There has to be a swamper around here somewhere."

"What is a swamper?" Mukhtar said, tilting his head to one side.

"A jammer," Quinn said. "It sends out a signal to confuse cell phones—keeps them from talking to the tower. A swamper that would work on an area as big as this park would have to be fairly large. It might look like a rolling suitcase with a bunch of antennas sticking out the top."

The Iraqi boy grew animated and he gave an emphatic nod, his face a shadow in the darkness. "I have seen such a device. Abu Saqr took it toward the waterslide at the beginning of shift this afternoon."

"That waterslide?" Thibodaux whispered, looking

toward the Dead Drop, looming high above the rest of the park, black against the gray backdrop of night.

"Indeed," Mukhtar said. "Abu Saqr is assigned to maintenance, so I thought nothing of him having that odd case."

More gunfire split the night air, followed by Terry/Tariq's shrieking voice on Ibrahim's radio.

"I told you to conserve your ammo! Is that so impossible to understand?"

Quinn had no idea what the boy looked like but could picture spittle running down a crazed face.

No one replied, but the shooting trailed off, leaving only the wails of the dying through the ghostly stillness of the park.

"Does it seem like the shooters are starting to crumble to you?" Quinn said, half to himself.

Thibodaux grunted. "Like I said, amateurs. Wouldn't surprise me if they start blowin' each other's brains out here in a minute."

"Yeah," Quinn said, his lips tight. "We can dream, I guess."

He studied the dead man's radio. It was a heavy-duty but off-the-shelf 22-channel FRS/GMRS unit with a range of around a mile and a half. Serviceable, but nothing sophisticated.

"I know that look, *l'ami*," Thibodaux said. "You're about to mess with their minds. What do you think? Tell these bastards we're coming to cut their heads off? It's not like they're gonna start shootin' more than they already are."

"I'm tempted," Quinn said. "But I have another idea." He shot a glance at Mukhtar. "The music they play around the park during the day," Quinn said. "Where does it come from?"

"I'm not sure," the boy said. "I would guess from the main park offices. I think I saw some kind of sound system there during employee orientation."

The hollow whump-thump of an approaching helicopter grew louder in the distance, adding weight to the stone that pressed against Quinn's gut. Tariq had told the others to wait for the media to arrive. But what for?

"Take us to the park offices," Quinn said, checking his watch. Thirty-four minutes had elapsed since the initial blast of the suicide belt. "These guys are falling apart. Maybe we can use that to our advantage."

"Tricky business, Chair Force," Thibodaux said through a tense sigh. He turned so he could eye his friend with his good eye. "What's your plan?"

"I'm thinking a bit of psyops. Like you said, mess with their minds a little, add to the confusion." Quinn let out a slow breath. "Then, we'll go save our kids and stack some bodies."

Chapter 11

Mattie Quinn hit the water hard, landing on her back and sliding off someone's clammy shoulder to go completely under. It was freezing cold compared to the hot night, and she had to fight to keep from gasping in a lungful of water as she fought her way to the surface. She and Dan had made a run for it as soon as their log slowed down enough for them to clamor out—hoping to get back to the pirate ship where Dan's dad had told them all to meet up if they got separated. They didn't even make it back to the restrooms before they met two of the terrorists coming around one of the little concession stands. Mattie almost peed herself she'd been so scared, but instead of killing them, the men had poked them with rifle barrels and marched them into the darkness in the opposite direction of the pirate ship—and then had thrown them in the wave pool with at least a hundred other people.

The wave pool looked like a giant bowl of human soup. It was well over her head, and the danger she might be held under by some flailing grown-up, panicked out of his mind, was a real possibility. The cold water shocked her heart. Chlorine hurt her eyes and stung her nose. She came up sputtering, lungs burning and bursting with fear. Blinded and disoriented, Mattie treaded water as she cried out for Dan Thibodaux. She'd heard a shot when they'd thrown her in and was scared they might have killed him just for fun.

"Hey, Mattie." His quiet, sure words were nearly drowned out by the hum of other frightened voices and the splashing movement of all the people in the pool. "I'm here. Right beside you."

He put a tentative hand on her arm, taking care not to push her under. "Are you okay?"

Though most of the park had gone dark, the lights in the pool still worked, making the shimmering blue water stand out starkly in the night. Hundreds of terrified people bobbed in the water. At least a dozen bodies floated facedown amid clouds of blood. Mattie had counted three men with guns when they'd marched her to the pool. The men had forced almost everyone into the water, but she'd seen a bunch more standing around the edge, their hands tied in front of them. Some were men, some were women, but all the people around the edge were grown-ups.

Mattie wiped the wet hair out of her face and nodded, suddenly unable to stop shivering. Her teeth chattered. She blinked hard, trying to clear her eyes and stay above water.

Dan tapped on her shoulder and pointed to the shallow end. "I don't think there's an inch of space between anybody down there," he said. "We're gonna have to swim for a while." He sounded an awful lot like his daddy when he was tense.

"I'm fine," Mattie said, still sputtering. She wiped her face again. Her teeth still chattered uncontrollably. "I can float pretty good."

"I see three guys with rifles," Dan said, swirling his arms in the water to spin slowly around without actually going anywhere.

"I wonder why they have some people standing up there out of the water," Mattie wondered out loud, as much to herself as to Dan Thibodaux.

"I can't figure that out," Dan said.

Mattie leaned her head back and peered up through the darkness at the helicopter hovering above. She could see the flashing lights of another one flying in from a long way off.

"It's a police chopper," Dan said. "See the spotlight?"

Mattie nodded, blowing water out of her face and trying her best to stay calm. She looked at the men with guns, and then at Dan. "I wish our dads were here. You think the police will start to shoot the bad guys soon?"

Dan shook his head, sniffing and squinting his eyes from the heavily chlorinated water. "I don't know," he said.

"I think our dads would shoot them," Mattie said.

"They might," Dan said. "But I'll bet these guys will start killing more people if the police don't get them all right away. My dad says it's pretty hard to hit anything from a helicopter."

Dan was starting to shake, too, but Mattie couldn't blame him. It was impossible not to be scared bobbing there in the swimming pool next to so many dead people.

Someone bumped into Mattie's back. She thought it might be one of the bodies and spun hard, pushing away. It turned out to be a blond lady in a black-and-white checked swimsuit, treading water behind her. She looked like she was about Ronnie Garcia's age, only heavier and with much paler skin. She held a pink foam swim noodle just below the surface.

"Sorry to bump into you," Mattie said.

"Don't worry, sweetheart," the woman said, forcing a smile. A trickle of blood oozed from a gash on her pale shoulder. She grimaced, obviously in pain. "How old are you?"

"Eight," Mattie said.

Dan swam up beside her so they were shoulder to shoulder. "I'm ten," he said. Mattie could tell he was protecting her, and she liked it.

"Eight and ten years old," the woman said, shaking her head in disbelief. "Y'all are holding it together better than most of the adults around here tonight." She pushed the foam swim noodle out to Mattie "Here, take this. You need it more than I do."

Mattie took the end of the float, grateful for the chance to give her arms and legs a rest. "Are you sure? It looks like you're hurt."

"I'll be fine," the woman said, dabbing at her shoulder. "What is it they say? It's only a flesh wound. And heaven knows I have enough flesh to keep my head above water. My name's Sarah, by the way."

"I'm Mattie." She looked around. "Are you all by yourself?"

"My date and I got separated in the dark," Sarah said, looking lost and sad. "I just met him on Tinder, so I hardly knew him anyway. To tell you the truth, I think he probably swiped left and saved himself."

"What?" Mattie asked.

"Nothing," Sarah said, sounding sad.

Mattie moved the pool noodle so Dan could lean on

one end, and then kicked around to maneuver so the other was directly in front of Sarah. "Stay next to us, then," she said. "We're alone, too."

Sarah's eyes clenched shut and she took a deep, shuddering breath. Mattie thought the poor woman was going to cry, but instead she moved in closer, eager for the friendly company.

Dan made the mistake of looking at one of the gunmen a little too long—a teenager with a sparse black beard. The man raised his rifle and pointed it with a harsh glare. Dan and Mattie both turned, relaxing only slightly when no shots came their way.

"Yeah," Sarah said, touching the wound on her shoulder again. "They don't like it when you stare. I can vouch for that."

"There's a whole bunch of us and just a few of them," Dan said. He kept his voice low, though there was no way the terrorists could hear him over the whimpering moans that rose from the pool. "It seems like a bunch of grown-ups should be able to rush them and take away their guns."

Sarah scoffed. "Grown-ups don't often work together so very well—"

The abrupt twang of an acoustic guitar with a heavy, clapping beat poured in from the darkness. The sudden noise caused everyone in the pool and the gunmen surrounding it to turn back and forth, looking for the origin. It took a minute to realize the music was coming from speakers all over the theme park.

Mattie perked up as she listened. "That's 'Beat the Devil's Tattoo,'" she whispered, recognizing the song immediately. "Black Rebel Motorcycle Club."

Sarah stopped treading water, cocking her head to look at the nearest shooter. "Listen," she said. "The music's playing over the speakers, but it's also on their walkie-talkies. I wonder where it's coming from."

Mattie gave Dan's ribs a happy nudge as a wide smile spread across her face. "I bet you it's coming from my dad's phone," she said.

Chapter 12

Jericho Quinn pressed his belly flat to the dirt and watched his daughter through the leaves of a Japanese boxwood shrub seventy-five meters from the wave pool. He squeezed the wooden stock on his rifle until he thought it might shatter. Thibodaux lay to his immediate right. Mukhtar waited another twenty meters back at a concession stand that rented swimming tubes, ready to sing out if anyone came up behind them. "Oo ye yi," the big Cajun whispered. His breath kicked up bits of dust and leaves beneath the bush in front of him. Quinn half expected his friend to leap up and charge the pool at any moment. Instead, he took a couple of deep, cleansing breaths and nestled down behind his rifle. "The little boogs are still alive, praise the good Lord for that." His whispered voice was muffled against the wooden stock as spoke. "I count three shitbirds on the pool deck—and two of 'em have better rifles than us, if you can believe it."

"I can see that," Quinn said from behind his own gun. Two of the men carried what looked like AK-47s, the other, some kind of shotgun. He wondered if it was just luck of the draw or if they had planned it that way. It didn't bode well for the people in the pool.

"Alrighty," Thibodaux said. "Let's get this show on the road. You take the turd on the left and I'll take the one on the right. We can both shoot the one at the end if it makes you feel better."

"Hang on," Quinn said, continuing to scan back and forth with his rifle. "Something isn't right. See one, think two . . . see three, think four . . . or five or six."

"Or maybe these three knuckleheads are just stupid enough to stand out in the open like that with the choppers overhead."

"I'm sure there are at least a couple more hiding somewhere, out of sight," Quinn said. "Any law enforcement snipers on the ground are likely to have infrared or at least basic night vision. All the hostages these guys have standing around the pool as decoys will make it difficult to tell good guys from bad at first glance."

Thibodaux rolled on his side to look Quinn in the face. "Well shit, Chair Force, if the cops use infrared and start shooting guys in the bushes with guns, you and me ain't gonna last very long."

"True enough," Quinn said. "But for now, our bad guys seem to be holding off any police response."

"Reckon their long game is to wait for the news choppers to show up, then murder everyone in the pool?" Thibodaux said.

"I think that's exactly what they plan to do," Quinn said.

"Looks to me like the news chopper is just hovering out there, tryin' to inch his way in close. Shit-for-brains media gonna be the cause of the story they want to cover."

"They're probably trying to get clearance from law

enforcement to get closer," Quinn said through clenched teeth. "The powers that be will likely grant it if only to get more eyes on the ground." As important as it was to gather all the information he could about the scene, it was almost impossible not to focus on Mattie. Tearing his eyes away, Quinn watched the gunman nearest him and Thibodaux. "See how this guy on the end keeps looking up at the top of the Dead Drop?"

"Waiting on a signal from Terry/Tariq," Thibodaux mused. "Your little trick steppin' all over their radio traffic makes sure they can't communicate—for a minute anyway. How about this for an idea? I'll stay put and take out these three if it looks like things are about to ramp up. You get to the top of the slide and throw that son of a bitch down here so I can have a talk with him."

"Sounds like a plan I can live with." Quinn passed the Mini 14 rifle to Thibodaux. "Let's trade. Your little .30 caliber is a war winner for close work, but this one will reach out a little better."

The Cajun handed over the stubby M1 carbine. "I ain't arguing with that . . . hang on . . ." He rolled onto his side and reached into his shorts to bring out the tiny .380 pistol, handing it to Quinn before taking the larger rifle. "I reckon all the bad guys will start to work their way here for the big finale. Send our young Iraqi friend back to tell Camille and Ronnie to take the boys and haul ass."

Quinn held the pistol in the palm of his hand and nodded. "Good idea," he said, already inching his way back on elbows and toes, taking care to be as noiseless as possible in the litter of leaves and twigs. There was no time to come up with another plan.

"Watch your grape, *l'ami*," Thibodaux said, already behind his rifle and back onto target.

"That is Abu Saqr," Mukhtar whispered, standing in the shadows beside Quinn as they watched the lone gunman pace back and forth in the blue shadows at the base of the Dead Drop tower. "He is the one I saw with the . . . what did you call it? The swamper . . ."

Saqr brought up a two-way radio and tried to call out. A swaying, bluesy number called "Ten Cent Pistol" now poured from the radio, preventing him from getting any message across. Exasperated, the young jihadi threw the radio against the concrete building, shattering it to pieces. He stepped back and craned his head to stare upward, waving his hands as if to get the attention of whoever was at the top. In the end, he took something from his pocket and moved to a darkened doorway at the side of the building.

"He's going inside," Quinn said, preparing to sprint after him.

"There is an elevator," Mukhtar said. "The park makes those who wish to ride Dead Drop climb the one hundred and eighty-nine steps to the top, but employees can take a lift from the basement, as Abu Saqr is, or the main floor behind the gift shop. He would have a key, since he works for maintenance."

"Okay then," Quinn said, already working through the idea of what he had to do. "Go now," he said, handing Mukhtar the little .380 Ruger. "You know how to use this?"

"I do," Mukhtar said.

"Remember, this is a pipsqueak gun," he said. "If you have to shoot once, shoot three times to be sure."

"I will die before I let you down," Quinn heard the Iraqi boy say as he sprinted after Saqr. "You have my word!"

Chapter 13

Bile burned the back of Quinn's throat as he wove his way over and through a pile of bodies at the base of Dead Drop, apparently cut down one by one as they ran from the stairs. Skidding around the corner to make up time, Quinn entered the building at the front, one floor above Saqr. He breathed a sigh of relief to find the elevator doors in a small alcove at the rear of the abandoned gift shop, right where Mukhtar said it would be. Rattling cables and squeaking gears told him the car was already on the move. He used his fingers to pry open the elevator's outer safety doors to expose the shaft. He'd hoped the car would be at the top since Terry had likely been the last to ride it, but it must have already been at the bottom when Saqr reached it. Quinn was just able to jump through the open safety doors into the shaft as the car flew up to meet him from the floor below. Quinn wanted to land on a support beam and simply shoot the jihadi through the elevator ceiling, but necessary haste gave him no time to plan or aim his leap. Both feet hit square in the center of the light fixture, sending it crashing down on top of Saqr with Quinn following right behind. The wooden stock of the M1 carbine caught crosswise on the ceiling braces, jamming in place and leaving Quinn hanging in the elevator as if from a chin-up bar.

Piking his legs, he kicked a surprised Abu Saqr square in the face with both feet. The teenage terrorist bounced off the elevator wall, dazed enough to give Quinn time to kick him again. Reeling from the blows, Saqr dropped his rifle and fell sideways, causing Quinn to have to release his hold on the carbine and spin to continue to face him. Amateur that he was, the young jihadi still had the forethought to draw a dagger from a sheath at his side and thrust it wildly upward. The long stiletto blade caught Quinn in the front of his thigh, piercing meat and scraping bone. There was no searing pain, only the sensation of a heavy punch, and the sickening shiver as the blade glanced off the thighbone and exited the outside of his leg, punching a small hole in his board shorts.

Instinctively, Quinn lowered his center, capturing the hand that held the dagger and turning it back on its owner. Falling, as much from nausea as any martial arts technique, he drove the dagger into Saqr's chest. He felt the familiar pop as the blade punched through the cartilage connecting the man's ribs to his breastbone, and slid into his heart.

Quinn left the quivering knife where it was and pushed away. He scooped up the dying man's rifle, a short AK-47 carbine with a folding stock, and then stood to test his damaged leg. He could put weight on it, so that was a blessing. The entry wound was located just below the hem of his swim trunks. It was a good two inches across, made deeper by the lateral movement of the double-edged blade when Saqr had stuck him. The exit wound was small enough it could be covered with a Band-Aid. Quinn didn't want to think about the damage done inside. A more experienced man would have slashed the inside of the leg, severing the femoral artery, bleeding Quinn out in a matter of minutes. As it was, his wound wept a steady flow of blood. But nothing arterial, Quinn thought. That was blessing number two.

The elevator doors chimed as they slid open behind him. Quinn spun to find a muscular man with a black beard peering over the railing toward the base of the slide. It was Kaliq, the young jihadi who had laughed while he shot dead the group of UVA students. Music from the Black Keys still played from the two-way radio in his hand. His gun was parked against the rail ten feet from where he stood.

Blessing number three.

Bodies lay strewn around the concrete deck—groups of teens, families, middle-aged couples—arms and legs tangled, stacked as if they'd been dropped on top of one another. They'd been trapped at the top of the waterslide when the shooting began—and eventually murdered as they tried to run.

The top floor of Dead Drop was wide open but for the trapdoor entrance that gave the slide its name. A two-foot-wide column beside the hard plastic door was home to a small panel that housed the simple controls: a green light to signify the bottom of the slide was clear, and a large red button that tripped the door like a gallows, sending the rider on a near vertical drop for the first ten of the twenty-one-story journey. Wooden stanchions and yellow rope, meant to keep people in line as they queued up for the ride, were now a tangled knot, over-turned by the stampede of victims as they attempted to flee back down the stairs. Those who had made it out the small doorway accounted for the pile of dead he'd passed at the bottom.

Saqr's AK at his hip, Quinn aimed at the jihadi's belly and pulled the trigger. Fresh out of blessings, he heard nothing but the resounding click of the firing pin on an empty chamber.

Chapter 14

Ronnie Garcia had long since given up hope that anyone crowding around her in the belly of the pirate ship would stay anything close to calm. Instead, she tried to keep the noise down to a level that might, if they were extremely lucky, keep them undiscovered and alive. She knew from experience that few people could keep still, let alone quiet, when they were afraid. The more heightened the sense of fear, the jerkier and more vocal the human body became—as if every muscle and bone was crying out in terror. Breathing became ragged, knees jumped uncontrollably, teeth chattered to the point of breaking. Pent-up words hummed and buzzed, struggling for release behind pursed lips. Children and adults alike sobbed and shuffled, embarrassed at not being able to control their bladders. Jericho called it terror-piss, and the smell of it was overpowering in the dank surroundings, adding to the misery—and the noise level—of the little band of refugees. Thankfully, the port side of the vessel faced away from the concrete pathways and concession vendors, open to the shallow wading pool. In less violent times, this gave parents a place to sit and watch their toddlers play in the water, protected from the sun and general hubbub of the park. Slides came down from the top deck into the water, and ladders made it possible for small children to climb up from inside the ship's hold. A half dozen plastic picnic tables were situated around the toddler-size play equipment below. It should have been a fun place, full of splashing and laughter, but hope had vanished with the breeze. The fans that normally kept the shady playground cool had clicked off with the lights shortly after the shooting had started.

Forty minutes had passed since the first explosion. The gunfire had slowed, but errant shots and screams still popped and wailed throughout the park, ripping at the last shred of Ronnie's nerves and keeping everyone huddled in place.

Though physically sick with worry over Jericho and Mattie, Ronnie had no children and could only imagine the stress Camille Thibodaux was going through. So far, the tough little brunette had been a rock, working to fight what had to be bone-crushing despair while she faced the realities of keeping her remaining six sons as quiet and upbeat as possible.

"Mama," Denny whispered, his voice as frail as he looked. "My nose is starting to bleed again."

"Hush now," Camille said, drawing her little boy closer. She removed the sheer cover-up, making her look all the more vulnerable wearing nothing but her swimsuit. Blood dripped onto her bare thigh. "Just hold it there like that. You'll be fine."

One of the men in the back scoffed. "Fine?" he mumbled. "That's laughable. We're a long way from fine, kid. It's only a matter of time—"

Camille glared daggers at the man, her intent clear even in the darkness. He turned away and melted back into the crowd.

"I'm thirsty," a little girl who couldn't have been over three whimpered.

Her mother, a near catatonic young woman who had watched her husband and in-laws murdered just minutes before, patted the child on the back, but said nothing.

"I could get her some water from the wading pool," twelve-year-old Shawn Thibodaux whispered. "It's gross, but it would be better than nothing."

"It might come to that," Camille said, giving her eldest boy a proud smile. "Let's give your daddy a few more minutes before we venture out. He'll take care of this, I prom—"

"I am sorry," Ms. Hatch said, speaking through lips pulled as tightly as her gray curls, "but that gentleman is right. We are in serious trouble, and it's time we admit it."

Ronnie held up the shotgun as if to illustrate how aware she was of the dangers. "What do you think we're doing?" she said.

Ms. Hatch rolled her eyes. It was obvious she was used to being in charge and the fact that someone else was calling the shots had crawled up under her skin and galled her.

"It seems apparent to everyone in this place except you two that your men have been . . . taken . . ."

"You mean murdered," Camille said, her chest heaving, chin quivering. Ronnie knew the poor thing was beginning to crumble. And who could blame her? Her little boy, and now Jacques.

"I didn't say that, my dear," the woman said, as

disingenuous as ever. "I only mean to say you might want to season your hope with a little dash of realism."

"You have no idea what my husband is capable of," Camille whispered.

"If he's smart," the man in the Blue Jays hat said, "he's found a way out of this shithole and saved his own ass."

Shawn stood and squared off at the man. "My dad would never—"

"Shut your piehole, kid," the man said. "If your daddy ain't gone over the wall, then he's got his ass shot off. We're stuck with nothin' to protect us but the hot tamale with a shotgun. End of stor—"

Camille flew at the man like a woman on fire, spitting and clawing at his face. The otherworldly wail of a woman who'd lost her child made the hair on Garcia's neck stand up.

The idiot backpedaled, barking at Camille to leave him alone, and doubled his fist to hit her. Before he could swing, Mr. Larue smacked him in the side of the head with a piece of broken concrete, knocking him to his knees.

"I'm scared," Larue said, straightening his pirate hat, "but not scared enough to listen to that."

Camille stood over the man, one bare leg cocked back as if ready to fly at him again. Her dark hair was mussed, her chest heaving. The right strap of her swimsuit hung off a shoulder. Ronnie didn't know if she'd ever seen such a burning intensity from another human being.

Blue Jays looked up at Ronnie with squinting eyes, mouth opening and closing—teetering on the verge of a scream. A trickle of blood ran down the side of his head in front of his ear. "You . . . you're supposed to be some kind of law?" His voice rose in tremulous anger and indignation until it became a ragged scream. "What are you gonna do about this? Huh? Are you just gonna stand there and—"

Ronnie answered his question with a quick thump to the face with the butt of her shotgun, knocking him out cold. "Hot tamale, eh?" Ronnie said, fire flashing in the depths of her eyes. "No, *postalita,* I am not going to stand around and let you give us all away." She gave Larue a wink in the darkness. "A necessary evil. He was making far too much noise."

"I hate to say it," Larue said, eyeing Ronnie and keeping his voice to a judicious whisper. "But it is true that your friends aren't back yet. It's been over a half an hour. We may need to try another option."

Ronnie took a deep breath. Maybe the man was right. Jericho and Jacques had been gone too long.

The scrape of a boot on gravel outside the ship caused Ronnie to wheel back to the porthole. She held up her left hand to silence everyone in the crowded ship, and pointed the shotgun out the porthole, toward a man wearing a park uniform approaching from the shadows.

Fadila Baghdadi watched as a flower of orange flame erupted like cannon fire from the side of the wooden ship. A hundred feet away in the trees, she clutched her pistol and watched as Abu Nasser pitched forward into the darkness, cut down by the sudden blast. She'd witnessed many deaths that night, and expected to witness many more. Her own death was inevitable, part of the plan—but she still found it painful to see her friends die.

This was not part of the plan at all. Abu Nasser was not supposed to go yet. They would all go together when the cameras arrived and police stormed the park in a final, glorious battle. But somehow, someone inside the ship had gotten their hands on a gun.

Fadila kept to the shadows, working her way toward the dark hulk of the pirate ship, stopping alongside a wooden shack that smelled of sweets, less than twenty yards away. There were definitely people inside, several of them from the sounds of murmuring—hiding there, waiting to cut down her friends as they walked past. The thought of it set a hot ball of rage alight in her belly.

She wondered if the people inside the ship were the ones responsible for the incessant music that had cut off their communications and rendered the radios useless. Hers was off, but she abandoned it on the sidewalk anyway, realizing it would give her away.

Lifting the black polo, she shoved the pistol down the waistband of her khaki shorts in front of her hip bone. She took a deep breath to steel her resolve, then pulled a green egg-shaped object from her front pocket and held it in her open palm, staring at the oblong outline of a RGD-5 hand grenade. There were only two. Tariq had one and she had the other. They'd planned to use them together, taking many infidels with them at the time of their own deaths. Not as powerful as the American grenades, the Russian weapon was far cheaper, and much easier to obtain. It would most certainly kill anyone hiding in the stupid ship.

She stuffed the grenade back in her shorts, leaving it

high in her pocket so she could reach it easily. The fuse would burn for less than four seconds, so Fadila knew she would die as well—but that was of no consequence.

She mussed her hair to look as if she was also being hunted, then affected the terrified expression she'd seen on the faces of the people she'd killed that night. Americans were quick to trust a woman in jeopardy. Whoever was in the ship, police or otherwise, would believe her long enough to give her the opportunity to kill them all.

Chapter 15

Quinn gave the base of the AK-47's magazine an upward smack with the flat of his hand, and then racked the bolt and pulled the trigger. Years of training had embedded the tap, rack, bang drill in his brain for a failure-to-fire malfunction—Tap, rack . . . but no bang. Quinn chided himself for not checking the chamber when he'd picked up the weapon, realizing Saqr must have run it dry.

Abu Kaliq turned out to be much more athletic than the others in his group and jumped sideways at the first sight of Quinn, as if to try and dodge his fire. The jihadi smiled when the gun malfunctioned, and then dove for his own rifle that leaned against the wall. Quinn threw the useless AK like a spear, crashing in behind it with the point of his shoulder.

Quinn felt the other man's rib cage bend inward as they came together. It would have been a devastating blow, but the knife wound in Quinn's thigh throbbed as if it had been stuffed with hot coals and robbed him of a considerable amount of power as he sprang forward. Still, it knocked the wind out of Kaliq long enough for Quinn to get him rolled back on his heels—for the moment.

Quinn saw the black plastic box that had to be the cell phone jammer and tried to work his way to it, but Kaliq circled, putting himself in front of the device. Tariq was nowhere to be seen, but Quinn didn't have time to worry about anyone who wasn't trying to kill him right then and there.

Battle, especially in close quarters, was frenetic and unpredictable—but for a victory, it had to be fought with an end goal in mind. Inflicting pain might slow down the opponent or redirect his energy, creating a different avenue for attack. But pain didn't stop a determined fighter. In the end, blood or oxygen to the brain had to be interrupted, from a correctly applied choke, a bullet, a blade—or the sudden fatal meeting with the concrete after a fall from twenty-one stories.

Quinn pressed forward, shoving Kaliq backward toward the rail, driven by momentum and rage. But the young jihadi had other plans, and stepped off-line to slow Quinn's attack. At the same time, he reached over Quinn's shoulder to yank the T-shirt up his back toward his neck, gripping all the gathered fabric from neck to hem in a stout fist. Crossing his forearms, Kaliq snaked in to grab a second handful of shirt and collar on the other side of Quinn's neck—and then squeezed.

His turn to push, the heavier man drove Quinn backward as he pulled his forearms together, bashing Quinn into the clear Plexiglas tube that covered Dead Drop's entry. The flimsy tube was meant for safety, not security, and it separated from the wall under the force of Quinn's body. Tipping sideways like a tree, it rolled across the concrete to expose the trapdoor.

The collar of Quinn's own shirt pressed against the

arteries at the side of his neck, cutting off the blood to his brain. With only seconds until he passed out, Quinn shot his left arm between Kaliq's elbows, putting the flat of his own hand to the side of his head, wedging open the jihadi's grip with his arm and shoulder—a simple but effective choke escape called "answering the phone."

Quinn felt the tingling rush as blood returned to his brain, and he used the renewed energy to pummel Kaliq's open left side with a series of brutal uppercutting hooks, digging deep into the soft underbelly just below the man's rib cage. Kaliq struggled to put some distance between himself and the brutal beatdown to his spleen. Smart enough to know he shouldn't run, the jihadi mounted another attack the instant he felt any relief from Quinn's punches. Injured and fatigued, the kid lumbered forward, intent on using his greater mass. Quinn side-stepped, throwing out the inside of his forearm like a club and letting it thud directly across the brachial plexus on the left side of Kaliq's neck. The disruption of nerve impulses caused the jihadi to gurgle unintelligible sounds as his feet outran the upper portion of his body. He tried to regain his balance, but found himself caught in an explosive flurry of hooks and crosses that sent him staggering back directly over the slide's now-exposed trapdoor. Slamming against the control column, his back collided with the red button and the door fell away, sucking him out of Quinn's grasp.

Unwilling to let Kaliq escape to the bottom and alert the rest of his crew, Quinn dove in before the door could swing shut, following Kaliq headfirst into the gurgling darkness of the tube.

* * *

As the name implied, Dead Drop's tubular slide fell away at a stomach-churning near-vertical drop for the first ten stories, or ninety feet, with riders' bodies gradually coming back into greater and greater contact with the slide itself as the angle increased with each passing foot. A steady spray of water greased the way.

Diving headfirst with his arms outstretched, Quinn was in virtual freefall, coming into far less contact with the slide and producing greater speed than Kaliq, who slid on his back, feet forward. Obviously terrified, the young jihadi screamed at the top of his lungs. He flailed wildly as he slid, causing him to careen back and forth inside the tube, slowing him down even more.

Rocketing down the slide near highway speeds, Quinn gritted his teeth, arching his neck to keep his nose above the jet of water that rushed down the base of the slide. A rooster tail of spray flew up behind Kaliq as he slid. Quinn's fingers curled around a knot of his trailing hair two seconds into the ride. The jihadi went apoplectic, screaming even louder, a hollow, otherworldly sound inside the close confines of the plastic tube. He'd had no idea Quinn was behind him, and flailed wildly when he felt something out of the darkness grab his hair.

They reached fifty miles an hour about the time the angle of the slide rose up to meet them. Quinn pulled himself forward with Kaliq's hair as if it were a rope. Both men careened up on the side of the tube as it curved sharply to the right in a series of two downward spiraling corkscrew loops. Unable, or at least unwilling, to put his arms up over his head and fight back, Kaliq jerked his head from side to side as he sped along, in an effort to shake off the unseen attacker. Quinn tensed his core, locking his ankles and tucking his shoulders to gain as much speed as he could. Kaliq's fighting only slowed him all the more, allowing Quinn to move forward enough to slide his right hand over the screaming face, groping forward to claw at the man's eyes. Thrashing like he was out of his mind, Kaliq arched his back, inadvertently allowing Quinn to sink his fingers into the man's eye sockets up to his knuckles. Kaliq tore at his own face with both hands, but it did no good. Pain and physics made his efforts hopeless. Quinn gripped the young terrorist's face like a bowling ball, allowing his legs to come apart slightly, slowing him, forcing Kaliq to drag him along by the eyes.

The jihadi screamed a broken scream. Quinn's stomach fell away as the two men shot out of the final loop and plunged downward another twenty feet. The angle decreased and the top of the slide opened up to form a trough instead of a tube. What had been a lubricating spray became two feet of water, slowing the men's forward motion as surely as if they'd deployed a parachute. Eighteen seconds after they'd dropped through the trapdoor twenty-one stories above, they reached the end of the Dead Drop.

Maintaining the claw grip, Quinn arched his body and let his legs fly past the thrashing jihadi, flipping on his belly and clamoring onto the man's back to hold his face underwater. Expecting to be shot at any moment by one of Kaliq's compatriots, Quinn locked his legs around the man in an effort to quiet the sound of splashing water. It was over much more quickly than Quinn expected it to be and he lay there on the man's back, holding him under long after he'd stopped his struggles.

Drenched and oozing blood from the knife gash in his leg, Quinn left the dead jihadi floating facedown in the slide. He took a quick moment to look around and gather his thoughts, finding himself alone in the shadows. A blue glow from the lights in the wave pool flickered up through the trees to his right. Apart from the music coming from the speakers, the park was eerily silent.

He'd hoped to find Terry Spencer at the top of the slide, kill him, and disable the cell jammer. The immediate scrap with Kaliq had left the swamper operational—and Terry hadn't even been there. Quinn took a series of deep cleansing breaths, trying to make sense of things. Terry wasn't at the top, but he had to be somewhere.

The Lynyrd Skynyrd version of "Call Me the Breeze"—another song from Quinn's playlist—began to play over the speakers.

If Terry Spencer had any knowledge of the park at all, he'd go straight for the office to fix the problem with the radio and reestablish communication with his team.

Quinn kept to the shadows and sprinted toward the park office. Once more he found himself without a rifle. The Benchmade folder had slipped out of his shorts during the slide, so now he didn't even have that. He saw two shooters as he ran, loitering in the trees just inside the side gate. He noted their positions, but gave them a wide berth.

Fifty meters out, Quinn saw the front door to the park offices swing shut. He dug in, ignoring the sickening ache from the wound in his thigh, and picked up his speed.

Mattie and Dan were still in the pool along with over a hundred other hostages—all surrounded by cruel men with their fingers on the trigger, waiting for an order.

Chapter 16

Ronnie Garcia watched the dead jihadi for over a minute. She'd seen him topple over in the shadows but wanted to make sure he was going to stay down. At just under twenty-five meters away, most of the nine lead pellets had slammed into his chest and neck, rendering him DRT, as Jericho would call it—Dead Right There. Garcia thumbed another shell into the shotgun, topping it off. The tight yellow swimsuit offered no pockets to store extra ammo. She'd tried to tuck a couple of shells down the front of her cleavage, but they'd both become irretrievable without stripping off the suit. In the end, she'd asked Camille to stand near her with a handful of shells, passing them to her as needed. She didn't trust anyone else. "Any more out there?" Camille whispered, almost reverently, leaning forward to peer through the porthole. Her broad shoulders suddenly tensed, as if she'd seen another threat.

Ronnie didn't want to expose their position by sticking the shotgun out the window, so she had to lower it in order to get a wider view.

"What is it?"

"Someone else," Camille whispered.

"Shoot him!" An unidentified voice, but the murmur rippling through the crowd said it was the general sentiment.

"Hang on," Ronnie said. "It looks like a girl. She's got nothing in her hands."

Ms. Hatch crept up closer to one of the portholes. "She's a park employee," the woman said. "That means she's one of them."

Mr. Larue scoffed. "I'm a park employee," he said. "Not all of us are part of this."

"She looks the part," the woman said. "If you know what I mean."

Ronnie raised the shotgun, but glared sideways at the bony woman. "Because she has dark skin? You need to keep a lid on your trash, *calaca*." Literally, skeleton. "I'll shoot who I have to shoot. Killing isn't quite as simple as you make it sound."

The woman ruffled like an angry hen. "Well, dear, you seem to know a great deal about it."

Outside, the young woman walked past the porthole with tentative steps. She approached the door with her hands in the air, looking back and forth as if afraid she might be shot. Garcia felt a sinking feeling burble through her gut, but reminded herself of the boy who was helping Quinn.

Garcia nodded to Camille, then glanced toward the porthole. "Do me a favor and keep a watch for more bad guys."

"Roger that," Camille said, sounding like her husband.

Garcia turned, moving to put the rest of the group behind her. The threshold of the door was made of metal, likely the best cover on the entire ship. She cocked a hip out to steady herself against the frame, allowing her to peek out at the approaching woman without making herself too much of a target. Some might have felt overly exposed, dressed in nothing but the tight yellow bathing suit, but Garcia had gotten over such a notion a long time ago. She knew how to use her body—and the temporary lapse in judgment it caused—to gain the upper hand.

The tactic worked most of the time, but when she stepped into the doorway holding the shotgun, the young woman who approached the ship seemed to look right past her. When Ronnie called out in challenge, she realized that what she had perceived as fear was actually anger.

"Stop right there!" Ronnie gave a whispered hiss. "Let me see your hands."

The young woman dipped her head submissively. She was close enough that a blast from the shotgun would cut her in half, but she hardly seemed to notice it. Apparently oblivious to the gun, she shot furtive glances over her shoulders, then back at Garcia.

Garcia raised her head, giving the girl a jaundiced look, and kept the shotgun trained at her belly.

"What's your name?" Garcia said.

"Fadila," the young woman said. "Please, I am frightened." She cast another look over her shoulder. Ronnie couldn't tell if she was afraid or waiting for backup.

"Please," the girl asked again. "May I come inside?"

Garcia didn't budge from her spot by the door. "You work here?" she asked.

Fadila nodded. "I know the people who have done this," she said, her voice breathy. "They are killing everyone. I only just managed to get away." She leaned forward. "Whichever of you shot that one out there certainly saved my life."

Garcia took a step back, holding the shotgun up with one hand and motioning the girl inside with a flick of her wrist. "Get in before someone else sees us," she said.

Fadila let out a long sigh. Her shoulders dropped. "Thank you," she said, stopping just inside the door.

She stood up straighter as she surveyed the crowded interior of the ship before looking directly back at Garcia. "There are so many of you," she said, as a dark smile spread across her face. "It is good." Her eyes crawled up and down Garcia, appearing to see her for the first time. "Are you not ashamed?" The words came out on a hateful whisper that caused the tiny hairs on the back of Garcia's neck to stand on end. "How can you walk around dressed like that?"

Garcia took a half step back, but it was too late.

Fadila didn't seem to care if she lived or died, stepping directly across the muzzle of the shotgun. Ronnie's finger searched for the trigger and fired, but the blast went over the girl's shoulder, missing her by a hair, and doing nothing but deafening everyone inside the ship with the concussive boom. Throwing herself at Garcia, Fadila grabbed the shotgun by the end of the barrel and thinnest part of the stock, just behind the trigger guard, attempting to wrench it away. Ronnie held tight, but Fadila brought her knee up in a vicious series of rapid kicks, slamming into Garcia's groin. Garcia doubled over, feeling as if her pelvis had been broken in two. She clenched her jaw, grinding her teeth from the pain and gulping back wave after wave of overwhelming nausea.

Women screamed and children began to howl at the sudden violence. Garcia heard the muffled cries of several men shouting for Fadila to stop her attack. But no one stepped in to help—no one but for Camille Thibodaux.

The fiery brunette crashed in as if she was protecting her own child. She hit both women with such force it knocked them to the ground and sent the shotgun flying against the ship wall with a plastic thud.

Both arms pushed up over her head, writhing on her back, Garcia tucked her knees to her chest and bucked her hips, keeping herself from being crushed but unable to get Fadila off her. Past injuries to her shoulders at the hands of a madman made the angle impossible to escape. She could feel the hard imprint of a gun against her knees, tucked under the young woman's shirt.

Ronnie outweighed Fadila by at least forty pounds, and bum shoulders notwithstanding, she was plenty strong enough to hold on to the girl's hands, putting the two women in a sort of stalemate—each holding the other, Ronnie unable to wrench free because of her shoulder, Fadila unable to reach her pistol.

"You killed my friend!" Fadila hissed. Her lips pulled back as she gnashed her teeth. Spittle flew from her lips and she threw herself back and forth, craning her neck and trying to bite Garcia in the arm and hands.

Garcia was strong, but she knew she couldn't hold on forever. Beginning to worry, she searched desperately to locate Camille. The rough concrete floor scraped her neck and shoulders. Tresses of black hair puddled around her face, adding to the darkness. A glimmer of hope hit her when she saw Camille had the shotgun.

Fadila screamed like a crazy woman, redoubling her efforts to tear her hands free. Instead of trying to escape, Garcia held what she had and let her legs separate around the woman's back, wrapping muscular thighs around her waist. Hooking her ankles together, she did her best to squeeze the life out of her attacker.

Camille raised the shotgun to her shoulder. "What do you want me to do?" she yelled over a screeching Fadila.

"Shoot her!" Garcia snapped, bearing down with her thighs. She was pretty sure she felt a floating rib snap, but the enraged woman refused to let up.

"I can't," Camille all but screamed. She stepped to the side, then back again, all the while keeping the shotgun trained on the two women. "You're moving around too much! I'm afraid I'll hit you!"

"Just shoot!" Garcia said, grunting from exertion and the weight of the other woman. "She's got a pistol in h—"

Fadila gnashed out again, nearly biting a chunk out of Garcia's wrist. A moment later she relaxed. She looked down at Garcia, and a gloating smile spread over her face—as if she'd already won. A small metal pin hung from a silver ring between her clenched teeth. Still on her back, Garcia let her head fall to the side, looking up at the young woman's right hand to find it held a green metal egg. Garcia recognized it immediately as a Russian grenade. Her grip on Fadila's smaller hand was the only thing that kept the spoon in place—and the grenade from going off.

Garcia tried to scream. "Camille, wait!" But Fadila came up on her toes, pressing her weight against Garcia's chest. Her words came out as a breathy moan. Garcia knew she might survive a piece of buckshot or two, but even a slight wound might cause her to lose her grip. If the grenade fell away, it would kill or maim everyone within twenty meters.

"Grenade!" Garcia gasped, unsure if Camille or anyone else in the ship could understand her. "Get out! All of you!"

Fadila threw her body from side to side in an effort to free her hand. Still smiling, she seemed to know it was only a matter of time. Garcia held fast, squeezing harder with her thighs. She knew she was doing damage, but her grip was too low, catching the girl around her middle rather than her ribs. Crushing liver, spleen, and gut, it had to be extremely painful, but she was too low to put a quick end to things. Garcia had to pin the girl, cut off her air, or somehow wrench the grenade away without it going off in order to win the fight.

Fadila had only to open her hand.

A dark shadow suddenly rose up behind Fadila. Garcia cursed, thinking one of the stupid men had finally decided to step in and help her. If they dragged the girl away, she'd lose her grip—and Garcia and anyone close to her would be turned to red mist in a matter of seconds.

Garcia felt something press against her locked ankles and Fadila suddenly grew heavier, as if she'd gained a hundred pounds. The young woman's head flew back and she began to thrash even more wildly, trying to throw off this new threat. Garcia caught a flash of movement in the darkness above her as three shots popped in quick succession. They were too quiet to be the shotgun. Fadila's eyes flew wide, then rolled back in her head as her body went slack.

Mukhtar's head poked over Fadila's shoulder, skin pale, lips trembling. He looked at Garcia, blinking.

"Are you alright, miss?

Still on her back, Garcia grabbed the Russian grenade in both hands and peeled Fadila's fingers away, taking care to keep the flat metal arming spoon in place.

"Thank you," she said as she wriggled out from under the body, rolling her sore shoulders. She bent to retrieve the pin from the concrete beside Fadila's slack lips.

"I'm okay," she said, breathing easier after she'd reinserted the pin. "Thanks for saving me." She sat back on one of the picnic benches and nodded, still panting from the fight. "For saving all of us."

Mukhtar held up Jacques Thibodaux's .380 pistol. "Mr. Quinn said this is a pipsqueak gun," he whispered, looking down at the dead girl. "If you're going to shoot once, shoot three times . . ."

Chapter 17

Lynyrd Skynyrd still played over the park speakers when Quinn pulled open the door to the main office, the electric guitar riff helping to mask his approach. The inner lobby was just as he'd left it, the body of the park manager slumped at the front desk. His assistant, a woman named Tiffany according to Mukhtar, had been shot in the back, where she'd cowered in the corner, curled in a fetal position. The door to the back hallway stood ajar, the feeble glow of emergency lighting coming from the manager's office where the public-address system was located. Quinn paused at the threshold before going in, getting his bearings, remembering the layout of desks, doors, and windows from when he'd taped his phone to the handheld radio and placed it next to the PA microphone. More light spilled from the open door on the right side of the hall, less than fifteen feet away. He heard a rustle of movement, footsteps on carpet, and a nervous cough.

"I gave you what you needed," a male voice said. "And this is what you give me?" It was gruff, and direct, accustomed to being in charge.

"Yeah, well," a younger voice said. "You know how it is, Uncle Frank. It just looks better this way."

"Hang on—" Two distinct cracks from a rifle came from inside the room, cutting off the older voice midsentence. It was dark enough that Quinn could see the flash of each shot.

Padding with quiet purpose down the hall, he stopped before he reached the office, stepping sideways inch by inch to get a glimpse of the interior without giving up his position. Cutting the pie, they called it.

The console against the wall across from the door came into view first. Quinn's phone and the radio were still there, right where he'd left them. He took another half step, revealing the feet and legs of a prone man— the recipient of the recent gunfire. The dead man wore the gray slacks and navy blazer of park security. Blood plastered a thick mop of blond hair and broken skull to the carpet. A Glock pistol lay on the floor, inches from the man's glazed eyes but too far from Quinn to do him any immediate good.

The squeak of metal from the other side of the desk drew Quinn forward another step. A low whistle followed the squeak, then whispered words Quinn couldn't quite make out.

Quinn had opened enough safes in his life to know the sound of a door swinging open. A burglary? It was a stroke of cold and evil genius to hide a simple theft in the middle of a massacre of hundreds by religious zealots.

Another step brought the entire desk into view. A young man wearing the black polo of a park employee knelt in front of a box safe by the wall off the end of the desk. He stuffed banded stacks of money into a small black duffel. Apparently satisfied that everyone else in the park was too busy to bother him, Terry Spencer had leaned his rifle against the wall, a good five feet behind him, after he'd murdered his uncle. Focused on the money, he'd set a Russian RGD-5 hand grenade on the desk beside him, obviously intending to use the little green egg to blow up the place and cover his tracks when he left.

Quinn reached the desk in three quick bounds, snatching up the grenade and pulling the pin before Terry Spencer even knew he was there.

The boy spun at the noise and raised his hands as he tried to get a grip on the situation. He cocked his head sideways, then glanced at the rifle he'd left leaning against the wall.

Quinn held the grenade in his fist, the spoon under his fingers rather than the proper grip with it toward his palm.

"What are you going to do with that?" Terry smirked. "You toss a hand grenade and we both die."

"Maybe so," Quinn said, his voice low, almost a whisper.

"Those other guys out there . . ." Terry said, giving a bored sigh. "They can't wait to be martyrs." His eyes narrowed at Quinn and he shook his head. "But you don't strike me as the kind of guy who wants to die."

"All this for a robbery?" Quinn tamped back the rage. At this point, unbridled anger would only slow him down.

The kid smiled, taking Quinn's question like some kind of compliment. He kept his hands up but wagged his head as if bragging over some touchdown pass he'd just made. "I know, right? The park's so deep in blood right now, I get away with a couple hundred thousand cash and no one's the wiser. Admit it. It's pretty damn slick. They'd write books about me if they knew who I was."

"Dozens of people . . ." Quinn whispered. "You planned all of this in order to cover a theft . . ." He wasn't really surprised. Nothing another human did surprised him anymore.

"Two birds," Terry said. "My friends have a little cause, and I simply jumped on board for my purposes. My uncle had connections to get us a few grenades. He was also nice enough to lend me a few of his guns . . ."

"And you kill him for it," Quinn said, suddenly very tired.

"Who gives a shit about an uncle?" Terry scoffed. "Anyway, he was in on it, too. Listen, this has been fun, but I gotta run." His eyes shifted again to his rifle.

Quinn waved the grenade again. "I wouldn't do that, Terry," he said. Cockroaches like these enjoyed darkness and anonymity, and speaking their names out loud often disrupted the loop of their thought process.

The boy gave a slow nod of pride. "You know who I am then?"

Quinn opened his hand to let the spoon fly off the grenade. Terry Spencer's eyes flew wide at the sound of the muffled pop as the fuse ignited.

"Not really," Quinn said. He pitched the grenade underhanded, past Terry Spencer and into the open safe, before diving sideways behind the desk, hands over his ears, mouth open.

The thick body of the safe acted like a mortar tube, focusing the force of the grenade's blast out the open door, directly into Terry Spencer's face.

Grenades were deadly, but they were nowhere near the massive explosions Hollywood made them out to be. Out of the line of the blast, Quinn was able to roll during the detonation and come up with the Glock. He was stunned and half deaf, but absent any permanent damage.

He turned immediately to cover Spencer but needn't have bothered. The force of the blast had taken off much of the left side of the boy's body. White tiles from the suspended ceiling littered the carpet. Bits of charred cash in various denominations fluttered down in the dusty air. The grenade had demolished half the room, but the PA system remained undamaged. Lynyrd Skynyrd played on uninterrupted, and the last few bars of "Call Me the Breeze" twanged away over the speakers.

Quinn now had two working guns, but was too far away to run back to the wave pool. The other terrorists had surely heard the explosion. He needed to contact Jacques before they worked out what had happened, but with the cell jammer still up there was no way to get him on the phone. Quinn staggered to the public sound-system console and stared down at the two-way radio he'd taped to his iPhone, working out the pros and cons of what he planned to do next.

Chapter 18

Mattie Quinn expected the men around the pool to start shooting any minute. She'd been in the water so long that her fingers were getting all pruney, something she'd always found funny in the past. Now, she could only feel sad. In scary stories, the people always worried about getting killed or hurt, but all Mattie could think about was her dad and Ronnie Garcia, and poor Mrs. Thibodaux and her little baby—and what her mom would do all by herself. Dan Thibodaux leaned closer, coughing to clear his throat from the constant slosh of water. "We should get closer to the edge, maybe," he said. "The minute they start to shoot, we can jump out and run."

Their new friend Sarah wiped a strand of wet hair out of her eyes and gave a resigned sigh. "I suppose it would be better than just floating here and getting shot. I have to be honest with you, though. We're still likely to be shot."

"Not if a bunch of people go at once," Dan said. "We can swim around and spread the word. Some people might be too scared, but some might not . . ."

"Worth a try," Sarah said. "We'll just go slow. Don't make them any more nerv—"

The music suddenly stopped. All three of the men with guns stood completely still, staring back and forth at each other as if they were afraid of the quiet.

Then, Mattie heard a sound that made her begin to sob. Her dad's deep, sure voice suddenly blasted over the speakers.

"Jacques Thibodaux, Jacques Thibodaux," her dad's voice boomed. "Drop them! Drop them all now!"

The bad guys looked up at the loudspeakers. Three quick pops later and they all lay dead on the pool deck.

Mattie held her breath, waiting, fighting back the tears she'd been holding inside.

The speakers boomed again, all over the park, almost as soon as the last bad guy fell. It was even louder now, but Mattie was so excited she could hardly hear it.

"Off-duty federal agent on the inside to any law enforcement who can hear this. You have two armed hostiles in the trees twenty meters in and approximately ten meters to the north inside the east gate—both male, with dark hair. Both wearing park employee uniforms."

Everyone in the pool fell silent, in shock from their ordeal and entranced by the voice that seemed to be on their side. There was a flurry of gunfire somewhere in the distance.

"The shots came from the east gate," Sarah said, nodding with satisfaction. "Sounds like the cops got them."

Mattie's dad spoke again. "And there will be a female hostile somewhere. Also a park employee. Name of Fadila Baghdadi . . ."

Ronnie Garcia's voice came over the speakers next,

strained and breathy. "Fadila is no longer a problem, Quinn."

Sarah looked at Mattie. "Quinn?" she said, blowing water out of her face. "Isn't that your name?"

Mattie closed her eyes and began to cry in earnest. "Uh-huh," she said. "That's my dad."

Epilogue

An hour and a half after the first explosion, Quinn adjusted the grip of Mattie's arms around his neck so she didn't choke him to death. Ronnie wasn't much better. Wrapped in wool blankets to combat the onset of shock from the ordeal, neither had let an inch of space come between them and Jericho since the police had swarmed the place and escorted everyone to the waiting medical triage facilities that had been erected in the parking lots. First responders now lined up like taxis outside the main gate. The most critically wounded were still being loaded into what looked like an endless number of ambulances from the five closest hospitals and police cars from every jurisdiction within an hour's drive. A medic insisted on wrapping Quinn's wounded leg, threatening him with all kinds of horrible infections if he didn't get it cleaned and checked. Ronnie promised she'd get him to a doctor as soon as the more seriously wounded were taken care of.

A commotion of strained voices from three tents down drew Quinn's attention. Stepping away from the glare of portable construction lights, he could see Mukhtar seated on the tailgate of a pickup truck. Three men in suits stood in front of him, peppering him with questions. As Quinn moved closer he could see the boy was cuffed behind his back.

Garcia tensed at the sight and stepped away from Quinn, peeling off her blanket to reveal the tight yellow swimsuit—the chest and belly of which were smeared with dark blood. Quinn handed Mattie to her.

Mukhtar lit up, nodding brightly at Quinn. He tried to slide down from the truck but one of the men caught him and shoved him back.

"There's been a mistake here," Ronnie said over the top of Mattie's head, addressing the men in suits. "He helped us. He doesn't belong in handcuffs."

The eldest of the three men gave her a condescending smile, spending just a little too much time studying the ups and downs of her swimsuit, to Quinn's way of thinking.

"Mr. Brooks says he could be cooperating with the shooters," the oldest agent said.

"Who's Brooks?" Ronnie raised a dark brow.

"That's me." The man in the Blue Jays hat stepped up beside the truck and puffed out his chest. "You can't tell me this haji son of a bitch isn't a part of all this."

Ronnie rolled her eyes and looked at Quinn. "That's the guy I was telling you about."

"A hot tamale?" Quinn said, bouncing the man's head off the side of the truck. Brooks staggered, then slid to the pavement in a heap.

Two of the suits advanced on Quinn but he raised his hands. He stepped over beside Garcia and took Mattie back to show he wasn't a threat to the suits.

"You just knocked that guy out," one of the agents said.

"Sorry," Quinn said. "Guess the stress of this got to me . . ."

One of the men stooped down to check on a muttering Brooks, who looked like his pride was hurt more than anything else.

Quinn looked at Mukhtar and then the senior agent. He assumed they were DHS or local detectives. If they'd been FBI they would have told him already.

"Look," he said. "It's easy to see why you'd think Mukhtar might be involved, especially with upstanding citizens like Brooks giving you your intel, but I'm the one who called you guys over the PA. This man helped save a lot of people in there—including my daughter."

"It's not as simple as that." The older agent shrugged. "I think we—"

"It's exactly as simple as that." Quinn stepped in, nose to nose with the man. "I don't know who you are, and frankly, I don't care. I'll give you a number to call, but I'm warning you, you're going to wish you'd taken the cuffs off before you called it."

Quinn's boss—the man on the other end of the number he gave the agent—happened to be sitting in the Oval Office when he took the call. Mukhtar's father had been waiting frantically in the outskirts of the parking lot. He was finally let through the outer perimeter and allowed to collect his son.

Ronnie Garcia exchanged numbers with the boy with the promise that she and Quinn would join his family for dinner in a few days. Mr. Tahir then wisely whisked his son away from the crowd, which was still jumpy about anyone with dark skin wearing a Buccaneer Beach Thrill Park uniform.

Exhausted to the point of falling over, Quinn held both Mattie and Garcia close as he staggered back to the triage tent where Jacques waited with his family. The ringing in Quinn's ears made it difficult to hear everything that was being said, but he could tell Camille Thibodaux was busy alternately chastising Dan for running off on his own and showering him with hugs and kisses.

"A burglary, Chair Force?" Jacques said from where he sat in the folding chair next to Quinn, shaking his head. "I'm hearing estimates of a hundred and three dead and twice that number wounded . . . All this killing for a little dab of cash?"

Quinn shrugged. Mattie sat in his lap. Garcia sat in the chair beside him. He took a moment to give her shoulder a squeeze and sniff Mattie's hair before he spoke. "A park as big as Buccaneer Beach could rake in a quarter million in receipts every day," he said. "And that's not counting the concessions."

"Wouldn't a lot of it be credit card receipts?" Ronnie asked, batting exhausted brown eyes at Quinn.

"Some of it would," he said.

Thibodaux rubbed his jaw in thought, following the logic. "But if he rounds up a bunch of guns from his uncle's safe and a bunch of radical yahoos take care of the shootin' spree that covers his crime, this little sociopath had no upfront investment and no accountability. Even half the daily gross in cash would be free money."

"Exactly," Quinn said.

Thibodaux leaned back in his chair and shut his eyes. "I guess they all got to die as martyrs," he said.

Mattie lifted her head from Quinn's chest. "What's a martyr, Daddy?"

Thibodaux gave a low groan, his eyes still closed.

"Martyr is another word for dumbass," he sighed. "Go ahead and quote me if you want to, darlin'."

Quinn hugged his daughter and chuckled. "We'd better not mention that definition to your mom," he said.

Mattie pulled back, blinking huge blue eyes, her mother's eyes. She sniffed, flashing a beautiful grin—the type of grin that made him want to buy her things.

"Sorry I scared you, Daddy," she said. "But there was this guy with a gun, and you always told me I should run from a guy with a gun. Then Dan said we should run, too, so I did."

"He was right," Quinn said. "And so were you."

"Did you see Dan made a bow and arrow out of a piece of plastic pipe?" Her beautiful eyes grew even bigger. "And it really worked."

"I saw that," Quinn said, squeezing her as if she might fly away. "I'm just glad you're safe."

Mattie went on talking without taking a breath. "Then the bad guys threw us into the swimming pool. And it was really deep, and we treaded water, but Dan said we should stay out of the shallow end because we might get trampled."

"He did?" Quinn said, shooting a sideways grin at Ronnie.

"It was really, really scary, Dad." Mattie gave an emphatic nod, her arms still around Quinn's neck. "We thought they were going to shoot any minute, then Dan told me and my friend Sarah that we should swim close to the edge and run—"

Jacques looked at Quinn, smiling broadly, mouthing his words so Mattie couldn't hear him. "Well, Chair Force," he said. "Looks like she got over Shawn . . ."

If you enjoy the Jericho Quinn novels,
you'll love the new series from
bestselling author MARC CAMERON.

OPEN CARRY
AN ARLISS CUTTER NOVEL

*Law enforcement veteran Marc Cameron
brings an explosive authenticity to this
powerful new U.S. Marshal series.
Arliss Cutter is a hero for our times. And his hunt for
justice cuts straight to the bone . . .*

U.S. Marshal Arliss Cutter is a born tracker. Raised in
the Florida swamplands, he honed his skills in the
military, fought in the Middle East, and worked three
field positions for Marshal Services. When it comes
to tracking someone down—or taking someone out—
Cutter's the best. But his newest assignment is taking
him out of his comfort zone to southeast Alaska. Cold,
dark, uninhabited forests often shrouded in fog. And
it's the kind of case that makes his blood run cold . . .
the shocking murder of a Tlingit Indian girl.

But the murder is just the beginning. Now three
people have disappeared on Prince of Wales Island.
Two are crew members of the reality TV show
Fishwives. Cutter's job is to find the bodies, examine
the crew's footage for clues, and track down the men
who killed them. But it won't be easy, because the
whole town is hiding secrets, every trail is a dead
end—and the hunter becomes the hunted . . .

*Keep reading for a special excerpt of OPEN CARRY,
on sale now wherever books are sold.*

Prologue

The maze of deadfall was higher than her head, as if God had walked away from a massive game of pick-up sticks.

In the darkness behind her were the sounds of a predator.

Boots shuffled on dusty ground, stopped abruptly, and then moved closer. Millie pictured the cloud of vapor around a nose, sniffing the chilly air. Her rubber boots made little noise on the carpet of decaying spruce needles. It didn't matter. The scent of fear was enough to give her away.

A branch snapped, somewhere in the shadows, flushing the girl from her hide like a panicked grouse.

Floundering over snot-slick moss and through thorny stalks of devil's club, she fell more than she ran. She thrust herself forward somewhere between a frantic scramble and a scuttling crawl. Blood oozed from gashes on her streaked face, dripping off her chin and onto her T-shirt. Her knees and palms were raw and ravaged. Few of the logs made passable bridges over the rubble, pathways to gain precious ground toward her skiff. Most crumbled at her touch, rotten and soggy, sending her clamoring for a foothold before she impaled herself.

Millie Burkett was Tlingit, people of the tides and forest, and these giant trees had been her friends for all of her sixteen years. Their groans and snaps were normal, and their mottled shadows a perfect place to hide. Her earliest memories were of playing at the mossy feet of the great trees as they watched over her like a kindly grandmother. But now, the Sitka spruce, Western hemlock, and yellow cedar loomed like hateful villains from a movie. An eerie silence pervaded the forest. Rain clouds pressed through the dense canopy, adding a sinister air that chased away the light.

Wheezing and winded, Millie ducked around a massive spruce, at least eight feet across. She yanked a curtain of black hair away from her face and pressed her back against the rough bark. Straining to hear over the thump of her runaway heart, she listened to the sounds of the forest, like her mother had taught her. A branch cracked in the cathedral-like stillness.

Redoubling her efforts, Millie crashed through a wicked tangle of leaves and ropy stalks twice her height, oblivious to the scourging. Her camera swung back and forth from a strap around her neck, snagging on the vegetation and threatening to hang her. A spruce hen exploded with a drumbeat of wings to her right. She cut left, into a jagged, half-rotten limb as big as her wrist, that slashed at her belly. Startled, she tried to jump again, but the gnarled branch seemed to reach out and grab her, clawing at the loose tail of her wool shirt, tearing away a strip of plaid cloth and nearly upending her.

She knew these forests. Her people had called them

home for thousands of years. The stony silence of Bear, the chiding of Squirrel, or the drumming *whoosh* of Raven's wings—they were to her as the patter of falling rain or the lapping of ocean tides.

But today was different.

She should have known better than to come alone. Tucker had warned her. He ventured out alone all the time with his camera, but he was at least ten years older, probably more—and he knew the risks. She choked back a sob. If only she'd listened.

Head spinning with fear and fatigue, she ducked under, over, and around the towering, tilted trees, many of them two or three meters wide. It was still light enough to pick her way through, but dark enough that there were no shadows.

Millie's lungs felt ready to explode by the time the giant spruces began to give way to thicker undergrowth. There was more light here, and a spit of rain. The odor of rotting bull kelp and low tide swirled on the breeze, filling her with a sudden rush of hope. Her skiff came into view as she ran, at the edge of the water less than two hundred yards below. If she could just make it to the boat, she might have a chance.

Long legs in freewheel down the steep incline, the Tlingit girl was sure she was beating her best cross-country record. Her heart sank when she saw the tide was out. It left the bow of her aluminum skiff on the gravel slope, but the stern still bobbed in the shallows, and the shore fell away quickly into deep water. She prayed her little outboard would be able to pull her off the rocks.

Air chambers in the carpet of bladder kelp popped and

snapped beneath the soles of her boots as she hit the tide line. She fell twice between the line of driftwood flotsam and the edge of the water. Broken shells and barnacle-covered rocks tore her shredded knees and hands, but she didn't care.

Sliding to a stop on the slick rocks, she pulled the anchor line off the large stone where she'd looped it and clamored over the side of the little aluminum boat. Her back to the shore, she sat on an overturned five-gallon bucket that made up her seat, and worked to coax the reluctant outboard to life. She pumped the bulb on the gas line, opened the choke, then put her back into the starter rope. The thirty-horse Tohatsu coughed on the first two pulls, as it always did, and she didn't hear the crunch of gravel behind her until it was almost on top of her.

Millie Burkett turned to see a face she knew well, smiling at her.

One hand still on the starter rope, her eyes shot to the dark woods above the beach. "What are you doing here?" Unwilling to take the time to explain the gravity of their situation, she turned back to the motor to give it another pull. "Never mind," she said. "Just get in, we have to—"

Something heavy struck the back of her skull, knocking her off the bucket. Reeling, she flailed out with both hands, trying to catch herself, grasping nothing but air. A second blow, more powerful than the first, drove her to her knees. A shower of lights exploded behind her eyes. Molten blades inside her brain spun with sickening regularity, pulsing with each beat of her heart.

She pitched forward, against the cold deck, vaguely aware of splintered wood and the copper taste of blood.

The fleeting image of a rubber boot passed inches from her face, and the heavy ache in her skull dragged her into blackness.

The terrifying realization that she'd been stuffed in some kind of sack hit her all at once. Panicking, she jerked from side to side, finally realizing that only by moving her face away from the rough cloth could she get any air. Her hands were bound in front of her, low, at her waist. The rough cloth was there as well, against her hips. The thump of lapping water on an aluminum hull told her she was on the floor of a boat. Nauseated, she pulled her knees to her chest, trying to keep the world around her from spinning out of control. She wanted to scream but managed little more than a pathetic whimper. The effort was just too painful. The back of her head felt as if it had been opened with an axe. She remembered that there was someone else at the boat when she'd been attacked—a person she knew—but the face escaped her.

The boat rocked heavily to one side and someone grabbed her feet, hauling them up on the metal gunnel. Good. They were getting out. A disembodied voice muttered something she couldn't understand. The boat rocked again as her body was hauled roughly upward. She strained to recall the face.

"Where are you taking me?" Her father had told her stories about what happened to young girls who were kidnapped. "Please . . ." Her chest was racked with sobs. "I don't . . . I don't know anything. Please, just let me go."

Now sitting on the edge of the boat, Millie heard a

splash behind her. A line zipped over the aluminum gunnel filling her with deadly dread.

An anchor.

An instant later the rope went taut, yanking hard at her ankles and dragging her off the edge of the boat. She sucked in a final, desperate breath before she went under, but shock from entering the frigid water drove much of the wind from her lungs. Intense pressure pushed at her eardrums as the anchor pulled her down.

Millie Burkett screamed away her last breath as the anchor slammed into the muddy bottom. She remembered, and the name of her killer rose toward the surface on a stream of silver-green bubbles.

Chapter 1

Viam inveniam aut faciam.
I shall find a way—or make one.
—LATIN SAYING, often attributed to HANNIBAL

Supervisory Deputy US Marshal Arliss Cutter knew how to smile—but it took effort and, often, came at great expense. More than once, the flash of his killer dimples had sent him crashing headlong into an ill-advised and short-lived marriage. The dimples were a genetic gift from his mother, but he'd also inherited the resting "mean mug" of his paternal grandfather—whom everyone called Grumpy. The mean mug turned out to be perfectly suited to a man who hunted other men for a living.

Cutter stood beside his government-issue Ford Escape—the irony of the name not eluding him as a manhunter. The hood of the small white SUV was surrounded by the seven other members of his ad hoc arrest team, each of them dressed in the full battle rattle of law enforcement on a mission. The three Anchorage PD officers looked bedraggled, having spent the last six hours of a ten-hour shift shagging back-to-back calls for service. One had a mud stain on the thigh of his dark blue uniform, like he'd slid into home plate. Anchorage could get rough after midnight. The two special agents from the DEA, along with the two deputy US marshals assigned to the Alaska Fugitive Task Force, had the damp hair and scrubbed-pink look of people who'd showered and rushed out the door in order to make it to the 5:00 a.m. briefing. One of the DEA guys still had a bit of tissue paper stuck to a shaving cut on his neck. These two sported neatly trimmed, matching goatees, though one had more salt and pepper than the other.

Counting his time in the army, Cutter had almost twenty years of experience tracking evil men, but this position with the Fugitive Task Force was new. He was a hands-on leader, and would be hands-on during this first op in Alaska.

The chilly breeze teased at his sandy hair, pushing a Superman curl across his forehead. He took a deep breath, drawing in the spring smells of flowing birch sap and new spruce growth. He was a long way from his home state of Florida and its comforting familiarity.

There was a real upside to working fugitive cases in the Last Frontier—at least during the spring and summer. The hours of darkness were few and far between now, so the bandits spent most of their time running around like cockroaches trying to find a place to hide. In Cutter's experience, stomping roaches was easy when they ventured into the light. There had been plenty of cockroaches in Florida and it turned out there were a few in Alaska that needed a bootheel as well.

The roach of the moment, Frederick "Donut" Woodfield, had a criminal history that said he'd gone peacefully during each of his seventeen previous arrests. There was no reason to believe that today would be any different. Cutter checked the BUG—or backup gun—

in any case. It was a small Glock he wore in a holster over his right kidney. On his hip, he carried a stainless steel Colt Python revolver with the Florida Department of Law Enforcement badge engraved over the action.

Arliss Cutter was fresh to the District of Alaska—and as such, the two deputies assigned to his task force were fresh to him. All three were still in what Grumpy Cutter had called the "butt-sniffin' stage." They were untested, getting to know each other's ways, the good, the bad, and the stuff that might get somebody killed. The deputies had yet to see Cutter lead, and he'd not seen either of them in a fight. That too was apt to change. The pursuit of violent fugitives virtually guaranteed it.

Deputy US Marshal Sean Blodgett stood to Cutter's immediate right. Bull strong but thirty pounds on the heavy side, Blodgett's thick forearms rested T. Rex–like on the magazine pouches and personal trauma kit on the front of an OD-green armored plate carrier he wore over a tight navy blue T-shirt. A subdued green and black circle-star badge was affixed over his left breast. A short-barreled Colt M4 carbine hung vertically from a single-point sling around the deputy's neck. Bold letters on the back of the vest said "POLICE: US MARSHAL."

At twenty-six, Deputy Lola Fontaine was what Cutter's grandfather would have called a "healthy" girl. Naturally thick across her hips and shoulders from her Polynesian roots, she took her fitness to the extreme. Decked out in the early morning light, she reminded Cutter of something from an advertisement for tactical gear. Similar to Deputy Blodgett's, her vest identified her as a "US MARSHAL," but her intense countenance and chiseled arms screamed "badass." She kept her dark hair pulled back in a tight bun that highlighted her wide cheekbones and made her look more mature than she actually was. Chestnut eyes issued a challenge to anyone who met them for too long. She was around five and a half feet tall, but Cutter didn't have to guess her weight because she kept a record of it on a piece of printer paper taped to her computer. Yesterday, she'd scrawled, "134 pounds of blue twisted steel." She had proclaimed this her "fighting weight" and no one in the task force offices argued with her. Cutter had heard her tell war stories in the squad room about the fights she'd been involved in, and considering the swagger with which she walked through life, he was inclined to believe her.

Boiled down to its core, manhunting was a straight-forward science. Deputy US marshals cared little for the *what*, *when*, or *why* of a crime—but focused with a laser-like intensity on *who* and *where*. In theory, now that they had a location on Donut Woodfield, it was a simple matter of closing in and scooping him up. But in practice, few theories survived first contact with a fugitive.

Cutter glanced at the two seasoned agents from the United States Drug Enforcement Administration: Simms and Bradley. Each was dressed in a thin blue raid jacket pulled over an olive-drab tactical vest. Each topped off their extra ammo, personal trauma kits, and other tactical gear with two flash-bang grenades.

A little over the top for someone not in a SWAT unit, but it was hard to argue against taking extra gear as long as it didn't weigh you down.

The DEA guys appeared to be capable enough, though Simms, the younger of the two agents, made a lame joke that Lola Fontaine was a stripper's name. Cutter did what any good supervisor would do. He quietly led the man away from the group and threatened to kick his ass if he heard that kind of talk about one of his people again. Although it took a few minutes away from the gathering, it was time well spent. With a six-foot-three, two-hundred-forty-pound supervisory deputy making sure he watched his p's and q's, Special Agent Simms became a picture of decorum. Deputy Blodgett had also made fun of Lola Fontaine's stripper-esque name—but in private and as part of the USMS family, so Cutter had let it slide with nothing more than a raised eyebrow. Even that had the same effect.

As per their standard operating procedure on a raid, both DEA agents wore black balaclavas, ready to roll down over their goateed faces just prior to booting the door. The other five members of the team—the three uniformed APD officers and the two deputy marshals—were young, pitifully so in Cutter's mind, young enough to make his forty-two-year-old bones ache. He was at least a decade older than anyone else there. But young didn't necessarily mean inexperienced, especially for the coppers. Serving a population of three hundred thousand, these APD officers witnessed enough human conflict and unmitigated stupidity every night to mature them at near lightning speed.

Out of habit, Cutter touched the small leather bag tucked into his belt, and then leaned over his Ford to get one last good look at the floor plan drawn there in erasable marker—a mobile whiteboard. It was just before five-thirty in the morning but the other members of the team cast stark shadows across the hood.

He was satisfied that he had a solid mental picture

of the apartment complex they were about to hit, but as supervisory deputy, Cutter positioned himself to face the rising sun, making certain everyone else could study the diagram before they went in. He'd seen too many good people die over some piddling mistake—and wasn't about to let it happen on his watch.

The oldest of the APD officers, a sergeant named Evers, was likely in his early thirties. He shot a glance at the sad little cluster of apartments set among the white birch trees in the quiet neighborhood off Spenard Road, then looked back at the diagram drawn on the hood. "Anybody been inside this place before?"

"I have," one of the APD officers said, raising a black-gloved hand. "It's basically four floors of whores, Sarge." He looked as though he might still be in middle school but spoke with the conviction of a man ten years his senior, and this calmed Cutter a notch.

"The landlord lives in California," Deputy Blodgett added. "He's got a rap sheet as long as your arm for heroin distribution and use. I'm not even sure if he re-members he owns the damn thing."

Lola Fontaine shoved a powder-blue warrant folder across the hood toward the APD officers. It was thick with Woodfield's background information and known associates. She'd folded it open to the criminal-history page.

"Frederick James Woodfield," she said, tapping the photograph with the bright red nail of her index finger. "AKA Donut."

"That's a fit dude for a heroin dealer," Sergeant Evers said. "Doesn't look like someone named Donut."

Fontaine shrugged, wincing a little from the movement.

Even in the chill, she was still sweating from her 4 A.M. preraid workout and her arms glistened in the morning light. Both of the younger APD officers were mesmerized by her. It would have made Cutter smile, if he were the smiling sort.

"Whew," she gasped, half under her breath. "It was shoulder day this morning and I am feeling it." She glanced up at Blodgett. "I could barely get into my T-shirt at the gym. Know what I'm sayin'?"

Cutter cleared his throat, keeping her on task. "Donut?"

"Right," she said, rolling her shoulders again. "Not sure why, but that's what everybody calls him. He's got warrants out of California, Washington, and Alaska for distribution. Black male, six-five, two hundred and sixty pounds. He's got ties to the TMHG—Too Many Hoes Gang—one of the Crips affiliates out of LA. Maybe the name comes from them."

The APD officer nearest Cutter dragged his eyes off Fontaine's biceps long enough to study the photograph of their target and whistled under his breath. Officer Trent, a callow string bean who looked fresh out of the academy, tapped the line that showed Woodfield's date of birth and shook his head. "Twenty-eight. Isn't that ancient for a guy in a street gang?"

"True," Cutter said.

"So our guy's on the fourth floor?" Sergeant Evers repeated back information he'd already been given. Cutter didn't blame him. Cops were more terrified of hitting the wrong place than they were of flying bullets.

Cutter looked at Deputy Fontaine, letting her answer. It was a DEA warrant, but they'd turned it over to the

Marshals Service. Cutter wanted to make sure everyone here knew this operation was Fontaine's show.

"Correct," the deputy said. "Apartment four oh five. Three down after we top the stairs, on the south side of the hall."

Evers nodded. "I'd still be happy to bring in SWAT," he said. "If you think this guy's going to barricade."

"That's your call," Cutter replied to the sergeant, taking a half step back and crossing his arms. "If it would ease your mind. This is your city." Cutter knew that being able to personally slap the cuffs on a fugitive at the end of a long hunt was a point of pride with those who hunted men. He wasn't immune to the notion, but if there was any indication that Donut Woodfield was going to be a problem he would have stepped in and called SWAT himself.

All the men looked at Lola Fontaine. The two DEA agents shuffled a bit and everyone seemed to be holding their breath at this critical juncture. The whole operational plan could change with her next words.

Fontaine flashed a quick look at Blodgett, then confidently shook her head and pointed to the criminal history. "He's never put up any fight before. I think we're good with what we got." She flashed a grin at the APD officers. Cutter couldn't help but notice that even her face had clearly sculpted muscles. "I appreciate you guys coming along though. A uniform presence keeps the neighbors from going apeshit."

"And anyhow," Deputy Blodgett chimed in, "we got a pile of five more of these mooks around Anchorage that we're going to hit today. SWAT's got no time for that." Blodgett was from Nevada, but used words like "mook" and "perp" as if he'd grown up as a NYPD beat cop.

Evers gave a low groan, still mulling it over. "He's supposed to be alone?"

Fontaine gave a noncommittal shrug. "That's what we understand," she said.

"Okay." The sergeant stepped back from the Ford. "We seven rock stars should be able to handle it. Are you planning to knock and announce first?" He glanced down at the breaching ram resting upright on the pavement at Blodgett's feet. Fifty pounds of steel and painted flat black, it resembled a length of railroad track with two hoop handles and a flat plate welded to the end—because that's exactly what it was.

The older DEA agent coughed, drawing attention in his direction. "There's a good chance this guy's holding a fistful of black tar heroin. If it's all the same to you, we'd like to get inside before he has a chance to run it down the garbage disposal."

"Daisy will make that happen for us." Blodgett smiled and gave the ram an affectionate pat.

The sergeant studied his two officers, looking them up and down the way good field leaders do to make sure their people are squared away. Satisfied, he turned back to Cutter. "No fire escape on that end of the building. We can all go to the front door. You guys will handle the breaching tool, right? If my guys touch it, I gotta call SWAT."

Blodgett hoisted the steel ram to his chest. "Nobody's touching Daisy but me," he said.

Special Agent Simms threw a black nylon backpack over his vest. It held a pair of bolt cutters and a hooked breaching bar that resembled a hammer with one claw called a Halligan tool. It would be invaluable in the event Donut's door happened to open outward, or was too flimsy to make Daisy effective.

"Here we go then," Evers said, waving toward Donut Woodfield's four floors of whores. "We'll follow you."

Lola Fontaine led the convoy of six law enforcement vehicles off Spenard Road, parking behind the cover of the birch trees on the north side of the building, away from Donut's apartment. With no reason to dally, the team eased their vehicle doors shut, then moved immediately into the main entrance of the apartments. They stacked in the same order they would hit the door. Fontaine was in the lead, Deputy Blodgett behind her with the ram, followed by Cutter, the two DEA agents, and APD acting as over-watch in the rear.

The overwhelming stench of trash and dirty socks hit Cutter full in the face. Deputy Blodgett took a deep breath through his nose as if savoring a favorite meal.

"Hmmm," he whispered. "Yummy . . ."

The building had an elevator, but the team opted for the stairs, moving at a fast trot. They stayed close enough to reach out and touch, but just far enough apart so as not to bump into one another. Her Glock drawn and pointed at the floor, Fontaine indicated 405 with her free hand, confirming that was the apartment as soon as they reached it. Cutter had warned her about spending too much time on target. Rather than ramming the door immediately, she reached to gingerly try the knob. It was not the worst thing in the world to ram an unlocked door, but it was as embarrassing as hell.

It was locked.

Fontaine gave a whispered hiss. "Breacher up!" She stepped to the side, allowing Blodgett room to swing the heavy ram. She would take the lead inside once the door gave way, while everyone else filed in behind her. Blodgett, having dropped the ram and transitioned to his rifle, would follow at the rear of the stack.

The door was metal with a solid core, and from the looks of it, had a deep, reinforced dead bolt. There was a peephole at eye level, so Cutter gave a thumbs-up ordering them to make entry. Blodgett took his stance and swung Daisy back at the same time Cutter saw a camera mounted on the ceiling in the far corner of the hallway. He noticed it a fraction of a second too late.

The heavy door swung open an instant before the steel ram made contact, causing Blodgett to lose his balance and stumble forward. A dark and brawny arm grabbed the deputy and yanked him inside before slamming the door. The dead bolt slid home with a definitive clunk, leaving Cutter and the rest of his team standing flat-footed in the hallway—with no ram.

Connect with Us

Visit us online at
KensingtonBooks.com
to read more from your favorite authors, see books
by series, view reading group guides, and more.

for sneak peeks, chances to win books and prize packs,
and to share your thoughts with other readers.

facebook.com/kensingtonpublishing
twitter.com/kensingtonbooks

Tell us what you think!

To share your thoughts, submit a review,
or sign up for our eNewsletters, please visit:
KensingtonBooks.com/TellUs.